MIKE CHEN

LIGHT YEARS FROM HOME

Recycling programs for this product may not exist in your area.

ISBN-13: 978-0-7783-8694-0

Light Years from Home

First published in 2022. This edition published in 2022.

For questions and comments about the quality of this book, please contact us at CustomerService@Harlequin.com.

Mira
22 Adelaide St. West, 41st Floor
Toronto, Ontario M5H 4E3, Canada
BookClubbish.com

Printed in U.S.A.

For the ones who earn their forgiveness.

LIGHT YEARS FROM HOME

CHAPTER ONE

JAKOB

Everything in front of Jakob Shao was dark.

His eyes adjusted after several seconds, turning the void into a black sheet laced with brilliant white dots, countless stars coming into focus. Jakob raised a finger and poked at the nothingness, only to feel a magnetic pushback from deflective impulses. Force fields, really, as Jakob still used the Earth terminology gained from a childhood of movies and comic books. Whatever they were called, they kept the vacuum of space from sucking him out, freezing him, possibly imploding him.

The atmosphere dock of the Awakened ship wasn't much more welcoming than deep space. It didn't help that he stood barefoot and nearly naked, only an ill-fitting cloth halfway between a burlap sack and a poncho draped over him. The Awakened probably used it more to maintain their hostage's body temperature than comfort, and definitely not for fashion. But where were his captors?

Where was *anyone*?

Then a voice called out.

A familiar voice, a not-human one that strained to yell his name in a vocalization that came out halfway between a crow's caw and an electronic blip. The implanted chips between Seven Bells soldiers constantly translated for species, but nothing came through here. Something must have burned out the chip, leaving only natural expression, a human word forced into alien physiology.

It called Jakob's name.

Jakob ran to the voice, tracing the sound while rumbles vibrated the floor. Spouts of steam and vapor burst onto him, and his bare feet crunched on jagged debris. He turned a corner, and though different lights flashed and fluctuated through the dim space, he saw a familiar figure.

Henry.

The unmistakable silhouette of curling horns and humanoid frame of Henry's native species stood out against beams of light, and Jakob called out, "Henry!"—the simplest name he could assign to his friend, given the physical impossibility of pronouncing their culture's names. A harsh draft blew dust in his face, fragments hitting his bare shoulders as he charged forward. "Henry! We need to go right—"

Except Henry would not be able to go anywhere.

Stripped of his standard armor and clothing, his friend's set of eight eyes all focused on him, their face angling away. One arm reached out to Jakob, straining to move.

The other remained frozen, a statue pose as the crystallization took over, organic matter gradually desiccating from the bottom up. Jakob paused, slowly putting together what it all meant.

Jakob was in the Seven Bells's first wave of defense, but

his power-armor mech had been damaged, and he was captured in space. Henry was to lead the second wave, an on-the-ground defense squad that took advantage of their native planetary knowledge.

They must have failed. Which meant Henry's home world had fallen to the Awakened, their technology analyzed and usurped, their population and wildlife crystallized to be used as building material.

Jakob took his friend's hand, a pincerlike claw with small sensory tentacles in the palm. "I'm so sorry. So sorry," Jakob said repeatedly, taking far too much time given the exploding craft around him. Henry's shoulder froze, body solidifying from elbow to forearm to claws until the whole appendage stiffened and the sensory tentacles stopped moving. Jakob leaned forward as an invisible weight suddenly pushed on his skull, a pressure from the center outward. He looked at Henry, only their head and neck remaining, eyes closed, but tilted his way.

Jakob knew what to do, what Henry wanted. It was the way their species passed on generational knowledge during their final moments.

He let Henry in.

And several seconds later, Jakob absorbed information, secrets, devastation, all of the things that Henry saw and felt while Jakob had been captured. And a number.

A sixteen-digit number that could change everything.

"Go," Henry managed in their unearthly voice before the crystallization process inched upward, eventually taking over their entire head with a sparkly, dead texture.

Then his friend collapsed, their transformed body falling apart like a sandcastle imploding under its own weight. Henry's remains scattered, spilling everywhere and getting between Jakob's toes. When he turned, he felt it grind beneath his feet.

But there was no time to mourn or be disgusted. He needed to go. But where?

Jakob sprinted, checking all corners and hallways. But whatever had happened before he had come to had caused the ship to be evacuated, mostly ransacked of anything useful. At a hangar bay, his captured, half-wrecked mech sat, stripped of any useful tools. The only thing intact was a decryptor—a tool for espionage, not escape.

That wouldn't help here, though he grabbed the device, anyway—technically, a neural encryptor/decryptor—and looked for a way out. In the corner, a holographic interface flickered on and off.

That just might do it.

A closer look had Jakob laughing at his luck: the half-functioning interface was the ship's compressed-matter transporter system, something he was familiar with, since the Seven Bells regularly scavenged them from downed Awakened craft. He craned his neck up at the too-tall interface next to him, fingers flying over controls he understood just enough to operate. It hummed to life, a low vibration nearly eclipsed by the ongoing rumbles of various decks exploding above him. A white glow signified it was ready to fire him across space.

Him, and the knowledge he'd stolen.

But what destination would provide safety until the Seven Bells could recover him?

A star chart glowed in front of him, and the vast pool of space lay at his fingertips. One of those tiny dots represented a chance. He just had to figure out which one—fast.

Jakob scanned the possibilities, already tensing for the brutal gauntlet of compressed-matter transport: an invisible bubble sealing around the body, then throttling it through a newly generated wormhole that collapsed upon exit. He needed somewhere safe, somewhere primitive that the Awakened would completely overlook. Only then could he track his fleet without putting them in danger. Solar system upon solar system whirred in front of him, the options coming and going until he paused at one choice.

One obvious, hilarious, completely impossible choice.

Earth. The place he'd departed fifteen years ago.

Jakob zoomed in on the image, examining its projected rotation. Pure dumb luck handed him a win here; they were passing through within three light-years, perfectly within the edge of the transporter's radius. The holographic light pulsed, indicating the system was ready to go.

But what if the Awakened chased him, captured him again? He could hide his body, yet his mind still represented a risk: specifically, the device implanted in his head that connected him to the Seven Bells command fleet, activated only when speaking the right words. The Awakened were known for torturing to the point of unconsciousness, trying to pry secrets that might tip the war one way or another, except he'd been trained to protect the activation phrase with his life.

His life for the entire fleet's life.

But did the Awakened have other ways to extract that information, something more strategic than pain? If they tracked him down, could they try some type of mental probe or memory scanner?

Jakob turned to think, his bare foot kicking against a smooth object that suddenly caught his attention.

The decryptor he'd salvaged—a basketball-sized device that could scramble certain parts of his memory. A way to blank out the activation phrase from his mind, guaranteeing its safety—and thus, the fleet's safety—in any situation until the Seven Bells located him. Jakob calculated the risks. As one of the Seven Bells's leading engineers, patching up damaged equipment in the heat of battle was standard procedure. But scrambling and patching up his own mind?

There was a first time for everything.

Jakob held the decryptor to his forehead, pressing it firmly and *thinking* as hard as he could about the specific phrase to activate the skull implant's emergency communications signal. A very quick, very sharp zap hit him and, with it, scrambled that memory, now unlockable solely with this very device.

But he suddenly realized that if the zap's blast radius scrambled tangential memories, he might lose more: what had happened, what he needed, his whole mission. Jakob's eyes darted around, searching the broken space for something that might provide a way to give himself tangible backup clues.

The pipes on the walls.

Whatever liquid they contained might be as good as ink.

He grabbed jagged shrapnel off the floor and smashed the line, neon-blue dripping out. It didn't produce steam or eat through the floor. Good enough. His finger stung a little under the viscous liquid, and with it, he wrote words on his exposed skin.

SIGNAL. WEAPON.

Dizziness and nausea struck as details blurred out of existence, and Jakob knew disorientation would hit soon enough. He held the decryptor close, hugging it while activating the scan sequence of the transporter. A thin beam of light trickled over him, a tingle crawling over his skin while the transporter calculated the shape and strength of its protective bubble. It had nearly finished when sparks flew from the far side of the room, another shake knocking him off balance.

"Shit, shit, shit," he said while reinitiating the scan, uttering Earth curses that still stayed with him. The scanning beam reappeared, only to stop halfway down his body. He tried again and then again, but each time, it refused to move past the decryptor.

Jakob squinted at the repeated message on the transporter's interface, but without the supporting communications tech from Seven Bells on him, it was incomprehensible. He looked at the decryptor in his hand, then back at the interface, then over at the message.

Maybe that was it. Jakob *with* the device might be too much.

He set the decryptor on the floor and retargeted the scan beam. Several seconds later, a planetary image indicated a target destination. The decryptor shot off across space, a simple white flash as it vanished.

He'd have to find it. But what if the decryptor's memory fallout erased those details? What if the transporter veered him off course on his own journey? How would he even know where to start?

Jakob turned back to the holographic map: the decryptor had been sent somewhere on the west coast of the North American continent. The Bay Area. Images flashed through his mind, faces surfacing after so many years of disconnecting from that life.

Mom. Dad. Kassie. Evie.

Home.

Such a word felt weightless, devoid of any meaning now. But it gave a shorthand to the decryptor's location.

He jabbed his finger into the smashed pipeline, dipping into enough alien goo to write one more message. *GO HOME*, he wrote across his left shoulder. That would point him in the right direction, no matter where on Earth he started.

Jakob took in a deep breath, then hit the controls again on the transporter. The beam returned, scanning him up and down. Seconds passed and the air changed, like he was encased in a layer of plastic—pressurized energy protecting him across the vacuum of space. Around him, various hums and vibrations indicated the system would activate in moments.

The room shook as a hole tore open in the ceiling, fire and shrapnel showering him.

"Signal. Weapon. Go home," he told himself, repeating the words. If all the writing dissolved or washed off, he could try to remember these few words. He readied himself, and only now did he notice bits of crystalline sand stuck to his legs and feet. Nausea hit Jakob, but whether it came from the decryptor process or seeing Henry's remains, he wasn't sure. Fists formed with tight fingers and tensed arms, and he forced himself to picture Henry's crumbling body, a reminder of *why* he needed to do this.

"Signal. Weapon."

He had to make it to Earth safely. He had to retrieve the decryptor and contact the fleet.

Because he wasn't just a Seven Bells soldier trying to find a way back. Those sixteen digits Henry had chiseled into his mind would win the war.

He just needed to tell them first.

"Go home."

CHAPTER TWO

EVIE

We need to talk. This is huge.

Evie Shao tried her best to look slyly at her phone. She'd done so plenty of times during shifts, pulling it from her back pocket and returning it swiftly enough that most people failed to notice. The antsy cat owner across the exam table from her probably assumed it was all part of the job, a way for staff to communicate with each other.

It *was* a part of Evie's job. Just not this job. Not that she disliked her work as a veterinary technician; it paid the bills while her mental energy went to a much more urgent issue.

Proving the existence of extraterrestrial life.

And how it all connected to her brother Jakob's disappearance fifteen years ago.

Evie lingered on her phone, mind wandering from the exam room of the small Buffalo veterinary clinic. Usually a quick glance was enough; most things could be addressed later. And she had an unhappy cat to attend to. But this text from Layla wouldn't let her go.

> We need to talk. This is huge. It's so electric that it's lightning the mood.

Evie ignored the terrible pun, Layla's trademark form of communication. *Huge.* The word implied so much, so many possibilities from the normally calm, normally data-driven Layla. Her phone vibrated again, still in her hand.

> Seriously, call me ASAP.

The buzzing must have startled the nervous cat. At least based on the sudden "Oh no, I'm so sorry" from her owner and the sound of liquid dripping on the exam table.

Maxine yowled, the overweight dilute-colored tortie clearly upset about the situation. "Oh gosh," said Maxine's owner, a pale woman with a splash of purple in her short blond hair. "I'm so sorry." Maxine hissed at no one in particular, then dashed into the open cat carrier sitting on the exam table.

Evie froze, suddenly caught between two worlds. On one hand, the exam table was covered in cat pee, and Maxine had dashed back into the carrier after taking long minutes to be coaxed out. On the other, Layla from the Red Network had said to call ASAP. That in itself was unusual. Usually the Reds sent emails, maybe a text if Evie flubbed an edit on their web show or if their viewing metrics spiked. Unscheduled discussion was rare. Broadcasting hours of scientific theory behind alien abduction already involved a lot of time and talking, and they all had day jobs. This level of persistence meant something significant.

From the carrier, Maxine mewed again, pulling Evie back

to her responsibilities. Yes, she was there to help animals, but something urgent from the Reds might indicate something way, way, way bigger than an annual physical for a sweet-but-nervous cat.

Thin paper towels quickly absorbed the mess as Evie weighed her options. “Let me grab some real towels,” she said, exiting the exam room before Maxine’s owner responded. “‘Huge,’” she muttered under her breath. She bit down on her lip, the possibilities balancing in her mind. No one in the vet clinic was freaking out about news announcing alien life. So *huge* had to be relative.

“Evie, could you download the blood results for a dog named Leonardo from this morning?” Dr. Firenze asked while passing her in the hall. “Please forward it to my email. I have to review it for a follow-up.”

“Sure. Got it.” She waited for Dr. Firenze to enter an exam room, then pulled out her phone. At work. Give me a few. Her reply did *not* include a pun in return. Puns belonged only to Layla.

“Evie, can you give me a hand in X-ray when you get a sec?” another technician asked. “This Great Dane is huge.”

Huge. But a different type of huge compared to what Layla had.

“Yeah, okay. I’m in Exam Room B first,” Evie called, trotting to the linen closet, making an artful dodge around a patient nudging a nervous brindle greyhound onto the weighing scale. She grabbed a handful of towels and dashed back to Maxine. “Maxine, then blood work, then X-ray,” she said under her breath before catching her habit of thinking aloud. Doing that in her apartment was fine; at work was something else. She walked at a brisk pace, reminding herself to focus every few seconds—not because she skirted her responsibilities but because the sooner they were crossed off her list, the sooner she could call Layla.

Fifteen minutes later, Evie emerged out of the X-ray room and charged forward, even as the office admin tried to grab her. "Evie, can you—" he started, but Evie shook her head.

"Sorry," she said. "Family thing. I'm taking my ten-minute break."

"Wait, are you swapping with..." Even though the words registered, Evie didn't stick around long enough to hear them. Her thoughts already turned to the messages on her phone.

The office's back door opened, slamming her face with the frigid Upstate New York air, a light snow coming down, though the snowflakes melted into droplets before they graced the pavement with anything picturesque. The phone trilled in her ear as she waited for Layla to pick up, and a burst of wind caused her to shiver, tickling the shaved areas of her head enough to consider running inside and grabbing her coat.

"Hey! Where've you been?" Layla asked upon picking up.

"Working," she said, her voice far more playful than how she felt. "Some of us can't get by on puns alone."

"Hey, I save my best for you. They're sodium funny I slap my neon." Layla laughed, and Evie pictured her tossing back her long brown curls as she did.

"And you say I have more followers? Not with that material. Anyway, define *huge*. I'm on a time limit."

"Okay." She sucked in a breath loud enough for Evie to hear. "So there was an event that happened a few hours ago. The data scraper just caught it."

"All right. But we get an event every month or two. What's so special about this one?"

"Evie..." The longer Layla hesitated, the more Evie's nerves electrified. "I, uh... Look, I know why you started doing this. You know, why you're so involved with the Red Network."

"Yeah, yeah, to find my brother. Look, I've only got a few minutes and—" Before another word formed, the different puzzle pieces of the past few minutes suddenly snapped together.

It couldn't be.

"Jakob?" she whispered.

"Now, we're *not* sure—"

"Don't even joke about something like this. You cannot. I swear to you, I will one-hundred-percent stop being your friend if you do."

"I'm not joking. No puns."

Sprinkles of snow fell onto the top of Evie's head as she stood still, the tiny bits of ice eventually melting and making her short jagged hair damp while freezing the shaved undercut. The pounding in her chest intensified, each beat rippling from head to toe.

"Evie?"

Air caught in her throat, not allowing her to get any words out. Or was it her brain, unable to fully comprehend a one-in-a-million shot possibly coming true? "How do—"

"Look. Let's be clear. We're not *certain* it's him. All we can tell you is that the measurements are the same."

Not certain. Two little words caused Evie to deflate. "Which measurements?" she asked, though she knew the standard measurements of the Red Network. Their entire methodology was based on them.

"Temperature. Magnetic-field fluctuations. Atmospheric pressure. A sudden electrical storm—"

"Okay, okay," Evie spit out, in a tone harsher than she intended. "Sorry. It's just…a bit much. They're exactly the same?"

"Well, not exactly in the traditional sense." Every word made Evie's stomach twist and tie, her mind several steps ahead trying to interpret meaning before everything came together. "But the differentials are the same. It's a different time of year, so the starting conditions are different. But the amount they dropped and surged, even the time deltas on it, those are exactly the same."

"How exact?"

"Like, exact. Fluctuations are in the tenth of percentage points. But if all of these numbers are based on the volume of energy it takes to transport someone—"

"And their specific weight," Evie said. "And their specific body chemistry and typical body temperature." And all the other things that calibrated exactly to a person's physiology.

"We think it means something. Especially because..."

Layla's voice trailed off in a way that didn't imply good or bad but simply more. And more, Evie figured, meant something of significance rather than doubt.

"Spit it out."

"It's in Reno."

Reno. A short trip from where they'd camped the night when Jakob and Dad had disappeared.

From the lake where they found Dad a few days later.

As if on cue, Layla continued. "It's worth noting that the data curves from your dad's return follow very similar slope patterns as well. Enough to mean something. I think. And there was another event. Different metrics, but still. Detected minutes apart. In a city called Half Moon Bay. You know it?"

The beach town's name conjured up memories of cold, gray skies over beach bonfires, the smell of burning kindling mixed with s'mores. "Yeah. Half Moon Bay's like an hour from where I grew up." A decision snapped into Evie's mind, words escaping without thought or filter. "I'm going home."

"Wait, what? When?"

"I don't know. Next flight out. I'll figure it out. Look, I gotta get back to work."

"Edward is monitoring social media in the region. He's got some cool new tools. Apparently he's got a side gig freelancing for the FBI. Someone there likes our work."

"FBI, huh? Edward is big-time now?"

"Don't tell him that. It'll go to his head."

"Look, I gotta take care of a scared cat. But if Edward wants to use fancy FBI tools on Reno… Well, you know?"

"Hint taken. We'll let you know if anything pops up. I'm texting you the charts now."

The line went dead, and Evie checked the clock. Two minutes left on her break. Her fingers flew over the virtual buttons, loading an airline app for all flights to the Bay Area out of Buffalo Niagara.

And, of course, her bank account. That created a bit of a problem.

The phone buzzed, loading up five different graphs. The fine details were illegible on the device's small screen, but the dips and curves of the graphs lined up exactly with data she'd pored over, large printouts scrutinized in Layla's dim basement studio after a drive across the border to the west end of Toronto. Those shapes and slopes were burned into her memory: the gradual ramp-up in atmospheric pressure before snapping back to normal, the drop—then spike—in temperature, the shift in magnetic fields, the high-altitude electrical storm that lasted for only seventeen minutes. She saw it: the exact way each curve bent, dropped, rose, and plateaued in exact same proportions to the historic numbers.

Still enveloped by the chill air, Evie closed her eyes, and thoughts of Jakob flashed of the last time she saw him. Not just shared space with him but actually saw him for who he was.

The night *before* they left for Lake Kinbote. On that evening, she'd stepped into his childhood bedroom, which Mom and Dad had preserved despite Jakob and Kassie being at UC Davis. It started off simple, to quickly remind Jakob of Dad's plan for leaving in morning. Jakob stood, his unkempt hair bouncing as he sorted through a paper bag from his backpack, ultimately pulling out a tiny wad of plastic wrap in his hand.

She'd called him on it—with her usual teenaged self-righteousness, talking about his potential and why Kassie always called him a loser and how doing drugs proved it—and he'd smirked.

He always smirked, one side of his mouth going upward just enough to project genuine amusement, a warmth that felt totally foreign elsewhere in the family. Jakob had joked about how it was a *science* experiment, and of course Evie was a scientist even back then, as a freshman physics major in college, nearly fifteen years ago. His words stuck with her in startling clarity, every pause and inflection etched in permanence, a big speech equal parts charm and obfuscation that also appealed to her sense of order and logic and numbers. Jakob's default skill was explaining his own lack of drive and commitment as some sort of universal right, a fact similar to how every single facet of existence boiled down to one plus one.

But deep down, Evie always knew Jakob's happy-go-lucky bullcrap was a facade. And on that day, everything had shifted when he saw her *concern*, as though her discomfort activated his big-brother mode: the same gregarious vibe that disarmed people, except synthesized with a genuine bit of sibling protectiveness.

That afternoon, the cavalier braggart changed for twenty minutes, cockiness swapped out for empathy, an open mind about Evie's concerns. Jakob would still take the drugs, sure, but he wanted to ease her worries.

And the surprising thing was that it *wasn't* surprising. At least not to Evie. Kassie called her twin a deadbeat, never taking him seriously. But maybe if she had, if Mom and Dad had, they would have understood Jakob better too. In the end, it didn't matter, though. Once Jakob vanished, Mom sank into work, Kassie became frigid. And Dad… Evie just hoped Dad would be proud of the way she carried on her promise.

Snow stung on her nose and cheeks, reminding her of the task at hand. Evie shook her head, chastising herself for indulging in the past when there was work to do.

This moment needed her phone. She turned the camera to Selfie mode, then stared right at the image of herself before tapping the button. No smile, no grin, nothing worth posting on social media. Simply a moment captured in time, a single frame showing who she was when she learned that Jakob might have come home. And then she told herself to put those memories away for now, to keep them at bay until she had more data.

She returned to the small facility, ear pressing to the various exam rooms until she heard Dr. Firenze finishing up. The door swung open, and first stepped a girthy and smiling corgi, its back leg with a noticeable limp. Little tufts of hair swirled in the wind as it tugged on the leash, pulling an Asian man out the door. Dr. Firenze followed, meeting eyes with Evie. "Oh. Excuse me."

"Hi. Sorry, I wanted to catch you. I've had a bit of a family emergency, and I need to head out right now. I might need to have someone cover me for a few days. I'll use my vacation time, of course. Oh, and I forwarded you the blood work from earlier."

"Oh," he said, concerned creases on his face. "No, no. No worries about that. Family first. You take care of them, we'll take care of you." Dr. Firenze smiled, and a small voice within Evie chastised her for the fib.

Reno. Just a few hours from home. If this was by the Bay Area, if this was possibly related to Jakob, if this meant going across the country, then only one option made sense. Evie shrugged into her parka, then scrolled through her contact list until it highlighted the name Kassie Shao.

The last time Evie had gotten in touch with her older sister was probably about six months ago, and in the most undignified way—asking for money, of all things. This might be better, asking to talk about their family's past while slipping in a request to crash in her old bedroom. Or maybe it was worse. Given Kassie's penchant for cold stoicism, anything involving family might be quickly shut down.

Only one way to find out.

Evie tapped the name and began typing out a text to her big sister.

This *was* a family emergency. This was Jakob—somehow miraculously returned in the form of charts and graphs and scientific measurements. She just had to prove it.

CHAPTER THREE

KASS

Kass tried to hide her sigh as Mom repeated the words for a third, then fourth time. Because she knew Mom wouldn't put her through this if she could help it.

"It moved," Mom insisted, pointing in the general direction of the dresser under the window. Kass didn't need specifics to know what Mom referred to. She looked over to the object nestled between a dusty wooden jewelry box, a stack of yellowing paperback novels, and a Bluetooth speaker that Mom somehow managed to unpair without even trying.

Mom meant the closest thing to a Shao family heirloom: a small, seemingly innocent tube-shaped object.

An heirloom or family curse.

Kass's entire jaw clenched, the pressure building up to an intensity that she had to consciously let go. The last thing she had was the time or energy to deal with a cracked tooth. Maybe Mom's failing memory could work to her advantage, allowing Kass to sneak out for a quick smoke break. Five minutes away was usually all it took to reset Mom.

No. How dare she. How dare she even *think* something that cruel.

The Shao family, once a model nuclear unit in tech-driven Silicon Valley, now whittled down to this. And *this* was something she would hold onto. Not exploit.

Compassion, she reminded herself. The last three years or so had worn out Kass, so much so that she'd recently brought in hired help in the form of a caregiver named Lucy. And of course Mom didn't want that, not even when Kass and Lucy framed it as needing help to get through Kass's workday in a home office. Kass looked over at Mom, unable to tell if her eyes were the sharp eyes of the quiet-but-fierce woman who'd raised her or the lost stare of someone whose dementia symptoms got exponentially worse over time.

That was the problem with Mom. None of the Shao kids could ever tell what she was thinking until she opened her mouth. Years ago, Mom explained that her quiet exterior worked to an advantage in an industry filled with loudmouths. But now it just put her family—her whole, only family—in limbo.

The clock read 11:43 p.m. Or about an hour and forty-three minutes later than Mom's usual bedtime. The onset of dementia made many things unpredictable, but at least administering medications at set times created a rhythm with sleep schedules. Except for tonight. Lucy's early departure had affected her, and despite being surprisingly lucid for most of the evening, the divergence threw Mom off, causing a ripple effect that pushed her mood further and further off the rails until now they were debating something wholly impossible.

"Okay, I believe you," Kass finally said after fifteen minutes of circular arguments. She craned her neck to look at the thin object sitting on Mom's dresser, the thing that looked like a combination of polished stone infused with metal—the Key, going by Dad's nickname, as in the key to getting Jakob back. That detail seemed to have evaded Mom in her current state.

She assumed Mom meant that thing, and the lack of naming the object was *not* an attempt at irony, since Kass had always simply referred to the fucking thing as *It*. Dignifying it with anything further simply gave the thing power over their lives, gave *Jakob* power over their lives.

And Jakob had done enough damage.

"So It moved," Kass said, "and—"

"You see? I have to tell Arnold. Your dad's been waiting for years."

Kass knew the power of routine for someone with dementia, and how the most subtle shift might echo out for the rest of the day. She *knew* this, both as a mental health professional and from simply Googling the hell out of the topic when Mom's first blips of confusion and forgetfulness came three years ago. But despite every effort to use her training, give things the proper framing, and all of the other nuggets Kass spouted every day to her clients, tonight found her teetering on the edge of losing her shit. Maybe it was sheer fatigue. Or the fact that the conflict involved It. Or the fact that Evie had texted earlier about visiting, a message that she'd promptly deleted.

"I have to show Arnold."

That would be a problem, given that Dad died years ago. Kass bit down on her lip, trying to consider the moving target of Mom's mind. She didn't mention Dad often enough for Kass to have an effective strategy given that the context changed each time. And the only attempt at explaining "Arnold Shao, your husband, my dad, is dead" hadn't gone well at all.

Tonight came with an extra unique challenge: no prior time had involved It.

"Mom, you can't show Dad." Kass glanced around, scanning for any inspiration to bring the discussion to a close. The framed photo of the family at Evie's high-school graduation, its corner faded from catching too much of an afternoon sunbeam. The stack of DVDs, various TV medical dramas from the '80s and '90s—things that Mom still remembered in frightening clarity despite losing the space and time of where she was now. The printed sheet that listed a daily schedule to regulate her day and memory. The business suits in the closet never to be worn again. The notebook of pencil sketches, some as current as this week—somehow the lack of memory hadn't eroded her artist's hand.

None of those would help right now. "Fuck," she whispered, the curse word slipping out too easily.

"Language, Kassie," Mom said, as if Kass were a teenager.

Kass nodded, resetting with a soft smile while she looked for a way out. The clock. Maybe it was as simple as that. "It's too late. Look at the time." She pointed at the glowing blue LED numbers on the nightstand.

"Oh. Oh, Kassie, you're right. It *is* late."

There was movement in the right direction. Kass looked at her options here, playing off Mom's fix-it tendencies. "Remember how he went to bed early because he has a cold?"

Mom nodded, then sat down on the twin bed's flannel sheets.

"Maybe we should all go to bed," Kass continued. "As early as possible. So our bodies are all rested and we don't catch Dad's cold."

"When did you get so wise?" Mom said with a short laugh. She crawled under the covers, pulling the sheets up to her. "You know, I always worried about you."

This bit, however, was standard. At first, it had annoyed Kass, but now hearing Mom say it for the umpteenth time in months brought a certain level of comfort. They'd been through so much together, a life built around only them since Dad had died and Evie had run off to Buffalo. Hearing her say that meant Mom's mind lived in a place where none of that happened, where Kass was still on the verge of failing out of UC Davis and Evie was the one with her shit together.

"I know, Mom. I'm just getting better at listening." Mom's hands rested upon her chest, and Kass put one palm over them as well.

"You know, I think I'll get up early and make Dad waffles for breakfast. Real ones, not the frozen ones he puts peanut butter on."

"I think Dad would like that," Kass said. Dad's favorite breakfast. That was a new one from the timeless ether where Mom's mind spent most of the days. The mention brought up a flash of images, smells, sounds, a collection that hadn't been activated in her memory in years. She worked so hard to push her sentimentality aside, and now goddamn waffles with peanut butter made her teary.

"You look upset," Mom said, reaching up to caress her cheek. "We'll be better soon." Kass nodded, and before she could reply, Mom looked straight up and opened her mouth. "Hush, little baby, don't say a word," she sang quietly. "Mama's going to buy you a mockingbird. And if that mockingbird won't sing..."

"Mama's going to buy you a diamond ring." Kass joined in on the last line, the way she did when she was so little that Evie was a toddler. She watched as Mom stared straight up, seemingly no longer aware that her eldest daughter was kneeling next to her, and then just like that, Mom closed her eyes.

Kass hesitated for a moment, waiting for any sudden outbursts or rash words. But none arrived, and the circular arguments from earlier evaporated. She stood up, as quietly as possible, then crossed the room, only stopping when something caught the corner of her eye.

It.

All of the sentimentality and affection, the pain of watching Mom devolve into a collection of memory fragments tied together by fraying coherence, something surged in Kass, and she did something she'd never dared to do before, something she promised Mom she'd *never* do.

She grabbed It, the cold, textured surface tight against her palm as she snuck out, closing the door in near silence. Seconds passed, then minutes. Enough time that it meant Mom was safely down, and Kass could move forward. Her fingers curled, and she gave herself a small fist pump, a private gesture marking the day's milestone, then she stepped away from the door.

Kass set It on the kitchen table, grabbed the adjacent chair, and stared at the textures and details across the surface, all while keeping one ear tuned to the floor above. Several minutes passed with no creaks or footsteps, allowing her mind to dwell on the *thing* in front of her.

Not so much on formation or color or the textures but on how the object had landed in their family's lives. Of course Mom connected It to Dad.

Dad had brought It home on *that* morning.

The feel of the dew-filled air, the cool mountain breeze, the aroma of pine trees, they all lit up Kass's mind like she was still there, still in the moment when the Placerville County sheriff called her and Evie.

Some three days after Jakob and Dad had disappeared, the sisters returned to that same main road before veering off toward a picnic area on the far side of the lake, the path changing from smooth pavement to the crunch of a dirt path, yellow tape gradually coming into view beyond the clearing. A single police cruiser sat parked, and at one of the picnic tables stood a uniformed officer.

Next to the officer sat a person huddled in a blanket.

"Dad!" Kass had yelled even before she had fully unbuckled her seat belt. She sprinted over to her father, and behind her Evie took more measured steps.

There was Dad. But where, they asked, was Jakob?

Dad barely moved, even when Kass threw her arms around him. They jolted as a single unit when Evie did the same, but Dad returned to a silent upright pillar, like a bowling pin that managed to reset its balance. He stared ahead, random tremors rippling through the emergency blanket draped over his shoulders. Evie knelt down in front of them, shoes grinding into the dirt. She angled to see him face-to-face, to look him in the eye.

The relief that Kass *should* have felt immediately was counterbalanced by the dread of missing the other half of the equation. "Where's Jakob?" she asked, harsher than it should have been.

Still hugging her father, Kass craned her neck over to meet Evie's gaze. Any stoic resolve melted away, and for a minute Kass had wondered if she needed to put a brave face on for her younger sibling. They were both legal adults by that time, Evie a freshman starting at community college to save money, and Kass digging deep for her fifth year after nearly taking Jakob's lead of failing out, but a big sister was still a big sister despite a lifetime of being out of step.

Except Evie took the lead, standing up and putting her hand on Kass's shoulder. It lingered for several seconds, both sisters waiting for something to break Dad's mute expression.

The officer leaned over, voice just above the rustling of leaves. "We found him on the bench. He matched your missing person report, so we called you. He hasn't moved. He was shivering so I put a blanket on him. But that's it."

Kass tried again, searching to make eye contact with him. Despite being in his line of sight, his stare passed her, landing somewhere beyond. "Dad? Dad? It's us. We are right here. We found you."

She repeated herself, switching up words and phrases but with the same intent, a rolling urgency gathering momentum. Several minutes passed, and the officer's hand landed on her shoulder. "Miss?"

"Dad!" Kass yelled, loud enough to scatter a pair of nearby birds searching for their morning meal.

Whether through sheer volume or coincidence or sheer luck, something triggered, and Dad's eyes finally shifted. His whole demeanor, in fact, shifted. His shoulders relaxed, he blinked several times, though his mouth remained a grim line.

Evie noticed right away and joined Kass's side.

"Girls?" he asked, his voice cracking with dryness.

"Dad. What happened?" Kass asked. "Where's Jakob?"

"Jakob. Jakob..." His voice trailed off, vacant eyes gradually shifting to...something. Anger? Sadness? Confusion? Maybe a little of everything. Kass stared at his face, trying to decipher it. But the trembling continued, and so the emergency blanket shifted ever so slightly, just enough to expose Dad's hands.

In between his fingers lay something that looked like it belonged in a mall novelty store sitting next to neck massagers and wireless headphones. It may as well have been a fancy video-game controller with its contoured shape, grooves and notches embedded into the underside of its shell. On the top, light bounced off what appeared to be minerals, like someone cut out a granite countertop and jammed it into a game console. Dad shivered, his fingers showing the same small bits of condensation that dotted the device.

That was the first time Kass saw It.

And now, she could make this the *last* time she saw It. She couldn't reverse what It and Jakob and that night had done to their family, but she *could* erase the one last physical reminder of everything.

Kass stood up, the seat legs scraping the laminate flooring beneath them, and marched to the other side of the house, over to the sliding glass door to the back patio. She walked over paving stones and patches of moss to get to the large black garbage bin, her only company the sound of passing cars and the dots of starlight above.

It, a mess of metal and plastic and stone and whatever else, represented so much more, not just to Kass but to her entire family, like all of the confusion and pain and anger arrived in the form of a handheld object, probably a child's toy or a novelty device lost while camping. The wrong place at the wrong time for the wrong person: Dad, who needed *something* to believe in when a body was never located rather than just accepting that Jakob—flaky, unreliable, *selfish* Jakob—had probably just run off to travel the world while trying every drug in existence.

Because Jakob was a dick. He always had been.

Several years ago, Kass told Evie that Mom had thrown It away. That was the easier path, with Evie wanting photos and details about the stupid thing for her deranged alien web show. She'd held onto It, of course, since Mom's sentimentality was one of the few remaining parts of her cognition.

Part of her wanted to bury It in the garbage bin *right now*, under cigarette butts and used napkins and granola bar wrappers. But another part of her wanted to go further—find a rock or a brick or something to smash the device, as if destruction might undo the last fifteen years and restore things.

The hunk of junk deserved that. Mere disposal would be too easy.

She turned and took several steps, maneuvering in the dark backyard by muscle memory until she was inches from a paving stone, the one that refused to sit flush no matter how many times they dug it out and reset it. She placed the device as flat as possible, kneeling for so long that her joints ached and the circulation to her feet cut off.

In the dim light, It only existed as a faint outline; ridges and detail were absorbed into the evening's darkness. She reached over to grab a cold smooth stone, evening humidity making the porous texture slick, even needing some effort to jar the stone from damp soil. The stone's weight seemed strangely heavy, and maybe fatigue was getting the better of her on a draining day like today.

Or the weight just meant she'd grabbed the right rock.

With two hands, she held the stone about a foot above the device. Her breath danced out into the cold night, rolling into a cloud before disappearing, and Kass thought about this moment, like the ritual deserved more than a single swing and smash. Thoughts failed her, and instead, years of pent-up emotions bled into too many memories, and she hesitated long enough that a tremor ran through her arms from holding the weight up.

Then her back pocket buzzed, interrupting everything. Kass put the rock down and pulled out her phone: a text from Evie. She didn't even have to read it. Evie's mere digital presence shifted her thoughts, dissolving any intentions of destroying It. Instead, she returned the stone and picked up the device. She hesitated, her chilled fingers grasping onto It's smooth texture.

She should return It. The stupid thing was property of Sofia Aguilar-Shao, not her impulsive daughter. Kass started back, fully intent on sneaking into Mom's room and replacing It, but paused at the patio's plant stand, reaching down for a small wood box. She flipped open the lid and felt her way past pens and scraps of paper and other bits of miscellaneous bullshit for the emergency pack of filtered cigarettes stored there in case she forgot some on her way home.

Or, in this case, the momentum of It and Evie's late-night text proved to be too powerful and she just *needed* a smoke. The cigarette came alive with a burning glow, a single orange dot in the dim backyard, at least until the phone screen lit back up.

> Never mind on money. My friends threw in for this, heading to airport for super early flight. But I could use a place to crash. You mind? I'll stay out of your way. Hey, maybe I could even catch up with Mom. I'm such a bad daughter, I think it's been years since we had a real convo LOL.

Kass studied the message from Evie and let out a single powerful "Fuck" before taking in a cigarette drag and silently pondering how she'd explain Mom's condition to her sister.

CHAPTER FOUR

JAKOB

The smell of garbage brought Jakob to his senses. *Warm* garbage, the type of odors that happened when the afternoon sun from hot days met an open dumpster, releasing all the wrong chemicals into the air. Jakob shifted his weight and realized he should be grateful. At least tough plastic bags held the garbage within.

The disgusting sour odor of garbage from Planet Earth. Jakob laughed to himself, loud enough that it echoed off the metal dumpster walls. Oh, he missed garbage.

Even the worst smells felt like home after fifteen years away.

He'd made it.

Earth. It had been the goal. He wanted to get to Earth. But…why? His lips pursed as he ignored the smell and concentrated on his memories. Capture. Escape. Explosions. Then a hurried bit of using a system's holographic interface. The memories proved hazy, though he pulled enough out to deduce it had been a compressed-matter transporter.

That explained a lot. But why here? It wasn't a social visit.

Jakob shifted, and with the movement, plastic and paper and who knows what else crinkled. His naked feet flexed, toes wiggling in the air, and he looked down to see a hint of steam coming off his skin, despite the sun being angled directly above the thin alley. Though, when he turned his head skyward, clouds crept into view, their undercurrent of dark gray indicating that things were about to change.

The dumpster clanged as his arms and legs moved out of sync, trying to pull him out. His bare feet hit warm pavement, and he checked the state of the loose tunic wrapped around him. Dizziness put everything in slow motion, but then he saw it, and his attention sharpened.

Words. Scribbled on shoulders and forearms in big, bold letters. Some of them had all legibility smudged away, but two were clear.

WEAPON.

GO HOME.

His hands felt the cloth, draping over him like a poncho, something that may as well have been a discarded curtain or blanket. Regardless, it provided him some measure of modesty here in…

Reno?

Reno, Nevada. *The Biggest Little City in the World*, it proclaimed. From his alley view, only part of the sign's neon reflection was visible off a building's glass facade, but he knew what it said. He'd been here, back when things like gambling and drinking and grades mattered. Back before he understood life and death and the true horrors of an unfeeling and unrelenting enemy.

Back before he'd said goodbye and returned his father to Earth.

The sound of laughter came and went, people passing by

on the street without a look or care. Jakob's eyes focused despite the disorientation. Details remained, but the dizziness of compressed-matter transport and something else...it all created a gap in between his cognition and his memory. He told himself to focus, retracing the steps that brought him here, pulling specifics out of a murky haze.

"Woooooooooo," someone shouted from down the street, followed by chants of "Chug, chug, chug!"

Reno. The United States. Earth. He was safe. *Safe*, of course, was relative, given that no one on Earth had any clue about the battles that raged light-years away. And that meant he needed to rejoin the Seven Bells fleet as soon as possible. No one here understood what was at stake, and certainly not the men chanting *Chug* the way he'd done with his high-school varsity swim team years ago.

A lifetime ago.

Jakob glanced again at the writing on his body. *WEAPON*. The word gave him pause, his mind trying to catch up. That meant something, something about why he shot himself off to Earth. It was something...vital, something that might make a difference in the fight.

No. It was more than that. It could turn the tide. Those blanks started to fill in, and when coupled with *GO HOME*, a path formed in his mind.

It started with getting out of the alley.

Jakob surveyed his surroundings for clues that might help him strategize his return. Garbage cans, doors, a cat perched on a series of boxes. And then there was him, wrapped in a sheet and stinking of garbage.

It dawned on him that maybe the teeniest, tiniest bit of luck was on his side after all. Because he *was* in Reno. This look wouldn't be totally out of place for the party-gone-wrong crowd.

He grabbed a half-filled plastic bottle from the concrete and opened it just enough to sniff it. The odor of tequila—cheap tequila, he was pretty sure—stung his nose, and that would do the trick. He poured it over the words scrawled on his body, enough to smudge them into blurs. The accompanying smell helped fit the alibi quickly building in his mind.

He walked out of the alley with a wobbling gait that had as much to do with the transporter process as his cover story. People walked up and down the strip, most not even paying attention to someone like him. "Chug, chug, chug," continued the voices from earlier, and he spied a group of young men, probably in their mid-or late twenties, each holding three-foot pipes of beer.

The perfect group to exploit. "Hey," he said, stumbling over.

They stopped and looked at him, collectively puzzled, then with smirks on their faces. "The fuck happened to you?" one of them asked, laughing the whole time.

"I know, right? Here's a bit of advice—" Jakob sank into the person he was before all this: the slacker voice, the persona, it came easily. "Never go to your sister's bachelorette party."

"Ohhhhh," the group let out at once, and he knew he was in.

One guy in a black San Jose Sharks hat—similar to one Jakob had growing up—came over and slapped him on his bare shoulder. "Did they drug you?" he said with a laugh.

"No, man. They bet that I couldn't outdrink the dancer they hired. They were wrong," he said with a laugh. "I outdrank the bastard. And then I passed out."

Another collective exclamation of "Oh shit" and "Oh fuck" and "Oh no" came from the group.

"Dude," one of them said, "they wrote all over you." He pointed at the smeared characters stained all over Jakob's body, and as the group attempted to make sense of it all, more details snapped into place. Not the exact meaning of each note, but the memory of frantically writing.

"I think this one said *go home*," another one of the group read while squinting. "They did *not* give you a break, did they?"

"I think it means they actually left without me. Hey, look, I know this is really shitty, but I'm, like..." Jakob shrugged and pointed at himself. "I am *completely* fucked. Any one of you want to be generous and give me, like just some pants and a T-shirt to wear? And then I'll call my sister and figure out where I'm going."

The group huddled like a flag-football team. Voices mumbled, heads nodded, and the group broke up and came over to him. "What's your name, bro?" one of them asked.

"Jakob."

"What's your sister's name?"

Jakob sucked in a breath and hesitated. Given everything he'd seen, answering such a question should have been easy. And yet, the name was something he hadn't uttered in more than a decade. "Kassie. My twin sister."

"Your *twin* did this to you?" Laughter roared around him, along with more slaps on the back. "Okay, we've decided. As a group. It's our *duty* to not just get you in clothes, but we're all throwing in twenty bucks each for you. After a night like that, you deserve to gamble a little bit."

Reno. Of course it was lucky. "Gamble?" Jakob smiled. "Let's find a goddamn blackjack table." All those hours, all that money he'd lost gambling with his college friends instead of studying, it was finally going to pay off, literally. And he'd been in practice too, having programmed blackjack into the Seven Bells's recreational system and taught Henry how to—

Henry.

Flashes hit Jakob: their crystallized body imploding, the grit beneath Jakob's feet, the sound of their natural voice calling out. The sixteen digits Henry transferred into Jakob's mind.

"You okay, bro?"

"Yeah. Sorry. Tequila headache." Jakob nodded, his cheeks lifting with an artificial grin as he reset to his current mission on Reno's streets. "Let's fucking gamble."

Jakob walked with his newfound friends, laughing and yelling about a made-up night with a made-up party. The group explained how their trip had stemmed from a bad breakup, petty grievances and insignificant details, things that ultimately wouldn't matter and probably never mattered considering how the universe *really* worked. But Jakob nodded and played along, all while figuring out what he needed to return to his fleet. Some stability, access to the internet, and a car or some form of transportation. Maybe some money too.

Go home. Possibilities crunched, all pointing to one conclusion that caused him to grimace. Going home wasn't the issue. He bit down on his lip, contemplating the options in front of him, the obstacles that surfaced as thoughts raced. He needed to go home for *something*, but what he would find there, that would be the thing that stood in his way.

His family.

CHAPTER FIVE

EVIE

The woman in the adjacent seat snored loud enough to get past the noise-canceling headphones. Evie tried to ignore the noise, and instead flipped through the different movie options again. Two hours remained in her early-morning flight, which she'd barely made, first by having to go back because she forgot her laptop charger, and then by being so lost in data that she'd nearly missed her boarding call, distracted by a gnawing anticipation that bubbled under her skin all the way to the airplane seat.

She reached forward and pulled out the in-flight magazine, flipping open the pages to a picture of a smiling dog with the headline *Best Vacation Spots for Dog Owners*. But nothing underneath registered, and it wasn't because she didn't own a dog. The same thing happened when she loaded a movie or a podcast—any attempted concentration simply evaporated. She squinted at the text once again, but none of the individual characters came together to form words.

Finally, she shifted gears to *stop* trying so hard and gave herself permission to awaken unfiltered feelings and memories she'd dammed up years ago. They'd lingered under the surface for ages, thoughts of Jakob and Dad and their time as a complete family unit.

Evie reminded herself that she was a scientist, after all, and that meant sometimes instead of fighting it, she might work with it. If her past was going to hold her hostage, she could at least analyze it.

That was how the Red Network operated—not conspiracies, not internet conjecture, not impossible theories, but a truly data-driven approach. "All right, brain," she said quietly to herself after logging in to their secure server, "let it in."

Details scrolled past her tablet's lit screen, showing the initial metrics from fifteen years ago.

The temperature: cool, typical for February. Later, online records would show it to be about fifty-four degrees that night.

Magnetic declination: 14.49 degrees east.

Atmospheric pressure: 23.73 inches.

She knew those facts, having memorized them years ago, but they represented outlines of shapes, no true dimension or color to them. Evie took in a breath of the stale plane air and shut her eyes to the story behind those numbers, sharp-edged memories that she'd cut off whenever they crept in. A big exhale brought a release that finally let in her old life.

After all, she wasn't going anywhere for a few hours.

That night, light flashed from over the horizon. Once, twice, then a third time in rapid succession, silhouettes of tree branches coming to life from the brightness. The rapid blinking meant Evie's eyes needed several seconds to adjust, and she leaned back on the Shao family car's windshield, the hood beneath her still warm—relatively, as they were still out in the late-winter woods.

Another flash tore through the night sky, drowning out the stars for the briefest of moments. "Goddamn it, Dad," Kassie said from next to her. "What the hell are they doing there? Taking photos?" Evie's sister swung her legs off the hood, and she landed on the dirt patch, ruffling the tall grass around her.

"I thought they were just going pee. Are they hiking around the lake too?" Evie asked.

"No, you know Dad. He's using that as an excuse to talk to Jakob before we get to the cabin. Because he thinks he can convince Jakob to get his shit together. He doesn't seem to realize that Jakob's a dick," Kassie said. "That's not gonna change." Evie followed Kassie's move off the car, but instead of staring off into the night, she pulled open the door of their dad's decade-old SUV and settled in the driver's seat.

Dad had called it "a simple family outing" since the twins were home from college, but Evie had overheard the truth. Her parents never considered just how much she listened, and how much more aware she'd been of her parents' concerns when Kassie nearly failed out a year ago. With Jakob talking about taking a year off to backpack across Europe, well, that probably had Dad being a little proactive about things. This way, they wouldn't need a drop-in intervention like they'd had with Kassie.

They never told the kids that directly, but Evie knew. Most of the time, their conversations came muffled through several layers of closed bedroom doors, but the Shao's small house reverberated voices, so much so that she'd bought a three-dollar CD of ocean sounds and Peruvian flutes as white noise. But the rage that came out about Jakob, who wanted to "seek a new life direction" after years at college, that was louder than the rolling hiss of ocean waves.

"You'd think by now Dad would realize Jakob is a chameleon," Kassie said to Evie through the window of the SUV.

"He becomes whoever his audience wants him to be. I mean, shit, maybe if he had the work ethic to memorize lines, he should switch to a drama major." She laughed to herself, and from the darkness came the sound of crinkling paper. "He believes his own bullshit so much he could be a method actor." Another flash lit the night sky, the tree line creating silhouettes in the shape of jagged daggers. "This is one hell of a meteor shower," she said.

Evie suddenly picked up a different kind of glow, a tiny dot of orange tracking by Kassie's hand, complete with a distinct burning smell.

"Goddamn it, Kassie, you know I hate that."

"Hey, if they're disappearing for a few minutes, then I'm taking advantage. I waited this long, didn't I?"

"You know those things will kill you."

"So will hanging out in the mountains in fucking February, but here we are. And why aren't we staying at our usual campground, anyways? We are literally right here," she said, gesturing to one of the paths into the woods. "It's like Dad thinks a cabin ten miles farther will make Jakob act different. No, I know what it is. Dad planned all of this *just* so we could pause here and he could talk to Jakob. His master plan. Mom's smart to skip this." The cigarette's end burned brighter as Kassie took in a puff. "Seriously, what the hell is that flashing over there? I thought meteor showers were just, like, lines trailing from above."

Evie tried to ignore the smell, and the fact that Kassie pulled a flask out from her purse. *Don't say it, don't say it, don't say it.* The dashboard lit up as Evie turned the key, and the car's radio came to life, though only with static. "Jesus," she muttered before looking at her big sister. "All sorts of atmospheric—"

Silence interrupted her.

Not the silence of the night. The silence of *everything*, as if something had vacuumed out all the air in a radius around them. The car's dashboard LEDs disappeared, and just as quickly as the flashing in the distance had arrived, it seemed like the absolute inverse happened: what little light there was from the moon and the stars switched off into a void for two, maybe three seconds. Evie turned, but suddenly Kassie was gone too, her telltale cigarette fizzing out of sight.

"What the…?" she mouthed, though she tried to say it. No words wanted to come out, and electricity shot up her arm, a tingle that started from her fingers and worked its way up, crawling like a millipede made out of lightning—first up to her shoulder, then head, then tips of her hair.

A faint sound emerged to her left, a tinny frequency that gradually ramped up into the full-throated yell of Kassie's voice. "…eee?" she yelled. "Evieeee?"

Their eyes met. Kassie's cigarette dropped to the ground.

Evie cranked the car, but nothing happened, not even the click of a dead battery.

"What was that?" Kassie said wide-eyed as Evie kicked open the car door and ran to her sister. "Dad? Jakob?" Her voice echoed into the night sky, but at least there was a night sky. "My phone is dead. Is yours—"

"Everything went black. Not like black, but like…negative. Did you see that?"

"Seriously, Evie. What the hell was that?" Kassie spun toward the direction that Dad and Jakob had hiked some ten, fifteen minutes ago. "Dad?"

Brightness tore through the night, eating away the stars, the moon, the tops of the trees. Evie squinted, and even then she had to hold her hand up, but the brightness was everywhere, reflecting off the car's exterior and bouncing right back into her vision. "Jesus," she said. "Kassie?"

"I'm here. I'm here. But where's—"

A boom cut Kassie off. A boom cut everything off, shutting down the brightness and pushing Evie with a force that stole her breath. It took a moment for Evie to realize she'd fallen on her butt, though Kassie seemed to hold her ground.

Then quiet. Normal quiet, with wind moving trees and the distant rush of a car moving somewhere farther away along the mountain road.

Evie and Kassie looked at each other, their motions in sync. A flurry of questions appeared in Evie's mind, but the one that played in a relentless loop was *Have I ever seen Kassie scared?*

Her sister was four years older than her, which was close enough for them to still be scared of the same things as children for a few overlapping years. But not as a teen, not as an adult. Kassie was fearless—*careless*, as Mom would call it, a do-it-all attitude that got her into trouble when left unchecked. Her still, wide-eyed look seemed completely foreign, like an effect out of a movie rather than her semibitchy sister.

"Dad?" Kassie called out, finally breaking. "Jakob?"

Evie joined in the chorus. Her legs began churning, and she ran in the general direction her dad and brother had gone. They continued yelling the names, running down the trail, Kassie far faster with her high-school track-star legs, and as trees overtook the path, the only light came from tiny points of stars above.

"Do you smell that?" Evie said. "Something's burning."

"Burning. We'd see a fire."

Evie dropped to her knees, palm flat against the dirt. "This is warm. Why the heck would the ground be warm?"

Kassie dashed ahead, and Evie took a breath, reminding herself that whatever weirdness was going on, the most important thing was to find her dad and her brother. She crawled on her hands, bits of dirt and wood and pine needles sneaking into the crevices of her shoes, the heat coming and going but the charred smell getting stronger. "Kassie?"

"I'm still here," she said, somewhere off to the left.

"I think there's something here." Inches turned to feet, both the smell and the heat intensifying. She'd lost any sense of direction, only following what her hands and nose told her, like a scout trying to earn a tracking merit badge. The thick branches overhead made a dense layer between her and any natural light.

The tips of her fingers felt something different from bark and dirt, something firm yet ridged, almost a flat, textured plastic. She pulled at it, releasing it from the forest floor, and the strange odor of burning intensified though this thing, pliable as it was, felt cold—cold but without the stickiness of frozen things.

"Weird light, no sound, now weird weather, and a cold… *thing*," Evie whispered to herself, trying to kick-start her brain into piecing it together.

Maybe it was garbage. Maybe it wasn't. Either way, it was in this spot, this place along their path that fused cold and hot. But until she had light, she wouldn't know.

As if on cue, a bright beam appeared, this one sweeping from left to right, sending shadows of tall trees into motion. Except the source came from behind, not in front. "You see that?" Kassie called.

"Yeah. Checking it out." As she said that, her eyes adjusted to the balance between bright and dark, and a red glow became apparent. At first, Evie thought the rapid shift in vision created a trick, but as she stepped through the brush and tree trunks, it became clear: yes, it was actually red light. Her fingers held onto the flat, strange object as she pressed forward. Brush crunched underneath with each step, only to be confronted with a rumbling that caused the ground to hum.

Red lights.

Then bright beams, one by one piercing through the night.

"We've got someone," a voice yelled.

Evie put her hand up, blocking the direct blinding light until her eyes adjusted, and the form of a uniformed police officer came through, complete with jacket and hat. And in her hand, the strange flat object also came into view, though when she realized what it was, she nearly dropped it.

It was Jakob's blue UC Davis hoodie, or enough of it to show the logo across the chest and seams where half of a hood still connected. Except it was flattened and stiff, now almost compressed to a solid thin board. And the bottom edge, cut halfway down the material, flaked with movement, bits breaking apart like ashen dust falling off of Kassie's disgusting cigarette.

"Dad?" yelled Kassie. "Dad!"

"Jakob?" called Evie in a similar tone.

Ding.

"Jakob!"

The sound of the flight's public address beep jolted Evie back to the present. She blinked, waking to find her fingers clutching the thin arm rests of the economy-class seat and several sets of eyes looking back at her, even the ones framed by headphones. The snoring woman next to her managed to stay asleep despite Evie's jolt and apparent callout for her missing brother.

Evie blinked, the rest of the memory playing out in fast-forward as she came to. She and Kassie went with the Lake Kinbote ranger and county sheriff back to the station. They called Mom, which led to a blistering conference call where Mom barked orders to anyone who might listen: search teams, helicopter sweeps, and all sorts of absurd demands causing more problems than solving them. And when Mom said she was going to drive up, Kassie ran interference and suggested she stay home with their dog since the sisters were already there.

Kassie took charge. Moved forward. Talked Mom down—talked *Evie* down. Like she took the baton life had handed to her but then never let go.

Evie shook her head at how she finally managed to sleep on the plane *after* letting some of those thoughts and memories through. Maybe Kassie would have a professional take on that, assuming her big sister actually spoke to her.

She straightened up, first offering an awkward smile all around before taking a moment to collect herself.

"Are you okay, miss? Did you need something?" asked a flight attendant as he passed by with a black garbage bag.

"No. No, I'm fine," Evie said, craning her head to look through the tiny window at the bluish Bay Area morning floating by.

"We'll be starting our descent into San Francisco," a low female voice said over the intercom. "Please leave your devices in Airplane mode until we touch the ground. Should only be about twenty minutes or so. It's a beautiful, clear early morning in the Bay Area."

Evie's phone sat on her open tray table, which bumped up as her knee collided with it. Her fingers fumbled, trying to bring the screen to life before the flight attendants made their way down to order devices off. Her contact list loaded, and she scrolled all the way to *Kassie Shao.* Their message history appeared, a list of outgoing texts from her phone but nothing received—not in recent months and certainly not in the last few hours. She tapped the icon to go into Airplane mode, though before sinking into her chair for the flight's final descent, she snapped a quick selfie to mark the moment.

Kassie wasn't responding. And it wasn't because she had gotten a new phone or fallen off the planet.

Evie got the hint, though she considered her options. With the Reds each chipping in to fly her out here, giving up wasn't an option. She could stay in a hotel as a last resort, but for the sake of her bank account, only one option made sense.

It was worth a shot.

For Jakob, anything was worth it. Even facing Kassie.

CHAPTER SIX

KASS

Only one client was on the docket today. That meant today was a Real Life day, though Kass didn't know if that was good or bad. The positive was that she had time to deal with shit and didn't have to pay Lucy to come in and watch Mom.

The negative was that she had time to deal with shit while watching Mom.

Kass sighed, shutting her eyes. Calling it all *shit* didn't make things easier. Given the scope of things before her, she opted to put Evie in the category of Things That Can Be Dealt with Later and/or Ignored; the badgering and whatever her UFO weirdos wanted could wait.

More pressing issues needed her attention. Upstairs was thankfully quiet, and Kass looked at the clock. Last night, after Evie's final text, Kass had snuck It back into Mom's room. But her nerves prevented a peaceful sleep, and she awoke an hour before normal.

Between that and the empty schedule, Kass knew the large

packet with *Golden Apple Assisted Living* embossed across the front should be her priority. She stared at it during her first cigarette of the morning, during her first cup of coffee. Still no noises from above, and so far it seemed like Mom was back on schedule despite the bumpy night. That meant two hours before things started.

Maybe she'd postpone thinking about putting Mom in a home. Just for a little bit. Lucy gave her the packet two days ago upon telling her that she'd accepted a full-time position there, but even knowing that hadn't been enough to let her really dig in.

Though she brought the packet into the home office, Kass set it aside and instead fired up her computer, its two massive monitors sitting side by side. A quick set of keyboard taps brought both screens to life, still with the system's generic background of a sunset in some remote tropical location. A window appeared, informing her that her log-in password had expired and she needed to put in a new one. Her fingers flew with muscle memory, trying several of her go-to passwords. Red *X*s appeared each time, along with messages that each had apparently been used in the past two years and she needed something different.

Quite the life metaphor.

"Too early," she said with a sigh, then clicked the button that disabled password protection for now.

Another thing for the deal-with-it-later category.

Kass gave one more listen for any noise upstairs, then slid on cushy headphones and clicked the sword icon on her desktop, launching the start-up sequence for *The Ancient Runes Online*. A prompt appeared beneath an image of elves jumping out of a flaming turret, while choral chants blared into her ears. She typed in her character's log-in, and various boxes appeared as she assumed the virtual point of view of Aveline, a tall and thin elf with brown skin draped in a gray tunic with red flare.

A chime rang in her ears, soon followed by a message from the handle Dwarftastic. You're up early.

Dwarftastic, also known as Desmond.

Also known as her ex-husband.

A strange feeling came over Kass, and it took several seconds to realize that the sudden release of her shoulders and unconscious sigh translated into relief.

Shouldn't you be at work? she typed.

Off day. Surgeon's schedule, you know? Enjoying a nice Paris afternoon by staying inside and earning coin for my guild. What's your excuse?

Oh, you know. Kass laughed to herself, though her headphones drowned it all out. Family reunion.

An animated ellipsis icon appeared, indicating that Desmond had typed at least a single character, and it repeated its series of dots for well over a minute until the message finally appeared.

Evie's visiting?

Kass sucked in a breath and held it, and for the first time that morning, her lips escaped gravity enough to curl upwards. Of course Desmond would understand.

She's flying in. I don't know about "visiting" yet. She mentioned Jakob.

Whoa whoa whoa. Jakob???

This time, it was Kass's turn to type a few characters before deleting and starting over. Desmond must have seen the animated ellipsis as she considered what to say. Too much detail? Not enough? How she really felt? Playing it off with a joke?

In the end, she kept it simple. Desmond always saw through her bullshit, anyways.

> She thinks she's found some information about him. I haven't replied. My theory hasn't changed, though. Death certificate or not, it's gotta be barmaids in Europe. Or South America. One or the other. Not Evie's fucking aliens. But that's why she's coming out here. I don't need her shit with everything going on.

She hit the Enter key, and the message appeared on the game's internal chat, the length of her purple text shoving all of his green text out of sight. Her fingers punched the keys, the dam that held her thoughts and feelings about *everything* finally bursting through.

> Mom's getting worse. And Lucy starts a new job at a care facility in a few weeks. I haven't found a replacement for her yet.

On-screen, Desmond's character appeared in a puff of smoke, a stocky dwarf with a thick white beard and a giant ax. He shuffled over to her Aveline, and in the virtual space between them, he hugged her.

Another message appeared after the hugging animation completed. Is Evie going to help out?

Ha. Kass laughed in step with the typed word. You give Evie too much credit. I don't want Mom to see her. Evie doesn't know. She'll just make Mom more confused.

OK, Kass, I'm gonna play therapist here LOL. Desmond's character let out a hearty chuckle. She replied by clicking buttons to make Aveline give a thumbs-up. I know Evie's flaky. But she deserves to know. You can't let everything you feel keep this from her. Besides, she'll find out eventually. Better now than later.

The text on the screen burned into Kass's eyes, sparking a slow registration of what Desmond meant. Next to the chat window, Desmond's character sat down and remained still. No movements or funny dances or in-game gestures; he gave her space to digest it all. He knew exactly what to do. All those years of him listening to her practicing psychobabble must have paid off. Except understanding each other was never the issue. In fact, the issue was probably that they understood each other *too well.* Just like now.

So you did learn something from me after all.

The dwarf laughed again on-screen. The great thing about marrying a therapist is that every argument is like a therapy session.

The activity ellipses appeared again, though unlike before, the full response came even before the digital characters finished moving.

And I'm so sorry.

Kass picked up the packet from Lucy: the building's exterior, a combination of classic-looking brick with the sheen of tinted windows. Below it, an elderly man smiling at the camera, someone who was clearly posing for a piece of stock photography. Next to it, several people sat together, a basketball game on a TV ahead of them.

All the charm without any of the reality.

It *meant* something—Jakob and Evie and Lucy and the images of the facility above—it just had to. Kass considered herself secularist of the highest order, a devotee of the purity of science, but even still, she occasionally wondered if numbers somehow had a sense of irony. She glanced back at the game screen, somehow having missed another message from Desmond.

I have a few days off next week. Do you want me to fly out and help with this?

Distance had been the biggest issue in their marriage. So of course, playing as partners in a virtual fantasy world somehow brought them closer. Now, with her inner world facing turmoil that matched the chaos of fifteen years ago, he offered to drop everything and see her—despite the fact that they hadn't been face-to-face in several years now.

Could she say yes?

Her pulse quickened at the idea that this would mark a new beginning for her, a repair to her own life, their challenges of the past simply drifting away.

But no, dragging him into this wasn't fair to him, especially since they'd never fully resolved their biggest issue from a few years ago. And that was on Kass, but she had far too much on her plate right now.

No, but thank you. How about we go quest for the Hidden Blade?

I'd love to, but I have to get going. Desmond's dwarf sat down, then set his blade on the virtual floor.

What, you don't have a hot date with a Parisian model,

do you? Aveline blew a kiss at the screen, then her shoulders shook with stiff laughter animations.

The typing icon popped up, then disappeared, then popped up again. This cycled several times, far more than it should have for a simple joke. Kass realized her mind projected in too many directions and her professional sensibilities took over, a reminder that impulsive thoughts were merely grasping for control and stability within a storm.

Besides, Desmond didn't say anything about a date.

Well, she's not a model. She's in Operations at the hospital.

If Kass looked in a mirror, she'd know the expression on her face: pursed lips, chin rumpled, eyes averted. Desmond would call her on it too, if he'd seen it. She forced it into a smile, as if Desmond was right here in front of her and not sitting behind the avatar of an adventuring dwarf.

Look, I gotta run, he typed. But seriously, let me know if I can help. I have a few days off. Your mom was always kind to me. I'd like to help.

Kass sat, staring at nothing. First Evie came back with her bullshit. Then Mom and whatever bullshit was happening with It. And now this. One by one, Kass felt her personal shields withstand the blows, but the attacks came from all sides, leaving her defenseless and raw. If she could pause time and escape the whirlwind of family nonsense, where would she even go? What would she even do?

Seconds ticked by, Desmond's message awaiting a reply.

And then Kass did what she always did. She took in a deep breath and told herself to march forward—for everyone. Thanks, she typed back, except his avatar faded from the screen before she could hit Enter.

Suddenly, Kass didn't feel like playing anymore.

Kass opened the desk drawer to grab the weathered notepad sitting at the top, and she flipped the lined yellow sheets, page after page of questions scrawled in pen—most with lines striking them out. Halfway through, a fresh sheet lay ready for her.

Would Mom be better off in a home?

Is Mom a hazard to herself?

Do you trust Lucy to keep her safe?

Can you find anyone as good as Lucy?

Her fingers pressed the pen into the pad, turning a single dot into a pierce that tore through several sheets.

What good would come from answering Evie?

Patients always seemed relieved when she mentioned doing the Objective Questions technique herself. And it worked, at least most of the time. But this time, rather than being given some clear space to process her thoughts, every question burrowed deeper. No answers came, no release came, only memories compounding other memories of the last few years.

Are you okay with Desmond going

Kass stopped before finishing the question. No, not going there. She looked at her phone again, the text from Evie sent about an hour ago, probably when she touched down at SFO.

I'll be here for a few days. Maybe I can swing by.

The message infuriated her enough to stomp out of the room, Golden Apple folder in hand. She marched over to the kitchen counter where she grabbed her cigarettes along with a fresh cup of coffee. As she stepped onto the back patio, she took in the scene around her, the still vacuum of it all reminding her of *that* night.

Except it wasn't like that at all. A car drove by. Birds sang. Somewhere in the distance, a child laughed. There wasn't an absence of sound like before, no eerie feeling that all audio within the space was simply removed from the air. This time, it was within Kass. Evie had created the black hole in her, not weird atmospheric conditions or, as her sister insisted, aliens.

The irony.

And now she wanted to come over, to dislodge the fragile balance Kass had achieved with Mom.

The corners of the pack dug into Kass's palm, and she stood, considering her own self-imposed rule of one cigarette in the morning, one with lunch, one after dinner, and one before bed. A strict regimen to maintain control over the unhealthiest of habits, something she'd stuck to religiously for years.

Fuck it. She grabbed a cigarette from the box and put it up to her mouth. She held it there without lighting it, a slight pressure against her teeth and the hint of tobacco tickling her senses.

She shouldn't. She had rules that she kept, rules that, while not totally circumnavigating the health risks of smoking, at least kept it to a minimum, kept cravings in a structured pull rather than a brute-force tether.

Her second cigarette of the morning.

How dare Evie get her to break her own rules.

The thought repeated several times as Kass flicked the lighter, brought the flame up, and took in a deep burning breath. Several minutes passed in a battle to keep all those nagging demons at bay. She looked back, and suddenly the folder felt like another lifetime ago, despite looming over everything the past few weeks. Her slippered feet walked around the perimeter of the yard, pacing across paving stones—stones set some twenty-five years ago, back when they had moved to the suburb of Mountain View as a young family, Kass and Jakob just on the cusp of middle school and Evie in elementary school. She walked carefully now, mostly to avoid getting her slippers damp, not like years ago when she and Jakob challenged each other to see who could hop across them on one foot the farthest without falling.

Kass shoved the memory away and moved to the ceramic pot waiting for cigarette butts by the front gate. Above her, the sun reflected off the upstairs-corner window, her bedroom through high school but now the place where Mom slept. Based on the strict rhythm of medications, probably for at least another hour.

Would an hour be enough time to review the nursing home stuff *and* deal with Evie?

It would. Evie would take no time at all if her request was simply ignored. Kass nodded to herself, then turned to make her way back to the porch chair, packet finally open. Except that while the sheets with fancy photography and smiling faces were there, the massive intake form was not.

Of course. She'd left it in her car. She'd glanced at the insurance info last night when she'd parked and must have forgotten to stuff it back in.

A look at the back patio showed that steam still rose from her glass mug, the very thought of the coffee offering a reliable comfort. *First the form, then the coffee*, she thought, when the sound of a car out front caught her attention.

At this time, cars simply rumbled by, probably heading out to the highway or a nearby café for coffee and breakfast. But this one stopped, brakes squeaking before a door opened, and then a voice spoke.

"Thanks."

Kass stopped.

She *knew* that voice.

Folder still in hand, Kass pushed on the gate's latch and opened it just enough to see the shape of a woman tapping at her phone. She closed the passenger door and turned, looking up the same way Kass had seen hundreds, possibly thousands of times.

Goddamn it.

CHAPTER SEVEN

JAKOB

Jakob lifted the plastic cup, slamming it into the other cups from his new Reno buddies. "Three thousand," he yelled, intentionally slurring out the middle syllables. Gold beer sloshed from their cups into his, mixing slightly with the clear gin and tonic swirling around his transparent plastic cup. He sloshed it around, consciously spilling some over the brim, drops hitting the pavement below to lower the cup's volume.

"Three thousand," the group yelled in return, the number growing into a chant. "Three thousand! Three thousand!" With each refrain, Jakob shook his cup too, letting more and more alcohol fall out, his temporary friends too inebriated to notice *why* it got more empty over time. "Three thousand!" they shouted again, and Jakob held up a wad of cash close to that amount, unleashing whooping and hollering that caught the attention of some—but not all—passersby from the late morning crowd.

The number wasn't totally accurate, given he'd purchased a

pay-as-you-go smartphone while the rest of the group bought the first round, but still, the winnings from blackjack came courtesy of old gambling instincts using soldier-hardened hyperawareness that made card counting and calculations far too easy.

All of it seemed simple without the fate of civilizations at stake.

"Fuck your sister!" More cheers came, and then a huddle like they'd just won a basketball championship. Barely a drop of alcohol made it into his system, but their euphoria proved contagious, and for a moment, Jakob let himself slide into being an idiot again, being *human*, even holding up a thick wad of cash from his winnings.

And then it was gone.

His hand was empty, the money snatched away by a sharp pull. He pushed the guys back, a little harder than he should have, prompting a "What the hell?" He scanned the people on the sidewalks and street, one person walking markedly faster than the rest.

"That guy took the cash," he said before tossing his drink aside and taking off after the thief.

Only a few seconds passed before he knew for certain. The commotion of movement and the distinctive slap sound of running in flip-flops drew a number of eyes, but only one person actually responded by sprinting the other way.

Any disorienting effects from the transport process had faded away by now, and Jakob ran at a brisk soldier's pace. Except here, he passed people crossing the street rather than automated drones of the Awakened, dodging moving cars rather than blasts that petrified his colleagues into crystallized statues.

Compared to that, a man in loose pants and a weathered coat stood little chance. Jakob ran straight toward an oncoming car and leaped onto the hood, a two-step push that propelled him up and over the vehicle, cutting the thief's lead. Several strides later and the man came within Jakob's grasp on the sidewalk, terrified eyes looking back his way, coupled with a clear stink of grime.

He's desperate, Jakob thought.

But, then again, so was Jakob.

Jakob wrenched the wad of cash from him, then took a single hundred-dollar bill and placed it in the man's coat pocket. "Do something with this," he said calmly, before getting up and turning back to his party.

Variations of "Holy shit" greeted him as he walked calmly back to the group, and long-lost muscle memory put a crooked smile on display, arms out in a "Who, me?" gesture.

"What can I say?" he said with a laugh. "Still got my high-school legs." Which wasn't true. His high-school legs belonged in the water with the varsity swim team. Kassie had been the runner in their family, and at the time, he'd found the whole thing boring and painful. But training to survive marauding drones on slick, ice-covered battlefields changed things. He held up the cash, then offered a hundred-dollar bill to each member of the group. "Thanks for helping me out. But I gotta go home."

GO HOME.

Following their suggestion of loading the cash onto prepaid debit cards, Jakob bought a late-night bus ticket. The direction was clear, but the purpose remained vague. *Home* had to be to the Bay Area, to the Shao house, but why?

WEAPON.

That was the other scribble that survived the transport process. Jakob pieced together that he'd probably used a decryptor on himself. The sense of disorientation, the gaps in his memory, it all painted in details, but what was the bigger picture?

★★★

The long bus ride rolled along the highway, long stretches of nothing on either side, though Jakob found his mind crackling with possibilities, questions, even a few nerves. In his hands, he cradled his new phone, one far more powerful than any device he'd seen from fifteen years ago. The bright screen and the sparkling camera piqued his curiosity, despite countless hours dealing with holographic projections featuring tactile feedback. Yet here, he marveled at the device, leaps and bounds over his college friend's early-2000s Blackberry.

Why he needed to go home, he wasn't sure. He set that aside, compartmentalized for now, and his posture shifted as he realized a tension in his shoulders, a knot in his stomach. Both intensified with each passing mile of the ride, and it had nothing to do with intergalactic wars or getting to the Bay Area.

What to do about his family?

Even the last time he had come home—right before they went to Lake Kinbote—things had veered between messy and uncomfortable.

That afternoon, Jakob had stepped through the front door, Kassie a step ahead of him. She'd already announced that they were home from UC Davis, then yelled to anyone within earshot that she was going for a run and would be back soon. He did the opposite, casually walking in with his bag over his shoulder. Though from how things had gone, he might as well have been a pinball launched at the start of the game, fired straight into endless bumpers and walls.

The first hit had come from Dad. "Are you excited about this weekend?" he asked with so much enthusiasm that Jakob felt twelve again, when swimming for hours in Lake Kinbote was his favorite thing in the world. "It's a new cabin, about twenty minutes north. Cleaner, less people. A lot of great places to think. And talk. It'll be nice, just the family, no distractions." Jakob nodded through all of that, knowing immediately that Dad had targeted the weekend excursion as a means to talk about school yet again. He offered a disarming smile and patted Dad on the back before moving on.

The second hit had come in the upstairs hallway: Evie, who stood up with arms wide open. "Come here. Give me a hug," she yelled in a throaty, monster voice, and he let his little sister win the match, tilting back and forth like Frankenstein's beast pretending to struggle out of it. She held on extra long just to annoy him given his distaste for hugs, talking the whole time. "This weekend is gonna suck. I bet you and Kassie can't go an hour without fighting about something stupid. Like, seriously, twenty bucks on that."

Then came Mom, who said hello as he settled his things in his childhood bedroom. "Bring any homework with you?" Jakob responded with a laugh that was comfortable only on the surface, which prompted Mom to laugh too, the kind of dismissive I'm-joking-but-not-really laugh that she fired off with targeted precision. "But if I were you," she said before leaving, "I'd take some textbooks on the trip. Get a head start."

Several minutes later, Jakob stood by the upstairs bathroom door, Kassie already gone on her run, and Evie in her room, a soundtrack of new age Zen music accompanying her studies. But Mom and Dad, their hushed voices from downstairs escalated quickly. "I'm not going, Arnold," Mom said. "Do you think your plan will actually work? It's going to be three straight days of arguing. Jakob won't listen to you. I'll stay home and enjoy the peace."

As he stood there, Tiger walked by, the mini-schnauzer's nails clip-clopping on the solid floor. He dropped his favorite toy, a half-transparent nylon spiky ball, and sat with bright brown eyes staring. Jakob knelt down and presented his hand. "High five, little guy," he said, which Tiger promptly slapped.

"At least you don't give me shit," he said before rolling the ball down the hall. The mini-schnauzer chased it, stopping only because Evie picked it up.

"Hey," she said, Tiger following her steps. She dropped the toy for the dog, who laid down to chew on it. "You okay?"

"Who, me?" Jakob stretched his arms over his head, a wry grin defaulting on his face. Evie returned a half smile, and he forced out a quick laugh, something to disarm his little sister. "You worry too much," he said, giving her a light punch in the shoulder. "I'm always okay."

"Better not be lying," she said, hitting him back with a grin.

He was okay.

Even now, on this bus. He'd escaped the Awakened. He had intel from Henry. He had a job to do. And it required research, not nostalgia.

The virtual keyboard popped up on the screen, though it took several times for his thumbs to accurately type his twin sister's name. The results listed something slightly off from what he expected: instead of *Kassie*, everything appeared using the name *Kass*.

A therapist website. An article in a psychological journal. Several social-media accounts, all of which had only sporadic postings over the course of nearly a decade with generic clues: a photo of a circle of redwood trees, a stylized photo of a cup of coffee, a few mentions of a video game called *The Ancient Runes*, some reposts of her quotes in articles from *Psychology Today*.

Only one post stuck out, a single line with no accompanying photo: *Guess I'm getting married tomorrow. Here goes nothing.*

Jakob reread the line several times. It came without context other than being dated about seven years ago, and a few celebratory comments—one of which mentioned the name Desmond. No details filled in, no wedding photos or further mentions of this mystery Desmond. No pregnancy announcements or anything else. In fact, Jakob found far deeper info on Kassie's professional website. After he'd left Earth, she'd finished her psychology degree at UC Davis, then had gone on to get her master's in counseling at Cal State East Bay. He loaded up her professional headshot.

Kassie and Jakob had shared a womb together, entered the world together. Their cheekbones, their noses, their eyes, they shared those too—a blend directly between Arnold and Sofia. And yet, this photo seemed to come from a different person altogether: the straight-ahead stare, the slight smile, the tired lines, it showed nothing of the Kassie he knew growing up and certainly far removed from the self-proclaimed Queen of Jell-O Shots in college.

This was sedate, businesslike, everything tuned down, and despite clearly being a professional photograph, she felt out of focus.

Was that what had happened when Kassie had become just Kass?

Evie, on the other hand, was everywhere. Literally, as in her face popped up in countless search results associated with something called the Red Network. On the surface, she looked the same—older, of course, her hair dyed blue and styled in a much different way, but her inquisitive eyes remained. Yet when she spoke on-screen, the way she punctuated the air with waving hands and a fierce nod, the way all of her words palpably fused with true belief, created a greater whiplash than Kassie's turn as a mild-mannered professional.

He paused the video, leaving Evie's wide-eyed stare burning through the screen. He flipped through, episode after episode, picking random moments to try to gauge who and what this version of Evie really meant. "And here," Evie said, "within this cluster of sightings over central Ohio during this span, we see extreme magnetic-field changes within an hour of each reported sighting." Numbers flashed on the screen in two columns. "The amount of change in magnetic declination is proportional to the documented length of sighting periods."

None of it made sense or touched on the true nature of what happened outside of Earth's reach. None of it *seemed* like the Evie he knew, his younger sister's blend of goody-two-shoes naivete and studious science nerd. And now she spoke with lively expressions and her voice pushing louder and louder so that Jakob worried the noise might bleed out of his newly purchased earbuds and wake up the old couple across the aisle.

An advertisement for website hosting interrupted Evie, followed by another for a travel website promising the lowest prices online, the dissonance jarring Jakob back into the reality of being on a creaky bus rolling along Highway 80. He shook his head and thought of the *other* half of his family. Despite experiencing the most extraordinary circumstances, the most devastating losses and unbelievable victories by Earth standards, his pulse quickened at the mere thought of his parents.

Within seconds, he was no longer a soldier, a survivor, and intergalactic traveler. Tight shoulders, hesitant breath, and a dozen ready responses all loaded in, as if he were going to get admonished about his grades or his attitude or the cost of college again, the sense of failure coming laced with a weary spite.

But none of that mattered now. He was a different person. *They* were different people. Jakob started typing.

His search for Sofia Aguilar-Shao came back with nothing, a handful of people who shared the same name as his mom and one ancient mention of her on a dated real-estate site. Jakob tried Sofia Aguilar and that proved to be even less fruitful, no results approaching anything remotely close to her. He clicked, page after page, scrolling from top to bottom and then onto the next page, diving deeper without any trace of his mother.

The information he wanted, the choices and mistakes recorded by history for Mom, simply didn't exist anymore. He sighed and changed focus to the last member of his family.

Arnold Shao.

Jakob closed his eyes, picturing the last time he'd seen Dad, the last time he'd seen any member of his family. A hallway in the Seven Bells ship. An argument. Dad's pleas. Just like Mom, page after page of results returned with little useful information. One headline from the local newspaper referenced Dad's reappearance at Lake Kinbote, but the link itself brought up a page that displayed an error code. Dad's history, it turned out, was as vacant as Jakob's own memory.

The fog in his brain crept in, and a blanketing effect over his mind. Not just memories but the gears that usually cranked out plans and strategies slowed, most likely thanks to the decryptor. Even a numbing layer covered whatever feelings resurfaced about Kassie and Evie, Mom and Dad.

Jakob blinked, for a moment forgetting where he was and why he was there. *GO HOME. WEAPON.* He forced himself to see the images of scribbles on his body, but those memories phased in and out too.

They were too important to forget. "Go home. Weapon," he whispered repeatedly, the act of physically speaking the words bringing some stability to the phrases.

"Go home." For what? Something… But for now, he'd done all he could. Jakob checked the time before powering down his phone and shutting his eyes, going over the various ways he might be forced to interact with his family again—and how they might be able to help him figure out what he needed.

Either way, he planned to speed past any entanglements once he accomplished his goals.

He had much bigger things to worry about than family.

CHAPTER EIGHT

EVIE

The house looked different.

Evie couldn't quite put her finger on it. Six years had passed since she'd been home. She'd flown back to the Bay Area a handful of times, but those usually involved staying in San Francisco or Berkeley and meeting with people connected to the Reds. Home, it seemed, was always too far away. That distance meant that *something* looked different, but the specifics remained uncertain.

Was it the way the trees were trimmed? The different car sitting in the driveway? Little details synced up between her memory and what sat in front of her until she realized that the house had had a new paint job, changing the accents to a slightly darker shade of green. Off to the side, the garden hose that once had sat on a metal reel now hid in a dark brown box, and the first floor's angled roof held solar panels that reflected the early-morning light.

"Evie!"

The whisper came with the urgency of a yell, a hiss loaded with a harshness that Evie *should* have expected but hadn't. She looked over to find Kass in slippers and bathrobe, one hand carrying a folder and the other pointing her way. Though she merely stood in front of the backyard gate, she carried the authority of a school principal on a power trip.

"Kassie! Don't worry, I'm not assuming—"

"Keep your voice down."

Evie looked around her, trying to determine if Kassie's words were meant for someone else. Why would she have any issue with what Evie said?

"I, uh..." Evie started. Kassie tilted her head, her eyes refusing to blink. "Can I whisper?"

Kassie looked up at the house's second floor and pointed. "Don't wake Mom," she finally said.

"Doesn't Mom go running in the morning?"

"Wait right there." Three quick words came out, then Kassie spun on her slippered heel and disappeared around the backyard gate. Evie's mind switched gears, and rather than ponder the ways the house looked different, she pivoted to Kassie.

Her sister looked the same, but different—not the fact that she was in a robe and slippers. "What is it, what is it?" she whispered to herself. Kassie's axis had shifted when Dad had died, inverting her *screw it* attitude into a wary diligence, her playful snark now loaded with a caustic bitterness. But this felt beyond a leap in maturity. Something about this version of Kassie Shao carried a tension: a brow that furrowed a little more, a gait that stepped a little faster, shoulders that held a tad tighter.

Evie was pretty sure it was that, and not her older sister's attire. And she'd put all her money on Kassie still being a smoker. Despite knowing that those things would kill her.

Kassie came storming back, still in bathrobe and slippers, but now with a key ring hanging on a finger. A beep came from the car in the driveway, one chime at first and then two more in rapid succession as Kassie tapped the fob quickly. She pointed at the passenger side, then jumped in the driver's side without a word.

Was Kassie returning her to the airport?

"You can't just come here unannounced," Kassie finally said before Evie even shut her door, hands planted on the wheel though the keys weren't in the ignition.

"I didn't. I texted you."

"And I've been busy with work. I didn't have time to respond."

Evie adjusted in her seat, teeth digging into her bottom lip. "You didn't have time to…respond to a text?"

"I told you, I've been busy with work."

"Kassie, I'm not…" Evie paused, then reached under her to pull out a sheet of paper. *Golden Apple Assisted Living* was printed across the top, and it looked like some sort of intake form.

"That's a client's. Confidential." Kassie snatched it out of her hand.

"Okay. Look. I'm just saying, I'm not here for fun, not here for a vacation." The facts and figures had all lined up, ready to support the idea that somehow Jakob had been transported back to Earth. Evie had started preparing the details while standing in Buffalo Niagara's TSA line for domestic flights. "We detected an event. Yesterday afternoon. The readings—"

"Don't. If you're here to ask for money, you don't have to wrap it up in bullshit about aliens."

"Kassie, I'm telling you with, like, a billion-percent honesty that I'm *not* here to ask for money." That was nearly all true. She wasn't there to ask for money. Though asking for a place to stay was still related to money. But she'd work that part in later. "There was *another* event in Half Moon Bay. Different numbers. But similar circumstances."

"So you're working?" Kassie asked almost absentmindedly as she pulled out her phone. The screen lit up for a mere second before she clicked the side button to turn it black again, either a nervous tick or time check, or maybe both.

"Yeah. I'll be working. I want to go to Reno for a day or two. Shoot some video for the show and also take a look around, see if any of the locals have interesting leads. Then go to Half Moon Bay. I came here first because, well..." she took in a deep breath "...I thought it would make sense as a home base of sorts. Look, it'd save money and I'd probably just sleep here. You wouldn't..."

Evie's voice trailed off, the sudden shift in Kassie's demeanor stopping her. It was subtle, something only experienced eyes might detect after growing up in the room next to someone for years. After watching that person evolve into an adult.

After seeing that person go through *that* night.

"You can't come in," Kassie finally said. "I don't want to wake Mom. She's...under the weather. And I have client calls."

"I'll be quiet. You won't even notice me. Besides, I just need a place for my stuff—"

"Mom is sick. She shouldn't be exposed to any other germs right now. Especially since you were on a cross-country flight."

"It's not like I was in the air *that* long. And the flight was mostly empty—"

"I said no, Evie."

Evie had expected some measure of resistance from Kassie. Some hemming and hawing, possibly some passive-aggressive snark, some other crap that would make Evie work for it, in a way that little sisters had to. Kassie had always been aloof and prickly in the way that often felt the complete opposite to her twin brother's natural warmth. Even with all of that, Evie didn't expect a flat-out no.

"I'm—"

"The answer's no."

Kassie said it with such bold assurance, like she threw down the law from Mount Olympus with a thunderbolt.

"Well, can I at least use the bathroom?" Evie finally asked. Not that she really needed to. That had been taken care of at SFO when the plane landed. This was more about needling Kassie and her weird firewall.

"No. You can't come in. I can drop you off at a coffee shop a few blocks away, but that's it." Keys rang out as Kassie pulled them from her pocket and cranked the ignition. "We have to go now if that's what you want."

"Wait, Kassie. This is ridiculous."

"For fuck's sake, Evie. I told you no. Mom's sick right now."

"Wait a second." Cracks appeared in Evie's internal promises, things she'd told herself to keep the peace. *Agree with Kassie. Say nice things to Kassie. Don't get worked up about the past.* But Kassie's harsh demeanor, the way her words felt like massive bricks rather than mere language spoken aloud, activated long-buried feelings. Her cheek twitched, an involuntary contraction that completely threw her off her game. "You can't do that," she finally said.

Screw it. This was about principle now.

"Do what?"

"*That.* Keep me from coming in. This is my house too. I grew up in it, before and after Dad. I have the right to go in and at least pee." Evie strategically omitted that it'd been probably two years since she'd talked to Mom and probably five or six years since they'd had any meaningful exchange. Mom's sharp tongue and scornful looks *still* carried the power to make her feel like a small child, pushing any thoughts of repairing her residual anger continuously downward on the to-do list. So *that* probably wouldn't be great to bring up. Other excuses came to mind, adult topics that she probably should have understood but didn't quite grasp. "I mean, I'm gonna be on the deed one day with you, so you can't pull this type of bullshit."

Kassie looked at the time again, a different expression chiseled onto her face. That slight bit of tension, the hints of creases and furrowed brow, like she wanted to give in to it but fought desperately to maintain calm. But why?

"What?" Evie finally asked.

"I have shit to do. Do you want to go to a coffee shop or not?"

Evie examined her sister, the strange vibe she carried, the feeling that right beneath the still exterior was something ready to either burst or collapse, she didn't know which.

"Oh, that's what you're gonna do. Just like always. Try to plow over everything in your path. Not even listening to what I need." Evie couldn't help it. It just came out.

"Plow over everything? Use the bathroom at the goddamn coffee shop."

"You know what I mean."

"Damn it, Evie, you're the one who ran off to Buffalo—"

"To look for Jakob!"

"You. Are. Not. Looking. For. Jakob." Kassie's eyes widened with a surprising intensity. "You're making money off idiots who want to believe in bullshit. You're a…a con artist."

"Me? You're getting paid a hundred bucks an hour to say 'tell me how that makes you feel,' and you say I'm the con artist?"

"I am helping people through their problems—"

"Right, and that works so much. Clearly. I'll ask Desmond how that went."

She shouldn't have said that. Part of Evie took pure delight in dragging that up, ripping the scab off that wound, payback in the form of a verbal bullet for, well, everything.

But it was also just freaking mean. And she knew it. "Kassie," she said, her voice suddenly soft. She *should* apologize here. Even an attempt at the word *sorry.* Something wouldn't let those syllables form, and instead she said the next thing that popped into her head. "Just let me in. This is ridiculous."

"No. Evie, you're *not* on the deed." Kassie yelled the statement, complete with a slam against the steering column that triggered the car's horn. Her cheeks burned bright, visible despite the front yard's cypress trees casting a wall of shade on the driveway. "Mom changed it two years ago," Kassie finally said to break the silence. "It's just me."

"Wait, what?" Evie eyed her sister to see if this was a joke, a retaliation for Evie crossing the line. But no, it wasn't. She *knew* from watching Kassie's expression, or lack thereof. "Shouldn't Mom have, like, told me?"

"Maybe if you'd actually called her in the past five years—"

"I've been busy! It's not like she called me either." Heat flooded Evie's face, though her thoughts remained disjointed, collision-prone. How dare the family make a decision like this without her? Except, though she loathed to admit it, Kassie was right. But on the other hand, it's not like they'd reached out to her. They'd never once even asked her about visiting. Like, yeah, Buffalo wasn't that great, but there was plenty to see driving to Niagara Falls and Toronto.

"Evie, you *don't* understand what I have to deal with here."

"Doesn't help if you never tell me."

"And what? When we have problems you're going to stop chasing delusional shit and fly out here? Come on."

Didn't they realize that all of this—quitting school, joining with the Reds, doing the show, studying atmospheric data, so much more, all those thankless hours—all of it was *for* their family? To make it whole again?

That stung more than anything else. More than the wood and concrete and drywall that apparently was no longer her inheritance.

Kassie looked at her phone one more time, then turned the key. The car roared to life, the sound of the motor rumbling between them. "Evie," she said, her voice quiet and gravelly, "I'm going to shut up and take you to a coffee shop. And then—"

Behind them, another car rumbled up to the house, slowing to a halt, its brakes squeaking. Distracted, Kassie watched it in the rearview. Evie's phone buzzed, and she pulled it out to see some texts from Layla asking how things were going, even a silly photo of Layla and her cat in an alien costume with the caption *I'd say more but my cat got my tungsten.* Evie started her reply, the phone's feedback pulsing into her fingertips when she heard Kassie suck in a breath.

"You've got to be fucking kidding me," her big sister said.

CHAPTER NINE

KASS

He's not dead.

A little slimmer than before, his once-thick dark curls now shorn into the stubble of a buzz cut and his complexion slightly paler than she remembered, though it still had that blend of Dad's Chinese and Mom's Brazilian color, the same rich gold-olive tone they all had.

Kass caught herself, recognizing a tornado of feelings whipping around too fast to identify individual bits. There was relief, for sure. Because as much as Jakob was a dick, she never wanted him dead. Incarcerated, though—that seemed more likely than dead anyway, and she lingered on that thought for a fraction of a second.

He *should* be in jail. Even if all he did was charm tourists and con spring-breakers around the world, his real crimes were here, the fallout from Lake Kinbote rippling all the way to their suburban family home.

Relief disappeared, making it easier for Kass to see what

lay past it: rage, regret, and more rage. And an urge to say *Fuck you* to all of it.

Kass considered leaving the scene and hiding upstairs, headphones on and logged into *The Ancient Runes.* Maybe Desmond was online and they could go questing for the Hidden Blade together or something. Or she could actually read the paperwork for Golden Apple. Prepare some questions for Lucy about it. Or do some client billing. Or emails. Or something else before Mom woke up.

Anything that offered a way out of this mess, because spending the morning with both Evie *and* Jakob was *not* in her Top Ten of anything. But there he was, seemingly out of thin air, or at least a rideshare, right on cue.

Behind them, the car door slammed, and Kass turned around fully to see if her eyes deceived her.

But as soon as he locked eyes on Evie, something changed. Not immediately. First Jakob froze, appearing more like a statue than their flesh-and-blood brother. Then things snapped into place. He raised an eyebrow, that little acknowledgment that Jakob saw you, knew you, began the process of trying to charm you.

Though if she needed further confirmation, it came from Evie's sharp inhale and "Oh my god." Her phone fumbled, slipping through her fingers and tumbling by her feet, and Evie bonked her head on the dashboard bending down to grab it. Before Kass managed any kind of response, Evie was outside, a chill breeze coming in through the door she forgot to close.

It couldn't be.

It simply couldn't be. Not Jakob. Not on a day like today, the morning after Mom went down a rabbit hole of It, the same day that Evie came and disrupted the fragile routine that was already imploding under its own weight.

Kass turned in the driver's seat to see Evie hugging Jakob,

a full-body envelopment. And to prove that he was the genuine article, Jakob's mouth formed a crooked line of discomfort before his shoulders bounced to shrug her off. Evie kept holding on, and Jakob replied by offering light pats on the back, arms and elbows at awkward angles.

Their little sister either forgot that Jakob hated hugs or just didn't care.

Jakob shouldn't be here. Evie shouldn't be here. The mere sight of her twin brother and her younger sister together formed a snapshot out of context, a single blip of family reunion that shouldn't exist.

But for a blink, Kass wanted to jump out and join them. Jakob aside, did the Shao siblings ever hug? It didn't seem that way. There was certainly no reason to, not for any event or milestone, and the rare times they'd been together before Jakob disappeared all came with their own weight. After Jakob, only Kass's wedding would have been hugworthy, but Evie hadn't even bothered to show up to that.

Kass stepped out of the car and took in the sight: though he was visibly older, she wouldn't say he looked more mature. Not for Jakob, especially in a getup of cargo shorts, flip-flops, and a T-shirt that made him look like he'd walked straight out of a frat party. While Evie held on, Kass saw it: first one side of his mouth tilted upward, shifting his lips into a slanted line before releasing a full-mouthed grin and bright eyes.

Whoever he was, whoever he'd been since that night fifteen years ago, that single gesture proved he was still Jakob.

For better or worse.

She closed the car door behind her, then walked around to shut the door Evie had left open. As she stepped over, a tapping noise from above caught her attention. The blinds in the upstairs window rustled, their edges bumping against the pane of glass.

Not now not now not now.

"I can't believe this," Evie said, brightness bursting through her tone and catching Kass off guard. Her sister's voice pierced her defenses, grounding Kass in the instinctive whimsy that came with looking at old photographs or reminiscing about childhood Christmas mornings.

Kass felt that crack turn into an opening, something powerful enough that she opened her mouth to say something. What exactly, she wasn't sure. But something needed to released.

Except Evie got in her way. "Of all the days," she continued. "He's here. He's here, on the same day I'm here. Can you believe—"

The window rattled again. Kass realized that the familiar pitch and cadence of each Shao sibling probably triggered something in Mom. And *Mom* was more important than any false nostalgia. Besides, Jakob would probably just shower them with more lies and stupid grins.

"Goddamn it," Kass said under her breath. "You two. Stay right there. And be quiet." They both shot her a confused look. "It's early. People are sleeping. Have some respect for the neighbors."

The blinds bounced up and down with a rapid frequency that set Kass off on a hurried march to the side gate.

People were sleeping, as in Mom, who would launch into who knew what with another day that broke her routine. Hearing Evie *and* Jakob would make things exponentially worse. As Kass trotted up the stairs, her fingers tapped on her phone's screen, an urgent message to Lucy.

I know it's your day off but a bit of an emergency today. Can you come now? And stay late?

Kass stepped carefully in the hall, listening for any movement. A thump came from upstairs, then another, and another. The noise triggered stomach knots as her pace picked up, floorboards creaking with each step. Her hand gripped the doorknob, palm resting long enough to warm up its metal surface. She turned it slowly, and with her free hand, she pushed it open in a slow, controlled motion so as not to startle her. "Mom?"

"Oh no, no, no, no," Mom said to herself.

Kass pushed the door open farther, then told herself to remain calm at the ring of blood soaking Mom's sleeve at the wrist. "Mom? Is everything okay?" she asked, though clearly things were not okay. Especially when Jakob's voice rattled through the window.

Goddamn it, those two never listened.

"Kassie? Kassie, what are you doing home from school?"

"Mom, you're bleeding." Gentle voice, soft tone. Why was Mom up early? It had to be Evie's arrival. But her hand—how had she gone from a pleasant slumber to bleeding? "Your hand."

"Don't be silly, Kassie. I would know if I were bleeding."

"Mom, look. Just look."

"You think I can't take care of myself." Mom turned from her and stepped to the window, toward the voices of Evie and Jakob.

No, she couldn't see them now. The mountain of confusion from that would just explode an already-bad situation. Kass's eyes darted around the room, much like they had the night before, but this time they searched for the possible source of Mom's wound. Dim shadows from the low-morning sun and thin sheer curtains didn't help, but at least they obscured the view *out* the window. Kass moved swiftly, angling almost in front of Mom to run interference, when she spotted the culprit.

A mug. A ceramic mug, or at least half of one. The piece

sat on the dresser, a jagged spike curving out of a broken cylinder. On the laminate floor lay several smaller pieces, including the mating side to the mug's handle.

"Mom, the mug. It must have fallen, and I think you cut yourself picking it up. Let me see."

"That's ridiculous. I was, I was, I was..." Mom blinked, then looked down at her hand, then over to Kass. "Oh, Kassie, good thing it's a Saturday."

"What? No, Mom, it's Tuesday," she said reflexively. Which she shouldn't have. She knew better than to argue about details. Things like that only happened when her guard was down.

"Don't be silly. No school on Saturdays. That's why you're here. Now." She leaned in close and put her hand out for Kass to examine. "Don't tell Dad, but I think I broke his favorite mug."

Dad's favorite mug.

Did Mom even realize that in the end, the mug was just another object to Dad, all of its sentimental value gone?

Several weeks after the sheriff's department had found Arnold Shao, life had *not* returned to normal. Kass took spring quarter off from school to help at home, with plans to return for summer, while Evie lost hours commuting to school. That mostly meant weeks of dancing around Dad's strange impulses. Or acting as a peacemaker between her parents.

Sometimes both.

On a Saturday afternoon that should have been like any suburban June weekend afternoon, Kass had gone to find her father. Opening the door to the garage proved that it wasn't a normal weekend. Natural light flooded her eyes, the glare harsher than usual, and she looked out to see why: Dad had backed the family SUV into the driveway to make space. Instead, a towel covered the floor, objects on each corner to weigh it down. A drill, a hammer, a level.

His favorite mug.

And in the center, that *thing* he'd recovered from Lake Kinbote.

Kass felt her lips purse along with the natural instinct to roll her eyes. She forced herself to stop, to have some measure of compassion for Dad.

Which was hard, given the ever-present stare, whether on a Saturday afternoon or in the middle of the night as she passed him in his office, typing away, while she walked to the bathroom. She knew trauma affected people long-term, but Dad seemed like a physically different person, someone completely new inhabiting his body and mind.

Mom and Dad were pulling apart, in many different ways.

"Hey, Dad? Mom needs you for something."

"Tell her I need a few minutes," he said, walking over to the damn object without a second glance. He moved a digital camera on a tripod to the left before angling it down. "Can you do me a favor and scoot that toward me slowly until I say stop?" He leaned over the camera and pushed buttons on its back. "Just trying to get it into focus."

"Which thing?" She knew what Dad was referring to, of course. But this obsession, the way every single conversation was about the device or Jakob or aliens or something extraterrestrial created a never-ending loop, and she didn't want to dignify any of the shenanigans with legit responses. Not when there were real adult conversations that needed input.

"The Key. Please scoot it forward."

She was not going to use that stupid name that he'd given it. That Evie used. Even Mom referred to the damn thing as that. "Move it?"

"Yeah. I need to zoom in, and the camera's not focusing. Trying to do it manually."

"Okay, I'll scoot It forward." In that moment, the word *it* became the name *It*, if for nothing other than her own amusement. She nudged It an inch forward. "But Mom really needs you."

"What about? I'm busy here."

"Dad," she said, her voice draped in a forced calm, "Mom wants to talk to you about Jakob's death certificate."

"What?" That got his attention.

"She needs it to be finally processed for his school enrollment."

"No, no, no. He is not dead. I told you, I was on that starship with him," he said, pointing up to the sky. "He's not dead. He's somewhere, and we've got to find him. His enrollment status should be *Deferred*, not *Deceased*. This is—"

"The Key to finding him," they said together. Dad completely missed her tone.

Fucking aliens.

Technically, Dad was right. Jakob was still considered missing months after that night. *Missing* seemed like such a subjective term when it involved Jakob—Mom and Dad didn't go to college with him. They didn't understand that he went supposedly missing for days at a time, only to turn up with a group that had gone to Tahoe for snowboarding, been on a road trip to Santa Barbara, gotten lost in Chico smoking weed for forty-eight straight hours. Usually forgetting to charge his phone to boot. One time, she got an email from him from goddamn Moline, Illinois, because of some strange whim of his.

Yes, it had been months. But why would this be any different? Jakob tiring of academic nagging and saying *Fuck it* to responsibilities still presented as the most realistic explanation, even though no one believed her.

So was Jakob dead or missing? Her brother never did anything cleanly or simply, so Kass doubted any clear resolution here.

"You told me yourself, you don't think he's dead. It doesn't make sense, right? They searched the area. They dragged the lake. They questioned the locals," he said, hands on hips. Kass gave his rant space, testing to see if he'd mention the expensive private investigator he'd secretly hired. Several seconds passed, and Dad left it solely with on-the-record evidence to support his beliefs. His pose held, his only movements from short, shallow breaths.

Kass tried to remember if she'd ever seen Dad as intensely focused as this, but no, not even cheering her on during county track championships. Losing Jakob cracked Dad's sense of balance, tilting him from mild-mannered to tired, wide eyes and aggressive posture. "Are you going along with this?" he asked.

She'd kept the PI thing quiet after she'd found a stray document on the floor a few weeks earlier. But after this outburst, maybe now would be the time to tell Mom that he'd cashed out some of their 401k to pay for it. "Not necessarily. I mean, I'm pretty sure Jakob's at some bar in a tiny Central American village with no Wi-Fi."

"You see? Why does Mom want to do this now?"

Mom never gave a definitive response on Jakob, but she didn't have to. Kass knew this was more about the practical aspect of moving forward. Which, based on the class she'd taken on grief and bereavement, made a lot of sense to Kass.

This was Mom's way of fixing things when she couldn't fix Jakob.

"Well, look, I think Mom just doesn't want to deal with the school anymore. It's paperwork. It doesn't change whether he's out there or not. You know? Keeping his paperwork status in limbo doesn't do anyone any good. Can you come in?"

"I can't. I've got to finish this experiment now." Words poured out of Dad, things he'd told the entire family before about It. How he'd grabbed It from some space creature shortly before the aliens forced him and Jakob apart. How he'd landed back at Lake Kinbote with It in his hands. How It had glowed and radiated a strange heat for the first hour after he'd returned. The diatribe went on long enough that Kass could have snuck in a cigarette break. "I'm certain. Kassie, I am so certain. I just need to find the, the, the…the frequency or, or, or…spark or something to get it going again. I'm close, I know it, and now that I've got the camera set up for slow-motion video, I can capture the specific parameters to activate the Key."

The afternoon sun angled just over the houses and trees, and she felt an urge to step into the beam, let the warmth wash some sense of normalcy back into their lives. Yet she knew that wouldn't accomplish anything. She couldn't control that. Or Dad. Or Mom, for that matter. But if Mom needed something, that was one thing she *could* do. "Okay, Dad. I understand," she finally said. "You know what, I'll help Mom. Don't worry about it."

Dad barely responded with a silent nod, the only noise coming from whatever his tinkering was about. Kass's foot accidentally brushed by Dad's empty mug, tipping it just enough for it to fall sideways on the towel. She bent down to set it straight but didn't look over at Dad.

She knew then he wouldn't have even noticed.

In Mom's mind, that was still Dad's favorite mug, as if none of that had ever happened. And for this current flow of time in which she lived, she'd just shattered it. Kass took Mom's hand, pushing the sleeve back and turning the palm upward. Blood oozed from a one-inch gash on the edge of the palm just below the pinky finger—thick, coagulated blood that showed a natural slowing even though Mom probably hadn't applied pressure.

"It's okay, Mom," she said as she met her gaze. Mom's mouth became the smallest of smiles, more an acknowledgment of Kass's presence than anything else. They met eyes for several seconds, and Kass told herself that to react like this was no big deal, like she was still in high school and simply coming to help Mom out on a Saturday morning. And though they stayed focused on each other, Mom's brow furrowed, and the light behind her eyes shifted.

Kass knew this. She should have expected this. This was an entire class in her graduate program on senility and aging: the gap between where Mom's mind sat and the image of an older, wiser, and much more tired Kass creating the kind of dissonance that jarred her further from reality. Kass moved quickly, pushing the spotlight back to the wound. "I'll get a towel. We need to clean this up." Which risked that Mom might reset by the time she got back. But desperate times and all.

A buzz came from her robe pocket. That's fine, the text from Lucy read, I'm close by, just finished at the gym. Be there in five.

Come in the back, Kass wrote in a reply with the thumb of her left hand, her right hand still joined to Mom's.

Ignore the people out front, she added in a final message.

CHAPTER TEN

EVIE

The moment wasn't quite like what Evie had imagined. Given how they'd found Dad shivering by the lake years ago, Evie had imagined Jakob would arrive in similar fashion. But it wasn't shocking, or desperate, or mysterious.

His T-shirt that said *Reno Is for Winners* definitely qualified as something else.

Yet it wasn't just how Jakob was dressed. Emerging from a rideshare as if this were a family barbecue, Evie thought of the theories that Kassie had insisted upon for years.

But there had to be more.

She *refused* to let Kassie's skepticism and anger fill in the gaps. When she hugged her brother, Evie offered the embrace with a full commitment to *her* truth. The hug was validation and victory and reunion all in one.

Even if Jakob tried to get out of it.

She'd been right all along. Jakob was alive, and given the data from the Reds, Evie breathed with a certainty that it was all related to extraterrestrials. It had to be. But she wouldn't press now. The truth would reveal itself eventually. Right now, his existence in this moment defined everything that mattered, and letting go was not an option.

As Kassie ran indoors to take care of…something, Evie held her brother like he was a fragile baby, not the older brother with a penchant for acting like he never grew up past high school. She focused so intently on his very existence, a need to ensure his appearance wasn't a trick or a delusion or dream, that Kassie's departure hardly registered. If Kassie explained why she went inside, Evie didn't hear.

And really, she didn't care.

Jakob was here.

And he was different.

Older, wiser, and definitely changed. His eyes carried a weight that said they'd seen much more than the happy-go-lucky person who'd nearly failed out of college multiple times.

Evie registered this as a fact right away, looking Jakob square in the eyes for *truth* as soon as she'd stepped out of the car. And despite giving that patented Jakob smile, something was off about it, no matter how much he looked like an unemployed hipster. During her years with the Reds, she'd interviewed countless people. Some were full of crap, simply trying to get attention. Some weren't quite sure but put forth what they thought they should say.

But the ones who truly believed everything they said, they showed commitment. Their eyes came with a different glow—not the light that arrived with joy or the spark that showed fear, but something further, an intensity that begged for understanding, for belonging.

Evie saw that in Jakob.

Hidden behind his disarming smile and stupid clothes. But still there.

And she wanted to know *why*.

Somehow, in some way, Jakob had arrived home on the very same morning as Evie. And Dad wasn't around to see it. Did this count as keeping the promise she'd made to him so many years ago? Evie squeezed her eyes shut, leaning into the hug. So many questions remained, questions that Dad would have wanted to ask, questions the Reds would want to ask, questions that she *needed* to understand.

But those could wait. For the first moments, all she wanted to do was hug her brother. And though he didn't return the embrace, she felt his tense body relax just a little. "I missed you," she said, and as she laughed at the sheer disbelief of the scene, he did too. She blinked several times at the tears quietly leaking through, despite trying to keep *everything* together. So many ways she'd prepared for this moment, and yet her momentum was stolen by a trickle of tears.

"Hey, it's all right. I missed you too."

"Oh, it's not that." Evie finally pulled back, wiping her eyes and nose. This was even more undignified than cleaning cat pee at work. "I mean, it is and it isn't. It's just…"

"I know. Where have I been?" Jakob nodded. "I'll get into it. Let's wait for all of us so I don't have to tell the same story a bunch of times. It's…" he paused, lips pursed in a sudden shift "…well, it's a long story. That's probably the best way to put it."

A long story.

"Actually," Evie said after a heavy pause, "I was just thinking. About something I told Dad."

Jakob's face contorted, his mouth slanting at an angle and brow furrowing. "I wondered how Dad would react. Do you think he'll be—" he turned his head and stared at the second story of their childhood home "—I don't know, upset? That I'm back?"

It was a good thing that Jakob faced the other direction.

He completely missed Evie's expression evolve with the gravity of his words sinking in. The smile that had felt permanent seconds prior shifted into openmouthed horror, accompanied with a sudden weight on her chest, squeezing out any capacity to breathe.

"He's usually up around now, right? Probably on his morning run with Mom. Is he retired yet? I can't imagine—"

"Jakob," Evie blurted out. Her big brother finally turned back, eyes meeting hers.

She had to tell him the truth. He'd know any instant now. Kassie certainly wouldn't pull any punches. And she had no idea what Mom might say; it'd been years since she'd had a conversation of any real substance with Mom, but time had probably made her opinions even more acidic than before.

"Yeah? What is it?" Jakob grimaced, blowing out a sigh. "Dad's pissed, huh?"

"Look, Jakob. Dad—"

Another car drove up and slowed to a halt in front of the curb, the engine cut, and the parking brake cranked. Evie eyed the woman clad in gym clothes who got out, glanced at the siblings, then walked through the house's back gate.

Like she belonged.

Springed hinges pulled the wooden gate back, its latch clicking back into place to leave Evie and Jakob in silence. Evie was pretty sure Jakob was also wondering *Who is this person and why did she just waltz into the house?* Their gazes shifted, hitting each other with puzzled looks, and in a way, it was just the thing that Evie needed. There they were, Evie and Jakob, connecting on a level that Kassie probably wouldn't understand and, in a way, never had understood.

"Who's that?" Jakob finally asked.

"I…have no idea."

They remained in silence. Birds chirped. A child yelled

from somewhere down the street. In the other direction, a dog barked, and somewhere around them, the air carried the sounds of traffic turning at a light. It came and went, and Evie hoped it would stay this way, with comfortable silences and random people going into their childhood home.

And no unbearable truths to reveal.

"Anyways," Jakob said after a minute or so, "what were you saying about Dad?"

There it was. She should do it. She should be the one. Not just because of how the others might handle it, but because of the promise she'd made to Dad. It was all connected, in some way, like the universe pulling threads together.

Or maybe just being extra cruel. It could have been either.

Evie took in a deep breath, the tears that had just stopped suddenly welling up again. This time, for a completely different reason. "Okay. Right. So—" From her back pocket, Evie's phone buzzed. A quick look showed that it was a group text from the Reds. Nothing extraordinary, just checking in. "One second."

But she took her time constructing her reply back. It gave her more time to think about how to explain to Jakob that Dad had died because of him.

CHAPTER ELEVEN

KASS

"Sure," Mom said, so pleasantly it was like Kass had just offered her an Arnold Palmer to drink, not a towel for a bloody gash. "Thank you, Kassie."

Kass wrapped Mom's hand and shuffled quickly out of the room, voices from the cracked upstairs bathroom window reminding her that goddamn Jakob and Evie had completely ignored her request to stay quiet. The medicine-cabinet door swung open, and while Kass made a first-aid stockpile to bring back to the room, the conversation grabbed her attention.

From outside, Jakob spoke at a volume too loud for Kass's liking, even if Mom was preoccupied. And though she assessed the different-size Band-Aids in their small cardboard box, her attention crept more toward her siblings' conversation.

Siblings. Plural. How strange to think that.

"You might say I was finding myself." There it was. This was definitely Jakob, not some sort of magical look-alike or impostor. Only Jakob would say something so meaningless and vague. She stepped out of the bathroom, hydrogen peroxide, towel, and Band-Aids of various sizes all balanced between her hands when Lucy's voice came from downstairs.

"Kass?" she called.

"Up here," she yelled back. "Mom cut her hand. I'm patching it up."

Footsteps clomped up the stairs, and Lucy came into view, clearly dressed for a day off in leggings and a T-shirt with *New York University Athletic Department* across the chest. A few drops of sweat remained on her forehead, all the more visible by her hair being pulled back in a tight blond ponytail.

"How bad is it?"

"She dropped a mug and cut the side of her palm on the broken edge. I don't think it's bad."

"You got company?" Lucy asked, moving in step with Kass.

"Yeah," she said. "You could say that."

"Well, if it's not bad, I can handle it. I'm assuming that couple is why you asked me here." They stopped outside of Mom's ajar door, Lucy holding a hand out to let Kass enter first.

"Kassie?" Mom called. "Don't tell Dad about his mug. I can fix it."

Fix it. She would say that. At least her inner drive to always find a solution to problems had remained. She was always asking her kids, "How will you fix it?"

The truth of the moment hit Kass. Maybe it was because Lucy stood there now. Or maybe her frazzled brain was still rattled from both Jakob and Evie arriving this morning. But that mug, it was exactly like Mom had said: *Dad's favorite mug.* Not exactly pretty or sturdy, and it didn't have a cool logo or change colors with heat or anything like that. But it was his—theirs, from the time Mom had dragged him to a pottery class.

And now it existed only in pieces, jagged pieces, incomplete and crumbling. Nothing could fix that.

Kass turned from Lucy, pretending to adjust the supplies in her hand. She faced the wall, not at any particular decor in the hallway or the small side table, but instead she found a nice blank spot, nothing but paint upon textured drywall. And then, only then, did she allow her dam to crack, the tiniest, slightest of punctures that caused her eyes to well with tears.

"It's okay," Lucy said, the warmth of her hand landing on Kass's shoulder. "I got this. It's okay to see your friends for a morning."

Friends. If only it was that easy. "Yeah," Kass said, allowing herself one strong sniff before straightening up. She turned, and Lucy took the supplies out of her hands. "Thanks for coming on such short notice. It was...unexpected."

"These things happen. This is my job. You already do enough for her."

My job. It *was* Lucy's job now, but that would change in two weeks when she joined the staff of Golden Apple. And then what would Kass do? Work while breaking in a new caregiver? *Find* a new caregiver? Kass considered the list of referrals Lucy had sent. They sat in an email, a constellation of names, phone numbers, and email addresses. All available to access anywhere, anytime from the comfort of the small device in her pocket.

So why hadn't she done it yet?

Kass told herself to focus on one problem at a time, then forced steps forward toward the *other* unfolding disaster. On her way out, Jakob's voice floated in from the bathroom window and stopped all of Kass's forward momentum. "Kassie said Mom is sick," he said. "Can't Dad take care of her?"

Kass's grip tightened on the doorframe.

"Jakob," Evie said, her voice breaking, "there's something you need to know."

"Know what?"

Could Mom hear this? If she did, could she reconcile *any* of it? Different instincts pulled Kass in different directions. Shout out the window for them to stop. Sprint to the bedroom and cover Mom's ears. Get in her car and drive away. No, put Jakob and Evie in the car and take them to the airport.

But it didn't matter. Nothing stopped Evie's words.

"Dad *died* looking for you."

A complete lack of response gave away how the news stunned Jakob. And while that probably should have elicited some measure of sympathy, Kass found herself wanting to scream *through* the floorboards at them. She needed a cigarette. She needed one *now*, something to soothe the nerves that suddenly fluttered with electricity.

Jakob didn't know. Of course Jakob didn't know, because he was too busy doing whatever the fuck he did. He finally spoke after several seconds, but by then distance had muffled his voice. Kass strode straight into her room with jaw clenched and unblinking eyes, changing from bathrobe to the fastest, easiest socially acceptable clothes in her wardrobe, all with one goal.

She wasn't going to let Evie and Jakob upset Mom.

"Who was that lady?" Evie asked as Kass stepped outside.

"She's my assistant," Kass said, quietly enough to not give away the situation to Lucy. The car in the driveway beeped twice, and she marched over to the driver's side, where only minutes ago she'd sat with Evie in her robe. "You two. Get in."

Jakob arched an eyebrow.

Kass settled into the driver's seat, then waited for her siblings to buckle into the car. "We're gonna have a family reunion. Right now," she said with a sigh.

CHAPTER TWELVE

JAKOB

This world is so small.

Jakob sat in the back of Kassie's car, observing everything from the dashboard's massive touch-screen panel to the tension between his sisters. Kassie's frustration burned hot enough that Evie clearly felt it sitting there. Evie, though, remained more inscrutable. From his view in the back seat, he could see her jaw clench and then relax, the occasional sigh coming from her as she scrolled through her phone.

Around them, the streets surrounding their childhood home had barely changed. Storefronts swapped out, like how the strip mall's laundromat had become a pet groomer, and a few new office buildings emerged out of the ground, looming over the city like glass-paneled overseers. But fundamentally, things had remained. The traffic light turned green, the car moved, and a familiar rhythm came to the passing blocks. Jakob even had a hunch as to where they were headed.

All those people, coming and going. Completely unaware

of so many bigger things happening beyond the sky. Jakob watched a man pacing on the sidewalk, one hand holding a phone and the other in large, animated gestures while he complained about *something.* Something trivial for sure, something clearly not about life and death.

But there *was* a different kind of death from what burned in space.

Dad.

Dead.

The word rooted itself in his mind, refusing to leave. Death was a part of the war against the Awakened. It fused into every moment aboard the Seven Bells fleet. He'd seen countless colleagues beyond Henry die, some merely hours after they'd suited up for their first mission, colleagues that looked nothing like him and communicated in ways he barely understood.

This was different. *Dad died looking for you*, Evie had said.

Looking for Jakob. Except Jakob was the one who'd made the decision to send Dad home. And he'd never questioned that decision until now.

About two standard days after he and Dad had disappeared from the surface of the Earth, they'd found themselves on a Seven Bells ship—specifically, the aftermath of a battle that had gone very wrong for the ragtag Seven Bells alliance. The ship was limping back to the fleet rendezvous point, swinging far wider than usual to avoid detection, and scanning for resources on any planets they passed.

Like Earth.

And Jakob happened to be in the right place at the right time and, more importantly, the right height and size to fill the equipment of recently deceased soldiers, some of whom Jakob saw as soon as he regained consciousness: alien, organic tissue turned into strange crystalline material—in some cases fused directly into damaged mech limbs. Tools hummed and equipment vibrated, an entire process to reclaim whatever armor and parts might be salvageable.

That was why they'd targeted him. Something about a combination of age, size, and physical condition. And for a crew of motley species, these recruitment parameters were one way to make sure no equipment went to waste.

Dad, however, was caught along for the ride. Literally, as the transporter settings were meant for one human. They were lucky that it didn't disintegrate Dad on the way.

For Jakob, it meant days where time had no meaning, one life-changing revelation after another. Were there aliens? Yes, there were *so many* aliens, a number so overwhelming that even now he still didn't know the name of every species working under the Seven Bells flag. Were there *bad* aliens? Yes, and it turned out that Dad's sci-fi shows got some of those traits right—plus mechs from the few years when he indulged in anime—along with holographic displays, faster-than-light speed, smart communication tech that quickly adapted to English, and other things.

It was all of that mashed into one overwhelming reality, something that made him question if he hadn't taken the best/worst drugs of all time.

Except the experience was more powerful than drugs. For someone who'd always felt rudderless, almost fearful of having purpose, the cumulative impact of all the revelations snapped things into focus. The universe suddenly offered so much more, and the weight of that responsibility pushed Jakob in a way like nothing else had.

After the whirlwind of information, as the crew of the Seven Bells ship let Jakob see and feel things for himself, only *then* did they reveal that they'd accidentally caught Dad in the transport radius as well.

"I'm going to stay here," he'd told Dad. They stood in a

thin hallway in one of the fleet's smallest cruisers. He stepped toward his father, still marveling at the way the artificial gravity felt different from the Earth's standard gravity, each motion like a clumsy pull.

"What?" Dad stared at him, wide-eyed. Jakob never knew if Dad had fully grasped where they were, what the Seven Bells were up against.

"They want me here." That wasn't an exaggeration, given the outcome of their recent skirmish, and having recruited several humans over the past decade, their database recognized a human in peak physical condition. "That's why they identified and transported me up here."

Dad turned, facing the walls and putting his hand against the smooth rock-life surface that seemed to be everywhere on the ship, from the control panels to the weapons to the ship's hull. "You can't. What about us?"

"Dad," Jakob said with a polite scoff, "this won't be any different than when I'm at school. You won't even notice that I'm gone." The claim came with so many caveats and asterisks that Jakob didn't even believe it himself, but he recognized that he'd put up a reasonable argument based on Dad's reaction. "Pretend this is grad school for me. It's better than just backpacking around Europe, right?"

"No, it's not. This is dangerous. The things I've seen. I won't let you do it."

"What do you mean, you won't let me?"

"I won't let you. It's too dangerous. Look, you're replacing a creature that is roughly your size and shape? Stepping into this role? You know what that means? You're cannon fodder. They're plucking people like us off random planets, showing you the wonders of all this—" he gestured around them "—and then telling you your life isn't worth much. I can't let you do that."

"I've made up my mind." Jakob thought back to all the times he'd tried to blow off his parents, deflecting and evading their questions about his future. Now he had a simple, true answer, and all he got in return was pushback. "I have to do it," he said, the words filled with purpose. "You've always told me that I'd know when I found my path. This is it. I feel it in my bones."

"Jakob, listen to me. My whole life I've been trying to steer you back on track. I know I've been tough. I know I've been annoying." Dad's eyes grew wide with an unblinking desperation. He reached over, taking his son's hands. "I know it's been a lot. But you can't just disappear on us. What about school?"

"School? Dad, look at this." Jakob pulled away from Dad's grip and motioned to one of the interfaces nearby. The floating holographic message fluttered as he waved his hand through it, a message in unknown glyphs fizzling out before coming back to bright, empty existence. "There is so much more out there."

"No, you listen. You are *my* son."

Within Jakob's inner ear, a message rattled, one that only he could hear, having been outfitted with a communication device a few hours ago. "Shao Jakob Human. The ship will leave this sector in forty-one of your time measurements."

"Dad, listen. You need to go." He pointed at the small docking station across the hall. "That's called a…um, it's some type of transporter. But it'll put you back down at Lake Kinbote."

"No, Jakob. We're leaving now." Dad grabbed him by the arm as if he were still a little boy, but Jakob shrugged him off before doing the most unexpected thing.

Jakob hugged him. Partly to keep Dad contained and focused, but also the reality of the situation had sunk in. He held Dad close and tight until two other beings stepped toward them, both bipedal, one that looked like a metallic bird merged with a human and the other with elegant appendages, etched lines in its coral face, and ganglia at the base of its skull. The birdlike one yelled something in a surprisingly human voice—though that may have been the internal communicator translating for him—telling colleagues to watch his calibrations while he sorted this out.

And the other, in a calm, measured tone, suggested that they apply a decryptor to his dad.

The different possibilities played out to Jakob. His dad wouldn't know the truth. He'd be confused, groggy when he landed, and given that the decryptor required such a device to restore scrambled memories, it was likely that Dad would never recover what happened.

Which meant he'd be back home and safe. And Jakob would be free to act on this newfound feeling of… Was it purpose?

The thought rippled through his body, and his simple decision landed with a far more massive weight than the reality of standing on a faster-than-light spaceship with two aliens trying to subdue his dad.

"Yeah," he said to the open channel quietly. "Let's do it."

Over the following years, Jakob had sent soldiers—colleagues, friends—to their deaths. He'd sent himself, volunteering to run into the field to fix equipment or recover gear. But Dad, he'd sent him *away* from war.

Only it hadn't kept him safe. Maybe just the existence of aliens wouldn't have done it. Or the idea of Jakob walking away from their family. But both? That had proved to be too much, unraveling him in wholly unexpected ways.

Logically, that revelation should have gutted him, and the guilt should have weighed enough to sink his spirit. The fact that it *didn't* felt notable to Jakob, but he told himself that he didn't have time to deal with that.

He was on a mission. And the memory itself uncovered

something: Dad was never able to fully recall what had happened because the decryptor used on him remained with the Seven Bells fleet. Jakob knew the gaps in his mind must have been from such a device, but he just realized why he might tell himself to go home.

The decryptor was somewhere around home.

Learning about Dad's death gave him cover from his sisters, an excuse to sit back and consider how he might identify the location of the device and what it might reveal about himself, about the circumstance, the mission, all of it. Since Kassie had come out of the house in a huff, they'd all piled into the car, barely any acknowledgment among each other.

And now here they were. A family reunion, as Kassie had said. Though he didn't know if that was a joke or if their destination was meant to rub it in. But it seemed like a strategic time to say something to his sisters.

"Didn't this place used to be the Rook House?"

Of course it did. He knew because Dad used to suggest the Rook House for weekend brunch, then Mom would reply that it was overcrowded and not worth the hassle for a mediocre diner. Half the time, Dad would relent, and they'd go elsewhere. The other half, Dad would insist, saying that it was the only spot that served breakfast burritos.

"When did the Rook House become—" Evie squinted at the fancy font on the restaurant sign "—Kosmos?" Evie asked.

"Last year." Kassie pulled the car forward over speed bumps. They turned into a parking spot as she sighed. "Better coffee. Quiet. It's close."

This led to small talk between Kassie and Evie, which provided Jakob with even more observations about his sisters. Their individual tics remained, such as Kassie's pursed lips when annoyed or Evie mumbling while she figured things out. In a way, seeing their little idiosyncrasies felt most like coming home.

Like a teacher leading pupils, Kassie unbuckled and led the charge, Evie tentatively following her older sister and Jakob moving one step behind. A bell jingled as the front door swung open. Kassie passed, but Evie stopped, turning to wave Jakob through, and for a moment, the tension eased. Evie beamed a bright smile, her short hair disheveled in a way that looked completely different from her videos. Jakob met her gaze, and Evie quietly said, "I still can't believe you're here."

Her excitement didn't generate nostalgia or regret in him. "Should have come back sooner," he said. Did he mean it?

"Yeah, you should have. There are things called phones," she said, giving a soft punch to his shoulder before looking at Kassie.

It was a small gesture, something so benign that most people wouldn't notice it. But that hint of sibling playfulness caught Jakob off guard, the way he and Evie fell into their old rhythms, and he felt himself seize up from within, a surprise pull of emotion before he buried it.

There were bigger things at stake than *feelings*.

Kassie turned around, her mouth neutral as the restaurant host handed over menus and pointed them to an empty corner of the dining room. Kassie walked forward without waiting, and the host followed.

"This way," the host said, motioning them through. "Can I start you with something to drink?"

As his sisters ordered, he looked at them. Kass, all tense shoulders and tired eyes. And then Evie, who seemed propelled by an effervescence just beneath the surface.

Jakob sucked in a quick, sharp breath, enough to clear his mind and reset his heart rate. He'd made it here. And now he was going to do anything to get back to the fleet, even if it meant mining his sisters for whatever resources they could provide. Ultimately, they were tools to help him find the decryptor. That started with playing *exactly* into their expectations of who they thought Jakob Shao was: unreliable, irresponsible, idiotic. And then he'd assess from there, based on their reactions.

Because the truth would break them.

He whispered to himself as quietly as possible, "Go home. Weapon."

CHAPTER THIRTEEN

EVIE

By now, Evie had been awake far too long, especially considering that most of the West Coast was still having breakfast or starting their day. She checked the time while they all thumbed through their menus, watching to see that Kassie didn't catch her stealing glances at Jakob. It still seemed impossible. Her *brother*, sitting next to her, a restaurant menu in hand. After all these years, and the way he'd returned, the way that he looked the same but different, she sensed a shift in him. His gestures were the same, his expressions were the same, his freaking *smirk* was the same. But his eyes—something weary lingered there, but what might have caused it?

She knew. It *had* to be what she suspected. The things he'd seen, that he must have experienced. And the event in Reno—and his shirt! It all lined up.

Reno Is for Winners. Indeed.

"Coffee. Fresh pot," the waiter said, handing Kassie a beige ceramic mug. She looked up, flashing a polite smile and waving off the little creamer tin he offered. "Coke," he said, handing Jakob a large glass, "and herbal tea with lemon."

"Thanks," Evie said, immediately pulling the tea to her nose. Steam tickled her senses with the warm aroma of lemon, and in that moment everything felt like the world was perfect.

Except for one world-shattering issue: she'd told Jakob about Dad. He'd retreated into his shell once Kassie had come back outside, and not a single question, not a single word had come out about Dad since.

Evie warned herself to contain her own joy over the morning. Hearing news about Dad had clearly shocked Jakob, and she wanted to give him proper space to process all of it.

She took a slow slip and a deep inhale of the tea's steam.

"So," Jakob said, "I have a little bit of money. I can treat."

"Oh, you're chipping in," Kassie said right away.

"It's the least I could do."

"Noted."

Something inside tugged at Evie, urging her to yell at her sister. *This is your twin brother! Home at last!* She wanted to scream it with enough ferocity to shatter the windows around them, possibly every dish in the building.

But once again, she tempered her emotions, telling herself to enjoy the moment. Even *bickering* between Jakob and Kassie was a little miracle in itself. Her eyes met the waiter's, who clearly felt the familial tension. "I'll have a club sandwich with fries. I'm on East Coast time. It's lunch for me."

"Biscuits and gravy," Jakob said. He shuffled in his seat, eyes suddenly bright. "Over-easy eggs. And a side of English muffins, please. Kassie?"

"Granola parfait," she said, folding the menu and holding it up. The waiter nodded, taking the menus and disappearing, and the farther away he got, the more Kassie's presence seemed to loom over them. So many things that needed to be said. And asked. And answered.

Evie watched Kassie's expression as it changed, knowing she was about to go on the offensive.

"All right, I'm just gonna cut the bullshit," Kassie said. Her words bit through the gentle morning noises of the mostly empty restaurant. "Jakob, where the *hell* have you been?"

"Okay. Okay, I deserve that."

"Deserve that? Who runs off without a trace for fifteen years? And you come back, and you think buying us *breakfast* will make it okay?"

"No," he shook his head. "Of course not. It's just breakfast. An olive branch."

"Olive branches don't bring back Dad." Kassie stared at Jakob without blinking, a clear challenge across the table. Growing up, she'd never fought with such direct blows. She usually attacked with quiet pettiness, saying things just out of earshot or infusing her body language with a stiff apathy, even when something deserved at least a drop of feeling.

Kassie, who Evie had barely spoken to over the past five years—and really, that was *Evie's* fault—wasn't going to pull any punches here. Not with Jakob.

"You overheard us." Jakob stirred the straw in his Coke, ice rattling around.

"I asked you to keep it quiet. You didn't respect my request. Like everything else. 'Oh hey, I'm Jakob. Mom and Dad can't say no to me. All the pretty girls think I'm charming. All the dumb dudes think I'm cool.' Then you vanish. And now Dad is dead. Your. Fault. Yours." Kassie's cheeks flushed, and her eyes glowered, though despite her tone, this wasn't fury.

Evie wasn't a psychologist like Kassie, so her clinical judgment might be off—she spent her days weighing sick animals and wiping their pee off herself—but her gut knew her big sister was giving in to something besides rage, like if Kassie let up for a split second, then the raised voice drawing the attention of the restaurant would immediately slip into every other emotion.

"Kassie, that's a little harsh," Evie said.

"Is it? Am I supposed to dress this up? What would make it better?" Kassie laughed, fingers tented against her forehead. They threaded through her hair, pulling the strands all the way back as she sighed. "And don't say *aliens*, Jakob. Don't get Evie started on that bullshit. No. Fucking. Aliens."

Evie shot her sister a glare. "There is plenty of scientific evidence showing visitations not of this Earth. That night lines up with other findings of suspected—"

"Evie, this is not your show. Turn off the performance art."

"What the crap, Kassie?" She slammed the table with her words, causing the silverware to rattle and her tea to shake within its stained ceramic mug. "If you just took the time to understand—"

"Maybe if you just took the time to check in, you'd understand." Kassie's words came out terse, and rather than look up ready for a fight, all her bravado from earlier inverted, shrinking her into the diner booth with a sudden deflation.

"What's that supposed to mean?" Evie asked, now feeling the need to be the aggressor. She had her own questions for her family, and they had nothing to do with questioning life choices—and though the story of the day was Jakob's return, she sure as hell wouldn't pass up what Kassie had just walked into. "You got *our* house for free. That's right—" she turned to Jakob "—guess who's on the deed now. She convinced Mom to do that. Hey, some of us have to pay rent."

"That has *nothing* to do with this. Or *him*." Steam still visibly rose from Kassie's mug as she took a sip, then set it back down. "Actually, maybe it does. You have so much to say, then go on. Tell him how Dad died."

All eyes were on Evie now. The weight of Kassie's attention compounded with an intensity from Jakob—not judgment but a pensive curiosity.

He wanted to know this. Probably *needed* to know this.

Whether that was a good or bad thing, she couldn't say. This new Jakob proved harder to read.

She blew out a sigh and scanned the room. Even the wait staff, who were hiding behind folding napkins and sorting silverware for the morning, seemed to be waiting for her answer. "He...drowned."

"Drowned where?" Kassie asked pointedly.

"Lake Kinbote."

"And what was he doing there?"

Kassie may have known the answer to that in simple facts from the police report, like how they'd found the Key and surveying equipment in Dad's car or in what part of the lake they'd found his body. But what he had been doing there only Evie knew. Because they had talked about it, in one final quiet moment at home before Dad had died.

Six months after Dad returned *without* Jakob, he'd gradually slipped from being the same old Arnold Shao that everyone knew, watching science-fiction repeats and going for daily runs and staying up late with overtime hockey games to someone who spent all his free time online. And it wasn't just diving deep into blogs on UFOs and alien abduction. He'd started chatting with people, posting on forums, sharing photos and information, sometimes pushing through the night before stumbling into his office job and fudging his way through the day.

This shift rippled around everyone. It was as though Jakob had been the center of their solar system, and his disappearance was a supernova event that had knocked everything out of alignment. Kassie called regularly from her summer classes at UC Davis but increasingly grew irritable with Dad, more often talking with Mom. And the tension between Mom and Dad, Evie felt it: even though they weren't particularly talkative to begin with, dinners somehow evolved into even quieter affairs. Half the time, Evie didn't even bother coming home after her summer job at the downtown branch of Books Inc. The nearby cafés offered a friendlier environment for her to sit with her laptop.

Where she, like Dad, began researching alien abduction.

That night, they had had a heated discussion about a new thread, a discussion of historical environmental data recorded since the mid-1990s, how the burgeoning access of data allowed a network of people to put together consistent tracked shifts in relation to reported disappearances.

"Look at this," he'd said, swiveling in his chair to the glowing computer monitor. "This is recorded atmospheric pressure on the night we were abducted. And humidity levels," he said, clicking over to another browser tab, "and electromagnetic activity. You see how the values change?"

"Just like in the findings by the *Animus* blog." Not exactly—the blog's hypothesis had slightly different data curves. But close enough that Dad seemed onto something.

"Exactly. And look, a few days later when you found me, similar drops. Different starting points because the initial conditions are different based on weather." He leaned back in his chair, then grabbed *that* thing from the desk's hutch. He put the object on piles of printouts and charts that now blocked out the row of Kassie's track and Jakob's swimming trophies. "This. I'm not kidding when I say this is the Key. It *has* to be." Dad launched into his foggy recall of the alien ship. *With* Jakob for part of it. But Jakob had been ushered elsewhere.

And then the rest became large blurs. As he hit the unknowns, Dad's eyes welled with tears, but his mouth slanted with fury, a previously rare emotion that had become more frequent for him since Lake Kinbote. "What were they doing to him?" he asked, shaking his fist. "They let me see him. But he was different. I could tell. They *did* something to him, I know it. He came in and gave me a hug. That's how I knew something was wrong. Jakob *never* hugs. And he squeezed so hard," Dad said. "He said something, and I just can't remember it. It's all hazy from there. I remember being grabbed and pushed into a…a chamber of some kind. They kept pushing, and their grip—god, it was unlike anything I'd felt. Not human. I remember the feeling of floating almost. I don't know if they'd grabbed my legs or if it was something else in their technology levitating me. I remember grabbing something: it was on a cart or nearby table. They have tables in space," he said with a laugh.

"Everyone needs a table. Even aliens," Evie said, completely serious.

"I remember grabbing onto the Key, and it was being pulled from me. And then Jakob—it *was* Jakob, I'm sure of it—shouted, 'Let him go.' 'Let him go.' I still think about that. He told them to let me go, and they didn't. They didn't listen to him." They sat in the quiet office, the *whoosh* of traffic and the occasional passersby the only noises between them, and Evie had reached over and held Dad's hand as he stared at his stack of papers. "The Key. Why is it so important? Why would they fight me over it?" He tapped the smooth surface of the object in his hand. "I know it's all connected. I can feel it in my bones. I'm taking a few days off from work. Gonna drive up to Lake Kinbote in the morning."

Behind him, Mom crossed the hallway with a bag of groceries in either hand. She shot them a glance that Evie caught before her face returned to neutral and she marched to the kitchen.

"We're gonna find him, Evie."

Dad's eyes locked into hers, a pleading behind them that felt more like a question than a statement. Not the quiet ignoring from Mom, not the heavy sighs from Kassie. He believed that statement with every fiber of his being.

What he needed at that moment was for someone to give him permission.

"We will, Dad. I promise you."

Despite the euphoria of being around Jakob again, of watching him sit stoically in their corner booth, Dad's questions lingered. She didn't need to ask Jakob about where he'd been because she knew; she felt it in her bones and breath. But how, why, what it all meant, *that* mattered.

Kassie had told Evie she'd thrown the Key out a few years ago, and if she hadn't, maybe Evie could have inspected it with her equipment from the Reds. But she told herself to fret about that later, not as she sat with Jakob in the face of Kassie's question. Her sister loaded it with a vindictive tone, but Evie answered it the way she would have had she been livestreaming: matter-of-fact, scientific, calm. "Dad was at Lake Kinbote looking for you. Not *you*. Like, he didn't think you were out camping there or hiding underwater. But looking for clues about where you went. He'd looked up magnetic-field data and atmospheric-pressure data and wanted to see for himself."

"Did you hear that, Jakob?" The question came at nearly a shout. "Dad died looking for you. Something about your disappearance got him back at Lake Kinbote and then in the water. They found him two days later. Do you know who had to identify the body?" Kassie finally let go, her voice breaking despite its raised volume. She pointed a finger at Jakob, and it failed to hold steady; it jabbed in the air with each word, a tremble rippling through it. "I saw him. I saw Dad after two days of being in the water. I can never get that out of my head. So tell us, Jakob, where have you been this whole time? Because Dad would want to know. Dad *died* trying to know..." Evie watched her older siblings eyeing each other, the people she'd spent her youth with now sharing a table as weathered adults, twins with their connection severed by both time and space. Kassie's jaw tightened, and though the words and the emotions behind them were launched at Jakob, they seemed to bounce off him, like he processed it all and reset to zero in seconds. "So I think you owe us that," Kassie finally said, falling back to her seat.

Jakob looked at his sisters, focus bouncing between them.

Then he shrugged.

Of course he would. That was how he handled conflict, anything from their parents begging him to take school more seriously to the fallout from semi-illegal shenanigans with his swim buddies.

Except he didn't follow with his usual response, and *that* threw Evie off. There was no curl of the lip, no glow in his eye, and maybe that stemmed from the serious nature of the conversation.

It wasn't every day you learned your father had died searching for you.

"Excuse me," the waiter said softly. Evie turned to find him balancing three plates of food along his left arm. "Club sandwich. Biscuits and gravy. And granola parfait." He set each one down, then backed away before Evie could correct his placement. Instead, as they awaited Jakob's reply, she pushed Kassie's glass bowl to her and pulled her own sandwich plate over.

"Okay." Jakob looked down at his food, then back up at his sisters.

Evie's entire body tensed. Her breath narrowed, and her

pulse quickened, Dad's words echoing in her mind. *He was different. I could tell.* How much detail would Jakob give? Would Kassie believe him? What secrets did he carry, and—she just realized—what could she tell the Reds?

A stinging sensation came from the inside of her lip, and she realized that her top teeth were digging in. She told herself to unclench and wait, every fraction of a second stretching out interminably.

Here it came. Confirmation of extraterrestrial life. Confirmation of where he'd been. Confirmation of *why* he'd been away. Evie practically felt Dad's presence next to her, leaning forward in anticipation.

"I was backpacking," he finally said.

Evie blinked, trying to comprehend what *backpacking* meant as the balance of her mind tilted.

"In Europe," he added.

Evie held herself, unsure of what she'd just heard.

Did he say *Europe*?

"What can I say?" And then her wide, frozen eyes caught it: there—finally—was the trademark Jakob smirk. "I had a good time."

Though she *wanted* to say or do something, every part of her froze. Even thoughts failed to appear, and instead only a deep nausea gave away how she felt.

CHAPTER FOURTEEN

KASS

Kass *knew* it. She knew it so deep in her soul that the response she'd planned for years somehow sputtered. Because it would have been all too goddamn easy.

"Europe?" she finally said with dry exasperation.

All of Jakob's years of impulsive and stupid excuses—missing classes because of impromptu flings in Tahoe, disappearing for weekends in college because his high-school swim idiots visited—they all came roaring back, and under the table, a fist formed, fingernails digging so deep into the meat of her hand that the sting lingered after she finally released.

"Yeah. Um, all over, really. And a little time—"

"Fucking *Europe*?"

But of course Europe. Jakob ran away to go flirt with barmaids and do whatever without a care, without a worry, because *he could not get his shit together.*

"Yeah, and a little bit in Asia. Northern Africa. All over, really."

"For fifteen years?"

"Well, I stayed in some spots longer than others. I went with the flow," he said. Kass watched his every move, every change in position from the smallest of muscles. His voice shifted, gaining a playful lilt, and as if on command, his old self took over, the right side of his mouth curled upward.

Textbook stuff. Getting her master's afforded her a lot of insight into human behavior, but for now, all of that work led to this moment as she watched Jakob become the bullshitter he'd always been.

"*Stayed* places, if you get my drift," he said.

Right on cue.

Kass sighed, but this time, it was followed by an even heavier one by Evie.

"But…you're serious?" Evie asked. Disappointment draped across her face, and Kass could see the tide turning. Part of Kass felt an inherent satisfaction of I-told-you-so victory, probably more than she liked to admit. "All this time, that's all you've been doing?"

"I'm guessing you weren't exactly helping Doctors without Borders, were you?" Kass said.

"The longest I spent in one place was two years. Little fishing town on the Mediterranean. I don't even know how to properly pronounce the name. You should have seen it." Jakob's head tilted up, and his gaze veered over Kass's shoulder, as if he saw his Greek holiday through a portal over by the restaurant bathroom. "Blue water. Photos don't do it justice. It's this brilliant blue, trees on one side, white sand on the other. Perfect quiet. Humidity sucks, but nothing's perfect. Her name," he smirked, "was Alexis. And sometimes when the engine would stall and we'd be stuck for an hour, she'd get all riled up and curse *'Malaka!'* into the wind."

With each detail, Evie's face fell a little more, as if every word poked holes in the balloons holding her up. She looked straight down, nibbling on a single fry. On the other hand, Kass practically smelled the fumes burning off her own stare, and though she didn't move until the very end, the headshake of disapproval was more like Mom's than she would have ever admitted. "That's romantic," she finally said.

"It was," he said, as wistfully as possible. "It was a good time."

"Were you with her before or after Dad died?"

After a long pause he said, "After, I guess." Neither of his sisters responded, and Jakob began eating from his plate, like he hadn't just made a mockery of years of family suffering.

"What happened to you that night?" Evie asked, her voice barely audible.

"Okay." Jakob put his fork down, a tuft of gravy-soaked biscuit still hanging off its tines. "Okay. Here's what happened. That night, I ran. I hitchhiked out of there." He took in a breath, then a sip of his soda. The words came out flat, neutral, Kass unable to detect truth or lies in her twin brother. "Dad was giving me grief about school, and I just told myself to go. And then I did when the time seemed right."

That night. The cold wind. The blanket of unlit forest. The lights of police cars. Evie shouting out to her.

No. Not just that night. All of it. Telling Mom at the sheriff's station. Dad's return at Lake Kinbote. Evie and Dad's dive off the deep end. Mom's ensuing silence. The work Kass had to do to *break* that silence, months and months after Dad died and Evie hid in Buffalo.

All of it.

Heat flushed Kass's cheeks, a rage that lacked any firm description. So many things deserved her anger that boiling it down to one single thing felt impossible.

"Dad was distracted. Or lost track or something. I ran

through the woods. It was a spur-of-the-moment thing. Like, I knew I didn't have to run from him. But it just seemed easier that way."

Still, something didn't quite add up. The search, the media coverage at the lake, the sheer despair combined with Dad's delusions—all of that didn't happen to someone who simply went hitchhiking. "Hitchhiking across the country doesn't mean you ignore us for days, weeks when there's a search party. When Dad returns and is babbling nonsense. Or when Dad dies." Kass couldn't get the last four words out without them shaking, cracking. Evie sat still, eyes trailing out the window. "So were you in prison? Buying drugs off the street? Joined a cult? You *chose* to ignore us."

"Well, I mean, there were a few pit stops along the way. I didn't know about Dad. I mean, obviously, right? I was completely out of touch. I didn't want anyone to have any trace of me. So I ran. And walked. Followed the side of the road until morning. Then hitchhiked east. Later that day, I took out what money I could. Got in a van with some people who had the best shit." Kass *knew* it. Of course it was that. "Like, tripping for days. It was amazing. But I lost my phone during that. Didn't matter, though. I saw the coast. I figured you guys wouldn't miss me. A few days later, I fell in with a group of graduating seniors going cross-country. That was it. I left with them. We had a good time."

"Why now?" Kass said, her hand slapping the table so hard that an unused butter knife rattled off it.

"I was passing through. I wanted to say hello. I'm only going to be here a few days."

"Did you..." Evie started. "That night. When you...left. There was this weird thing that happened. Like, um, all the sound gave out around us. Like it was absorbed into the air.

And the air got thick, humid. And the ground got warm to the touch. Did you get all that too?"

Still on about the alien thing. Still. After everything she'd heard. Kass supposed it made sense, given the career path her sister had chosen. She wouldn't just let it go even if Jakob admitted to bullshitting.

Jakob sipped his drink before scrunching his brow—his *thinking* face. Kass knew it well, since its appearance had been the butt of many jokes in college, given how little he attended class.

"No," he said. "No, I didn't. Not sure what you're talking about."

Evie's face fell, and all the praise and excitement from her now evaporated. In fact, all three of them stopped talking. All those years ago, Evie claimed the sound had been absorbed into the air, and now practically the same thing happened, except this didn't stem from any sort of environmental phenomena or whatever bonkers alien theory Evie cooked up.

No, this was just three siblings with nothing to say to each other.

Kass looked at Jakob, who resumed eating his biscuits and gravy like he'd fallen into a Denny's after a swim meet, and Evie, who just *sat* there, a statue with a single French fry still gripped between her fingers.

She didn't have the energy for this drama. There were bigger things to deal with. Things like Mom at home with a sliced hand, Lucy adapting to the moving target of the day, and the Golden Apple papers. Family drama left with Evie years ago, and now it came crashing into her life on the exact wrong day. "You," she said pointing at Jakob, "are *still* a dick." Her hand dove into her purse, instinctively feeling for the pack of cigarettes and lighter. "I need a smoke."

CHAPTER FIFTEEN

JAKOB

Evie didn't flinch at Kassie's suggestion that she and Jakob stay at a motel, which worked out just fine for Jakob. They walked to Kassie's car with few words, not a single discussion about what they were going to do while Evie and Jakob were in town.

The car rolled out of the strip-mall diner's parking lot and over toward the other side of their suburban hometown, the small stretch where motels housed visiting business travelers. For a few days, this would mark his base of operations to try to locate the decryptor, maybe even plan for his next steps. He'd have preferred not to cut into his Reno winnings for motel fees, but resources gathered in the field were for necessities like this, particularly while he was still orienting himself.

Evie raised an eyebrow at his offer to pay but didn't ask further. She didn't even note his lack of luggage, though probably more from his history of couchsurfing and occasional ill-advised hitchhiking than anything else. If his sister had anything on her mind, she didn't say. Jakob opened the door, then glanced at her, though she stepped through without meeting his eye. "I'm gonna—" he started, but the *thump* of her dropped backpack interrupted him. "Hey, I think—" he tried again, but she fell face-first on the bed, replying with a muffled grunt. "What was that?" he asked, still standing in the doorway.

"Jet...lag," she said, with a loud edge that clearly showed it wasn't jet lag.

The last ten minutes or so had played out this way too, Evie turning a cold shoulder to him since leaving the restaurant. He looked over the room, first catching the clock before checking the street behind him, orienting his location by memory with options and possibilities.

Evie's silent treatment might be the best thing for his mission right now.

"I'm gonna take a walk." Evie didn't reply, her face still buried in the bed's comforter. "See how things have changed." He slid the room's key card into his back pocket and looked back at his sister, her only movement from the gradual rise and fall of her breath. "Back in a bit."

But instead of exploring how Mountain View had evolved, Jakob walked to the nearest library to look up all the data that was too hard to read on his phone. Temperature variations, magnetic declination, things that might pinpoint where the decryptor was. He made a stack of notes scribbled down on the back of coloring sheets lifted from the children's section. He'd also made a quick stop at an auto-supply shop and its neighboring hardware store, assessing materials should he need to craft any tools.

Reconnaissance wound up taking several hours, and by the time Jakob got back, the sun was beginning its late-afternoon descent. The key card slid into the slot above the doorknob, and as he stepped into the over-air-conditioned room, the recycled air gave a warmer reception than his sister, who looked up from sitting cross-legged on the bed, laptop in front of her.

"You're back." The twin bed squeaked as Evie adjusted.

"Yeah." Soft hinges shut the door behind him, and he lingered on his feet, suddenly unsure of what to do. Every moment of his return came with a strategy, a plan to get closer to his goal, even though the location of the decryptor remained unknown. But this—a room with the sister he'd crushed with a few simple lies—left only an unease that didn't exist in the vacuum of space or in the cockpit of a mech. "Good nap?" he finally asked.

Evie kept clicking away at her keyboard, and Jakob watched the bedside clock tick by three minutes before she finally broke her silence. "I have to take a work call. And yes, it's about extraterrestrials. I don't want to hear a single word about it."

Evie's web show had proved to be too rambling and incoherent—and jarring, considering how he knew his younger sister—for him to be able to watch much of it during the long bus ride from Reno. And given that pretty much every UFO conspiracy theory he recalled from his Earth years was *very* wrong, any further thought seemed worthless. He looked Evie over, and it finally hit him: he didn't mind his younger sister being mad at him, but he didn't want her to get sucked into the vortex of online trash.

She was too smart for that. She was too *good* for that.

"Do you," he said in an even voice, "actually believe all that?"

"I said not a single word. You don't get to do that." Evie straightened up, fury in her eyes. "You wanted to hike around Europe and party? Really? *Really?* Are you that selfish? I thought you were *taken*. That you had no choice. Dad thought so too."

Dad.

Those final moments in the Seven Bells ship corridor with Dad flashed by. And his look when Jakob explained the situation, what was at stake between the Seven Bells and the Awakened.

The way Dad's eyes dilated when the decryptor was used on him.

But no, Jakob wouldn't let himself go there. He couldn't.

"He said he was with you for two days, that you two were captured. He had so much faith in this, and no one—*no one*—believed him. Except me. That's how I got hooked up with the Red Network." The Red Network, he presumed, had more people like Evie. "That's why I started *The Bright Light.* Because of you. And now you're telling me that it was all bullshit, that Dad probably just hallucinated from hypothermia or whatever, and you were just off prancing through Europe, women on your arms, the old Jakob charm stealing their time and money until you decided to move on. So yeah, I'm mad. And you know what? Regardless of *your* bullcrap, I know aliens visit. The evidence proves it. So even though Kassie stuck us in this room together, *I* don't have time for you. I'm here to work." A chiming sound interrupted them through the laptop's tinny speakers, and a box appeared in the corner, green and red icon buttons within.

"I gotta take this," she said, grabbing the laptop without looking at him or his sheets. "Layla, you're up late." Half the screen filled with the pixelated face of one of *The Bright Light*'s cohosts.

The woman smiled under her dark brown curls, a smile that seemed a bit too bright for them to be talking shop after hours. "Everything okay?" she asked, concern lacing her voice. "How goes the family bonding?"

"It's fine," Evie said with a heavy sigh. "Really, it's fine. What do you got?"

"Are you sure? We can chat if you need to. I'm not going anywhere right now," the woman gestured around to her dimly lit space and laughed.

Jakob felt Evie's daggered eyes before she turned back. "Maybe later. Right now, I think work is better for me. What do you got?"

"Okay, okay. You know, family bonding is overrated. Chemistry is the better way to form bonds." The woman laughed, which triggered a chain reaction of Evie's matching chuckle, and even Jakob stifled a response at the terrible pun. "We've got more numbers now. On both Reno and Half Moon Bay. We've confirmed Reno. We've seen measurements like this before. But with Half Moon Bay, there was something different. Reno was exactly like the records on your original night at Lake Kinbote. But Half Moon Bay, it's different."

Though Jakob pretended to be lost in thought, the names Reno and Lake Kinbote grabbed his attention. He shifted, an attempt to look casual while focusing on their conversation.

"Different how?" Behind the video chat box, Evie loaded up two spreadsheets and a chart. "Which metrics? I've got them up now. Sharing my screen."

Jakob squinted, trying to discern any time stamps on the charts. The small font proved difficult to read, and he leaned forward, angling to get a better view of her screen, which showed 12:04 p.m. Sometime around then, yesterday, in Reno. Imprecise data, but close enough to mark his return to Earth, his first moments in the dumpster.

Evie highlighted a line on the screen. "That one," the voice said. "Yesterday at noon in Reno."

The pieces locked into place.

The Reno event was *him*.

"Emailing you a summary. Half Moon Bay was actually earlier. Like, only ten minutes earlier." Half Moon Bay *had* to be the decryptor.

"Hey," the woman on the screen said, "way off topic, dude, but your hair looks nice like that."

"Oh," Evie's blush was visible, and Jakob took the distraction to get a better look at the data. "I mean, it's just messy and faded from a long day."

"It's cute. You know, just in case you ever want to change it up before you drive up for our next recording."

"Oh, is that all I'm good for?" Evie asked, a bounce back in her voice.

Half Moon Bay. How far was that?

"I mean, the brain helps too, but Evie's hair is what gets the audience." They laughed together while Jakob reached into his memory for drive times on family beach outings. An hour away? Had he sent it there purposefully? Or was it inaccuracy stemming from chaos?

"Go home," he said to himself. "Weapon."

"Okay, okay. Hair tips noted. But look, if it's up to me," Evie said, "I'm still going with Reno. Known quantity. The other one, I mean, that could just be, I don't know, a lightning strike. Plenty of reasons to explain atmospheric changes out by the coast."

Jakob sat quietly, strategies and calculations running through his mind while the two continued joking about Evie's hair. The other event *had* to be the decryptor, the very device he'd launched minutes before he hurtled himself across space. Things lined up too closely for it to be something different. It launched around the same time as him, it had roughly the same trajectory, and its physical composition was different: size, density, electromagnetism, all of that. Perhaps that explained the readings.

The woman's image disappeared from the screen, and Evie remained still on the bed, her eyes staring somewhere beyond the motel-room wall. "Reno," she said to herself after a long pause. The laptop screen flashed, soon changing to an interactive map complete with driving routes. She glanced over at him and smirked, probably thinking his T-shirt was the most amusing coincidence. Evie was right in that it might have been something as natural as a lightning strike. But *he* knew Reno would be fruitless, both for him and for her: the best she'd get would be stories of a guy who dropped into downtown wrapped in a sheet. The room filled with keyboard clicks, and Jakob saw two paths before him.

Nothing prevented him from telling Evie the truth. His original commitment to secrecy stemmed from a survival instinct, a desire to stay undercover during operations for the Seven Bells, when any revelation about his true identity would have resulted in arrest, capture, perhaps torture and death. Earth didn't offer as extreme a threat, but his gut had told him to keep his family out of it, to use their resources and move on.

But now Evie *was* a resource. Light-years away, countless beings fought and died against the merciless weapons of the Awakened. If telling his sister the truth meant a way back to them faster, he should take it.

Besides, it was up to her to believe what he said.

"Evie?" he asked, voice wrapped in a serious tone.

"Not now, Jakob. I'm figuring this out."

"Evie," he said again, this time with greater force. He grabbed some of his notes and stood up.

"Dang it, Jakob, can you just be quiet? I have—"

"Evie," he said for a final time. "Don't go to Reno. It'll waste your time. Go to Half Moon Bay."

"Oh great, so now you're eavesdropping on my conversations. Thank you, basic human politeness."

"Listen." Jakob stood up, the motion catching his sister's attention. "Go to Half Moon Bay. I'll come with you. Don't go to Reno. You don't need to. You won't find anything there," Jakob said, looking Evie directly in the eye. "Not what you're looking for. Because *I* was the event in Reno."

"You know—" the sound of typing stopped, and Evie's brow furrowed, lines creasing across it "—I really don't like to swear that much. But fuck you, Jakob. Fuck you and your stupid Reno shirt. I can't believe you're making fun of me. You've changed. You weren't..." she said, a mix of confusion and disdain lacing her words. "You used to *listen* to me."

"I'm not making fun of you. The event that your scans picked up was me. I landed there. Materialized in a compressed-matter transporter wave. And I'm on a mission to locate something important. Half Moon Bay. We need to go there."

Evie looked him over, then away, then back again, mouth slightly open but only hesitation coming through. "Stop it," she finally said before turning back to her screen.

"I promise you, I'm not—"

"Kassie gives me enough grief. I don't need it from you."

"I'm not giving you grief. I—"

"You just ruined our whole family reunion by telling us that you were off frolicking with country women on the Greek coast while Dad *died*."

"I *lied*." Jakob held up his sheets. "I lied, Evie. I lied to you, I lied to Kassie. I lied because I didn't want to get my family involved. Not until now. Look." He waved his notes in front of her.

Evie's eyes narrowed, her head inching forward. "Jakob, I can't read your handwriting. Why did you use *Frozen* coloring sheets?"

"Okay, look," he said with a laugh. "I needed paper, and it was all the library had. Look at the numbers I wrote."

Evie gave an exaggerated sigh worthy of Kassie, then took it from his hands, eyes absorbing the scribbled ink on them before flipping to the end and restarting. "Air pressure, magnetic variation, temperature drops," she said quickly under her breath before voice became louder and stronger. "These numbers. Not just air pressure, not just temperature, and I mean, I don't even know what this column says, but..."

"You see?"

"Jakob, your handwriting is still terrible, so I'm making some assumptions." The air in the room shifted, and she looked up, face as bright as the first time they'd seen each other that morning in the driveway. Maybe even brighter.

"Ask me anything about the last fifteen years." They locked eyes, and the trust that they'd had, back when she was the academic prodigy and he was the fuckup and they had *nothing* in common except for how they cared about each other, that returned. Jakob's posture tilted at this realization, and he told himself to pull back, an internal tightening that pushed any nostalgia or feelings aside.

He would give Evie the truth, but only to lead him to his goal. Anything further would just slow him down.

"About space. About aliens. About *war.* Ask me whatever you want to know. Because I'm here for a reason. And it's not for a family reunion."

Her fingers rested on the upper edge of the laptop screen before guiding it down, locking with a *click.* She nodded to herself, small at first, but then a full-body affirmation that she was giving in to this new idea. She held the sheets up, fully absorbed in what his scrawl had to say.

"Go home," he whispered before letting the moment take too much space. "Weapon."

"What? Did you say something?"

The words he'd written down, the repetition he used to keep himself focused—should he explain that? If there was one person he could trust, it would be Evie, right? Jakob opened his mouth, about to tell it all, or at least what wasn't made fuzzy by the decryptor.

Evie's phone buzzed, grabbing her attention and pulling them out of the moment. "More data from the Reds," she said. "Hold on, it takes a minute to download from our secure server. I should upload your sheets to them."

Her network. No, he should keep *everything* between the two of them for now, in case they were more trouble than they were worth. He straightened up and looked her straight in her red eyes. "Let's not involve them yet. My fleet is called the Seven Bells."

CHAPTER SIXTEEN

KASS

The squawking audio jolted Kass awake. First she looked at the clock—1:41 a.m. Several blinks later and it registered that, yes, this was indeed the middle of the night. Given the course of the past twenty-four hours, she'd expected heavy dreams to process the car-crash of a family reunion that had taken place. But instead, it had been the most pleasant sleep: not joyful or flirty or fantastical dreams, but the deep empty nothingness of exhausted sleep.

Her favorite kind.

Except now she was up in the middle of the night. She blinked again and turned to the small device next to the clock. It looked like a walkie-talkie sitting in a charger, but she'd picked it up in the clearance section of a baby store earlier this year. Since things had started to really devolve, Mom occasionally startled awake. And Kass had learned the hard way that the confusion could lead to far worse accidents, including one near-tumble down the stairs, an incident she'd prevented by sprinting in her pajamas and catching Mom right on the precipice of slipping.

So now, she had a baby monitor by her bed. Just in case Mom woke up in the middle of the night.

This was her life right now.

The noise was incoherent at first, words jumbled together. Maybe this wasn't an actual wake-up event, though she half figured something might happen given the disruption to the day's routine. Kass rolled onto her elbows, eyes focused on the monitor's receiver. Part of her appreciated the irony of the scenario: it was playing out exactly like a cartoon from one of her human-development textbooks, the first panel showing parents taking care of babies in a crib, and the second showing adult children taking care of aged parents in a bed.

A minute passed, then another, with only small bursts of Mom's indecipherable low chatter. Maybe she simply mumbled in her sleep. Kass rolled back over, adjusting the covers in a vain attempt to fall back into the previous lovely void.

Several seconds later, a scream pierced through the monitor, overloading the speaker with static. "What the fuck?" Kass said, twisting to pull herself out of bed. Her bare feet hit the floor, and she hustled down the hall, the screams now coming behind a muffled door. "Mom?" she called out. "Mom, hang on," she said, hand already reaching out to the doorknob.

"Mom?"

Mom didn't respond. She sat motionless on the side of her bed, knees planted on the floor and arms folded around as if cradling a baby. No further screaming came, and instead Mom started whispering—faintly, like someone was wrapping gauze around her words. Kass hovered undetected, and though her knees popped with the gesture, she crouched enough to lean forward, inching further to hear the words.

"I can't remember. Really, I can't remember."

Kass exhaled as she straightened up, her hand grasping the doorframe to steady herself. Was this a moment of lucidity? Like it just dawned on her that gaps existed in her memory? It happened sometimes to dementia patients—unpredictable and rare, but possible. In those cases, the advice was to be extra careful and empathetic. She shifted into professional mode, despite the situation being deeply personal.

"Mom?" Kass said, her voice soft as she clicked on the corner lamp. "Tell me what you can't remember. Maybe I can help."

Mom's head tilted like a dog hearing the front door. She blinked, then her arms loosened, revealing the object she'd been cradling.

It.

Instant fury rippled through Kass, knocking her calm professionalism off its center. She should have smashed the fucking thing. Smashed it and thrown the remaining bits out into the street, where oncoming traffic could pulverize it more.

Or just tossed it out years ago, like she told Evie she'd done.

"Kassie?" Mom said, looking up. "I just can't remember it anymore."

Several recentering breaths later and Kass willed the anger aside. *Gentleness. Empathy.* "That sounds frustrating. What can I do to help?"

"Oh! Maybe you know."

"Maybe I do." Her lips turned into a gentle smile, one that felt more real in the moment than just a trained disarming technique.

"This," she said, presenting It. "I know Arnold told me how to turn it on. I just can't remember."

Kass nodded, an instinctive move that masked the fact that she had no goddamn clue what to say. Or maybe no further energy to deal with It—or her siblings at this point. Her eyes shut, the push and pull of the last twenty-four hours nearly enough to get her to leave the room, leave the house, get into her car and leave the Bay Area of her own free will. Stopping wherever she wanted. Sleeping till whenever she wanted. Maybe she'd even ditch her phone, freeing herself of the ties and responsibilities constantly pulling at her.

To just breathe. What was that even like?

But no. That's what Jakob did. That's what Evie did.

She would not stoop to their level.

Kass reached over, a soft hand on Mom's shoulder. "I don't think it works," she said matter-of-factly. "Remember, Dad's never been able to get it to work."

"That's not true. It just moved."

Not this again. She never should have brought it back the other night. "It's the middle of the night. You were probably dreaming."

"I heard it. It moved and fell off the desk. Look."

Mom's thin finger rubbed a gash in the outer shell, a line that dug about a millimeter in and ran an inch in length. Kass inspected the damage, and while there *was* a notch… Well, she'd dropped Dad's mug earlier too. The same thing might have happened here, easily.

No sense in trying to rationalize it, especially not at this time. Rather than argue or debate or theorize, Kass simply put her hands on Mom's, palm resting over the still-bandaged wound. "You're right. It probably did move, but I can't remember how to turn it on. So let's sleep and try in the morning." In one motion, Kass managed to get It out of Mom's hands while guiding her to the bed. "I'm sure we'll figure it out then."

"That's right, Kassie. Evie will know how. She's good at computer things."

"Evie?"

"Or Jakob. If we can catch him before he runs off again. He's always on the move."

Mentioning one sibling was a coincidence. Mentioning both? Kass bit her lip. She met Mom's eyes, and despite the feeling that Mom somehow looked past her, she found comfort in her brown irises. "I'm sure you're right. Good night, Mom." She leaned over and planted a gentle kiss on Mom's forehead. "Let's try to get some rest."

Kass sprinted forward, pushing the limits of her speed. From above, hellfire glowed, lit embers raining down all around, and she scanned for help.

Not fast enough. The ground shook, knocking her onto her knees, and the flat, grassy terrain in front of her erupted to reveal a giant rock-formed beast, arms hanging forward like a gorilla, the cracks in its body dripping with lava.

Lava that would take off at least thirty hit points per second, so she should definitely avoid it.

Kass slid the mouse back and forth, turning the camera's view to look for any other players. But no one was around, and maybe the *Ancient Runes Online*'s largely North American player base was mostly asleep at this time. Or she'd just made the very poor decision to go into a raid by herself.

The beast slammed the ground, spewing rock and lava in all directions. Kass rolled to the side and ducked, finding cover behind a patch of rocks before checking the lair's entrance—in this case, a cave that game-level's designers used to funnel players toward an overpowered beast. Most of the time, any raid marked on the map with an inverted red triangle meant one thing: extra difficulty for extra rewards. That needed research, planning, perhaps coordinating with a few other players to join along.

But not now. Not at this time, not after dealing with Mom

on consecutive nights. After finally settling Mom, Kass went straight for her computer. This was what she would have advised a client to do—in cases where anxiety trapped thoughts in a loop, the best thing to do was switch gears until they released and sleep was feasible again.

That usually meant reading a chapter or having a cup of tea or watching a short TV show. Healthy people would write in a journal. Unhealthy people would scroll through social media, which she always advised against.

Apparently, she didn't know how to take her own advice, opting to aimlessly sprint through the digital continent of Mystheos until the challenge icon goaded her into a *Fuck it* approach. She dashed in without reservation.

That was another warning she told her clients: be self-aware enough to acknowledge bad ideas. So there was that. If she had the time, she would have written out her Objective Questions to gauge her feelings and impulses. But now she had a volcanic rock gorilla to deal with.

The ground shook again, this time a giant boulder knocking her to the ground. As her character stood, her health meter blinked to indicate near-death status. Her magic bar shrank to empty as she cast a protection spell and a blue orb enveloped her.

Run away. Running away was acceptable when the odds were overwhelming.

Kass held down the Shift key and moved her character toward the cave, the light from the game's virtual sunset piercing through. Seconds later, a *boom* rattled through her headphones, along with a sudden chanting noise. In front of her, rocks fell, blocking the only way out.

And on the other side, the beast approached—now tethered by magical beams and several hooded figures pulling it along.

Text suddenly appeared on the screen. You know this cave is recommended for a party, right?

On the other side of the cave-in, a purple eyeball icon appeared. Beneath it, a player's name.

Dwarftastic.

"I could use some help here," she said into her headset, using the game's Speech-to-Text feature. The dialogue box filled with her comment except *here* was replaced by *hear.*

Yeah. I'm not enough to help you out.

"Thanks."

However, I can move those rocks.

The chanting intensified, and from behind, a flaming rock flew by, narrowly missing Kass. "Do it. Go, go, go."

Stand back. You're going to get hit.

"I don't care. I have a protection spell. Just do it. They're closing in."

A deep muffled voice shouted a made-up language, and the boulders flew out, one hitting Kass and causing her protective blue bubble to extinguish. Flaming figures appeared, tailing her, and as she ran, she took several steps onto a rocky side path before jumping back into the main road, timing it so her pursuers fell into the chasm below as they tried to course-correct. Purple twilight wrapped around her as she emerged and ran over barren plains and cracked dirt until the cave sat a safe distance away.

The office chair squeaked as Kass leaned back in it and pulled her headphones off, blowing a few strands of hair out of her face while she gave herself a little fist pump. On-screen, green swirls surrounded her character, and her life meter filled up.

There. Feel better?

Not really, she typed, headset hanging around her neck.

Don't worry about it. The reward for beating the rock-ogre cult really only helps if you're a druid or a monk. On-screen, Dwarftastic mimed a big roar.

It's not that, she typed, though several seconds ticked by before she sent the message. Did she want to get into this now? Other options were available, like saying bye and heading back to bed. Or taking a smoke break outside. Or doing that *then* heading back to bed.

But no, her professional self reminded her that discussion helped with processing. Even if it took the form of an online chat in *The Ancient Runes Online.* She hit the Enter key and waited for Desmond's response.

Figured it wasn't insomnia. Wanna get on voice chat?

No, Kass typed, I don't want any noise to possibly wake up Mom.

Dwarftastic nodded, and the next few minutes passed with Kass summarizing it all in large blocks of text: Evie, Jakob, Mom's injury, the breakfast debacle, and Mom's battle with It. Several paragraphs filled up the dialogue box, enough to push previous messages out of view. Kass wasn't sure if Desmond actually read everything or if he merely skimmed, but typing it at least helped sort the pieces out in her head.

Silver linings.

How do you feel about this?

Kass smirked to herself, one that probably mirrored Jakob's. They were twins, after all. You're just asking that because I taught you to respond that way.

Yeah. So?

A creak came from upstairs, and she sat a moment, head in hands, half listening to see if Mom had got up again and half just blocking everything out. I'm not sure, she typed after enough time passed. It's just all so fucked-up.

An ellipsis showed up in the dialogue box, indicating that Desmond was typing. Seconds ticked by, enough that both of their characters started cycling through their idle-player animations. Okay, first, holy shit, Jakob is back. I know you always suspected it, but that's gotta mess with your head.

He's a liar, Kass typed. Or not well. Or both. Something's off about him, but I can't tell what.

Or maybe you're just mad? Desmond's reply prompted a snort from Kass.

Fair point.

Dwarftastic raised his ax in a victory pose, then the typing resumed. Okay, forget Jakob. Or forget that he's a liar or whatever. Tough-love time. I think you've got an opportunity here. You say that you don't want Evie and Jakob judging about what happens with your mom. But they have no idea what you've been through. What happens if you show them now? What is the worst thing that could come out of it? If it's as bad as you think, they'll only see what pressure you've been under.

In the virtual sky above, stars shimmered between the three moons. A group of four other players passed, their characters kicking up digital dust with their dragon mounts. She began to open the desk's drawer for a notepad but then caught herself.

Kass read and reread the text from Desmond. That was as good as the Objective Questions.

Probably even better.

I'll think about it, she typed. Which was a lie. She'd made up her mind already, but admitting to it so quickly would make Desmond cocky.

Good. Now more importantly... On-screen, Dwarftastic flexed his muscles and roared. Do you want to go recruit those players to fight the rock-ogre cult together?

Kass glanced up, staring the ceiling between her and Mom, and a sudden fatigue washed over her.

Nah, she typed, I think I should get some sleep.

Strangely, she *didn't* feel like a smoke.

CHAPTER SEVENTEEN

EVIE

Years ago, Evie had tried to convince Mom and Kassie that pursuing Jakob—pursuing aliens—would be the right thing. Not just for herself, not just for Jakob or Dad, but for all of them.

It didn't go well, of course. Evie had expected that pushback to some degree. *Time off* generally meant something like *I'm taking a quarter off from school to find myself*—though, to be fair, both Jakob and Kassie took quarters off to reset after nearly failing out, so a bar had already been set. But Evie's announcement was not a lifestyle change, not a decision to get a puppy or a cat, not taking a few months off.

This would change the course of Evie's life. And she knew it.

Mom would disapprove. And, since Kassie happened to be home, she'd probably give her own level of grief. Possibly silent, knowing Kassie. She'd do that whole pursed-lips-and-slight-eye-roll thing, but whatever.

Dad would want this. Evie felt it in the pit of her stomach, in the core of her soul. Dad would encourage her to do whatever it took to understand what had happened to Jakob.

"I have something I wanted to tell you two," Evie said.

Kassie looked up from her phone, then sipped her postdinner cup of coffee. "Hold on," Kassie said, tapping away at her phone. While they waited, Mom offered a fortune cookie from the take-out bag.

Why not? Evie thought, taking the cookie and snapping it open. She flattened the small strip of paper and read the printed words.

The world needs to hear what you have to say.

The fortune cookie said it, not her. Deep breaths. Deep, controlled breaths. Evie inhaled and began the words she'd so carefully practiced in the bathroom mirror. "I'm taking time off from school starting fall quarter," she said. Might as well blurt it out. "I'm moving to Buffalo. I leave next week."

Kassie stopped texting.

Mom's eyes bored into her, and though she normally would feel the urge to back down, Evie reminded herself why she was doing this, what it meant, who it was for.

"What do you mean, *moving to Buffalo*?"

There it was, Mom's usual blunt approach. Evie had expected that, even planned out what to say, and yet her mind blanked on all prepared responses. "I have a job lined up," she finally got out.

"A job that is more important than your degree?"

"Well, kind of." That answer was true. The job itself was not important—an administrative role at a veterinary clinic. But it provided her with stability to be close to the group of online UFO enthusiasts she'd been chatting with over the past year. Not conspiracy theorists, not tin-foil-hat-wearing losers, but real students of the science behind sightings, of examining the plausibilities and data and looking for actual evidence beyond blurry footage of little green men. Most of them were based in Toronto, one was in Buffalo, and they agreed that if they could figure out how to do it, they might even be able to make a blog or something with this. They'd even given themselves a nickname—Real Extraterrestrial Data Nerds, or Reds for short (despite the lack of an *N* in there; it was easier to say). "It's a different type of education."

Mom's face didn't move.

"What the fuck is *a different type of education*?" Kassie asked. Mom skipped chastising Kassie for swearing and instead continued to stare at Evie in silence.

"It's complicated. I have a, um..." What was the word she'd prepared? "A mentor. And in the meantime, I'll be working at a vet hospital to pay my rent. So you don't have to worry about anything."

"You can't quit school," Mom finally said, her eyes narrowed. "I won't allow it."

"Mom, I'm twenty-one. I'm self-funding this."

"We paid for three years of college for you. Do you know how expensive that is?"

"The credits don't go away." There it was, the familiar justification. Evie felt herself slipping back to that, the need to prove herself despite being a full-grown adult, despite nearly two years passing since Dad had died at Lake Kinbote. "I can always go back if I want to—"

"You're throwing everything away."

"I looked at this. In fact, I could finish my degree at a school there—"

"You disrespect your Dad this way." Mom stood, a swift motion that seemed so unlike her that Evie drew in a harsh breath. Mom's fingers trembled as they gripped the top of the chair.

Evie held still, both body and mind ready to use the explanation she'd prepared days ago. "Please, listen. Dad would want this. Mom." She looked at Kassie, and part of her knew even mentioning him risked any remaining goodwill in the conversation. But it might be the only way for them to see the bigger picture. "I'm continuing Dad's work."

Mom's lips moved in unexpected, uncontrolled ways, though no sound escaped, like Evie's proclamation had broken her gears.

Kassie, on the other hand, seemed ready to fire back. "Really? The fucking aliens, Evie?"

"Dad would want this," she said, her voice turning, no longer a mere discussion with family, but begging to the universe and anyone else who might be listening. "We set out to do something together. I need to finish it."

Mom's entire demeanor changed, but not the way Evie had hoped. Rather than soften and draw her back in, Evie's mention of Arnold Shao's dreams turned Mom cold, draining her face of color and stiffening her posture. The chair nearly toppled over as Mom pushed off and stormed out. It teetered on its back legs before slamming back to a rest. Footsteps stomped up each stair before a door slammed so loud that the charm hanging off the kitchen window rattled.

Evie looked at the fortune sitting on the table. *The world needs to hear what you have to say.*

Kassie picked up her phone and started tapping away at the screen. "Are you for real with this?"

"I am," Evie said after a gulp and a pause. "Plans are made."

Kassie shook her head, still staring at her phone. "You fucked up." She turned her back as she shuffled through her purse until she snatched out a small gold-and-red pack. "Are you trying to break Mom?"

"No, I swear. This is what Dad wanted. I promised him—"

"Dad is dead, Evie." The plastic wrap around the cigarette pack crinkled as Kassie tore it. "We're still here. Think about that."

"This is for all of us."

Kass sent her a look, a fiery glance that only lasted for a flash before she grabbed a lighter out of her purse, an unlit cigarette dangling from her mouth. "No, it's not," she said through pursed lips. "This is for you. If you're serious about going, you should leave as soon as you can. Seriously. I'll drive you."

"But what about Mom?"

"I'll take care of Mom." Kassie strode out of the kitchen.

That night wasn't the smoothest start to her journey for the truth. But look at her now. In the end, her decision had been the right one. Evie's cheek muscles hurt from how much she'd been beaming. And she'd barely gotten any sleep.

Aliens.

Not just one race, but dozens, possibly hundreds, all entangled in an intergalactic war. On Jakob's side, a desperate ragtag coalition called the Seven Bells that recruited soldiers and scientists from any planet they passed by while scavenging for resources and materials. On the other side, ravaging marauders called the Awakened, a relentless species that waited for civilizations to awaken to useful technological prowess before usurping that, then eliminating the population with something Jakob called crystallization—apparently some sort of energy weapon that converted organic matter into sand-like crystals. Which was then used by the Awakened for construction and research.

Talk about a threat.

Space genocide and a fight for resistance. Desperate battles and unlikely victories. Plus, Jakob flew *mechs*, a kind of form-fitting power armor loaded with weapons. The way he described the details—the pressurized energy wrap of the compressed-matter transporter, the weird stone-based technology of the Seven Bells, how the kickback felt within the mech armor when it launched projectiles from its shoulders—it wasn't just straight out of a science-fiction movie, it was vivid and real. In fact, the moment Jakob blinked back tears while he explained the fate of his alien friend he'd nicknamed Henry caused Evie to think she'd never seen Jakob so sincere, so raw in all their years together.

And to think, *her brother* in the middle of it, as a soldier and field engineer. Fighting *and* fixing things under a sky riddled with energy blasts and exploding vehicles. Captured, beaten, probed, but refusing to give up vital information, information so crucial to the Seven Bells's survival that he risked his life and scrambled his own brain to do so. All to deliver intel from his dying friend.

Intel that could win the war.

This whole thing was better, wilder, than Evie could have ever imagined.

"When will they come for Earth?" Evie asked, leaning forward in rapt attention.

"They come for everyone. Everywhere. They're always monitoring. We thought Henry's planet had time, but something about their technology caught the Awakened's sensors. We'll never know why. So I think Earth has decades, maybe even centuries. But who knows? If we can push them back, even stop them, then you'll never have to find out." He rubbed his temples, letting out a sigh. "If this works, the galaxy can thank Henry."

Henry's intel, yes. But Jakob—*her* Jakob—would be the one to deliver it. Despite Jakob's solemn air, this may have been the happiest Evie had been, like, ever.

The conversation flowed, their old rhythm framed by this new, terrifying, completely awesome context. They spent so much time picking over Jakob's encyclopedic knowledge of the war, Evie realized that Jakob didn't ask a single thing about her personal life: job, moving away, none of that. She almost forgot to take a selfie to cement the moment—not a smiling selfie of brother and sister but a capture of her standing in front of the motel room.

Now, as they throttled up Highway 101 in a rideshare, they continued the mission together. The idea of the Awakened eventually swarming the Earth like locusts was frightening, but that type of murder-harvesting seemed generations away. Instead, this was all about being in the moment with her brother. Such giddiness fueled her every breath that she even snuck a message to the Reds, I was right, this is bigger and better than we could have hoped, typed in the group-chat thread last night while Jakob took a bathroom break.

Great, Edward had replied. Send details ASAP. We'll get to fact-checking before we go live with anything.

The term *fact-checking* had caught her off guard. Didn't they trust her judgment? In most cases, they did fact-check each other, a bit of peer review like all scientists should do. But at the same time, this was *her.* And this was Jakob. But maybe Edward got extra finicky about those things since getting an FBI friend.

Evie didn't respond, honoring Jakob's request for secrecy for now, and instead they'd spent most of the morning looking at ways to fine-tune the estimated location of the other event. At some point, she'd have to jot this all down. Jakob was on a mission to get back to his fleet, and that meant the clock was ticking on their remaining time together. But surely he'd be willing to do an interview for *The Bright Light* before he returned.

If not then, surely after he saved the galaxy.

In the back seat of the rideshare car, the heat from her laptop on her legs was still palpable despite it sitting on her backpack. She tapped through charts and graphs, then overlaid map data to identify whether they should head to the south side of the small beachside community. Technically, data from the Reds' secured server was only for their core team's eyes, but Jakob had actually been to freakin' space, so that gave him a pass. She'd zoned in so much with this that she'd failed to notice something about Jakob until they got past the windy lanes that led to the coast.

He looked ill.

Not just, like, food poisoning or a hangover, but very sick. She glanced quickly to avoid being rude and also to avoid alerting their driver, just enough to check that what she thought she'd caught in her peripheral vision wasn't a trick of the light.

In fact, it was actually worse.

Was he *talking* to himself?

Fingers pressed against his temples, and while the rumble of the small hatchback created a measure of white noise, Jakob's whispers were audible, a pattern that created a chantlike rhythm. She zeroed in on his words, trying to hear.

"Are you okay?" she finally asked.

Jakob straightened so abruptly that the open laptop nearly teetered over in the cramped back seat. That caused her heart to leap more than his behavior, though anytime someone whispered a chant, it was concerning.

"Are you, um, like, hearing from your fleet?"

"What?" He shot her a look, the easy Jakob smile coming once again. It flipped on so *suddenly* that it jarred Evie, causing her to do a double take. "Oh, I'm fine. Just tired." He folded his hands across his lap. "How long do we have?"

"It says twenty minutes, according to the map. But half of that is going to be side streets. We're almost done with the highway portion. Anything look important?" she asked, referring to the variety of notes she'd printed out at the motel's office station before they left. She looked up to see a large sign with *Welcome to Half Moon Bay* carved across it.

If the Reds were lucky, they got emails and texts from readers and viewers from within a hundred miles of an incident. Driving into an event was a bit of a new experience.

"Not really. The data from your team still shows those coordinates on the beach. Doesn't look like any new relevant data over the past few hours. I'm assuming there's some lag in it. But let's start there." Jakob laughed, a quiet chuckle that seemed out of time, as if the universe had copied and pasted her brother's high-school self right after making a pot joke and brought him here.

"Hey," Evie said, reaching over to pat him across the knuckles. "I'm really glad you're here. Look at us, right?"

"Family bonding, right?" Jakob's voice carried a low calm, though he kept looking ahead without blinking.

"Right," she said, with her own awkward laugh.

The car turned left at the first big stoplight, and despite not seeing, not even thinking about them, for years, Evie recalled how the roads led to the southern beaches and downtown area. The scenery must have gotten to her, and perhaps some of the memories that flashed by. Evie shoved between Kassie and Jakob on drives out here, cold gray beach days spent collecting shells rather than swimming, long waits for beachside restaurants that Mom would call *overpriced*.

It took Jakob's voice to bring her back to the present. But it wasn't something he'd said—or said to her, at least. "What was that?" she asked. Jakob didn't hear her, his hands pressed against both sides of his skull. And the whispering again, something just out of reach for Evie to hear.

They hit a stoplight, a crowd of families crossing from one side to the other. "Come on," Evie said, fingers tapping against the side of her bag. "This light is taking forever. It's a weekday. Why is there beach traffic?"

Jakob whispered again, almost like a mantra, with eyes shut, head against hands, seat belt tugged forward with his lean.

From the front seat, the rideshare driver gave him a look. "Does he need a doctor? If he's not well, he should wear a mask."

"I'm fine. Just drive. Don't worry about me," Jakob said with a strain in his words that hadn't been there a few minutes ago. But then he turned to Evie with a wide-eyed intensity. "Don't worry about me," he said again, this time directed at her. "We're close. I can feel it. Literally feel it. Just trust me." He reached over and grabbed her hand with clammy fingers. "I'm asking you to trust me."

CHAPTER EIGHTEEN

JAKOB

They were close. Jakob *knew* it.

"Listen." Jakob took in the view while Evie held her phone up, trying to orient themselves against the coordinates from the Reds. "I promise you, I'm fine. These headaches are just a sign we're getting close to the decryptor." A longer explanation existed, technical details about how the device synced to his brain-wave patterns during the encryption process, so the headaches indicated a repeating attempt to lock back onto the signals, like a Bluetooth headset seeking a paired phone. That didn't, however, explain why the pain exceeded the sync process's usual light pressure and heat. They stood on cliffs overlooking a thankfully empty leg of the beach. Above them, beams of sunlight cut through clouds, while high winds and harsh ocean waves hit the shore. Several paths headed from their roadside spot down to the beach itself, from a sand-sprinkled collection of worn rocks to a rickety staircase built into the cliff's lowest spot. "It's not supposed to hurt this much, but decryptors aren't supposed to be shot through space either. The headaches have become more frequent since we've parked. And stronger. We're heading in the right direction," he said, withstanding another pressure burst inside his skull. "Don't worry about me."

Evie's mouth twisted as she continued staring at the screen. "It's not that. I just got a text from Kassie. She's invited us to dinner tonight." She flipped the phone around, the characters barely visible in the glare of the sun.

> You and Jakob come by around 5:30 for dinner. I have something to show you.

In another life, that message would have meant something. But not now. Too much was at stake to be concerned with family squabbles. "What does that mean?" Jakob asked, choosing the most normal reply.

"I don't know. But it can't be good. Did you catch the part yesterday about how she's on the deed of the house? I mean, I know it's pretty low on our list of priorities. You know, because you've been in freaking space. But, yeah, she's tricked Mom into giving her the house. Didn't even tell me. Can you believe that? I swear…" Her voice drifted off, and she shook her head, then swiped at her phone again.

The pressure returned, and Jakob's knees buckled. He fought back, forcing himself to stand straight.

Evie didn't notice.

"Whatever," she said. "It's fine. We're here for you. Your mission." She pointed toward stairs built into the rock face. "Coordinates point that way." They walked in silence, Jakob focused on searching for the decryptor—not so much any visible evidence of it, given how it may have impacted into the sand but a *sense* of it. Down they went, step-by-step, and Jakob still wearing the flip-flops he'd been gifted in Reno. Despite their lack of grip and bits of dirt and sand getting under his feet, he stormed forward, the pressure growing in his head.

"What are we looking for?" Evie yelled across the beach.

"Well," Jakob said as he strode forward, "the decryptor's about the size of a basketball. But we may not need to find it. It might have hit anywhere nearby. The water, the sand, embedded into the cliff. But that's okay, it just has to get close enough to sync—"

As his foot dug into the beach, heavy bricks knocked him in the face. Or at least it felt that way. But his nose wasn't bleeding, his teeth weren't jarred loose, and the only ache in his ears came from the stinging cold.

No, this was all inside. He fell to his knees, an impact slamming him down. His hands dug into the sand, fine grain going around fingers and slipping under his nails. Suddenly, he was elsewhere, the grit beneath his toes the crystallized remains of Henry, his surroundings the frigid hallway of an Awakened transport. Henry's last word echoed in his ears, and all around him the ship rumbled.

Another impact hit Jakob's face from the inside, bringing him safely back to the beach's surface. He blinked and checked his surroundings: sand, wind, the ocean, birds overhead, tourists far away. He was searching, not back on the Awakened ship. His hands dug, throwing back sand onto Evie behind him. Each thrust of his arm brought a pain indicating he got closer and closer, though it was the best pain he'd ever felt.

He saw Henry again, but not in a catastrophic flashback. Instead, clear memories returned—vivid, coherent, and in proper order.

Each strike brought more, and despite the pain, he knew he was locking in. Arm-deep in sand, his fingers flexed until a tip grazed something smooth, a rounded shape that could have been cut from a kitchen counter made of expensive stone.

Got you.

He grasped through the sand and pulled his arm out, a heat radiating from the piece, but when his hand emerged, he only gripped a sliver, about the size of a sand dollar. But he recognized it. The smooth polish, the speckled colors.

"Jakob, that's a rock," Evie said as he jammed the sliver into his pocket. It *looked* like a rock. But Jakob knew better. It was part of the outer shell of the decryptor, something that had probably chipped off upon impact. The actual device likely lay far beneath, and if he'd found this piece of shell, then some of the device's inner workings might be exposed, possibly damaged. Which might explain why the sync process hit way harder than it should have. "No, Evie. No, it's—" he started before collapsing face-first in the sand.

Evie yelled something, and he knew she approached, but it didn't matter. Nor did the wind or the salty sea air or the sound of birds overhead.

None of it did. The only thing that mattered was the flood of images rapid-firing, memories at full volume unloading into his mind's eye. And in an instant, he understood.

He understood it *all*. Everything locked into place. The pain stopped, and he took in a breath, then another one. His sister stood behind him, a hand resting on his shoulder.

"Are you okay?" she asked.

He didn't answer. Not yet. More breaths as he took in the memories. *Go home. Weapon.*

Signal.

That was the missing link.

He whispered them aloud, the full set of words he'd written as desperate reminders to himself. But he wouldn't need them anymore. Not with the decryption process complete. Because everything he needed was there.

The information in his head. The alien hardware implanted in his body. The sheer importance of getting back to the Seven Bells, the weight of having the fate of the galaxy in his brain.

Henry's dying wish.

It all suddenly made sense. The decryptor hid his means of connecting with the fleet, something that had to be protected against all costs. But now that he was safe on Earth with memories restored, he saw the path ahead with startling clarity. He squinted, the light around him flooding his pupils, and though he first wondered if the decryptor had overloaded his senses, a much different memory came to mind: his pupils being dilated when getting his eyes checked in middle school.

"This is it. I have everything I need," he said, standing up and shutting his eyes against the brightness. "I have to activate a device in my head to contact the fleet. I have information that can win the war." Evie may have reacted to such a statement; he wasn't sure with his eyes closed. It didn't matter. He had to leave. Now. Too much was at stake. "These lights, what do they all mean?" he said, using the activation phrase he'd committed to memory.

Except nothing happened.

"These lights, what do they all mean?" No sudden warmth at the back of his head as the transponder turned on. No strange microvibrations as it transmitted a communication ping across space to the roaming command fleet of the Seven Bells. None of that, despite Jakob uttering the phrase he'd specifically chosen to activate his personalized transponder. It'd take some time to get a ship within transportation range, perhaps even a few hours. But that required contact, and that crucial first step wasn't happening.

Jakob opened his eyes to find Evie's puzzled stare, her hair whipping around in the wind.

Instead, a different kind of pain emerged at the back of his head, not the rhythmic pressure of the decryptor but an intensity drilling down toward the base of his skull. His hands went to the back of his head, his knees buckled.

"Are you..." Evie asked, taking a meek step forward "...okay?"

"Yeah. I'm fine," he said through gritted teeth. What was this? Was the transponder damaged, lacking power?

"I think we should take you to a hospital. You don't look well."

A hospital would only slow him down—or worse. Jakob summoned all his willpower to stifle the sudden strange pain as well as the confusion about the disabled transponder in his head. He needed time, possibly resources to figure this out. "I'm fine, I swear. Just...lingering effects of the decryption process. See?" He stretched his arms over his head and threw up a mock muscle flex. "Totally fine."

He wasn't, of course, but if Evie was considering the hospital, he couldn't trust her. His mind fired off plans and next steps, while he turned on the same facade he'd played in Reno. "I promise, things are fine." He reached into his pocket, a new idea to distract his sister coming to mind. "Here. In case you ever wanted some alien tech," he said, handing over the chip of the decryptor shell. Evie's cheeks lifted with a grin, and she held the small piece with both hands, seemingly transfixed at the most benign of objects. "Should we meet up with Kassie?" he asked.

CHAPTER NINETEEN

KASS

Kass pressed the play button on the remote control, and the TV screen faded in to show a field of stars. *Captain's Log, Stardate 46357.4: We have rendezvoused…* came over the speakers, and Mom settled into her favorite living-room chair, creases of anticipation framing her face. She turned to look up at Kass.

"Oh, this is Dad's favorite. You want to tell him it's on?"

Kass stood behind Mom, then placed a thin blanket over her lap. "I think Dad's still working," she said quietly. "Can you watch and help him catch up when he gets home?"

"Of course. You know how upset he gets when he misses *Star Trek*."

"Yeah. I do." As if by instinct, Mom leaned forward, letting Kass fluff the pillow behind her, something that they didn't do until the last two years or so as Mom's awareness faded. How such a thing had become part of her instinct Kass wasn't sure. But it provided a crackle of hope that somewhere within the swamp of Mom's cognition, she understood. Mom settled back, squishing the pillow behind her, and Kass knelt down to her level. Mom turned from the screen, locking eyes with her daughter. For a moment, Kass wondered if some lucidity had broken through, something more than a repetitive gesture for sofa comfort, something that might have even been triggered by yesterday's chaos.

Maybe even a sense that something in Kass had tilted off-axis, and that tonight was going to be very different.

But then Mom returned to the TV. She leaned over to the side table, first grabbing the sketchpad at the top, flipping the pages until a blank one appeared, and removing the pencil held in the top binding by a small binder clip, the motion so much like her old self that Kass nearly expected her to start talking about her old real-estate job. Mom quietly stared at the story unfolding in front of her while beginning to doodle something completely different, seemingly unaware that the episode streamed over the internet onto Kass's gaming console, not cable TV from the '90s.

At least this worked. Kass gave herself a little fist pump before the imminent arrival of Evie and Jakob occupied her. For so many years, it had been only Kass and Mom—not just in the house but as a unit.

And really, that unit had gradually whittled down to just herself, living in a house built for a full family. So many arguments filled the space, circular debates as Mom's thoughts and memories crisscrossed until Kass started changing her approach. Had it been three years? It felt like three weeks but carried the weight of three decades. Which perhaps was fitting, since Mom lived in different eras all at once.

A knock at the door interrupted her thoughts. Four knocks, actually, followed by a muffled laugh that was unmistakably Evie. Kass straightened up and told herself to stay calm.

★ ★ ★

"Things are…different," Kass said. "Just watch."

Jakob hovered behind Evie, his eyes in a weird squint, and they both remained in the hallway just beyond the family room. TV noise came through, but Mom was silent. Kass walked in and glanced behind to see her siblings inching to the threshold of the space but failing to cross.

Were they asking permission in their own way?

"Mom?" She knelt down beside the couch and spoke gently. "Mom?"

"Oh, Kassie. I'm so glad you're here. Look," she said, lifting the pencil in her hand and pointing to the screen. "It's *Star Trek*. You want to tell Dad? You know how he hates to miss an episode."

A cautious stillness came from Jakob and Evie, the lack of sound creating such a vacuum that it acknowledged what was playing out before them.

Kass glanced at the sheet in Mom's lap. It was, like many of the drawings in the sketchpad, of their mini-schnauzer that passed away eight years ago. "I think Dad's still at work. Can you watch it for him and tell him what he missed when he gets home?"

"Of course. That's a great idea. You know how he hates to miss an episode."

"Yeah," Kass said, biting down on her lip. "I know." She glanced back to see Evie's mouth agape, eyes fixated. Behind her, Jakob kept a completely neutral face—no turn of the mouth, no crinkle in the brow, not even a blink, not a single ounce of his bullshit. Maybe he was beyond processing proper emotions. Who knew how many drugs he'd taken in the past fifteen years, and even though she wasn't certain of it, his pupils looked dilated. She wouldn't even put it past him to have slipped in a pill while Evie wasn't looking.

But tonight wasn't about him. Jakob was simply part of the equation—the flaky, apathetic, possibly-on-drugs part. She gave her siblings a nod, then turned back to Mom. "Mom, I have a surprise for you."

"What's that, Kassie? A surprise?"

"Yeah. Mom, look. Evie and Jakob are here to see you."

"Oh!" Mom's demeanor instantly brightened. "They're back from school?"

"Yeah, they're on break." She waved a hand to motion them over. From the corner of her eye, she saw Evie hesitate before stepping forward, Jakob letting her lead. "I got pizza. Thought we could have a family dinner."

"That's wonderful," Mom said. She moved mechanically, as if her actions from before simply reversed: first the sketchbook closed, then the pencil slid into the binder clip at the top, then the whole thing got placed on the side table. "Can you tell Dad that *Star Trek* is on?"

"Sure. We'll let him know. But how about we get started on dinner first?"

Mom stood and came over, walking with a confidence that betrayed reality. From behind Kass, Evie gasped, and she turned to see Jakob with a brotherly hand on her shoulder. They waited quietly as Mom stopped midstride to look them over.

Did they see Mom? Or did they see some unknown form of Sofia Aguilar-Shao?

Kass lingered between them, equal parts buffer and simply caught in the middle of two opposing forces. Mom's mouth opened slightly, and behind her the *Star Trek* episode continued, filling the room with a dramatic speech between uniformed officers, their voices rising and flowing with Shakespearean precision. In front of the TV, though, the entire Shao family played out an entirely opposite scene: quiet, still, passionless, all of them out of place.

"Jakob, you came home," Mom finally said, rushing forward and completely sidestepping Evie. "Look at you." Her arms went wide. "Come on, don't be difficult about hugging." Kass watched as Jakob did his usual shrugging off of Mom's hug, amazed at the muscle memory at play here: Mom's blurry mind somehow recalling Jakob's weird aversion to hugs, and Jakob looking so much like himself with the awkward embrace that it seemed almost caricature. "Did she do this to you?" Mom asked as they broke apart.

"Do what, Mom?"

"Your hair." Mom reached up, fingers sliding over Jakob's close-cropped hair. "Did she convince you to do this?"

"I'm, uh… No, I chose to do this."

"Well, look at her. I'm glad you're interested in the artistic type now." Mom turned to Evie, her hand extended. "I'm Sofia, Jakob's mom."

Evie's eyes widened before turning to Kass. Was that questioning or a request for intervention? Or a plea for help? She needed *something* right now, though all of Kass's out-of-practice instincts for being a big sister drew a blank. "Mom," Kass said, stepping over to Evie. She pushed out a smile, a pleasant turn that lacked all sincerity. "Evie's back from school. Here she is."

"Oh, no, Kassie. I think you're mistaken. This is Jakob's new girlfriend. I'm sorry, your name is?"

"I…" Quick breaths came from Evie, short and sharp enough to hear over the ongoing TV episode. "I'm… Mom, I'm…" Her eyes glistened over, and Evie began rapid-fire blinks before turning to Kass.

"Look, Mom," Kass said to intervene, "Evie's home from college too. We're all here. Lucky you! How often do you get all of us visiting at the same time?"

"Oh, hello," Mom said again, turning to Evie. "I'm Sofia, Jakob's mom. I must have missed your name."

"Mom, it's me! I'm..." she said, tapping her fingers against her chest. "I'm Evie." Desperation clung to her voice now, the reality of the situation seeming to clash with the sheer lack of logic in the conversation.

"Jakob, who is this? Why is she pretending to be Evie? And what did she do to your hair?"

"Mom, it's Evie," Jakob said. Kass studied him as he spoke. His whole demeanor had changed again, the stuck-in-neutral pose suddenly gone, and instead, the cadence of his usual charms returned, only with bits of confusion and urgency sprinkled in. And his eyes, up close she could see they'd remained dilated. He glanced around in quick bursts, looking all about the room. Kass reminded herself not to judge or assume, but fuck it. This was Jakob, and of course he'd probably handled this while on some mild psychedelic or something.

Still, at least he was working with the situation. As opposed to Evie, who just let her shock overwhelm her. It was too bad she couldn't livestream this for Desmond. Explaining it all via *The Ancient Runes Online* chat later was going to be a nightmare.

"I decided to drop by," Jakob continued. "We all did. We thought a family dinner would be nice." He took in a deep inhale. "Pizza smells good."

That part was sincere. Kass had partied with her brother enough that she recognized his tone about snacks, as though he hadn't had pizza in years. Maybe he'd been gallivanting in some tiny European village eating goat or whatever.

"Mom, it's me. *I'm* Evie."

"Jakob," Mom said with a frown, her tone turning noticeably stern, "who is this? First she has you shave your head, and now she's impersonating Evie."

"Mom, look at me." Urgency began lacing her voice, ratcheting up with each passing word. "Look at my eyes. It's me."

"Don't be ridiculous. My Evie would never look so absurd." Mom gestured at Evie's colored hair and the shaved side of her head. "She's a good girl. A *smart* girl."

"Hear my voice. I'm Evie."

"Well, I— Kassie, did you invite her? This woman needs to get out of here. I'm not spending my precious family time with someone who…who *impersonates* my daughter." Mom turned her back to them. "Get out of my home."

"Mom…" Evie started, but Kass put a hand up to stop her.

"Do you see, now?" Kass asked her siblings quietly. "Things aren't how they used to be. Look, you two get started with pizza, this might take a while."

"Kassie?" Mom said. "Is Lucy here? She should tell Dad that *Star Trek* is on. He doesn't want to miss an episode."

"Mom!" Evie tried again. On one hand, Kass appreciated her desperation as she grasped at vapors, her world suddenly inverting.

But on the other hand, if Evie had bothered to call at any time over the last few years besides asking for the occasional loan, this wouldn't be such a surprise.

"Mom," Jakob said, his voice steady, "can I help?" He swooped past Kass, then took their mother's hand and guided her back to the couch. And Mom, she moved with a responsiveness to Jakob far quicker than Kass usually experienced—or Lucy, for that matter.

Kass told herself to *not* give in to the bitterness that came with such a realization. But seriously, what the fuck?

Jakob talked quietly with her, first unrolling the blanket, then tucking her in. She reflexively reached for the sketchbook, and Jakob handed it to her, his eyes fully engaged. Mom smiled, the type of peaceful expression that usually only happened at the very end of the day—and only on good nights. "How about you two get started? Think I'll talk to Mom for a bit."

"I, uh, need to clear my head." Evie headed out to the hallway, and Kass heard the front door opening and shutting.

"I don't need pizza," Kass said, though she was unsure if anyone remaining listened to her. "I need a smoke break."

"You should talk to Evie." Jakob nodded at the front door before turning back to Mom. "This is all a bit of a shock for her."

It was a good thing that Jakob wasn't looking her way, otherwise he would have noticed her skepticism in the form of pursed lips and raised brow. "Yeah," Kass took in a deep breath, reminding herself to process only recent events rather than just yell at her siblings for not being there. "If only," she said so quietly that Jakob either didn't notice or didn't care.

She opened the door to find Evie sitting on the front step, suddenly looking much more like the teen who had moped around when Kass would visit from college. Evie tapped away at her phone, staring at some charts and graphs on her screen. Kass leaned against the porch's large post, fingers digging through her purse as she watched a large gray van across the street rev to life and cruise away.

Kass stood for several minutes, taking puffs on her cigarette and choosing *not* to think about anything. Evie never looked up from her phone.

CHAPTER TWENTY

JAKOB

During his time with the Seven Bells fleet, Jakob developed a keen sense of opportunity, of recognizing when a situation's chaos aligned in a way that created an opening. They trained him to constantly scan the space around him, to glance quickly in all directions to take in a steady stream of details and options. Then it just took the right moment.

This was one of those moments.

Jakob waited until he heard the door shut behind Kassie. No voices came from the front porch; perhaps they were simply waiting out there for a sense of normalcy to return. It wouldn't, of course. Everything was different now, and with Jakob's memories fully restored, he knew what he had to do.

The issue, though, was *how*.

What would he need? He hunched over Mom, craning his neck to look around. A power source, for sure. Something to properly identify the location of the transponder. Tools, of course. Perhaps a mode of transportation. A means of communication, which would have to be built, but he could—

The pain at the base of his skull returned, knocking him down to his knees with a *thud*. Mom turned to him, aware enough to notice. "Jakob?"

"I'm fine, Mom."

She looked, really looked, at him, examining in a way that transported him back decades, those quiet moments when she'd pause between sentences and just *dissect* him, gears turning in her head to figure out why he wouldn't study harder or take his responsibilities more seriously—the opposite of how Dad tried bargaining to bring Jakob back from the edge. Growing up, bonus father–son bonding nights at hockey games were the reward, despite only putting in half the effort Kassie did. In high school, promises of a new iPod if he just kept his GPA up. In college, pleas to stay in touch and let them know that he was going to class.

Even at Lake Kinbote, on that last night.

There was that look again, barely visible through the moonlight as they walked. Dad had taken the lead into the woods, a trail barely visible under the shine of his phone's LED flashlight. "It's such a nice night, we should walk," Dad said, offering a smile equal parts meek begging and hopeful care. "Mmm-hmm," Jakob replied, reaching into his back pocket. How quietly could he undo a bit of wadded-up cellophane wrap? His fingernail dug underneath the fold, then he searched for the individual pills underneath.

Normally he wouldn't have brought something on a family outing, but the cabin they were staying at—some distance north of Lake Kinbote rather than their usual campground here—came with all sorts of stuff that seemed to excite Dad and Kassie: hiking, mountain biking, and the like. Evie said she'd use nature to study, and Jakob, well, he knew what his role was here.

On the surface, it was a long weekend with the family, something Mom and Dad had suggested given that they all had the time off. Then Mom claimed that some work thing had come up, though Jakob knew better. Dad, on the other hand, simply said he missed family time, though his ulterior motive surfaced quickly. "So how's everyone's classes going?" might as well have been "Are you failing?" By their fourth year of college, Kassie had recovered from her disaster quarter of partying too hard, whereas Jakob preferred the slow descent into carefree mayhem.

All credit to Dad; he really tried.

And this excursion into the woods—under the cover of having to pee, but now extended into a night stroll all the way to the edge of the lake—was obviously going to be a more direct discussion. He'd suspect this even if he hadn't overheard Dad's phone call to Mom during a rest break.

Thus, it made the choice easy. Extra easy. Super easy. The last time they stopped, he dug out the pills from his suitcase, tore off some of the plastic wrap and kept it in his back pocket. It'd definitely help with any discussion on the topic.

"Smell that forest air. You just don't get that at home," Dad said.

"I gotta tie my shoe. I'll catch up," Jakob said, dropping down to one knee. The flashlight turned his way, but he gave an overexaggerated reaction, hand up to block out the light. "Dad, you're blinding me."

"Sorry. Sorry. Okay, just be careful in the dark. Lots of stuff to trip over."

The moment Dad stepped forward, Jakob took off his hoodie and dropped it on the dirt path, shoving his hands under it to smother the sound of undoing the cellophane wrap.

He freed one of the pills and quickly popped it under his tongue. This was a new batch, fresh from his roommate's hookup in San Francisco, and Jakob closed his eyes to ease into it. It'd probably take an hour to feel anything, but it wasn't like they mass-produced them under strict quality control.

Despite shutting everything out, Jakob sensed a flash of some sort. He opened his eyes—maybe this shit was just really potent? Or a sudden lightning storm? Ahead, Dad's flashlight was barely visible, maybe thirty or forty feet ahead, closer to the sand and rocks sprinkled across Lake Kinbote's shore. But then that disappeared too, a flicker of some sort, and suddenly a harsh flush came over his body, like he'd been wrapped in a thick parka even though his hoodie remained at his feet.

More flashes came, and with each one, the light trailed as he turned his head from side to side. His sense of balance started to tilt, and though he wanted to stay upright, his body moved as if all of the weight tilted to one side. His face hit the ground, and he only knew that because he discerned further flashes of Dad's phone light when he dashed back. Dad was yelling...something, then the brightest light he'd ever seen or felt seemed to envelop them, absorbing Dad's phone light like raindrops falling into a river.

The light was overwhelming, an intensity that forced his eyes shut yet somehow stayed within, trailing and bleeding everywhere he turned until he blacked out.

The next time he woke up would be with a different type of sensory overload. Lights, colors, and sound came at him in an overwhelming mess of fiery input, but it became clear from his first conscious moment that he no longer was on a forest floor.

He'd woken up aboard a Seven Bells craft.

And somewhere across the strange room they were in, Dad lay knocked out as well.

"Jakob?" Mom asked again, bringing him back into the Shao family living room, the only aliens on the TV. Her eyes narrowed slightly, and lines of concentration formed around her brow, a familiar combination of defiance and shame growing in the pit of his stomach, no matter how much he'd tried to maintain some level of distance from anything family-related.

Go home. Weapon. Signal.

"It's okay, Mom. I'm, um, just going to get a glass of water." He cleared his throat, then straightened up despite the jab within his skull. "Do you need anything?" he asked, scanning the room for potentially useful equipment, only stopping when something grabbed his hand.

He looked down to see Mom's thin fingers wrapped around his. "Jakob," she said, "you should come home more often. Only if it doesn't take away from your schoolwork."

Everything he'd done since landing on Earth had been about the mission. Every decision, every action was laced with purpose. Even conversations with his sisters were driven by that, their surface affection purely strategic. He tried to maintain that level, picturing Henry's disintegrating body and mangled final pleas as a means to keep himself centered.

But the frail weight of Mom's hand against his paused the world. The Awakened, the Seven Bells fleet, the fate of countless beings. Something even more powerful took over, however fleeting.

The rare moment when Sofia Aguilar-Shao let her guard down.

Perhaps the war might spare him a minute. Henry, of all the beings in the Seven Bells, would forgive such an indulgence. Henry would have even given him playful grief about it during a round of blackjack.

Jakob knelt back down, his hands clasped around her fingers. "I'm sorry I've been away," he said, the gravel in his voice as unexpected as his words. He squeezed her hand, sinking into her presence as the wall clock ticked over sixty seconds.

Time was up.

Jakob started in the kitchen for things that might trigger power-up sequences of extraterrestrial equipment: batteries, wires, needles, syringes, perhaps some good old duct tape for binding. Drawer after drawer, cabinet after cabinet, he wrenched all of them open, but the only useful thing came in the form of some AA batteries and a blue canvas bag.

Scissors? Scissors would always help, even safety scissors, probably to minimize risk around Mom. Jakob grabbed them and tossed them into the bag. Just in case. He closed his eyes, revisiting all of the details he'd caught when he walked in.

The garage next? It was the best bet, but it wouldn't work with his sisters on the front porch. Instead, he moved behind and past Mom quickly, thumbing through an end table and the TV stand's drawers, only to find game controllers and a small library of Blu-rays. He shoved a few excess USB cables into the bag and moved on; nothing too helpful, though Jakob did wonder when Kassie had become a gamer.

Outside, the chatter picked up, Kassie's voice louder and clearer than Evie's. He stepped around Mom, who didn't notice at all, and scanned for more options until his eyes locked on the old family office, but when he turned the knob, it refused to budge.

Strange that it'd be locked.

In the dim hallway, a thin beam of light poked through beneath the door. Probably a computer screen, and if this was Kassie's home office, probably more. A fast computer. Perhaps he could order specific materials he needed, even find a place that would give access to a metal shop, a 3-D printer. His debit cards weren't loaded with too much, but there *had* to be some sort of work-around. Every second counted. Information, money, of course, and perhaps a few other key pieces of—

"You can stay or you can go. That's not up to me." Kassie's voice rang out followed quickly by the slam of the door. "But this is my life now."

Jakob glanced around before nearly being struck down by the sting at the base of his skull again. He shoved the bag behind a potted plant and tried to straighten up.

A pair of footsteps clacked against the entryway tile, the voices getting louder. "I don't get it. How could you not tell me she was like this?" Evie asked.

The sisters stopped, both looking at Jakob as he steadied himself by the office door. "Sorry," Jakob said, "I was looking around to see how the place had changed."

"That's my office."

"I thought it was the family office. Where our high school trophies are."

"For fuck's sake, is your head still in high school? You haven't been here in a *long* time, Jakob. That's my office. I lock it to keep things safe when Mom wanders," Kassie said, and though he expected some level of vitriol, the sharpness of her tone caught him off guard. "Wait, did you leave Mom alone?"

"Just for a minute, she's watching her show."

"That doesn't mean anything." Kassie strode forward, Evie in tow. "Goddamn it, why did I leave her with you?" Jakob followed, his eyes resuming a second look for anything useful he might have missed. "Mom, you should eat something. We got pizza."

Mom turned to the elder Shao daughter and said something just out of earshot. Kassie nodded, replying with a similarly inaudible response. Jakob motioned Evie ahead, not out of politeness but to hide the intense pain at the back of his head.

He kept his balance, staying steady despite the battle inside his body.

"Who is she?" Mom pointed at Evie, her ferocity seemingly worse than thirty minutes ago. "What is she doing in my house?"

"Don't," Kassie whispered back at them. "Let me handle this."

"Maybe I should go," Evie said. "I have work to do."

Though his sisters didn't notice it, Jakob's body tensed.

Opportunity.

If Evie left and Kassie tended to Mom, that bought him more time to gather resources. He'd need to encourage this, though. Espionage against the Awakened wasn't quite like navigating sibling rivalry.

"If it's okay," Jakob said, "I'd like to stay a little bit. I can always take a rideshare to the motel." He eyed the clock, making note of the time, how long he'd been awake, how much rest he'd need at a minimum to function. Evie had served her purpose, and now he needed distance to ensure she wouldn't try to get him to a hospital.

"That's fine," Kassie said with a sigh.

"Actually," Evie's words came out tentatively, "could you give me a lift to the motel?"

"What?" Kassie's eyes darted to each person around the room. Evie. Jakob. Mom. Back to Evie. "Take a rideshare. Don't tell me you need money for that."

"No. No, I… I just want to talk. As sisters. It's just a few minutes away."

"Sorry. Can't leave Mom alone." Kassie shot Jakob a look. "She needs someone with her."

"I can do it," Jakob said, his mind already churning with ideas.

"You already tried."

"No, I mean, I can do it. I'll sit with her." He looked at Mom as his thoughts turned to the battles far away from them. *Go home. Weapon. Signal.* He had to do this.

"I won't move," he said, putting on his best Jakob Shao charm. "Promise."

CHAPTER TWENTY-ONE

EVIE

As soon as the car door slammed shut, Kassie went on the offensive. Evie told herself to be steady: not defensive, not a jerk, and not overly emotional. But hold her ground, absolutely. Most importantly, expect all types of passive–aggressive jabs.

"I don't want to hear any shit about the deed, Evie."

Or straight-out aggressive jabs.

The car came to life, and Evie settled in. How could she switch the topic from their family home to aliens and intergalactic war?

"Which motel?" Kassie asked as she tapped away on the screen.

"Origins Inn." *Jakob told me the truth, and I was right.* No, no, she shouldn't crow this over her big sister. *Jakob told me the truth, and it wasn't actually Europe.* Maybe? That was a softer place to start.

"Your destination is five…point…six miles away," the car's speaker droned.

"You know..." Evie started as the car began backing out. *Just say it, don't overthink it.* "I know Jakob told us he was in Europe, but it wasn't that."

"Mexico? South America?" Kassie asked as she switched the car to Drive. "Jail? Rehab? No, he wouldn't go to rehab."

"No, Kassie." Evie's heart pounded in her chest at a surprising rate. She'd spent her entire adult life researching this *and* hoping Jakob would return. Was her body reacting to the fact that, for once, she'd get to speak out of certainty? Or was she afraid of her big sister's reaction? "I think... I mean, look, I know you're going to laugh, but just hear me out." *Boom. Boom. Boom.* The pressure hammered her chest, and Evie took in a slow, controlled breath to steady herself, not too speedy with what she said, not too aggressive in her enthusiasm. "I was right. It was aliens. Aliens took Jakob and Dad, and they sent Dad home." The words nearly left her lungs empty, the push to say them propelled by excitement. She took in a short breath to get the next part out. "But Jakob's been with them for fifteen years."

Evie expected laughter or vitriol from her sister. Maybe both. But instead, Kassie drove with a neutral expression, the dusk light creating harsh angles across her cheekbones. "Okay," she finally said. "Fine. Let's say that is true. How can you prove it?"

"Well, he told me."

"What makes that proof?"

"It was just so...detailed," Evie said, suddenly realizing how absurd that sounded. She tried, she really did, to back it up. All of the little bits of information Jakob had passed on, she recounted with as many particulars as possible. The Seven Bells and their desperate alliance and strange rocklike technology, the Awakened's marauding, the transforming mechs he piloted. The decryptor, the memory gaps, the way he progressively felt pain as they'd closed in on the decryptor. How Jakob had information in his mind to win the war.

His friend's dying wish.

All he had to do was get back.

"I mean, he said it like…like it was firsthand knowledge," Evie said. Minutes had passed of Evie offering specifics to tell Jakob's story, and though everything came together into one cohesive outer-space alibi, a tiny crack of doubt emerged. Saying it all aloud like a high-school book report created a different filter for the whole thing, and it stood apart from the weekly discussions she did for *The Bright Light*.

Kassie's reaction didn't help. Not because she poked holes in Jakob's story or mocked Evie for repeating it; in fact, her sister remained quietly steady the whole time, only asking questions with a clinical tone.

Probably because she *was* using a clinical tone.

The light ahead of them turned from red to a green arrow, and Kassie brought the car forward, leaving the downtown strip behind and heading onto El Camino Real.

"How was he behaving this whole time?"

"Fine. I mean, he's Jakob, right? So like Jakob, but kind of not. Much more serious. That's the other thing. Like, we've heard Jakob tell his stories before. But this wasn't like that at all. He's different. You can see it in his eyes. There's the guy we knew, he's still there. But it's like there's something built on top of it. You can see it. He's shifted." Evie adjusted in her seat and looked straight ahead as Kassie pulled into the motel parking lot. "He's grown up."

"I *did* see it in his eyes. His pupils were dilated." The car lurched quietly into an open parking spot, Kassie doing so without even asking where their room was. "Okay, look," she said as the parking brake clicked into place. "Have you heard the term *delusions of grandeur* before?"

The car continued to idle as Evie tried to formulate an answer. The right words failed her; they had to be smart, believable, sincere, a rebuttal without being defensive or condescending or frustrated. A precise target to pop Kassie's balloon before it flew too high.

But none of that appeared, leaving only a weak "Yeah" as Kassie shut down the car.

"Okay, let's take this step-by-step. This all sounds like stuff from Jakob's life. I was there." The old Kassie, the one who came back from college with tales of doing a row of Jell-O shots, would never present such a clear assessment, such a matter-of-fact summary. Each sentence landed like blades cutting through stilts, the house built on top of it beginning to crumble. "Mechs were part of his favorite show when we were, like, eight. And marauding aliens, come on, that's like every movie ever made. Seven Bells is a band he liked in college. They were called School of Seven Bells. I know this for a fact because we had a mutual friend who DJed at the UC Davis radio station. Jakob flaked on him for a local show, so I went instead. Not really my thing, but he bought the drinks that night."

"But the readings. Air pressure, magnetic declination, sudden temperature changes. In Reno. In Half Moon Bay. It matched that night. He even pulled a piece of the decryptor out of the sand. I saw it."

"What did it look like?"

"Well..." Evie knew what Kassie was doing, like cross-examining a witness into self-inflicted wounds. But that wasn't fair here. This was about both faith *and* facts.

The two could coexist. She was certain of it.

But dang, Kassie sure was trying hard to chip away at them.

"Okay, it looked like a rock. But, I mean, it fit what he'd talked about before."

"Look, Evie, I'm not going to try to understand what you do at your job. I'm only telling you what I see. You said he was talking to himself in the car."

"Well, yeah. But we were close to the decryptor. He said he could sense the signal was nearby."

"Okay. And you saw him collapse to his knees on the beach?"

"Right, when things restored. But," Evie said, swimming against the sudden torrent of Kassie's logic, "he said that his mind reactivated the details. So it was, like, overwhelming. And a little painful."

"And did you notice tonight? He kept looking around, wincing, taking a moment?" Kassie asked. "Like he—"

"What's your point?"

"My point, *Evie*—" she said, the emphasis on the name loaded with something she couldn't identify. Lording over the fact that Kassie was the big sister. Or that she was a licensed psychologist. Or that she just thought Evie was a gullible moron who traded in conspiracy theories (they *weren't*, they were facts!) or that she just wanted to get a verbal smack in because that was how Kassie rolled "—is that these are all classic signs of mental illness. Schizophrenia or possibly bipolar. Given everything you know about Jakob, what's more likely: he's the only space soldier who can win an intergalactic war, or all the drugs he's done have finally caught up to him? I'm gonna have a smoke."

Kassie unbuckled her seat belt and stepped outside without a word. Soon, the aroma of burning tobacco snuck through the window, and Evie got out. A chill wind blasted the shaved side of her head, and Evie pulled her hoodie over. "Jakob's never had mental illness."

"Uh, he did a bunch of psychedelic drugs all through college. Those can trigger schizophrenia if you're predisposed to it. And he might have even been on something today. Like I said, his pupils were dilated. And we both know Jakob hid it well when he was using."

"So you think he's lying?"

"No, not at all. I think he believes it. That's why he's acting with such sincerity. He really thinks he's a space hero on a mission to save the galaxy. He's synthesized things from his life for his delusions of grandeur," Kassie said, taking a drag of her cigarette. "He might be experiencing a psychotic break."

When she put it that way, of course she sounded right. Using textbook terms was cheating. "That's not fair."

"Look, I'm not going to bore you with the details, but you can look it up if you want. Schizophrenia often presents in young adulthood, men see it about ten years earlier than women. The drug use doesn't help. Delusions, hallucinations, brain fog, illogical thought patterns. High-emotion situations can trigger events. Jakob probably took something right before we went to Lake Kinbote."

Though she refused to let Kassie see it, Evie felt a gut punch, a mental impact so hard that she would have grabbed the side of the car to steady herself—if doing so wouldn't have given her sister the upper hand. She couldn't let Kassie know about the night before Lake Kinbote, that moment in the bedroom when Jakob her had shown her the little packet he was going to bring.

"I don't know why he came home now," Kassie said. "Maybe he really was in Europe with barmaids and decided to come home for whatever reason. Or maybe he just got out of prison. *Probably* he just got out of prison. Someone with this condition can phase in between perceived realities without proper medication, proper therapy. Jakob might be in crisis right now. And like I said, high-emotion situations can be triggers. It doesn't get more high-emotion than learning you killed your Dad."

She said it so matter-of-factly. Without any blame on Dad for his choices or the situation or anything else. Evie heard the words and processed the cold nature of her sister's voice. Kassie played the part of the clinical psychologist, but deep down, Evie saw it: she was mad at Jakob for Dad.

Was that independent of everything she said? It seemed impossible to separate the two.

"The way he acted on the beach, with those headaches and pauses and falling to his knees, it's textbook. The fallout from coming home, from talking to us, from finding out about Dad, it creates a ripple effect of brain chemistry. And it presents itself in different ways for that condition. Physical headaches, mental gaps, and delusions of grandeur. I promise you," Kassie said, taking a final puff before putting out her cigarette, grinding it into the ground, "you could make a list of his behavior, and any psychiatry professor would just put check after check on it. His whole life has finally caught up to him, and this is his mind trying to process it." She opened the car door, its rhythmic beeping announcing that someone or something should close it, though Kassie held on. "I need to go. I shouldn't have left Jakob there with Mom. Stupid, impulsive move."

Before Evie could respond, the door slammed and the car came to life. She stepped back, not sure if Kassie might just back out over her in her current mood. She zoomed out of the parking lot, barely slowing down at the curb before turning.

Another gust of wind kicked up, one so hard that it blew Evie's hood off. Behind her, the purple hue of dusk turned into the moody colors of early evening, a mix of darkening sky and harsh street lamps and the motel's neon sign. Cars roared past, coming and going down the busy street, and Evie looked up, straight up where a single bright star cut through the blanket of sky.

No. It wasn't a star. The light didn't twinkle. It was Venus, the brightest planet in the solar system, a static dot of white.

Evie walked across the parking lot all the way to her room on the far end. She slipped her key card into the lock, and it beeped twice before the door's mechanism unlatched. She stepped in and the door's hinges shut it, cutting off the ambient noise of an active Silicon Valley suburb. Car lights flashed through the window before angling away; probably some late-arriving guests who hopefully didn't deal with the same level of family drama as the Shaos.

The bed dipped and squeaked as Evie sat on it. She needed to talk to the Reds. She had data to research. And Layla's ridiculous puns always made her laugh.

But instead, Evie sat and stared at the wall ahead of her, wondering what to think. She almost—almost—got the piece from the beach out of her backpack, the one that Jakob claimed was part of the chipped shell from an extraterrestrial device. Not long ago, such an assertion would have felt completely factual, an absolute statement. But Kassie poked that confidence just enough to turn a breath of hesitation into something more. Several minutes passed before she finally pulled out her phone and turned on the Selfie camera to capture the moment. Because *something* important would come out of this.

She just didn't know what.

CHAPTER TWENTY-TWO

KASS

By the time Kass got home, dusk had turned into night. She pulled into the driveway to find nearly all of the lights dim, the whole time wondering *why* she'd even gone. Since Jakob's disappearance, simply having a sense of *control* over the variables had been a source of peace for her, if not pride.

Evie was a variable. Jakob was a variable. Mom was *the* variable.

And yet, she'd let Evie sweep her away, perhaps only for twenty minutes or so, but still away from Mom. She did feel for Evie, though. Regardless of their issues, no one deserved to be unrecognized by their own mother.

But that remained separate from the issues at hand. And while Kass kicked herself for leaving Jakob as sole caregiver, Mom seemed to calm down far faster with him than she did with herself or Lucy, no matter how much that irritated her. Maybe that tiny solace had tinted her judgment for a few minutes.

Kass tapped the lock button on her key fob. She paused for a moment, watching several children riding their scooters in a circle at the end of the cul-de-sac, the same place Kass had regularly beat Jakob in races all through high school. The constant churn of young families provided an extra level of idyllic charm to the neighborhood, but then again, Kass probably looked like a stock suburban professional to the outside world. No one could have guessed what her last however-many hours had entailed.

As she unlocked the front door, she listened for any hints of disaster. But there was no screaming, no signs of chaos or mess. In fact, when she cracked the door open, the only sound she heard was from the TV in the family room.

Kass inched forward quietly past the entryway and down the front hall, walking to avoid any floorboards that creaked. She crept ahead until she caught a glimpse of the family room: there was Mom, eyes closed and steadily breathing. The throw blanket from earlier rested neatly across her lap, one arm tucked underneath it. And on the screen, *Star Trek* continued playing, already into the next episode via streaming.

Though no Jakob.

Fury rose to Kass's cheeks, kicking herself *again* for trusting Jakob to keep his word.

Benefit of the doubt, she told herself. *He might just be getting pizza or using the bathroom.*

Besides, a relaxed stillness permeated the room. No signs of disaster or freak-outs or—more importantly—Jakob's bullshit. It was, however, about three hours before Mom's usual bedtime. Kass worried about a possible disruption to the schedule, though she reminded herself to have low expectations. The stress of the evening might have worn Mom out anyway; a short nap might be a good emotional reset for her after seeing Jakob and Evie.

Things were safe here. A minute or so passed while Kass stayed still, watching Mom. Then the brief wave of relief turned back to irritation.

Where the hell was Jakob? If he was just grabbing food, he'd be back by now.

Kass surveyed the rest of the room. No sign of anything else, other than Mom's sketchpad being open to a visibly torn sheet. She resisted the urge to call out Jakob by name for fear of stirring Mom, and instead tiptoed to the kitchen, where someone had broken into the pizza boxes. She moved as stealthily as she could back across the hall and had taken the first step upstairs to check the bedrooms when she heard something from behind.

A look behind her showed the door to her office ajar—and, in fact, part of the doorframe by the lock smashed in.

What the fuck.

Step-by-step, she approached, and while the mostly shut door muffled a lot of the noises, a distinct one came through. It was quiet, only audible by someone who was really listening for it, but Kass recognized it as soon as she heard it.

It was just a grunt, a vocalization of frustration. But it was Jakob. She knew his voice.

Kass debated between kicking the door open and sneaking in. She opted for the latter; her palm flat on the wooden surface, pushing it open at a controlled rate by an inch or so, enough to see what was happening.

Her stomach dropped in nausea at the sight of her private office being invaded. But then frustration roared at *herself.* Of course Jakob had broken in.

And of course on a day when she'd disabled password control on her system.

Kass bit her bottom lip.

A quick glance back at the family room showed no signs

of Mom stirring, so Kass tried to decipher what Jakob was doing. He sat hunched over the chair, brow twisted and hand at his temple. She recognized it immediately—that wince from earlier, the one she saw him try to stifle. This was the same reaction, except right now he didn't attempt to hide it.

Kass threw the door fully open and hit the light switch. "What the fuck are you doing, Jakob?"

Jakob stood up instantly, his knees banging into the desk, though the sudden movement caused him to wince again and hold his head. "Oh. Sorry, I just was looking up a rideshare. My phone doesn't get great signal here."

"You broke into my office?" She marched forward, and he leaned over and clicked on the mouse several times, the final time being accurate enough to close the browser window.

"Your office? This is Dad's. What happened to our trophies?" he asked, reaching down to grab something. Despite the limited light, she recognized the bag—blue canvas, just enough of the logo visible enough to know that it was from Kenway's Café downtown. Probably taken from the kitchen drawer. Definitely not something Jakob would have had with him or gotten from Evie. "Look, my phone doesn't load anything here." He looked out the door, probably down the hall. "Mom fell asleep," his tone adjusted, "and I thought I'd multitask since she was so peaceful. Hey." That stupid Jakob smirk popped up, but its charms had no effect on Kass, not now. "Mom and Dad always wanted me to be more efficient, right? Here I am."

"The door was *locked*. You smashed it open."

"No, I didn't."

"Don't lie to me, Jakob. The doorframe is busted. I always lock it so Mom doesn't wander in here and get into my work stuff."

Her brother's eyes darted around the room, controlled but

frenetic, until they settled on…something. He tensed, and his jaw clenched in a different way from his wincing earlier. "Work stuff," Jakob said. "Like this?" He reached on to the desk and held up the Golden Apple brochure.

Kass lost all her momentum. "That's not fair. Lucy is going to start there, and she asked—"

"Not fair? Kassie, what I see is you getting inconvenienced by Mom's condition, and so you're going to throw her to the wolves."

"Jakob, you do not know the situation." There. Not necessarily an explanation, but at least she could fight back. "And you've been off doing whatever bullshit you're into for fifteen years. So you shut the hell up right now about Mom." This time, it was *her* turn to let out a frustrated groan that scratched her throat and came out way louder than it should have. Eyes closed, she buried her head in her palms, thumbs pressing against her temples. "Listen," she said opening her eyes and ready to rip her twin brother apart, "I—"

And just like that, Jakob sprinted past her, bag in hand.

Goddamn it.

Out of instinct, Kass reached out. Her hand missed Jakob but managed to catch the bag. It pulled out, slipping between both of their hands with a *clang.*

Scissors?

Motherfucker. Kass wanted to scream the curse out loud, but she reminded herself to not disturb Mom's slumber.

She stormed out of the office, stopping only to scan for sights and sounds. Quiet greeted her, and no shapes whizzed by. "Jakob," she said in a harsh whisper, "where the fuck did you go?" She stepped out farther and turned the corner out of the hallway, only to catch sight of the front door closing.

More curses came out under Kass's breath, and she threw the door open. And though the evening sky had dimmed visibility, a clear silhouette sprinted down the street. "And stay the *fuck* out of our lives!" she yelled. A neighbor, mail in hand, stood on the sidewalk and gawked at Kass. She offered her best professional smile and waved, then went inside.

She closed the door.

And locked it.

Pizza. Jakob had taken *more* pizza on his way out. The sheer nerve of her brother. She took one piece herself, and while Mom slumbered, she brought the slice of mushroom/garlic/jalapeño to her office and brought up the web browser, then opened up its history.

A long list appeared, one much longer than she'd expected. Typical Jakob doing everything half-assed. If *she* were to break into a computer and use a browser, she'd at least have the sense to put it in Private Browsing mode. Her little bit of amusement shifted quickly as she processed the list of visited sites.

Shopping. He'd been shopping, but where would he even ship his purchases? It didn't really matter, given that it appeared he only put items in a cart, hadn't fully purchased. But the list itself was odd.

Surgeon's scalpel. Car battery. UV light. Fertilizer. Propane torch.

The bag she'd grabbed from him, which was now safely put away, had more than scissors in it. Batteries, USB cables, and two cigarette lighters—all things similar to his search history.

What would Jakob of all people do with a bunch of car parts and medical equipment? It didn't make any sense. Kass grabbed a pen and went through the shopping list again, writing down each item. It certainly didn't look like he was buying supplies for a Caribbean fishing trip.

She clicked the mouse again and again, page by page flashing on-screen, and Kass realized that several items went below the fold on the browser's history. She scrolled to the bottom, though she would have stopped there anyway as she realized what was on there.

Not another car-supply store but a bank. Eden Bank.

Mom's bank.

"No, no, no, Jakob. You didn't."

The bank's site loaded up, a large photo of a family enjoying a beach displayed on the header. Kass's hand shook, a combination of fury and nerves while she logged in. She typed Mom's email address in the first field, then *Elise12*, the name of Mom's cat she got at age twelve and the same damn password she'd always used, and which they kept using for her remaining few accounts now to keep it simple, on the off chance something happened to Kass.

Except nothing had happened to Kass. The preventative measures stopped nothing, but they let an asshole like Jakob come in and take from them, just like he'd taken from them fifteen years ago.

The screen blinked, Kass's foot tapping with an impatient rhythm while bits and bytes traversed over invisible signals. From the family room, a voice stirred. "Kassie? Tell your Dad that *Star Trek* is on."

"Okay, Mom," she yelled back with too much force for a simple confirmation. Because the simmering fury that had stayed capped for hours was finally boiling over, exploding into every muscle and every nerve in her body.

"Kassie?"

Think, think, think, she told herself. She had to talk to Mom and get her settled. And then she had to call the bank's 24-hour phone number.

Because there were six transactions, all to banks that she'd never heard of, but a quick search showed that they were routing numbers of prepaid debit cards.

Jacob had emptied the account.

On top of taking more goddamn pizza.

CHAPTER TWENTY-THREE

EVIE

The computer screen lit the dim motel room, and though Evie had taken the time to type out her notes and analysis, a summary of her findings—Jakob's incredible story—and probably several weeks' worth of material for *Bright Light* episodes, she hadn't been able to send it off to the Reds yet. Her email remained open.

In the next tab was her contact list, the core Reds grouped together for a potential video call—one or all six of them. She'd already missed several texts from them asking for updates: Connor saying that their secondary volunteer group of researchers were ready, Edward asking weirdly specific questions regarding location and Jakob's history, while Layla pushed in a gentler way: We haven't heard from you. Did a joule thief steal all your energy?

The Reds were all East Coast, meaning that midnight had come and gone for them. But they worked late, all except one having the luxury of single life with private spaces to conduct their research. Chances were, they'd gladly read Evie's report as soon as she sent it.

Yet rather than hitting the send button, Evie had spent most of the past two hours just *sitting there*. She *should* send it—all data had to be considered, even if Kassie had chipped away at her confidence. Even now, the bed squeaked as she shifted her weight, staring instead of hitting a single button. "What if she's right?" she asked aloud, and her brain didn't offer any clear response.

More importantly, what if the Reds confirmed Kassie's theory? Normally she'd make a crack at how Kassie studied soft sciences as opposed to real data, but her sister had presented an argument with clear, thoughtful evidence. So much so that any actual research Evie had pulled in the last hour had less to do with standard Red metrics and more to do with symptoms of various mental illnesses.

She wouldn't go so far as to say Kassie was right, but her sister's observations fell into the Clearly Feasible category.

And the weight of that idea caused Evie to procrastinate.

All she had were the notes scribbled down before Half Moon Bay. And now she'd transcribed them into her laptop, ready to fire away. Yet doubt sprouted thanks to Kassie, growing thick and messy and tangling into everything.

This whole effort was to discover what had happened to Jakob; the extraterrestrial part was just tangled into that quest. But they'd *found* Jakob, so now what? The truth mattered to the Reds. For herself? She wasn't sure. She had a brother to hug and laugh with, and wasn't that enough?

From the motel room's small circular table, Evie's phone buzzed, the rattle causing a pen to roll off and bounce on the floor. It continued, the ongoing vibrations of a call rather than a text notification, and she let it go. Probably Kassie saying she was finally driving over to drop Jakob off. Or that maybe Jakob was crashing on the couch there. Couchsurfing wasn't exactly out of Jakob's realm of experience, regardless of whether he'd been in space.

The bed bounced as Evie fell backward, a full flop onto it, leaving her staring at the decades-old popcorn ceiling above her. It didn't totally make sense, though. "Reno, Lake Kinbote, Half Moon Bay," she whispered to herself, trying to push it out of a circular rhythm and into a logical through line. The differentials in Reno? They were the *exact* same as the night they'd disappeared at Lake Kinbote. And Jakob's story had been *so* detailed. The Jakob she knew evaded questions so deftly that you didn't even realize he'd sidestepped the entire thing until he'd left the room. Not answers with precision, not such deep and vivid specifics that *anyone* listening would have found themselves convinced.

Even Kassie.

Evie had done the stupid thing, the dreamy awestruck thing, and forgotten to record anything yesterday. She'd been too caught up in having Jakob color in all of her dreams, answer by answer, both about his disappearance and what lay beyond the solar system.

The phone began buzzing again, the phone screen lit with the caller ID of *Kassie*, and this time Evie forced herself to roll off the bed, shaking off the fatigue that came with disappointment. She tripped over her kicked-off boots, and reached out to catch herself on the back of the room's lone chair. "Freakin' damn it," she said, then was doubly irritated at herself for giving in to cursing like Kassie. Not that she cared when anyone else did it, but she'd always prided herself on demonstrating a level of self-control that her older sister never could.

Feet flat, Evie finally grabbed the phone and reached over to swipe, except the screen reverted back to a tiled list of app icons.

Well, it must not have been too important, otherwise she'd text first.

Screw it, she thought, slipping the phone into her back pocket. Screw Kassie and her psychology degree and professional-textbook-whatever perspective, screw her disbelief, screw *her* for planting those seeds of doubt. This was *Jakob*, who'd always listened to Evie whenever Kassie seemed too busy or too distracted or too cool to do so.

She made a choice right then, thoughts taking root in her mind. She would believe Jakob. And she'd work with the Reds to prove it.

Evie sat, finger tracing over the laptop's touch pad until it brought up her email. The cursor slid over the send button and her finger rose to click, to launch this information into the world.

Right when her finger moved, her back pocket buzzed. "Figures," she said with a sigh. "Can't give up without an argument, huh?" She answered it without even looking at the screen. "Yes, big sister?"

"Evie?" Kassie's voice was different than usual. Not snarky, not dry, not annoyed or rushed. "Is Jakob with you?"

The question was asked in a detached tone, like the words floated instead of being propelled by an actual speaking person. There was only one time Kassie had ever sounded like this, her tone so unique it was burned into Evie's memory.

On that afternoon, several days after Dad went back to Lake Kinbote, Evie waited in the car.

Not fidgeting, not texting, not reading one of the books that just happened to be in the backpack at her feet while raindrops pelted the windshield. Kassie had said "Wait here," and that's what she had done.

Even looking back, Evie wondered if she should have insisted on going with her. When Kassie said "Let me do it," she could have fought harder. Kassie was pretty stubborn, and Evie'd learned very early in life to not argue with her.

Still, this seemed important.

Without warning, Kassie had emerged from the corner of the small stone building, and though her eyes hid behind large sunglasses, something about her seemed different. Her walk—normally with a bit of casual swagger—seemed stiff and detached, arms and legs moving in short swings that failed to line up with each other.

Evie had known the result right then.

"Hey," Evie called out, stepping into the thick late-summer air. Kassie responded by shaking her head. Evie extended an arm, the most obvious choice to comfort someone who'd just identified the drowned body of their father, but Kassie moved right past her and marched to the driver's side. Within seconds, she was back in the car, seat belt buckled, and keys in the ignition. The engine roared to life, and the radio's low music poked through the speakers, but the car remained idle.

They sat for a while, at least ten minutes, though Evie lost track. She'd opened her mouth to say something a few times, but she kept coming back to waiting. Kassie had told her to wait, after all, and though seniority didn't always mean wisdom—Jakob had been a perfect example of that—this moment kept deferring to Kassie.

Evie made a point not to give in to her instinct of whispering her way through the questions in her head. She didn't even ask Kassie what she'd seen or if their worst fears had come true.

She didn't need to.

"We need to move forward. We need to tell Mom." Kassie had said those exact words months earlier, when the sheriff reported that their extensive searches of the lake and its surrounding woods had failed to produce a body, ultimately categorizing Jakob as a missing person. Her response had been laced with irritation, a subtle tint giving away her opinions on Jakob's whereabouts.

In the car, though, Evie saw Kassie's frozen expression and statuelike posture. Several seconds passed until Kassie finally moved, her fingers fumbling as they tried to slide her phone out of her pocket. "Goddamn it," she said, the phone dropping to the floor. "Fix this. Fix this. Fix this." The refrain came out as a whisper, and it was the first time Evie ever recalled Kassie using their mom's favorite approach to problem-solving.

But while that may have worked with a botched recipe or a blown project, the scope of that moment far exceeded that.

"This is all Jakob's fault," Kassie finally spit out. She took off her sunglasses and tried to hang them off the top visor hook but missed. Her hands trembled as she exhaled, a slow, controlled motion to finally get them on there. "This is all Jakob's fault. None of this would have happened if Jakob just had his shit together." Her leg shifted slightly, the car engine giving a roar. "This is all Jakob's fault."

Jakob's fault. Kassie spoke it with the same detached cadence that Evie now heard over the phone while sitting in a motel room, as if all Kassie's emotions fought to a stalemate. Dread crept into Evie, a visceral reaction triggered simply by the way her sister spoke. Same tone, same cadence.

Kassie asked again. "Is Jakob with you?"

CHAPTER TWENTY-FOUR

KASS

Kass waited for a reply, her finger tapping on the arm of the patio chair. Small fidgets fulfilled her physical urge to do *something.* Better than smashing dishes and glasses. Or doing anything else she'd just have to clean up and repair later. Unless she saved that all for Jakob to do as a penance for the bullshit.

"I— What?" Evie finally said.

"Is he with you? Did he run to you?"

"No. Wait, what do you mean, *run*?"

"Evie, listen to me. Jakob's a fraud. I told—" Kass stopped herself, a reminder that of all the times to be in control of her emotions, this should top the list. Gloating to Evie, goading her into a fight, that wouldn't solve anything. "I had my suspicions. He may or may not have mental illness, but what I can tell you is that he broke into Mom's bank account, stole a bunch of money, and then ran into the night. Like literally, ran down the street." She took a quick drag on her cigarette, then puffed it out. "Fucking coward."

Okay, that last part had just slipped out. Kass gave herself a pass on that one. Pressure needed to released somehow.

"Evie? You there?" she asked after a minute of silence.

"Yeah," she said. "I'm looking out the window now. I don't see him. Just, um, streetlights and some traffic. A burrito place."

"Look, I know you had your hopes set on him being..." Kass went with the diplomatic approach "...something else. But he stole from Mom. He stole from Mom, Evie." Her voice cracked in a foreign way, like a different person had taken over. Every waking moment these days required shuffling, compartmentalizing. Control over which part of her slipped out, what that affected. Mom. Lucy. Patients. Juggling it all, slipping in and out of each mode like equipping different armor for Aveline's dungeon raids.

But right now, talking with Evie, cracks formed in the walls. "I just, I'm so..." Kass's voice drifted off as she searched for an appropriate thing to say. "I'm so *mad*."

Whether intentionally or not, Evie gave her space before responding. "I am too," she said softly. Kass let that revelation sink in, surprised at its simplicity. "Look. Any idea where he went?"

"No clue," Kass said, returning to herself. "He looked up a bunch of weird stuff. Like home-gardening supplies and medical tools. He did that all *after* he robbed Mom. And he took some pizza. I'm mad about that too." Kass only half joked about that, but it got Evie to laugh in response. "Look, Evie, there's something I gotta ask because it's going to define how we handle this." Kass took a final drag on the cigarette burning away between her fingers. "Okay?"

"Okay," Evie said, a gravity to her words that seemed to acknowledge that this moment might shift the course of their world. "Yeah. It's cool."

The next words came out carefully, her grip on the phone tightened, the burden of the moment suddenly evident. “Do you believe me now?”

CHAPTER TWENTY-FIVE

EVIE

Evie couldn't deny facts.

So much of Evie's adult life had been based around trying to apply facts and science to areas and discussions that often lacked that. Doing so created a sense of purity to the pursuits at the Red Network, something that set them apart from people who believed based on half truths or sheer desperation or somewhere in between.

Everything Kassie said pointed to a single fact. Jakob would not rob Mom if he was on an intergalactic quest. He would, though, if he'd pissed off people or blew his money or wanted to disappear again.

"I believe you," she said, the strength of her tone even surprising herself. Perhaps more surprising was the sudden change she felt, an urge to understand and fix things. "I'll help you. I promise."

Like she had with Dad.

"If he shows up here, what do you think I should do?" Evie asked. "Play dumb?"

"I… Here's the thing. I think there is a significant chance that he's schizophrenic. I mean, it is literally a laundry list of symptoms. But violent outbursts are pretty rare. That's more of a bad stereotype. It hardly happens. That doesn't mean you shouldn't be careful. You understand?"

"So…play along?"

"Honestly? Call the cops. Discreetly. He fucking stole Mom's money. And he may never forgive us for throwing him in jail, but it's the best way to keep him safe until he can get a psychiatric evaluation. He may even have a prescription, and he could just be off his meds."

"And what if he doesn't show up?"

Kassie blew out a sigh, and Evie wondered if all this exhaling stemmed from Kassie smoking yet another cigarette. "I don't know. Maybe we file a missing person report."

"Can we even do that?"

"I don't know. Mom had him declared dead even though we weren't convinced. I'm not sure how that works now. Let's just take it one step at a time, okay? I gotta make sure Mom gets to bed. And maybe have some of this pizza."

"Okay. I'll keep you posted." Meek farewells came out, seemingly more out of reflex than anything else. Evie held the phone up to press the red hang-up icon when a different urge grabbed her. "Kassie?" she asked, hoping that her sister hadn't hung up yet.

If the moment had passed, Evie wouldn't call her back. Not for this.

"Yeah." In a throwaway word used countless times in a day, this instance carried the weight of years with it.

"I'm, um, sorry I didn't…" Evie straightened up, her eyes trailing to the ceiling. "Sorry I didn't, you know…that I—"

"It's fine, Evie. We're here now. You know what Mom would say."

"'How will you fix it?'"

"Yeah. So let's do that. Look, I gotta take care of Mom."

And with that, the line went silent, the phone beeping to signal the end of the call.

Evie went back to the laptop, staring at the screen. Everything was a crossroads now, the unsent email a portal into her life *before* Kassie called. Her very existence felt different, as if one of her limbs had simply vanished from existence.

Who was she without her quest for Jakob?

And if she had been wrong about Jakob, then what else had she been wrong about? Leaving school? Joining the Reds? Committing to something that many considered a fringe conspiracy theory?

The laptop lid shut with a click. She wouldn't be needing that for a while. Instead, Evie walked over to the window and brushed the curtain aside, hoping something might appear to resolve all of this. Jakob with a really, really good explanation or something that proved this was all a bad dream, or a UFO landing right here in this parking lot.

But instead, she got a suburban motel on a suburban street. The parking lot itself offered nothing save some economy cars pulling in and the van that had been there since she'd returned—since the morning, in fact.

She stood and watched, a minute passing, then another, then five more. The night sky failed to give any clues or relief, and Evie found herself staring at a static parking lot, parked cars and signs.

Except…

Evie blinked to make sure her eyes saw accurately given the dim light and motel room's dirty window.

The van door opened. Someone got out. Which shouldn't

be an issue in most cases given that this was a *motel* after all, but the van itself had been sitting for a while. Why come to a motel parking lot and sit for hours?

Why come out now late at night wearing an official-looking suit?

And why walk toward Evie's door?

Evie glanced again to make sure that was *not* Jakob, then she slid back over to the door, watching only through the peephole. A woman in a pantsuit strode toward the door with purpose, a direct line straight like in video games when you tell a character to move to a targeted location.

This was definitely *not* Jakob. But did it have to do with Jakob?

A knock came.

"Ms. Shao?"

Holy crap.

They knew her name. And she was pretty sure that they weren't just a fan of *The Bright Light.* Should she open it? Call the police? What if they *were* the police? And if so, it's not like police were always trustworthy. Maybe she should call Kassie.

"Kassie or the cops?" she asked herself in a rapid whisper. "Kassie or the cops? Think, think, think."

Another knock. "Ms. Shao?"

Evie's fingers fumbled for her phone, fear and tension stealing her ability to have fine-motor skills. It took three tries to unlock her phone, then she hit her list of recent contacts when yet *another* knock came, this time its louder bang causing her to drop the phone.

"Come on, come on," she said to herself, bending down to pick up her cell.

"Ms. Shao, I need to talk to you. It's about your brother."

Evie paused, though her pulse was still racing.

It *was* about Jakob. But why?

"Ms. Shao, I'm Special Agent Jill Frye. FBI."

The FBI?

They couldn't *really* investigate UFOs there, could they?

Except Layla had told her; she'd said something about this right before Evie flew out to California. She said that Edward was freelancing for the FBI. But what could that have to do with anything?

And was it proof? One way or the other, Evie needed concrete evidence of *something.*

She gingerly stood up and steadied herself with a breath. "I'm here," she said, and her hand gripped the doorknob.

CHAPTER TWENTY-SIX

KASS

One of the things Kass always advocated for her patients was the idea of self-care, of setting time aside to deal with personal crises—or hide from them.

Today, Kass followed her own advice, which was something she often failed to do. Appointments? Canceled due to a *family emergency*. Coffee? Freshly brewed and piping hot. Cigarettes? She let herself have an extra for the morning and probably would allow the same indulgence later today.

She'd been doing that a lot over the past few days, much to the detriment of her lungs—and it didn't help that her usual workout routine had all but disappeared since the family bullshit had started. What was the correlation of spikes in bad habits and sibling visits? Most likely pretty high. Maybe later, she'd look that up. Probably good to know for her job.

Jakob had already taken so much from the Shao family. The first time, his disappearance had created a black hole that pulled everything into oblivion: Dad's life, Mom's warmth,

Evie's future, Kass's...well, everything. Each lost piece of the Shao family knocked individual members off balance, and there she was at the bottom, scrambling to save them from being sucked into Jakob's vortex of crap. And now, his *second* disappearance stole hours away. After she'd put a fraud report in to Mom's bank and had the abrupt phone call with Evie, he still lingered in all of her thoughts. Putting Mom to bed, having her evening smoke, simply lying in bed and staring at the ceiling—and her dreams offered zero solace from it. Every moment was a cycle of emotions *about* Jakob, something she understood on a textbook level as the brain processing a day's emotional peaks and valleys.

That didn't make it any easier.

The moment she woke up offered several seconds of blissful ignorance, but reality soon returned—and forty-five minutes before her set alarm time. Anger, frustration, sadness, even a little bit of fear for whatever Jakob may have gotten himself into, everything continued to cycle until she cleared her calendar and logged into *The Ancient Runes Online*.

Desmond was off-line this morning, meaning that her hour in a virtual fantasy world was spent relatively alone, mostly on the side of a mountain collecting rare herbs for a dragon-bait recipe. Jumping from ledge to ledge, digital snow blowing horizontally to obscure her character's vision, Kass let herself sink into a place where, despite attacks from mist demons, it seemed like a simpler life.

Until Mom's voice jarred her back into reality. Unlike before, it didn't come out of the baby monitor unit. Instead, she heard it come through the walls of the house, followed by a sudden *thud* from above. She was up. And about. Early enough, unfortunately, to throw today's schedule off. Kass dashed out, leaving her character standing on the edge of a gigantic tree branch some ten digital meters from a rare herb. "Mom?" she called.

The muffled yelling continued, and Kass followed the noise out past the screen door to catch Mom in the back patio, standing underneath the pergola that Kass and Jakob had helped Dad build when they were in middle school. "Jakob?" Mom called out, her voice projecting far into the early-morning neighborhood.

"Mom!"

"Kassie! Have you seen Jakob?"

"Mom, it's really early, and people are still sleeping. Come inside," she said, hooking Mom by the elbow and walking her back through the open door. Mom paused in half step while Kass closed the door behind her. "Look at the clock," she said, consciously stripping her voice of context or concern. "It's still early. How about we go back to bed?"

"Have you seen Jakob? I was just talking with him."

"Jakob..." Kass knew that memory retention was vague for people in Mom's position, and sometimes information slid out of context, slotted into the wrong time and space. She might have simply had a random dream about her son.

But yesterday's events almost certainly had left an impression on her, even on a subconscious level. Playing along seemed like the best approach to contain this. "I need to tell Jakob something," Mom said. Kass maneuvered in, steering clear of any breakable or sharp objects. She scanned the space, assessing for a safe path back to bed—if Mom only could be convinced.

"What do you need to tell Jakob?" Kass asked, her tone clear and steady with a forced brightness. "I'll tell him later today."

That part was actually feasible. Though if she did talk to Jakob today, it might involve actually murdering him rather than passing along any messages.

"When's he going to be back? He was here yesterday."

"Well..." Kass weighed her options, none of them offering much of a success rate. "He left. Yesterday."

"Did he leave with that girl?"

The question struck Kass as odd. Had Mom retained those specifics? "What girl?"

"The girl with the blue hair. They were here yesterday." Mom stopped shuffling and turned to Kass. Her eyes narrowed with a sudden intensity, a clarity that seemed impossible for her condition. "She's bad news, Kassie."

"Mom, that's..."

"Jakob makes bad choices. That girl has to be another bad choice."

Bite your tongue, Kass told herself. This was about getting Mom back to bed, not arguing over Jakob and Evie. "Well, I think she's gone now too."

"Good. Would you like some tea?" Before Kass could answer, Mom began filling up the kettle and searching the cabinet for a box of tea. She moved on autopilot, making tea as if she were her old self.

Or the time that she began to lose her old self.

On that afternoon, just about three years ago, Kass had witnessed something very, very wrong with her mother for the first time. It had started in the hallway, a fleet of plastic bags sitting in the entryway. Not exactly what you'd expect from a mid-January trip to pick up a prescription and a loaf of bread.

"Mom?" Kass had called out as she put her work bag down. She set it gently aside to protect the laptop and tablet in its cushioned walls, though sometimes she'd wondered if it just made sense to leave them at the office where she saw patients, since her gaming rig had access to her messages and files. "Mom?"

"Kassie, I'm in the kitchen."

As Kass stepped over the bags, she glanced down to see spools of…

Christmas lights?

She knelt to pull each bag open enough for a hint of contents. Lights, garland, stuffed Peanuts characters in Santa hats, and more decorations; bag by bag revealed holiday festivities with clearance tags on them. And in one bag, a lone item: a selfie stick.

Evie would need that. Not Kass.

"That's weird," Kass muttered to herself. It wasn't like they needed anything—their modest holiday celebration was a fake four-foot tree, a front-door wreath, and a life-size schnauzer plushy with a Santa hat. In fact, they'd never really been big holiday people, not even when Dad was alive and the whole family was there. Only Evie seemed to enjoy the pomp and circumstance of it all, and Evie hadn't been home for a Christmas in years.

Also, it was January.

"Mom, what's with all the bags?"

"Oh, I just got home. You know, it was so strange. Usually they put those on sale after Christmas, but they were clearing them out before Christmas."

Kass looked over her shoulder at the crinkled white plastic bags in the hallway, big red store logo distorted by folds. "I'm, uh, not sure what you mean."

"Well, I know we have some, but since Evie's coming home for Christmas this year and they were on sale, I thought it made sense."

The sheer break with reality in Mom's words froze Kass. She failed to respond, simply watching with a dumbfounded stare while Mom filled a kettle.

"Mom," she finally said, "it's January. Evie's in Buffalo."

"Don't be silly, Kassie. Remember Evie called last week to

say she'd be home for the holidays this year." The kettle settled on the burner with a clink, and Mom turned a knob. It clicked several times until blue flames licked into existence. "Since her internship wasn't going on their research trip," she said, starting to thumb through a tin of various teas.

What the fuck.

"Mom," she said cautiously. This couldn't be happening. Kass had read textbook descriptions before, case studies of onset, but she refused—she absolutely refused—to believe it was happening to them. Not after Dad. Not after Jakob. Kass watched the flames wave underneath the kettle, yellow and orange tips dancing at the edge of the blue. Never before had Mom's proximity to open fire seemed so risky.

No, no, no. It was not that. It couldn't be.

It wouldn't be fair.

"Mom, can you check your phone? I think I heard it buzz."

"Oh," Mom said, grabbing her phone off the counter. "No, no missed calls."

"Do me a favor, Mom. Look at the date. What does it say?"

Mom's brow and nose crinkled. "Kassie, you look terrified."

"I'm having a brain cramp about, um..." *think, think, think* "...the homeowners-association dues. I just realized it might be late. Can you check the date on your phone?"

"January thirteenth."

"January?" Kass said.

"Yep. January thirteenth." Behind Mom, the kettle started to whistle.

"January, Mom. It's..." Should she say it? Should she drop it? This was a fluke. Of course it was. Everyone made mistakes, got mixed up from time to time.

But the professional in her knew better, knew that little clues over the past few months suddenly made sense. Confusing Tuesday for Thursday. Paying the water bill twice. Missing dinner plans after a busy workday. She should have looked into it further when little things had come up every few weeks or so. Before it got to this. Before it meant being wrong about an entire season or a distance of years.

Or the age of her children.

Blood drained from Kass's face as Mom paused, midway through tearing open a bag of tea. The kettle's whistle kept going, steam shooting up and creating condensation over the microwave door. Kass sidestepped her mother and shut off the stove.

"Oh god, I just realized," Mom said. "We're out of lemon tea." She unlocked her phone and began tapping away at a list. "The next time I go to the store, I'll make sure I get it."

That afternoon, Kass had quietly put the shopping bags in the hall closet, and Mom had never mentioned them again. And since then, life had gradually changed, a weight on Kass's shoulders increasing with every passing day.

The sight in front of her looked timeless: Mom pouring her cup of tea, turning the kettle off, and sitting to look out the window as if the most fantastical and engrossing display sat just outside instead of their slightly unkempt backyard. A snapshot that masked the current reality, freeing it from any hint of danger or confusion or remorse.

From outside, a car door slammed, then another. Kass angled from her spot to peer down the entryway to the front window, silhouettes moving across the curtain. Another car door closed, and that probably lined up with two siblings wreaking havoc on Kass's delicately balanced life. And it was *way* too early to deal with *anyone's* bullshit. "Mom, I'll fix you something to eat."

It was a fifty-fifty shot, moving things as abruptly as that. Mom agreed with surprising ease, and maybe that went along with everything else that ran opposite of sanity right now.

The chair slid across the laminate flooring, and Mom settled in this time, moving with the detached precision of a character in *The Ancient Runes* animation. Kass grabbed a banana off the counter's fruit bowl and handed it to Mom. How long would this last? Perhaps long enough at least for Kass to step into the living room and peek outside.

Evie stood on the sidewalk, backpack slung over her shoulder. Did Evie *ever* get up this early?

But no Jakob.

Instead, someone else stood there, someone that Kass initially assumed was a neighbor getting into their car for the morning commute: a tanned woman with sharp eyebrows and a very professional pantsuit who got off her phone before joining Evie. Kass took a closer look at this person, the way her brown hair sat in a braid on one shoulder and how even beneath a jacket, she clearly had an athlete's strong frame.

Was she one of Evie's conspiracy theorists?

Kass didn't have time to consider more before they approached. At the table, Mom sat quietly, halfway through her banana. Then came the knock.

"Kassie, is someone at the door?"

This would not go over well.

"Hold on," Kass said. Her footsteps echoed as she dashed into the living room to grab Mom's sketchpad. "You know, I was just thinking about Tiger. What was that toy he always chased?"

"His squeaky ball."

"Right, how he'd bring it to wherever you sat and shove it at you. I wish we had a photo of that. Do you think you could draw it?"

"Oh, of course." Mom unclipped the pencil from the pad. "You know he's my favorite subject," she said, already beginning the outline of his head. The pencil moved in precise strokes, every action with a purpose, and for all of the ways that Mom seemed helpless now, her movements seemed to capture the essence of who Sofia Aguilar-Shao was and would always be. "I miss that little boy."

"Yeah. I do too." Another knock came, grabbing Kass's attention from the moment. "I'll be right back."

Kass held the door half open, hand still on the doorknob. "I can't let you in right now. I just got Mom settled. I don't want to disrupt her."

"So this is it, huh?" Evie asked. "She doesn't remember me."

"You haven't called, Evie. You haven't visited." Normally, there'd be more told-you-so in her voice. But whether it was the fatigue of the morning or the pain on Evie's face or their exchange last night, something allowed Kass to back off and speak with empathy. Evie nodded, a solemn realization.

"I hate to interrupt family matters," the woman said, "but I'm Special Agent Frye with the FBI. We have an issue with Ja—"

Kass shushed her before she managed to get the full name out. "Mom might be triggered if she hears that. Wait," she said. It was *way* too early to be dealing with the FBI.

"Kassie," Evie said before Frye could reply, "I was wrong. You were right. He's in trouble. Far more trouble than we thought."

Domestic terrorism. That hadn't been on Kass's list of possibilities for Jakob. But the security video on Frye's tablet was pretty irrefutable.

"Could this be a fake?" Kass asked. "Or a mistake, someone who looks like him?"

"It's true that facial recognition is not foolproof. But this," she said, moving the video timeline, "is as clear a shot as we're going to get." On the tablet, the man looked up from his kneeling position, then stood up, talking to himself for a minute before freezing and staring several degrees off-camera. Frye paused the video.

"Yeah," Evie said.

"Yeah," Kass repeated.

"And this was from Reno the other day, at a casino." This time, the video offered concrete evidence of Jakob, down to his stupid *Reno Is for Winners* shirt. Kass watched as Jakob sat at a blackjack table like it was college all over again, and as the dealer flipped over a card, the group of men behind him cheered. High fives went all around, though Jakob's face remained strangely neutral despite joining in. Something about him seemed much more grounded, more serious than the fuckup she'd known.

"Hold on one sec." Kass marched over to the office before returning with the note she'd scribbled on with Jakob's search history. "This list. He'd been looking at these items when I caught him."

"Well, fertilizer and fire are never a good combination," Agent Frye said. "You know about ammonium nitrate?"

"Oh, no." Evie's eyes went wide.

"Goddamn it, Jakob, you're crafting a fucking bomb." Evie winced, either at Kass breaking the agreed-upon rule of not using his name or at the sudden bite in her statement.

Agent Frye didn't react. "We have footage and facial recognition from the Upstate New York incident. Six years ago at a manufacturing plant. DNA samples match the sample in the missing-person database. Absolutely zero further hits on facial recognition, social media, anything since then. There were strange symbols carved into the concrete there in the remains of the advanced fuel-cell energy lab. Signs of zealotry, though we can't quite decipher what it is. Still concerning, though. We want your help bringing him in."

"Upstate New York?" Kass asked Evie. "That was right by you?"

"Wait, wait, wait." Evie held up a hand. "I remember that explosion. The news said it was an industrial accident. Like, a chemical fire. They made a big deal about how it happened after most of the employees went home and no one got hurt."

Frye shook her head. "It wasn't a chemical fire. Domestic terrorism."

"You're saying Jakob did that? He couldn't." Evie grabbed Kass's arm, fingers burrowing into her wrist. "He wouldn't, Kassie. He wouldn't do *that.* I know he's made a lot of bad decisions—"

"You're gonna arrest him?" Kass asked.

"We need to question him first. And confirm that was him in New York. We can't do that if he's loose. And if it *is* him, we need to get him before he hurts anyone else. If you're willing to help, we think it'll be safer for everyone involved."

"Kassie, what you said about his, um, condition..."

"Delusions of grandeur," Kass said. "Look, if it is schizophrenia, he probably won't be prone to violence. Zealotry, though, makes people do fucked-up stuff. You think he's still in town?"

"Most likely. A man fitting his description was seen stumbling around about three miles south of here on El Camino Real."

Despite twenty minutes passing over the course of Frye's further explanation, Mom remained quiet. Kass peeked into the dining area, and there she was, sketching away like her notebook and her pencil existed in a vacuum.

"Okay," Kass said with an exhale. "Let me call Lucy."

CHAPTER TWENTY-SEVEN

JAKOB

During all his years with the Seven Bells, Jakob had only considered the idea of returning home once. The question came from the only other human in the fleet at the time, a man named Alexios who'd worked as a banker in Athens before his recruitment. "What would you do if you ever went home?"

They'd sat together on the loading deck of a Seven Bells carrier floating in space, watching bipedal mechs get retrofitted to allow for the various sizes and shapes of their coalition, and Alexios recalled stories of visiting his brother, who'd eschewed modern life to hide away in a little Mediterranean fishing hamlet, a place without phone coverage and where the days and nights melted together. Jakob replied with his best pranks from high-school swimming days or lost hours on college snowboarding trips, both their tales carrying an otherworldly quality, like they existed in an impossible realm.

Jakob pictured the spark of relief in Alexios's eye as he told his story, describing the glow of the Mediterranean waters, the stillness of the trees, the layer of sweat caused by the region's humidity. Sometimes Alexios's thick accent and fumbling English made it difficult to grasp all the individual pieces, but whenever he stumbled, he'd shout *"Malaka!"* with a laugh—as Jakob understood it, the Greek equivalent of motherfucker.

"So, man, what would you do if you go home? Visit these ladies you loved and lost? Hide in the mountains, somewhere without all this—" Alexios gestured to the armada around them "—death?" His voice had dropped at that word, an overly dramatic tone betraying the frightening truth of it all, and the hangar bay echoed with their laughter. "See family?"

That moment still stood out, a snapshot not too long ago, though Jakob's decryptor-addled brain failed to place specifics—or perhaps weariness had erased those details. Because while Alexios carried on with his easygoing grin and wistful look, Jakob merely shook his head at the question.

"Nah," he'd said, trying to keep the tone light. "We don't get along."

The curtness of his reply seemed to end the conversation, and the discussion returned to fishing techniques. Several weeks later, Alexios suffered the same fate as Henry, petrifying under the Awakened's crystallization beam before blowing apart as dust, his only legacy being an inspiration for the lie Jakob would tell his sisters.

Jakob wondered if Alexios would appreciate the irony, in between stabs of pain within his skull as he stumbled down the sidewalk of Mountain View's biggest commuter street, desperate for options. He'd managed to rest a few times—at a park under a tree, in an alley against a dumpster, and in the patio of a closed café, at least until a guard kicked him out. Each time, enough strength returned to get both mind and body moving again.

His plan seemed simple enough: accurately identify the specific location of the transponder, then jump-start it by sending a jolt of electricity while he spoke the activation phrase. Storefront after storefront passed, the closest thing to fitting the criteria being a car-repair shop. He'd loop back if he didn't find any better options. But two blocks down from that, the answer became clear.

An animal hospital.

They'd have all sorts of medical equipment. Much easier to use existing items than try to build it himself—and without the foot traffic or security of a local hospital. Shortly after dusk, a little bit of stealth and good timing easily got him inside as the final employee left for the day. He waited in a room, holding still behind an exam table until he'd heard the back door open and shut one last time.

A quick study of the facility showed that he was in luck: from AED devices on the wall to drawers of surgical equipment to an X-ray table, suddenly much more was at his disposal, including a scalpel, which he held onto for basic defense purposes. Just in case. A good hour passed with Jakob stumbling through the office, pausing every few minutes to grit his way whenever the pain suddenly appeared. At the front desk, he bent over to sift through drawers and shelves, looking for empty sheets of paper to write down notes when another cranial shock wave hit him, knocking him down to one knee.

Despite the stinging in his head, he tried to think this one through: Why was this time so much worse? What had he done that might have triggered it?

Jakob stood still when the pain subsided, even holding his breath as he tried to retrace the exact steps and find a root cause when a noise caught him off guard.

Was that rumbling from outside? Or in his head?

His arms held him steady as more noises cut through, first several dogs barking on the other side of the building, then another low rumble, and then faint voices becoming more distinct. In fact, one sentence came with absolute clarity.

"Otherwise, fuck him."

It was Kassie.

CHAPTER TWENTY-EIGHT

KASS

Kass spent the whole drive to the animal hospital biting her goddamn tongue, despite wanting to blurt out *I told you so* over and over. She'd fought that urge all day, from the hours spent answering Frye's questions about Jakob's psychological profile to then going over the FBI's short history on their brother. With Lucy unavailable until the late afternoon, things moved twice as slowly as they should have, the disruption to Mom's normal schedule creating chaos in the house.

It didn't help that Mom *still* didn't recognize Evie. Kass almost felt bad for Frye, having to handle family drama when her job was tracking a domestic-terrorism suspect. And she did sympathize with her sister regarding the Mom thing, but watching Evie squirm while admitting that one of her alien-chasing buddies had ratted her out to the FBI was, well…if she had been her own client, Kass would have given permission to enjoy a sense of karmic justice. Especially because it went full circle: Frye had asked Evie's friend to research the symbols in the New York security video, and he logged the facial-recognition data on Jakob, then found a match when Evie insisted they research Reno.

In a way, Evie did find Jakob after all.

Kass didn't ask for the details of how Frye had pinpointed Jakob's current location, though she pictured him leaving a path of destruction typical of his college shenanigans: vomit, bottles, fast-food wrappers, and general destruction of property.

Honestly, she was a bit surprised they hadn't found him sooner.

"I can't believe we agreed to this," Evie said as the car pulled up to the loading space in front of the animal hospital's brick facade. To their left, Frye's car rolled down the side path to the back parking lot, her government-issued sedan moving with the headlights off. As she got past them, Kass locked eyes with the federal agent, a quick acknowledgment of what they'd discussed earlier: basically, keep Jakob talking.

"Which part is unbelievable?" Kass asked, the car lurching to a stop. The motor idled for several seconds, and she stifled the urge to take a quick cigarette break before they jumped in. "Wearing a wire for the FBI or bringing Jakob into custody?"

"Both? Legal breaking-and-entering?" Evie sighed, and the engine finally stopped. She held up the front-door key that the vet had turned over to the police. "All of it?"

"It's for Jakob's own good." Several steadying breaths came and went before she unbuckled her seat belt and cracked the door. "He's just lucky that Lucy was available tonight," she said after Evie followed suit. "Otherwise, fuck him." The last sentence caused Evie to wince, which surprised Kass. How could her younger sister *not* feel that way right now? "Let's just go." She took the small clear earpiece in her palm and put it into her ear; hopefully, between the dim lighting and her hair, Jakob wouldn't notice. Evie did the same, though she had way less hair to work with.

"Frye, we're here. Can you hear us?" Evie asked, her voice echoing through Kass's earpiece.

"Loud and semiclear," the agent responded. "Whenever you're ready."

Kass nodded and stepped out of the car. She slammed the door shut, though she wondered right away if she should have done that or gone for the quieter approach.

As she looked forward, she figured it didn't matter. "There he is."

"What?" Evie closed her door and took quick steps to catch up.

"Hold up." Kass squinted, looking through the vet's glass storefront. Through the lettering and animal silhouettes, shadows moved. It took several seconds to confirm it *was* Jakob—hand against the side of his head, hunched over, and seemingly searching for something on the front desk. "Do you see him? Front desk, behind the counter," she said, her voice dropping in volume.

"Jakob, what are you doing?" Evie whispered so low that Kass heard it more over the earpiece than in proximity.

"Let's just go in slow."

"Are we sure about this, Kassie? He's our brother."

"He stole from Mom! Hasn't he done enough? Fuck him," she said, probably louder than she should have. Evie shot her a look, a whole set of emotions caught together across her face. Kass recognized it, the same look clients had when feelings tugged them in opposite directions. "What I mean is…like, look at him. He's clearly not well. You know?"

Not well. Those words appeared to rattle Evie, or at least give her pause. Kass turned straight ahead, telling herself to stop analyzing her sister and simply wait until she was ready.

No backing out now.

"Right," Evie finally said. "Okay. Frye? We're going in."

"Acknowledged."

Kass glanced behind her, the two supporting police cars parked just within her view in front of the adjacent tire shop. She turned back toward the hospital's front, scanning for any movement. Several seconds passed until her focus settled on Jakob's hunched form by the front counter. "Well—" she started when the silhouette collapsed, quickly followed by the sound of metal clanging.

"Goddamn it, Jakob," she muttered under breath. She didn't care if anyone heard.

As Evie sprinted into the office, Kass kept a steady pace, constantly scanning for…something. Either Frye or the local police or Jakob with some trick up his sleeve; all of those seemed viable. "Jakob," Evie yelled, disappearing behind the counter.

Jakob may have been unreliable, lazy, even a dick. But he'd never shown any signs of violence growing up, and even if he was having an undiagnosed episode of psychosis, he was much more likely to hurt *himself* by accident than do something intentional to one of his sisters. Kass kept telling herself this, all the way up to the point when she turned the corner to see Evie hunched over him.

"All right," she started, "look, Jakob, we really—"

"Kassie, stop." Evie's command came with a sharpness that immediately put Kass on edge.

"You two," Jakob said, his voice low, "should leave. Right now."

Evie shuffled back before gradually standing at Kass's side, and even though Jakob lay sprawled on the floor, Kass realized why Evie pulled back: his fingers were wrapped tightly around a scalpel.

In the earpiece, Frye's voice cut through the silence. "Everything all right there?"

Jakob grunted as he tried to get back up, first making it to his knees before standing up with the help of the front counter. "Get out of here. There's something I need to do."

Delusions of grandeur, Kass thought. *Don't mock him.* "Jakob, it's Kass—Kassie. And Evie. We're just here to get you to safety."

"No. I have everything I need here. I'm fine. I know what's causing the headaches. This one's just a bad one, but it'll pass and I have to..." His voice faded away, though Kass failed to see why. But who knew with Jakob anyway?

"Is it—" Evie said, looking back at Kass. "Does it have something to do with the Seven Bells?"

"Yes. I have to," he said through gritted teeth, "use the X-ray machine here."

That wasn't what Kass expected. She locked eyes with Evie, who pointed to herself and nodded. Kass nodded in return and waited.

"What do you mean?" Evie asked. "I'm going to help you up, okay? Tell me what you need. Just, you know, trust me." She glanced over at Kass again, and Kass responded with a rolling hand. Frye must have read their minds, because she popped into the earpieces to tell them to keep going. "I'm a vet tech. We just didn't get around to talking about that during...everything. But I know how to use an X-ray table. Just... drop the scalpel."

Jakob propped himself up on the counter. Seconds ticked by, the three of them holding long enough for Kass to notice the tipped-over garbage can in the corner. That must have been the noise from earlier. "Okay. Okay." Sweat lined his brow, and though he was halfway up, he appeared unbalanced enough that a simple breeze could knock him back onto the floor. "You'll help me?" he asked weakly.

"I will. Just drop the scalpel."

"Okay. All right. Thank you." The scalpel dropped on the front desk, adjacent to the reception keyboard. Evie bent down, putting her shoulder under one of Jakob's arms. "That was the worst one by far. But I'll keep moving."

Frye spoke through the earpiece. "See if you can get him talking."

"Hey," Kass said, trailing but keeping some distance. "We'll help you. But we want you to be honest with us, okay?" Evie shot her a look, a mix of judgment and anxiety in the form of creases across her brow. "Have you ever been back before? And just didn't tell us?"

"I suppose you deserve to know," he grunted as they moved gingerly forward. No word came from Frye, though Kass assumed she was listening. "I was here before. On Earth. Like five or six years ago. I didn't reach out then. I owe you at least that."

Between the lack of light and Jakob's hunched body, Evie's face remained obscured. But her demeanor shifted, even while holding Jakob's weight. Something about her gait softened even though they seemed to pick up the pace by a hair.

"Where?" Kass asked, prompting a sharp look from Evie.

"New York. By Rochester. It was so fast. I was on a mission to retrieve a chemical. Our scanners detected it. In and out."

Delusions of grandeur. Kass followed behind, keeping her distance as Jakob pointed to a room down the hall. "Frye," she said in a sharp whisper.

"I heard that. We have it recorded. We'll come in," she replied. If Evie heard, she didn't give it away.

"Give us a minute."

"Understood."

An acknowledgment was better than expected from Jakob—much better than his usual shrug/smirk combo. And it *sounded* sincere. Kass had no doubt Jakob believed whatever delusions brought him here. But the fact was that in this quixotic quest, whatever it was, he managed to feel some genuine remorse.

Even if the rest of it was bullshit, that was nice to hear.

They crossed the room's threshold before Evie managed to get Jakob into a side chair. "You have to understand, I *need* to do this," he gritted out.

"What's *this*?" Kass asked.

Evie stepped over to what Kass assumed was the X-ray's control console, several feet back from the bulky structure in the middle of the room. A low hum kicked up, along with several whirs from the machine's start-up. The corner of the room brightened as the screen activated, illuminating angles on Evie's face, and she clicked away at the keyboard.

"I took the money. Because I have something in my head. And I needed tools to get to it." He tapped the base of his neck. "Here. Around here. It's a transponder."

The keyboard clicks stopped. Evie's head tilted, though the light from the monitor caused shadows that hid half her face, making her reaction nearly unreadable.

"It connects me to the fleet. We use it in case of emergency. It stays dormant until you absolutely need it. Otherwise, it might give away the current location of the command fleet. I know, I *know* this sounds wild and unbelievable. But if you just help me and take an X-ray, you'll see it. It's proof. I need its precise location, and then I have to power it up because it's damaged. That's what I was shopping for." Jakob hunched over, his breath deepening. "To build something that might activate the transponder."

Frye's voice cut through. "Keep him talking. See if you

can get any further details about the New York incident. The more evidence we get now, the better."

"Okay," Evie said, stopping there despite Frye's request, and the next minute passed with only the sound of Evie clicking on the keyboard, another whir of motors kicking in from the machine followed by a few rapid-fire clicks. She looked up, eyes connecting with her sister, and Kass hoped Evie caught her mouthing *delusions of grandeur.*

"I need to write down these settings. Kassie, can you go to the front and grab me a pen?"

That was effectively stalling. Kass gave Evie points for improvisation and played along. "Sure, I got it," she said, extra loud for Frye to hear. Evie nodded, though she stayed focused on the X-ray machine's screen. The hallway remained dark when Kass stepped out, her eyes needing a second to adjust even from the dimmed room. Her mind wandered as she walked past the several computers displaying screen savers. She needed a smoke.

Kass turned, just to check if Evie had the situation under control. Which, apparently she did.

Because the door was now closed.

Kass blinked several times to make sure the light didn't trick her eyes. No, she was certain of what she saw. Motionless, she stared, giving herself ample time to confirm that her vision and brain weren't out of step.

Kass told herself to control the quickening breath and sudden pulse, to *not* judge her sister right away. A good reason surely existed for this.

Seconds ticked by on the office wall clock and Kass waited, unsure of whether to sprint back or give Evie space to do… something.

As if on cue, a *click* sound broke the silence, the mechanical sound of a lock flipping into place.

Goddamn Evie.

CHAPTER TWENTY-NINE

EVIE

Proof.

The word echoed in Evie's mind. Proof. After the whirlwind of the last day, after the headaches and collapses at Half Moon Bay, after Evie taking in everything Jakob had said, *believing* her older brother despite his history of exaggerations—only for his own actions to rip apart fifteen years of faith—after all of that, now he offered *proof*?

When Jakob said it, she'd been pushing random buttons in the X-ray table's console. It didn't need anything in particular, just a handful of clicks. The rest of it was just for show, to give Evie time to process turning her brother over to Frye. Originally, she bought into Kassie's notion that this would deliver Jakob to the help he needed, while keeping him *and* the larger world safe.

But with the word *proof*, everything changed, like an old photograph going from negative to true color. If Jakob claimed that a single X-ray could provide irrefutable proof of his travels among the stars, if it could show that Europe was a cover story, then she had to take it.

Even though she knew Kassie wouldn't agree.

That last thought crossed her mind the instant Kassie stepped past the open doorway. She'd sent her big sister on a fool's errand. Originally, it was simply to have space to think. But as soon as Kassie had disappeared from view, an impulse emerged, something that told her everything she'd done led to this moment. All of the grief, all of the research, all of the hope among ridicule and scorn, all of it might be rewarded in stark black-and-white imagery.

She walked as softly as possible, leading with her toes and the balls of her feet as much as her thick boots would allow. She pushed the door with a delicate touch, minimizing any squeaking sounds and clicks of the latch. One second passed, then another, and no Kassie freak-out came, no jiggle of the doorknob or banging on the door.

Now they had to be safe. And quiet. Her fingers gripped the lock to turn it, but its mechanism had an industrial weight that clearly would make a noise upon flipping.

Not yet.

And Frye, she couldn't know what was happening. Evie popped the earpiece out and set it on the floor before giving it two good stomps, the second offering a satisfying *crunch*.

Jakob looked over, his eyes a little clearer than before. "What's happening? It's weird. Sitting still right now, I feel fine."

"Shh, just give me a minute." One tug on the paper towel dispenser accidentally pulled out two, but that was fine—extra insulation as she wrapped the crushed earpiece up and tossed it in the garbage under the side cabinet. If any doubt lingered about the earpiece's viability, that most likely took care of it.

"Okay, listen," she whispered, glancing at the door. "Stay

quiet. Let's try to do this before Kassie gets back." That seemed impossible, given the time needed to align and take several shots and examine them for clarity and accuracy. They needed to be safe. "Which part do you need x-rayed?"

"My head."

"Okay, um…" *Think, think, think.* She'd done this semi-regularly enough that the procedure had to be similar to their office, despite it being a slightly different machine. But that didn't usually involve the FBI, the local police, her estranged older sister, and possibly the fate of the galaxy.

Even if Kassie took a lazy stroll getting a pen from reception, they'd still need more time. She should have told her to take a smoke break. Instead, Evie went with the most practical choice: she decided to lock the door.

The handle switched from left to right with a click—a click loud enough to echo in the small exam room.

Dang it.

Several seconds later, Kassie's muffled voice came through from beyond the door. "Jesus fucking Christ, Evie."

"Come on," she said, helping Jakob up, though he shrugged her off like she was hugging him. A quick look around the room failed to show a protective apron but given the circumstances, she'd do without. "This way. It's built for large dogs, but it'll work. Just lie flat across it and hold still. Put your head immediately under it if you can."

Jakob nodded, but as soon as he went horizontal, his hands went to his head. "It's like," he pushed out, "lying down made everything ten times worse. Something's not right."

"Evie?" The doorknob jiggled, followed by several smacks at the door. "Evie, goddamn it, open the door."

"Something's not right," Jakob said with a huff. "Evie. The decryptor. It shouldn't hurt like this. Something's new."

"Sorry, Kassie," she yelled. "I gotta know."

"Cut the bullshit, Evie. He stole Mom's money. Did you already forget?"

Jakob groaned at Kassie's mention. "I know," Evie said. "I know. We're gonna figure this out."

Would Frye throw her in jail for this? Or worse?

The questions created hesitation, especially since Evie heard Kassie's voice coming through, most likely talking to Frye. "Come on, Kassie. Don't do this," she whispered, though she knew immediately that meant nothing. Of course Kassie would do this. She'd been positioning them to this since yesterday. "Listen," she said to Jakob, "I need you a little farther centered. Let's try to get the front view and both sides."

Jakob groaned, shuffling inches to a slightly better vertical but also slightly worse horizontal location. "Damn it," Evie cursed under her breath, running over to Jakob. Her fingers gripped his shoulders, pushing and aligning him the best she could before grabbing his jaw and holding him up straight, his prickly stubble scratching her fingers. "Okay. Stay there."

Her ankle twisted a little too much for comfort as she turned to the console. Hands and limbs moved far faster than her standard clip for work. For a task that required precision and patience, especially when dealing with squirmy dogs, Evie worked the opposite of her radiology-technician certification. Proper protocol got tossed aside in the name of discovery.

The mouse cursor slid across the screen, Evie taking in the interface that worked a little differently from the one at her job. "All right, that's one," she said, not even bothering to actually look at the result. Her phone buzzed as she snapped a picture of the image on-screen, then she shoved it in her pocket and deleted it from the system's history. "Turn your head to the left and hold still."

Jakob groaned, and while the machine reset to its ready position, he mumbled something to himself about getting upright. "Not yet, not yet," Evie said. "Come on. We need two more."

"I think I've figured the pain out. Finally," he said. "Thank you, X-ray table."

"Not yet. I need *proof.*"

"Evie?" Kassie yelled, banging on the door. "Evie, open the door. Frye and her team are gonna come in soon."

Move fast, she told herself. "Hold still. Head to the left." The machine whirred and groaned as the next image was produced. She waited on the circling icon to show a finished process, then the image appeared on-screen. "Head to the right," she yelled at Jakob. "Hold still—*crap*!"

Her phone tumbled to the floor, its silicone case breaking its fall. A memory flashed through her mind, Kassie calling her *butterfingers* because she couldn't catch a Frisbee in middle school while her older sister excelled at pretty much every sport on the planet.

This time, she deserved that tease.

"Come on," she told herself, picking up the phone. Thankfully the glass remained intact. The phone buzzed, capturing the image. "One more, Jakob. Turn your head the full ninety degrees to the right."

"Evie?" Kassie yelled. "Last chance. They're getting ready."

"No, I gotta be upright to control the pain," Jakob said as Evie took the next image. The machine groaned again, its gears and electronics squeezing off one more image right before Jakob shot up and got to his feet. Though he winced in pain, he moved with a frightening speed and strength for someone who had just been lying vulnerable. "They're coming in. What can I use? What can I use?"

"Jakob, don't fight the police," Evie said.

"I'm not," he said, scanning around. "I think if I just keep my head upright and steady, it won't... Yeah." He bobbed his head in slow, controlled movements, craning his neck until pulling it back with a wince. "Felt that." The gesture repeated, only a little faster but the wince appearing at the same angle. "It's repeatable." He reached, arms extending while his neck and head remained stable, and he pulled out the stool under the desk. "I think that's it." Stool in hand, he began to move across the room, a controlled but swift motion. "Will you trust me?"

"Yeah." Evie's voice came out in a quick, quiet whisper, her nodding head probably doing a better job of answering.

"Evie! They're coming in *right now.*" Kassie shouted more stuff, but the sound of Jakob smashing open the other door overtook it. Evie turned to see Jakob with one hand holding his head dashing into the next room. She peered in to see a supply closet, and with his free hand, Jakob used the edge of the metal stool to clear out a small window, shards of glass flying by stacked boxes of nitrile gloves and paper towels.

"Move out of the way, ma'am," a voice said through the main door—Frye, probably. "Evie, we're coming in right now. Jakob Shao is wanted on charges of domestic terrorism. Stand away from the door."

She turned to see Jakob, still holding his head, telling himself things like "Come on, soldier," and muttering about how this was just like...well, some place that Evie had never heard of, though she assumed it was a planet. He grabbed several folded towels off the shelf in the small storage space, threw them over the shattered bits of glass sitting on the window frame, and vaulted up.

A slam interrupted her as the door broke open and several flashlight beams cut through the dim room. "Hands up," Frye yelled, gun and flashlight in crossed hands. "Jakob Shao, we are taking you into custody." A local police officer ran by

Evie as she threw her hands straight up, followed by another, then Frye.

"He broke a window!" one officer yelled before grabbing his walkie-talkie and stomping back past Evie.

Frye and the officers talked back and forth about how to secure the perimeter, that Jakob was vulnerable but dangerous, and all of the other fancy law-enforcement terminology that she'd heard in movies before. But though the cross chatter continued, it all became moot when something much more pressing happened.

Kassie came in and marched straight at Evie.

CHAPTER THIRTY

KASS

Kass had seen the look in Evie's eyes before.

About fourteen years ago. Kass saw it right when she and Mom had come home.

Stunned wasn't totally accurate. Upset? Focused? Nervous? Maybe all of the above. Mom didn't seem to notice, though; she marched right on while reading from the printouts Kass had made for her earlier that afternoon. Whatever Evie was on, Kass didn't want any part of it, especially since her little sister had started staying up late tapping away at her computer. And it probably wasn't playing grow-your-farm-type games on social media. No, she'd developed that intense stare of too much caffeine and not enough sleep, the same look Dad showed in the months after Jakob disappeared.

No, thanks. She had an indoor soccer game to get to.

"So you exported to PDF," Mom said, "and then—oh, Evie."

Evie sat at the kitchen table, her college math texts open but also her laptop—and there, right *there* Kass saw it: her goddamn online forums talking about UFO bullshit. "Did you two get my texts?" Evie asked.

"Are we in trouble?" Kass took a drink from her protein shake, a move designed specifically to annoy her sister by being extra casual.

"I asked Kassie to help out with some office stuff." Mom's fingers flipped pages up and over the stapled corner to reveal line graphs next to photos of houses, bright red letters suggesting *Investing during the Subprime Crisis*, with *Sofia Aguilar-Shao, Realtor* below it in blue.

"I wanted to talk," Evie said. "Family dinner. I, um..." she marched over to the oven and pulled out a large aluminum tray and lugged it to the counter "...picked it up already."

Now that she mentioned it, the smell of garlic bread and tomato sauce did permeate the house. But still, Kass didn't have time for this. "Oh. Sorry, I missed the dinner part." Which was true—she'd seen her sister's question asking when they'd be home in the text, but nothing about dinner.

"Can we talk tomorrow?" Mom asked, tapping the papers. "I have to prepare for this presentation."

"Oh, shit, I gotta get changed for my soccer game." Kass chugged the rest of her protein shake and tossed it into the small bin they used for recycling.

"Language, Kassie."

"I mean, *Oh, no*." The response came out like a practiced comedy bit, though it reflected of the rhythm they'd developed by spending more time together since had Kass had graduated a few months ago. They both laughed too, something that seemed to needle Evie's intensity further up.

"Wait. Just wait." Evie's voice carried a force that moved past annoyance and into desperation. Kass decided to actually listen. "Today...do you realize what today is?"

Of course Kass knew. She'd known it as soon as she got up to do the early shift at Red Rock Café, she knew it when she looked at her grad-school applications on break, and she knew it when she popped by Mom's office to help out with computer stuff.

The date was burned into her memory, despite all attempts to move forward. One year ago exactly, they had driven up to Lake Kinbote. She could have also said how technically it was five months and fourteen days since the sheriff called saying, "We have unfortunate news about Arnold Shao," but that wouldn't do anything.

Kass looked at Mom, who didn't change expressions, then met Evie's eyes. "Of course I know. Are we supposed to have cake? Blow out candles?"

"No, wait." Evie flipped the laptop around. "Look, I've been reading."

Mom leaned forward, squinting at the screen. "What's Reddit?"

"That doesn't count as reading. Jesus, Evie."

"Please." Evie eyes widened, that desperation from earlier moving beyond her voice into a whole-body pull. But it had an opposite effect, as both Kass and Mom leaned back, like magnets pushing against each other. "From the minute they disappeared, we've been running away from this. We just *accepted* things about Jakob. But what if Dad was right? Remember the weird heat. The absence of sound."

Kass stiffened up, her mouth forming a thin line. "I gotta change," she said, checking her phone for no reason other than to brush Evie aside. "I have a soccer game."

"Not this again." Mom picked up her papers and shook her head. "Evie, you know how I feel about this. I am not revisiting it."

"Mom, you always ask us 'How will you fix it?' I'm trying.

Look, I swear, Dad was onto something." The laptop's screen flashed as Evie clicked through the different tabs. "That's what I'm doing. I'm trying to fix this."

That was enough of Evie's dramatics for Kass. She turned without a word and started down the hall, then paused at the foot of the stairs. Cabinet hinges squeaked and dishes clanked, then there was the sound of food trays opening. "I know what you're doing," Mom said, so calm, so certain, almost conciliatory. "We remember them in different ways. In our own ways. What you're doing here isn't fixing anything. You can fix things by concentrating on school. By helping out here." Forks and plates clinked together, and they ate in silence, the only sound from Mom flipping through the pages of her presentation.

About fifteen minutes later, Kass emerged from her room to find Evie sitting by herself on the stairs, the bright light from her laptop filling the dark space. Her fingers danced over the keyboard, moving at a hypnotic pace, but the screen showed her forums, not her homework. Kass stepped by without any acknowledgment, leaving Evie to double down on her own madness.

That same look was on her sister's face now in the middle of a closed animal hospital—the same overlap of confusion, frustration, and commitment. Years ago, Kass had dismissed her sister, literally walking away. Now, she told herself to ignore that instinct and try to do a little better. "Evie, seriously, what the hell? I thought we agreed to help Frye." Kass waited for a reply, but rather than say anything, Evie angled her phone and tapped it, taking a photo of…something…before reaching up and powering down the X-ray machine.

"Proof, Kassie." She exhaled, all her breath seemingly drained. All around, bright office lights blinked and then lit at full power. "He said it was proof."

"Schizophrenic people often believe their delusions," Kass said. She stood up, then offered her hand.

Frye marched over, gun back in its holster. Her flashlight clicked off, and despite harsh words, her voice mirrored Kass's softer tone. "That was a bad idea."

"Yeah, I know," Evie said. "He's just..."

"He's your brother."

The wild glint in Evie's eyes had tamed a little bit, calming down to a quiet tension. "We haven't seen him in fifteen years."

"I get it." Frye extended an arm, her hand resting on Evie's shoulder until Evie nodded.

"Did you find him?" Kass asked.

Frye glanced back as the officers milled around. "No, unfortunately not. He can't be far. He was having headaches?"

Evie nodded. "I'm not sure why. He was trying to figure out a cause."

"He's having an episode. Could be drugs. Could be a lack of medication. Could be an injury we're not aware of. But that will probably hinder him." Frye rattled off the possibilities like they were no big deal. "Do you two want an officer outside of your home?"

"No," Evie said before Kass could answer. She gave Kass a look. "He won't hurt us. He's not after us at all. He thinks he's—"

Kass took up the thread before Evie dug them into any further holes. "My professional opinion as a licensed therapist? He's got delusions of grandeur. I'd say he's much more likely to steal supplies from a hardware store than bother us. Besides, I don't want Mom to feel any disruptions."

"You sure?" Frye asked. Kass nodded, though probably for different reasons than Evie. "Look," she said, stepping back and addressing the sisters, "you two have been through a lot today. The past few days. Go home. Get some rest. I'll keep you posted. Just let me know if you see anything suspicious. We'll be right there."

They walked in silence step-by-step, moving through the hallway that led to the reception area. As they passed the front entry, Kass stopped to pick up the empty garbage can Jakob had knocked over earlier, then a few of the office supplies he must have scattered. Or maybe Frye and the police had knocked over.

Regardless, *someone* made the mess. And someone had to clean it up. She leaned down to pick up a spread of paper clips that had snuck under the chair's leg when Evie walked by. "Hey, can you grab those papers that fell down?" she asked, but her sister didn't respond.

Instead, she walked straight out the door. Her figure darkened into a silhouette against the night sky, leaning against the car's hood, staring at the emerging stars above.

CHAPTER THIRTY-ONE

KASS

By the time the car pulled into the Shao driveway, Kass realized she completely blanked on dropping Evie off at the motel. Evie apparently missed it too, because she didn't say a single word about being in the wrong location. In fact, neither sister spoke during the entire drive back. Instead, a wall of silence built between them, like the air in the car was suffocating any sound.

The car lurched to a halt, and though Kass shifted into Park, the engine kept idling. "I, um, forgot about getting you back to the motel."

"Yeah. I just noticed. It's okay, my backpack is still here, anyway."

"Sorry about that," Kass said. She looked over at her younger sister, trying to read the lines on her face, the stare in her eyes. "Look, how about—I mean, let me just check in with Lucy really quick, and then I'll bring you back."

Evie didn't respond, staring straight ahead. Kass let a minute tick by on the dashboard clock before she told herself that someone had to budge. It might as well be her. "I'm gonna have a smoke. Tell me what you want to do after."

The door clicked, then shut with a *thunk*, and soon the air filled with the familiar scent of burning tobacco. Normally she'd step into the backyard for this, but then again, not every night involved the FBI chasing after their long-lost brother.

That seemed to warrant a little bending of the rules.

From within the car, a brightness came, a light so sharp that it could only be from a phone. Kass didn't bother to look. She'd figured it'd be the X-rays—the *proof* Jakob claimed—and from how quickly the light disappeared, Kass already knew what Evie saw—or failed to see. She didn't even have to ask.

Halfway through her cigarette, the other door opened, and Evie's silhouette emerged. "That's fine. Checking in with Lucy, I mean. She's your assistant, right? I could use some water, and then we can go."

"Cool," Kass said, though of course things weren't cool. But maybe they were, in their own way? For fifteen years, Jakob represented the big mystery, the unknown that loomed over every element of their lives. And now they knew. Whether it was mental illness or just being a con artist—or maybe both—it was done. She didn't know where Frye would ship him off to, but maybe that didn't matter, not in the context of the big family mystery. It was answered and resolved.

Now they could move forward.

"Just to be clear, yes, Lucy is my assistant. Not for my practice. As in she helps out with Mom while I work." The cigarette nearly done, Kass smothered it on the ground and began the walk to the front door. "You understand?"

"I do." Evie opened her mouth, like she had more to say. She probably did—perhaps something to do with the last few hours. Or lamenting how Mom didn't recognize her. Or chastising Kass for not revealing more earlier. Or something else entirely.

Whatever it was, Evie dropped it, instead returning to a relaxed stance and looking up at the stars above them.

"Let's ease into this," Kass said, as much for herself as for her sister. She stepped in quietly and scanned the room for Lucy or Mom before moving completely inside. A few more steps in and the sounds of the TV emerged; further steps in and the glow of the screen became clear from the unlit hallway leading to the living room. "Mom?" She turned to Evie, holding up her hand to hold her back. "Lucy?"

"We're here. We're okay." Weary lines framed Lucy's smile, no matter how much she tried to hide it with her chipper voice. All of the erratic scheduling and the family drama, somehow Lucy managed to keep a steady attitude through all of it. Maybe she just felt guilty as the finish line approached. Either way, Kass made a mental note to send her a bonus or flowers or both. "The disruption to the schedule wasn't easy, but we managed to get through it."

Kass nodded, and as quickly as she admired Lucy's resolve, her own seemed to wither away. The weight of the day suddenly collapsed on Kass, and the fragile balance she'd held for so many years finally broke under the sheer *pointlessness* of it all. Their family grief, Dad's obsessive quest, years and years of silence—for this? For Jakob to be arrested?

She knelt down next to Mom, who sat comfortably on the couch, leaned in and put her arms around her. She hugged her mother harder than the old woman's frail bones probably should have taken. She took in her smell, the same familiar smell that defined who her Mom was, the underlying core of her essence despite Mom's transition from her previous work perfume to a gentle citrus-scented shampoo now; through it all something remained unmistakably Mom.

Kass held on as tightly as she could.

Lucy gave them space, but Evie shuffled behind them, seemingly unsure of what to do, possibly wondering if she should join in. But Evie didn't understand any of this. Evie didn't understand loss. She lived in speculation and fantasy.

This was real.

They'd lost fifteen years to this bullshit. Fifteen years that had eaten away at Mom, leaving her a shell of the person they'd once known. Kass held her, grasping onto the only thing that remained from their life.

About ten minutes later, the reality of the day finally caught up to Kass. Lucy couldn't stay forever; even if she could, she didn't deserve to get tangled into further Shao family drama. Her arm braced the door open for Lucy, and they stepped out together, the warmth of the house becoming the cool of the night. "Thanks again for coming on short notice," Kass said, looking behind her. Evie sat at the kitchen barstool, hunched over a glass of water and her phone, her lips moving like she whispered to herself. "I really owe you."

"I try when I can." Lucy dug through her purse for her keys.

"I promise I won't take advantage."

"It's okay. I know you have company in town."

Company. Lucy still didn't know. "Yeah. Sorry about that. It was all very..." Encapsulating recent events felt impossible, drilling all of the emotions and disasters down to a word or two. "Very sudden," she finally said.

"It happens. I'll always try my best for Sofia."

"I appreciate that. *We* appreciate that."

Lucy stepped forward, leaving the yellow glow of the porch. "I have colleagues, you know. People I can refer you to."

"This shouldn't happen again. I think we're done with the, um, situation."

"You know what I mean." Sometimes Kass wondered if Lucy went home and just did math problems to reset her mind after facing the illogical twists and turns of dementia brain all day. How was she so *together*? "I've only got two weeks left before I start at Golden Apple. You need *something*."

"Can I clone you?"

Lucy laughed, the color in her cheeks rising despite the darkness. "I wish. I wouldn't be so tired."

"Yeah, I know. Mom can be a handful."

"It's not her. I know how to handle Sofia. That's my job. Hey, I could say the same thing about you, talking to patients all day." Kass pictured the popular meme from the old Spider-Man cartoon, where identical Spider-Men on either side pointed at each other; it popped up occasionally on *The Ancient Runes Online* player forums. "Look, I'll try my best to make myself available. I can freelance from time to time. But things will be different."

"I know," Kass said. A look back at Evie showed her sister still sitting, eyes glued to her phone. Kass took it as an opening and reached into the purse still on her shoulder to feel for the familiar small box. "Do you mind?"

"Normally yes, but it's okay."

"I know, I really should quit," Kass said. Their mutual burst of laughter echoed into the night air, carrying far despite how quickly it came and went. The cigarette in her mouth came to life, and she made a conscious effort to assess which direction the wind blew before puffing out. A faceful of smoke would *not* be the best way to reward Lucy.

"I really want you to consider Golden Apple," Lucy said, and even without direct light, her face looked serious.

"I don't trust facilities. All it takes is one bad..." An unexpected laugh came out with a huff, leaving a small billow of smoke rolling through the air. "One bad apple."

"Golden Apple is a good operation. I promise, otherwise I wouldn't work there. I know the people. They're good people. And I'll be there. I'd take care of Sofia." Lucy took in a breath, and Kass cringed, worried that she might be inhaling some of the ambient smoke. But Lucy kept going like nothing happened. "It's funny. I actually see her more than my own family. When you look at the numbers. She means a lot to me."

From behind, the kitchen stool's legs slid out with a squeak. Kass glanced back to see Evie on her feet but still hunched over, and even Lucy angled to look at the noise. "I'll figure something out," Kass finally said, taking a long drag of her cigarette. "I'll look at your list, I promise. Now that everything's sorted out."

"It's okay to ask for help."

The cigarette ashed away in her hand while empty moments ticked by. "I'm the psychologist. I should know that."

"Well," Lucy said, "what would you tell a patient?"

Kass debated revealing her trick with the Objective Questions when a sound interrupted the flow of her thoughts.

"Holy crap." Evie's voice carried enough to be clear from the porch. *Now what?* "It is. It's there."

"I gotta go," Kass said, unable to stop a sudden eye roll. "I gotta deal—"

"Kassie?" Evie called. "Kassie? You need to—"

"Keep your voice down. Mom's gonna—"

"No, Kassie, you *need* to see this." Evie's voice got louder.

"I'm sorry," Kass said, turning to Lucy. "My sister's a bit of an asshole." The words came out harsher, more judgmental than Kass intended. She took the final drag of her cigarette, avoiding the stunned look on Lucy's face, then ground it out on the porch's concrete.

"Kassie, look, look, look." Evie's footsteps echoed as she made her way to the porch. "Look, look, look." An audible tremor rippled through her words and she held up her phone, though Kass's eyes had trouble deciphering the image given her sister's shaky grip.

"Evie, I don't care what your friends say about aliens. Unless they're gonna care for Mom or give me a lottery ticket—"

"No, Kassie, you need to look. Now. Like, right now." Her trembling hand steadied as she made it out to the porch. Fierce eyes looked at Kass, completely ignoring Lucy. Kass's focus adjusted, and she turned to the screen between Evie's fingers.

The X-ray.

"Proof, Kassie." Evie reached over and grabbed her sister's hand, as if no animosity had ever existed between them. "It's *proof*."

CHAPTER THIRTY-TWO

EVIE

Evie had told herself not to get excited *yet*. Not to tell Kassie until she was absolutely certain.

She had sat at the kitchen counter, staring at the X-ray images on her phone. Just like in the car, the first three images proved little. Not that Evie's experience with human X-rays amounted to much, but understanding how a typical human skull and collarbones should look, well, anyone who watched a standard amount of TV and movies could make that deduction. Cavities for the eyes and nasal passages, teeth and jawline, pretty standard stuff taken from all views: front, left, and right.

One issue existed with most of the images: Jakob's full head wasn't in the frame. When he'd flopped onto the X-ray table, she'd managed to hit the horizontal center, but he wound up a few inches higher than he should have. Yet, when he slid off the table to stand up, an unlikely benefit arrived: the rest of his skull came into the proper framing of the X-ray's camera.

And what she saw… She'd dismissed it at first glance, figuring that particular image offered little of substance given that it only captured from the teeth up.

Then she saw it.

"What is that?" she whispered to herself.

At the top of his skull, right near the center cap—a jagged *M*-shaped item that should not have existed. Evie even searched online for other skull X-rays to make sure human physiology didn't contain any significantly rigid and symmetrical pieces that she simply didn't know about.

But it didn't, which meant this strange fragment on a single X-ray offered infinite possibilities. It stared back at Evie, almost taunting her for ever having doubted her brother. She zoomed in and reset over and over to make sure the stress of the day wasn't making her hallucinate things out of sheer hope. Yet, each time she did that, the same unnatural shape appeared.

And the other images—the object was out of view on the first and third, but the second X-ray caught the very bottom of the object, which might be excused as digital noise or shadow or whatever. Evie swiped back and forth between the images, zooming in and judging its distance between the eye sockets to confirm a match.

It was real. It was *proof.* She knew it so deeply that she reached into her backpack to grab the chipped piece of extraterrestrial technology from Half Moon Bay, taking a moment to hold the sand-dollar-shaped *thing* in her palm, as if that would bring the world up to speed. Then she shoved it in her back pocket and focused on the next challenge.

Now she just had to convince Kassie.

And hope that it went better than the last time she'd tried to convince Kassie of something monumental, in Kassie's college car, on the way to the airport. It was one of those generic Toyota sedans that would run until the end of time with regular tune-ups and oil changes. That morning, Mom had claimed she had to work instead of going with them. Evie didn't believe her, but perhaps that was fitting, since Mom never believed Evie after Jakob disappeared.

On that afternoon, most of the ride up Highway 101 was fraught with a tense silence other than Evie's occasional whispers to herself about things she might have forgotten. It wasn't until the very end when Kassie spoke first.

"You don't have to do this, you know."

"What, like you want me around?" Evie asked before she could stop herself. But it was a legitimate question. Even before Dad had died, Kassie had treated their pursuits as frivolous, an annoyance more than serious research that affected their family. And after he'd drowned, well, Kassie and Mom started treating Evie's laptop like it was the actual reason for his death.

"I think," Kassie said, uncharacteristically quiet as she angled the car around the ramps surrounding SFO, "it would be good for Mom."

"Mom barely talks to me now. I told her about Buffalo four nights ago, and she hasn't even said good morning since then."

"She can't keep that up forever. She won't." Kassie's calm tone unnerved Evie. Was this the same sister who used the f-word hundreds of times a day? "But some distance might be good. As long as you try again later."

Evie processed the advice, letting it burrow deep within. That might have been true. It made sense, after everything they'd been through. But this wasn't about sense or putting Band-Aids over wounds. There were much bigger things at play here.

And a promise to keep.

The car rolled past the various gates for domestic departing flights until Kassie veered in past merging traffic to pull up to the curb.

"I'm doing this for us," Evie finally said. "So we can be whole again."

She waited as Kassie stared straight ahead, silent.

"Do you believe me?"

Still nothing from her big sister.

"Do you at least understand me?"

The engine idled long enough that the airport's traffic officer tapped their window to ask them to move. Kassie gave him a polite nod and pointed at Evie before shaking her head and looking down. Nothing else had to be said, and that morning, Evie stopped trying to convince her family. Instead, she flew across the country in pursuit of Dad's dream. And here, now, the answers were at home.

Jakob, the world, the whole freaking galaxy just had to catch up to the image now on Evie's phone. "Do you see it?" she asked. Kassie stood, her mouth at a skeptical line. Something moved behind her, and Evie just realized that Lucy still hadn't left.

Lucy may not have even realized who she was. She wouldn't put it past Kassie to not even tell her assistant that she had a sister.

"See what?"

Kassie was being purposefully obtuse. Evie *knew* it. She locked eyes with Lucy, who looked unsure about either the situation or whether to leave or both. "Hi." Evie threw up a hurried wave. "I don't think we've formally met. I'm Evie. I'm Kassie's younger sister."

Something in Lucy's expression shifted at those words. Her demeanor didn't change, her mouth didn't move, but the subtle crinkle in her brow demonstrated that gears turned and ideas connected.

She must have heard a *lot* about the Shaos.

"Don't involve her."

"No, we need an objective opinion. This X-ray," Evie said, holding up the lit phone, "is our brother. Jakob. Do you see anything…" The right word eluded her. What was that thing they mentioned in court shows? *Leading the witness.* Kassie would never see her side if she led the witness. "Noteworthy in this picture?"

Kassie blew out an exaggerated sigh. Evie ignored the passive–aggressive gesture and tilted her hand, adjusting the angle for Lucy. "Anything?"

"There's like… I don't know, a smudge here? The letter *M*?"

"You see? Kassie, she sees it too."

"I'm not blind, Evie. I see the M. I just don't think it's…" Kassie locked eyes with her, then turned to Lucy. She knew the next look that happened: lips pursed, chin rumpled, and the eyes looking up *just* enough to signify disdain. "I don't think it's *proof* that Jakob has been with aliens."

Evie chose *not* to look at Lucy's reaction.

"Okay. I get it. But look." Her finger slid to the other X-ray. "Look at the very top of the image. The notches. They're at the *exact* same vertical distance from his eye sockets. It's *not* digital noise in the image. It's not dirt on the machine's lens. It is something in Jakob's head."

Kassie snatched the phone out of her hands and held it up close, then zoomed in with her fingers. Lines formed around her eyes as she squinted, and seconds ticked by. The fact that her older sister didn't scoff and immediately hand the device back meant *something* churned. Evie opted to lean into the moment, not speak, not possibly break the tension, not risk this single thread on which everything hinged.

"Okay." The word came out at almost a whisper, and with it, Kassie's entire demeanor changed.

"You believe me? You see?"

"I *see*. I don't know if it's necessarily proof. I'm no expert. But..."

Evie waited, watching as Kassie's shoulders slumped, a single *but* seemingly deflating her entire body.

Kassie turned to Lucy. "I'm so sorry to ask for more, but do you think you could help put Mom to bed while we deal with this?"

Lucy's cheeks rose, something about her smile and tired eyes ringing as genuine. In one look, Evie understood why Kassie trusted her with Mom. "Of course."

"Let's go inside." Kassie motioned the women inside. "I know someone who could read these."

"It's not too late?" Evie asked, keeping her voice low as soon as they stepped in. From within, the TV still blared, and Lucy marched directly over to where Mom sat in the other room.

Kassie glanced at the clock, then pointed down the hallway at her home office. "Oh, he's probably just getting up."

CHAPTER THIRTY-THREE

KASS

Kass knew that years had passed since Evie had stepped into this room. Back then, it had been Dad's den, the dimly lit mishmash of clearance office furniture and supplies he'd taken from his job. Worn white walls that had come with the home, a desktop computer, a chair with electrical tape where, as a pup, Tiger had gnawed the cushion, and shelves mixed with hockey and NASA memorabilia among Kass's track and basketball trophies and Jakob's swim trophies, it had been a bubble of early-aughts Silicon Valley life. Thousands of home offices probably existed like that for middle-aged dads, but likely few of them had evolved into the leaning towers of paper and random electronic equipment that had surrounded Dad during his final few months.

Now, Kass kept it neat: a large desk with two monitors, an ergonomic office chair, one bookshelf with professional texts, another with polite decor against a navy blue wall; if it hadn't been for the handful of *The Ancient Runes Online* vinyl figures nested here and there, it might have been straight out of a home-store catalog.

That stark difference apparently captured Evie enough that she spent several moments taking in the space. Was she trying to resolve the chasm between the past and the present, or was she merely judging the aesthetics?

The screens came to life, and the computer hummed with activity as it loaded up *The Ancient Runes Online*. Behind her, Kass felt Evie's attention finally turn to her. "Are you mocking me?" Evie asked.

"What?"

"*The Ancient Runes.* Are you mocking me for being a geek? Why is this even on your computer? I…" Evie's voice trailed off. Kass looked back at her, then tracked her eyes to a vinyl figure of a unicorn rearing, clear plastic lightning coming out of its horn. "Phobos the Unicorn. You play!"

"I do. Is that surprising?" Kass asked, probably more defensively than it needed to be. "I mean," her tone softened, "Mystheos is better than the real world. Desmond got me into it."

"I haven't played in a few years. But still, I never would have guessed—wait, Desmond?" Evie's tone sharpened. *There* was the judgment, now verbalized. "As in, the doctor you married and divorced?"

"Yes, that Desmond." Kass closed her eyes while the game's start-up screens came and went. "He usually logs in over breakfast." She told herself to stay calm, to stay objective, like whenever clients accidentally brought up topics that hit too close to home. One exhale later and she typed in the game's dialogue box: */FIND Dwarftastic.*

"So I finally get to meet him. In *Ancient Runes.*" Evie snorted to herself, and Kass's objectivity slowly dissolved.

"It's not like you were around much during that time." The response came out swiftly, and with more teeth than it needed. Kass gave herself a mental high five for keeping the retort at that and *not* how Evie had missed their wedding for some supposed research excursion with her UFO buddies. Even still, Evie's sudden tension filled the space.

"Isn't it faster just to text him?"

"He'll check this faster." Just like that, a broad vista appeared, two moons visible in the purple sky and the chaotic sounds of battle echoing in the distance. Should she apologize? Would Evie? Had the moment passed? The questions lacked clear answers, their family floating in pieces without any tethers to common ground.

The Shao family had become a textbook case study in trauma. But with aliens.

Kass let it drop, instead taking Aveline over a ridge, and sure enough, colored blasts filled the screen as Desmond fought a horde of orcs with another player named AssassinCreep. Dwarftastic took out the two closest enemies before turning to her and waving with a canned animation gesture.

Late night? he asked. On-screen, Dwarftastic turned and raised his hand, causing the scene to shake as two lightning bolts zapped the ground, knocking a radius of orcs down.

Emergency. Can you do a video call? The keyboard clacked as she joined the fray, bow drawn and flaming arrows launching at the orcs. Behind her, a groan gave away Evie's impatience.

Okay. Dwarftastic vanished several seconds later—no funny animation, no additional text, simply the disappearance of Desmond's avatar from logging out.

If only everything between them had been that easy.

On the other monitor, a flashing icon appeared in the bottom left corner. Kass felt her pulse quicken, in a different way than all the stress and bullshit that Jakob brought, and she waited a second before double-clicking the icon.

The screen flashed, then a large gray box appeared, soon filled with Desmond's face. Flecks of gray hair wove into the stubble against his dark brown skin.

"Morning, Kass. Evening, I mean. Everything all right?" he asked, the vowels colored by his French accent.

The office chair squeaked as she turned it to center with the camera sitting on top of the second monitor. "Yeah. Well, no, not really."

"You look like hell. I mean that in a nice way."

"Yeah, shit is kind of fucked-up right now. So, um..." In the small self-view window in the corner, she saw herself and half of Evie standing beside her, with the camera cropping out at her sister's shoulders. "Desmond, meet Evie. Evie, Desmond." Kass thumbed over her shoulder, and Evie hunched over into camera range.

"Oh, Evie. The mysterious sister." A short laugh came out, one that didn't come from any humor but rather his own embarrassment. He ran a hand through his wild mop of hair before looking away. "I mean, nice to meet you."

"Hi. I play *Ancient Runes* too. Not the online version, the console one. So, uh...cool, you know?" Evie replied in a meek voice that landed much closer to the nervous teen Kass had grown up with than the woman who hosted an online show. Of nonsense. At least from the few times Kass had tried to watch it. "Um, good to meet you too."

His eyes darted around, and Kass realized that based on recent chats, he was probably looking for Jakob in the room. An urge came to sneakily use her phone for texting Way to be discreet to her ex-husband, though she resisted. That wouldn't accomplish much for anyone on the call.

"Look, we'll make this quick," Kass said. "You can read X-rays, right?"

Desmond's head tilted at the question. "Not as well as a radiologist. But sure, yes."

"Okay. Can we send you some images?"

"Sure," Desmond said. "Can you tell me what this is about?"

"Not yet." She turned to Evie. "Email them to me. I'll forward."

"Sending," Evie said while tapping away at her phone, and the images whirled around cyberspace.

Over the speakers, the sound of a repeated mouse click came through, and Desmond looked off-camera. "Nothing yet. I'll let you know." He recentered, peering at Kass with those deep brown eyes as if they were still sitting at a café, talking when they should have been studying for grad-school exams. "How is your mom?"

The floorboards creaked as Evie shifted behind her.

"Good. Relatively speaking. You know," she said, hoping her arched eyebrow communicated *Shut up, please* better than the words.

"Looks like something came through. Let's see here, and..." Desmond's eyes focused above to the left of the camera, the glare of the bright X-ray image visible in his glasses. "Hmm."

"Yeah," Kass said. She glanced back at Evie, and though her younger sister remained quiet, the sides of her lips curled up just enough to be visible.

He leaned in to the screen, the image of his face getting gradually bigger as the X-ray drew him in. Fingers rubbed against his scruffy cheeks, and even though an ocean and a digital divide separated them, his hesitant breath might as well have been next to them. "I'm not a radiologist," he said after far too long.

"But you are a doctor," Evie said. *Surgeon* was the technical term, though Kass held off on the correction.

He clicked the keyboard, and his glasses reflected a flickering screen, a blink to black as it loaded the other image. He clicked again, causing another flicker, and again and again, his squinted eyes grasping at what the images presented.

"There's a foreign body in the brain." Desmond pointed at the screen, the angle of his webcam distorting the size and shape of his finger. "Right here. I see it in both images. It's protruding into the brain tissue. What is this? Is this Photoshop?"

A weight landed on Kass's shoulder. It took a moment for her to realize that it was Evie's palm giving a gentle squeeze. Kass looked up to see her sister's cheeks twitch, and she could tell that Evie felt the need to hold back.

A full goddamn grin lurked under the surface. Evie must have been too polite to let it sneak through.

"No," Evie said. "It's real."

"Who is this?"

"It's—" Kass took in a deep breath "—Jakob."

Desmond leaned back in his chair, his brow furrowed and nose wrinkled. He grabbed a clear glass mug from off-screen and held it to his lips, as if his morning coffee might create some logic out of the impossible. "Wait, I'm… Jakob, is he dead? I thought you said he just returned."

"No," Evie said, "he's alive. I took these X-rays myself about an hour ago."

"This is recent?" he asked, pointing again at the screen. "This is from today?"

"Yes."

"This shouldn't be possible. This *object* here, whatever it is, it *can't* exist. It's within the brain. You can see here," his finger drew across the camera range, as if Kass and Evie were in the Paris apartment with him, "it rests right beneath the surface of the brain. These legs protrude down, they would pierce the parietal lobe, interfering with spatial sense. And this second piece here, it would have to have been buried individually. It goes deeper."

Evie jolted at the sentence, shaking Kass with her.

"A second device?"

"Or it was part of the main piece and broke off. But it looks too clean for that. This is implanted, so if it snapped off, you'd see some debris, even a small amount. And it's separated, by..." Desmond's finger and thumb came up to the screen "...maybe two to three millimeters. Like they were put in separately. But I still don't know how this could be done on a living person. It would damage the brain tissue. That would kill them." His hand came up and rubbed the morning scruff across his chin and cheeks. "This is Jakob?"

"Wait, wait, wait," Evie said. "Jakob said something about how it hurt more when he went horizontal."

"This." Desmond pointed at something that the sisters couldn't see. "I could see the smaller piece doing that. It's in a very tight area, and it's planted deep. Seems reasonable that orientation might affect it."

A second glow illuminated the space, this time from Evie's phone. She squinted at the screen. "I see it. You have to zoom in to really tell. I just didn't notice it before. But I see the gap. These pieces are separated. Look," she said, putting the phone in front of Kass. "See it?"

The lit screen caused Kass's eyes to sting before they adjusted to the sudden brightness. Evie had zoomed in so far that the context of the X-ray disappeared, leaving only black-and-white pixels that formed rough shapes.

And in those shapes, Kass saw it too: two distinct pieces.

"Yeah," she said, her voice an unintentional whisper.

"Desmond, would you say," Evie started, a waver rippling through her voice, "that we do not currently have the technology to do something like this?"

"You'd have to drill through the skull and implant both pieces. Getting into the skull is not easy. Anything dealing with the brain itself is extremely delicate with hardly any margin for error. I suppose it could be done, but I don't know how it's possible. Not with this precision."

"Are you convinced?" Evie asked, her voice also a whisper.

The three of them lingered, connected digitally across the planet, all still enough that the images on their video call could have been static photos instead of a live stream. In Paris, Desmond broke the stalemate by sipping his coffee. The reflection in his glasses blinked again as he tapped the keyboard and he shook his head with a befuddled grimace.

"We need to go. Thank you for this," Kass finally said.

"Is everything all right?"

"We're not sure. Possibly. But look, I'll tell you all about it when we're done." Desmond gave a look—*that* look. The one where his fingers tented at his lips and lines carved into his forehead, yet his eyes glistened with concern.

That look. She'd seen it so many times, but it had only petrified her like this one other time before.

When he had asked for a divorce.

"Promise," she said. Her fingers fluttered in a quick wave, come and gone so quickly the webcam may not have even caught it, and she clicked the red end button on the video call's corner.

Evie stood, and though Kass still faced the computer monitors, the reflection of the glass caught the slightest of movements: Evie holding a fist at her side, but bouncing it.

A private fist pump for herself.

Maybe she'd been paying attention to Kass after all.

Kass scooted the office chair back to stand, then let the moment breathe. Fatigue set in, a pressure that started with the day's happenings and finished with her mind trying to find *any* holes in Evie's theory. But nothing worked, and as that sunk in, the logic she'd lived by for the past fifteen years began to fracture.

CHAPTER THIRTY-FOUR

EVIE

This should have felt like a victory, like a culmination of fifteen years of arguments and begging and distance. Perhaps even a lifetime.

Finally, the balance in the family had shifted.

Growing up, Kassie and Jakob had commanded the headlines. Every freaking athletic endeavor on the planet seemed to boost Kassie's star, so many that they blurred together into one nebulous sports *thing*. No wonder she was able to smoke her whole life; her lungs probably took that on as a challenge compared to all the activity growing up. Mom and Dad driving her to practice, driving her to games, driving her to events, and *then* the long phone calls when Kassie just wasn't good enough to be on the college team beyond her freshman year. Even when Evie avoided the conversation, Kassie and her problems took the spotlight.

And Jakob wasn't that far behind. Despite being the best swimmer on the high-school team, one of the top in the county, he always just managed to carry on, teetering his very delicate house of cards on the edge of collapse. Somehow, he managed to get into honors classes, and somehow he managed to get into the same college as Kassie, but his potential always loomed over his reality. At least in Mom's and Dad's eyes.

Jakob and Kassie. Kassie and Jakob. Tied together the moment they arrived out of the womb as twins, always some form of yin and yang within the Shao family. And there was Evie—not as accomplished as Kassie but much more academic; not as charming or social as Jakob but much more reliable.

For her entire life, she'd lived relative to her siblings, unknowingly tethered to whether they succeeded or failed. And regardless, always *deferring* to whether they succeeded or failed.

If proof had fallen into her lap a week ago—before Jakob, before Reno—then this moment would have been about alignment, acceptance. Evie would have taken the information to the Reds, and Kassie would have reached some form of closure. She might have been able to dedicate an episode segment or something to it.

But that assumed proof remained in a vacuum, a binary piece of yes/no information that involved their brother's past, not his present. Now looking forward felt impossible without understanding the gravity of the situation at hand: Jakob was missing and, at best, injured. At worst, comatose, possibly dying.

Now, perhaps for the first time ever, Kassie deferred to *her*.

And, if Jakob *was* telling the truth, much more was at stake than sibling pride or the deed to the house.

"Here's the thing," Kassie said, her demeanor returning to her acerbic default. "Let's say that it was..." she closed her eyes and shook her head "...aliens. That doesn't explain the issue with the FBI. Domestic terrorism? How does that even line up?"

"We won't know unless he's able to tell us."

"It still doesn't totally add up," Kassie said, followed by pursed lips forming a frown.

"It *does* add up. Which part are you afraid of? Because there's *something* you're avoiding." Thoughts gathered momentum, accelerating in both sharpness and emotion to become something she hadn't expected. "Is it the aliens part? Is that too out-there to believe? Because I get that. I get that it seems life-changing, world-changing. It upends everything we've built our society upon." Her voice grew louder, letting the words take over. A heat came to Evie's face, things she'd wanted to say for *years*, ever since they'd parted ways at the airport.

So we could be whole again.

Or maybe so they could see the Jakob that she'd always known.

Sure, he'd never had his priorities right. And he shouldn't have done drugs, and he should have studied harder, and a single tiny piece of Evie still worried that he really *had* spent all those years drinking and charming his way across Europe. But growing up, he'd listened to her. Through all the mess-ups, through all their differences, her studious nature running completely opposite of his devil-may-care attitude, he'd listened to her.

And she wouldn't turn her back on that now. Not when she had a chance to do right by him *and* finally make good on her promise to Dad.

His last words at the animal hospital echoed in her mind. "Will you trust me?"

She would.

"You know what, Kassie? I don't think it's the extraterrestrials part." Kassie stood up, and now they were side-by-side. But though Evie had always been shorter than her sister, suddenly the roles reversed and she towered over Kassie. "This is about *Jakob*. You can't let go of him being a scapegoat. You can't accept that he actually deserves your faith this time."

Evie thought of all those times—at the dinner table, in the car, even on Christmas mornings—when Jakob would say or do something dumb and Kassie would shake her head and look away in irritation.

"You can't deny facts. Look at the facts."

Kassie had so far remained stoic, an impenetrable shell around her, even as she dealt with her ex-husband. It may have taken a thousand cracks in the armor before the defenses broke apart, because with Evie's final sentence, her expression finally changed.

To what, Evie couldn't say. Kassie moved too quickly for her to read her look. First to the window, where she stared for several seconds, then back over to the desk before throwing open the bottom drawer. She reached in and produced a pad of paper, countless lines scribbled on it. Page upon page were flipped over the top until a clean sheet appeared, and with swift precision, Kassie threw the pad down and began writing on it.

Okay, so maybe Evie had broken more than just Kassie's defenses.

It took tiptoes and a few inches of leaning forward, but Evie was able to peek at some of the scribbling.

Would Evie lie about this?

Is this beyond current science?

What do you need to be convinced?

The pen jabbed the dot on the final question mark, staying there long enough for ink to pool into a small blotch. Kassie stood straight again, then turned to Evie and locked eyes. "I need more proof."

"More?"

"Yes. You're the science person, you tell me. What further proof do you have?"

"More proof than X-rays?" The question landed with exasperation, despite Evie trying to hold it back. But Kassie didn't shift at all, and instead her eyes looked with a desperation so unlike her confident self.

"I just..." Fists formed at Kassie's side, and her gaze dropped, color draining from her cheeks. "I need more. *Something.*"

"Okay, look. Um..." Evie's mind raced. If not the X-rays, then what? "Metrics," she said. "The atmospheric metrics. Air pressure, magnetic declination. They were the exact same when Jakob landed in Reno as that night in Lake Kinbote. And there was a similar event in Half Moon Bay that the Reds detected, and that's what led us to the decryptor. And this," she said, reaching into her back pocket. "I don't know what this is, but Jakob pulled it from the beach and said it was, like, part of the shell of the decryptor device."

"That looks like a rock."

"I know, but... Okay, I grilled Jakob about everything he'd seen. The Seven Bells. The Awakened. Their technology, their communication, what they looked like. And he said the Seven Bells, they use, like, *rock* instead of metal. It's their material for stuff, they process geological material because it's easier to source. Those details, they were so specific. Too specific for someone like *Jakob* to just make up." A jolt ran through Evie, something connecting past and present in such a clear direct way. If she hadn't already been convinced, this would have put it over the top. "The Key. Wait, wait, wait, Dad's Key." Disbelief brought her hands to her temples. "How did I not put this together before? Things have just moved *so* fast. Do you remember what that looked like?"

Kassie spun around, and with her back to Evie, her arms crossed. "I...don't."

"It was, like, rock. A shaped rock, like something you'd buy at a gift store. That old place in the mall, Natural Wonders. That sort of thing, but it had these weird interfaces in it. Look," she said, holding up the sand-dollar-sized chip from the decryptor shell, "don't you remember? It *looked* like this. I think the color was a little different, but the texture and everything." A sharp breath exhaled, a sigh of frustration that filled the room. "If only Mom hadn't got rid of it." Images filled Evie's mind, hours of sitting with Dad, not just staring at it or holding it but wishing on it, begging it to please activate and provide some sort of link to Jakob. "Why did you let her throw away something that was *so* important to Dad?"

Kassie bit down on her lower lip, and Evie expected something defensive to come out. But instead, her big sister sighed again, then her palms massaged her temples. Evie nearly asked if she was all right—Kassie's low groan and cursing under her breath tipped that the topic hit much harder than typical sisterly jabs did.

A minute passed, which Evie confirmed by looking at the clock on her phone despite it feeling much longer.

"It's upstairs," Kassie finally said.

"What?" Evie's question wasn't asked out of outrage or any sort of protest. At least not yet. She needed to make sure she fully understood.

"It's upstairs." Kassie pointed above them. "*It.* Dad's thing. In Mom's room."

"You..." For everything that had happened in the past few days, Evie had kept her cool. Not just Kassie's condescending attitude, but the roller-coaster with Jakob, the incident at the animal hospital, dealing with the freaking FBI—she hadn't lost it. But this, *this* felt like a violation of the highest order, something more than a mere white lie about a trinket. This was a critical piece of family history, one of the only surviving bonds that connected them to Jakob—and Kassie had *lied* about it? "You lied about throwing it out? Why would you do that?"

"Because it was causing more problems than it solved."

"That—that's not an answer. That's not even saying anything."

"*You'd* ask about it when you called," Kassie said. "And I was tired of that being the only thing you cared about. More than how I was doing after a divorce, more than what Mom might be going through, more than any of it. I wanted it out of our lives."

"Why didn't you just *send* it to me, then?"

Kassie's eyes dropped to the floor. Her hand reached over to the desk, fingers propped out, like they were the only thing keeping everything from spinning out of control. She opened her mouth, but nothing came out at first. In fact, the only true reaction came from the smallest of head shakes and an even smaller voice.

"Because it means a lot to Mom."

And that said more than any grandiose speeches could have. In that moment, Evie realized two things. First, even though her sister seemed to sometimes operate solely on spite, the Key was just another part of Mom's burden she'd desperately tried to assume.

And second, getting mad about it was completely up to her. Evie had a choice to make.

"Forget it," she finally said, taking a deep breath in a way probably similar to the way Kassie advised her clients. "Where is it?"

CHAPTER THIRTY-FIVE

KASS

There were no more secrets among the Shao sisters.

On the kitchen table, It sat between Kass and Evie. In the other room, Lucy talked with Mom about going to bed. And somewhere, Jakob wandered alone—hopefully awake, hopefully safe.

Kass looked at It; she stared, looking at every inch of detail.

She'd *seen* It before, countless times sitting in Mom's room. In particular, this past week during bouts of fury and confusion from Mom. And she'd just told Evie about Mom's claim that It moved, whether or not that remained relevant.

The one thing she refused to do was use Evie's name for It. It would remain It, because fuck It and everything It stood for.

Mom's slippers shuffled against the hard floor with each step, led by Lucy. "We should say good-night. I've handled the evening's medication," Lucy said. "I'm going to walk you to bed tonight, all right?"

"Of course, dear. Kassie, have you met Lucy? She's so nice."

Evie froze, looking at Kass. Kass watched as her sister inhaled to say something before pausing, then shaking her head.

Kass stood, attempting to run interference before things got worse for any of them. "Okay, Mom. Good night." She gave the frail old woman a hug, marveling how the past several years had stolen Mom's runner's strength as much as it had her cognitive awareness. "It's not fair," she whispered aloud, though she reset to neutral before anyone might react.

Mom had had enough disruption for a while.

"Where's Jakob?" Mom asked as they shuffled away. Lucy's voice trailed from the stairs, soon drowned out by the sound of footsteps.

Kass returned and found Evie staring unblinking as she looked straight at her phone. Despite the fact that its screen was dark.

"Are you okay?" she asked. Her voice came out like a therapist's, the default way she'd asked that question hundreds, possibly thousands of times. Evie failed to respond, the words seeming to bounce off her. Kass had seen that look in countless patients: glazed eyes, steady breath, mouth slightly open, a combination of shock and fatigue and realization. And in this situation, her professional instincts told her to back off.

Yet something else gave the slightest pull, a frayed thread that somehow still remained, the same thing that pulled her to pick up the phone, answer the text, check in with Evie. Even if she didn't always act on it.

Right now, it told her to stop being a therapist.

She needed to be a sister.

Kass moved beside Evie as if they were children again in this very room. "Are you okay?" she asked, hand resting on Evie's shoulder.

"It's fine," Evie said after a long pause. "I know that's not Mom that doesn't recognize me."

"Actually," Kass said, her voice even and calm, but with a level of warmth that clients rarely saw, "that is Mom. Now." From above came footsteps, and Kass knew where each one was located: first a shuffle from the bathroom to the bedroom, then hitting the one floorboard that always creaked. Then the light *thump* as Mom settled into bed. "That's okay. I'm angry about it too. Jakob didn't steal her mind from us. Time did. I want to be mad at something, but I can't. I can't be mad at time and fate or whatever, you know?"

"Obviously you've never seen *Doctor Who*," Evie said with a laugh, focus returning to her glistening eyes. "People always fight time and fate on that show."

"Yeah, well," Kass matched her laugh, "too busy with Desmond, fighting beasts."

"Desmond," she said, and perhaps for the first time since they'd seen each other, her cheeks and brow softened. She straightened up and set down her phone, her hand accidentally knocking the small rocklike shell from Half Moon Bay a few inches farther down the table. "You two are really made—"

A rattling noise stopped the conversation, and both sisters turned their heads.

The rocklike chip now hovered in midair, and on the table, It rattled. And between them, a glowing yellow beam shot out of It's angled top, linking the device to the piece dug up from the beach.

Kass and Evie jolted up in unison.

The table bumped with Evie's quick movement, jarring It enough to roll across the table, the yellow beam trailing along. Evie's brown eyes went wide as she leaned into the space, her palm cutting the air underneath the floating chip. "Holy crap!"

Over. Under. All around. Kass kept shifting her angle, trying to find some sort of reasoning as to what was happening in front of her. Soon she matched her sister, waving her hand all around the shell to break the spell. "Can I?" Kass asked, her fingers closing in around the piece.

"Yeah."

Kass yanked on the floating chip, and it came free with the ease of a refrigerator magnets pulling off the door. She held up the sliver of…well, she thought it was rock or a broken chunk from a home-store countertop. Or maybe it really was a piece that had broken off Jakob's decryptor when the alien thingy had gotten buried deep under Half Moon Bay sand. Either way, she brought the chipped piece within It's radius, a sudden tingle dancing across her fingertips. From within the chip itself, a glow emerged. A thin vein. Deep blue. Just visible enough from her position given the kitchen lighting, a line that might stand out had they been in pitch-darkness. Here, it had the power of a fading light bulb.

But still. That *shouldn't* happen.

Kass moved the chip closer to It, slowly bringing them to each other until the sliver tugged and held itself, the yellow beam locking on the entire time. Her hand opened, fingers fully spread out, yet the piece remained.

Hovering.

"Proof," Evie whispered.

Kass got close, her face mere inches away when she noticed the smallest of gaps at the bottom of It. She reached up gingerly, almost afraid to break this spell, or whatever the hell caused this. But her finger nudged the family heirloom enough to show that there was, in fact, a clean separation: a base piece that had now unlodged itself from the larger unit. She tapped It's base again, something that Dad never managed to discover or activate, and the base piece floated about an inch away before dropping on the table.

"Yeah," Kass finally said. She stepped forward and hugged

her sister, holding her tighter than they'd probably ever embraced. "It's proof," she whispered into Evie's ear.

Evie nodded, her arms returning the hug, and the sisters gave in to the moment that their world veered off track. Or maybe it had course-corrected for the first time.

Kass exhaled, seemingly for both of them, then stepped back, meeting Evie with red eyes and quiet tears trickling down her cheeks. "Now what?" she asked.

"Hold on," Evie suddenly said, and Kass wasn't sure if that was an answer to her question or if her sister had bounced to a new thought already. "Oh no, oh no. What about..." In a blink, Evie's phone was in her hand, the X-rays loaded up. "I just realized something. Jakob, he'd said something wasn't right. When I was doing the X-rays. I mean, you saw him, he could barely move. He said that a decryptor shouldn't hurt like that. He figured out the pain depended on how his head was oriented." She zoomed in on the screen, then set it on the table for both of them to see. "Look. It's what Desmond noticed. Two objects. Why would there be two objects? And why would it hurt when his body is in certain positions? Forget that it's alien, just think logically. If his own team implanted one, then they'd make sure it worked. He can't be fixing things in battle if he's in debilitating pain some of the time. So this other piece, it shouldn't be there if it hurts him, if it doesn't fit properly. But there's two objects."

"One Jakob knows about—" Kass started.

"And one that he doesn't," Evie finished. "Kassie, I think Jakob's in big, big trouble." Heavy breaths raised and lowered Evie's shoulders, and Kass waited, giving Evie space to work this out. "We need to find Jakob," she said, her eyes alive with a fierce, steady glare. "We need to rescue him. Tonight." She grabbed the core unit of It and stared, like she was trying to decipher ancient text or will some miracle into existence. "What can we do with this? Dad was so certain about it," she whispered before her voice returned. "Here," she said, handing the chipped sliver to Kass. "Hold this. Stay right there. I want to test the range of the beam." She started walking backward, the light beam still tethering the device in her hands and the tiny piece in Kass's. "It's not magnetic." Evie waved her hand in front of the beam, breaking it before it arced up and over her palm to reconnect. "It doesn't burn. It feels like it's just…a guide." Her voice came from the front hallway. "I'm going outside," she said, followed by the sound of the front door opening.

The beam abruptly snapped off from Kass's piece.

"Look, Kassie," she called from the open front door. "Leave that chip inside."

Kass caught up to see the yellow beam still shooting out of It, but this time upward.

"We need to follow this." Evie's silhouette pointed to the beam as it fired off in an arc to…somewhere. "Get your keys. We need to follow this."

Kass did as requested, stepping back in to grab her car keys from the entry table. But as soon as the front door shut behind her, she paused on the porch. "Slow down, Evie."

"It's pointing that way," she said as Kass walked deliberately to the driveway. "That's…northwest. But how far does it go? What is the range?" Evie's voice dropped with that whole muttering-to-herself thing that she did to sort things out. "You know what? It doesn't matter. Let's just go."

"Wait, wait, wait. Go where?" Their tender sister moment evaporated, and Kass felt her instincts push straight into a defensive stance.

"Go where this is leading."

Kass looked upstairs at the lit bedroom window, where Lucy was earning the biggest bonus gift and/or apology of all time.

"This is absurd. Just because I'm on board with the aliens thing doesn't mean I'm going to join you on—" the keys rattled as her hands shook with emphasis "—whatever this is."

"It might be a compass. Or like a targeting sight." Evie waved It around, the beam tracking the entire time. "Or just like the line on Google Maps that brings you to your destination."

"Yeah, but to *where*?"

"Jakob! We need to get to him."

"*How* do you know it's Jakob?"

"That thing in his head. It's alien tech," Evie said. Kass *really* hoped the neighbors didn't hear them arguing about aliens in the driveway. "This beam points to alien tech." Urgency cranked up Evie's volume, and Kass's instinctive response was to go even louder.

"It could point to anything. Literally anything."

"No, Kassie. What else could it be? Jakob's on foot. And hurt. It's only been, like, two hours. He's within range. He can't be far."

"I'm not just running off into the night without a plan. This is ridiculous."

"No, Kassie, you listen. For once." Evie was at a full yell now, and if Kass wasn't so submerged in the moment, the whole thing would have proved to be extra amusing. "You don't get to be the big sister here. You *don't*. Because you don't know what we're dealing with."

"And you do?"

"More than you, yeah." The short sentence came out with a definitive ferocity, so much so that Evie seemed to deflate after that. "Come on, Kassie," she said, her voice suddenly back to normal. "This is our only lead. We can't just wait here."

Arguing with Evie just seemed so much more *natural*. But maybe that was the problem. Growing up, her old relationship with Evie had involved a lot of ignoring. As adults, it involved ignoring her *and* being mad at her.

Kass looked at her sister, who just minutes ago had managed to convince her of the existence of aliens *and* the fact that Jakob wasn't a deadbeat loser, and now she stood there holding Dad's most prized possession as it fired a yellow beam into the night sky.

What was one more leap?

CHAPTER THIRTY-SIX

KASS

Spending this much quality time—for lack of a better term—with Evie felt unusual, like walking out of step. With Jakob, it had been as easy as being twins. Even though he had always been a bit of a dick, their lives overlapped at each stage. In middle school, with rival friend groups. In high school, with the number of trophies they earned from sports. And in college, Jakob always succeeded at finding shenanigans whenever things needed an extra bit of enlivening, on-campus and otherwise.

Evie's age made those sorts of parallels impossible. Once, Kass got roped into dropping Evie and her friends at a movie theater, and the stilted, awkward conversation between a high-school senior and three eighth-grade girls made for an uncomfortable ride. The whole time, Kass suspected they'd tried to amuse each other by staying purposefully quiet, like a power grab through silent unity.

This time, the quiet car ride was different. Once again, Kass drove her younger sister, but in the end—and perhaps for the first time ever—Kass let Evie lead.

Science, after all, was her strong suit.

Evie's UFO pal—a woman named Layla who smiled way too easily on Evie's phone considering the circumstances—monitored the police band for them, and it sounded like no one had any sign of Jakob. But the light on the core unit of It kept pointing, angling in a consistent direction no matter how they held it or moved or drove. The thin beam of yellow light brightened the car, and at a glance, Kass saw it continuously oscillating between the car door and the window as they broke past the threshold of suburbia into the countryside of Silicon Valley.

Did alien light beams damage car doors? She'd bill Jakob for that.

Kass was about to suggest putting a blanket or something there just in case (though, really, would that catch on fire?) when Evie mumbled something under her breath. "What was that?" Kass asked.

"I'm just thinking to myself. What if I held it out the window?"

They drove among the hills west of the suburbs, a smattering of office parks and ranch homes in between the bike paths and long swaths of hills. "How do we know this beam isn't a fire hazard?"

"Well," Evie said, "we don't." She put her hand directly against it. "But I've tested it, and it doesn't hurt."

"Evie, please don't laser your hand off in my car."

"It won't. This is the, what, fourth or fifth time, and I still don't feel anything. I still have my hand. It's just for tracking or targeting or something."

"Okay, then please don't hit any buttons or switches that might fire at the target." The ridiculousness of what they were doing really sank in. For years and years, Evie had urged Kass to consider her quest seriously. She supposed it only took having an extraterrestrial compass—if it was that—and limiting her involvement to driving around the hills she'd run as a high schooler. "Okay, open the window. But be careful. We just finished wildfire season, and I don't think *using alien tech to find our missing brother* will fly as an excuse if we set it all off again."

Harsh wind blew into the car, tossing Kass's hair into her face. Evie unbuckled her seat belt and leaned with two arms outside the window. Kass concentrated on the road, though Evie angled the device enough to catch her peripheral vision.

"Kassie!" she yelled over the wind, "turn right whenever you can. I can see it tracking."

"Does it just keep going?"

"No, it's ending at a spot. Not sure if it's a range thing or what. But it's clearly pointing at something." Evie settled back into her seat, elbows propped on the side of the window frame.

"No signs of arson?"

"I think we're good. California thanks us for our concern."

Kass turned at the next small street and tracked the map on her dashboard. This wasn't a through street and, by the looks of it, had only a few houses standing several hundred feet back on the other side beyond the brush and lengthy driveways. She peeked at the beam coming from the device, and there it was: turning in real time, pointing not out but upward toward a hill.

"I think park here," Evie said. "Let's walk."

The car slowed to a halt, and Kass sent out a silent prayer to the parking gods or aliens that their illegal stopping point didn't get her a ticket. She looked at the small fence blocking off the hillside, with a clear sign that said *No Trespassing.*

That sign was up for a number of reasons Kass learned about in high school—mostly to minimize disturbances to wildlife and keep people from trashing the hills. But Jakob was never one for the rules, especially not now that he was apparently a space-army hero.

They trudged uphill in darkness. The ground shifted with each step, crunching dead weeds and dirt made soft from recent rainfall. The journey proved methodical and slow, slower than normal with Evie insisting they leave flashlights off to avoid flagging any attention. When they finally hit the top of the hill, the lights of Silicon Valley greeted them, and Kass took a breather, her thighs burning from the incline workout. She turned to see It's thin beam angled downward, and she tracked the light to the other side of the hill until it faded away.

"Is that thing not working?" Kass asked, blinking several times, then squinted. Ahead of them lay only a blanket of dark, their vision made even more difficult by the clouds obscuring any potential moonlight. Wind attacked from different directions, first blowing Kass's hair in front of her face, then tossing it back, and she tried again to figure out why the beam simply stopped, seemingly absorbed by the ground.

"No, I think it's fine. I think..." Evie sidestepped a few times, checking that the angle remained consistent. After several tries, she turned, and even though the night's darkness had been all-encompassing, her expression was clear enough for Kass to see. "I think that's him." Grass and leaves crunched beneath her feet as she took steps toward him. "Jakob?" she called out.

"Discretion, please," Kass said.

"Right, right. Jakob?" she said, her voice still too loud, but at least Evie put in some effort to containing herself.

The beam moved.

Kass took a closer look at It, making sure that Evie didn't pull a trick like teens using a Ouija board. But no, this was real. From her vantage point, the beam angled slightly to the left, then trailed up, then grew in intensity over several seconds. "Jakob?" Evie called out again.

The beam remained still, allowing Kass to follow it again. This time, it was clear: blended into the darkness, the silhouette of a person moved. Lumbering, not the fastest, with the occasional stumble, but the beam tracked each step. "There he is," Kass said. She held Evie's shoulder despite her sister's step forward. "Look, shit's really weird now. Let's be careful. Okay? If years of gaming have taught me anything, sometimes it's best to wait when encountering a new area."

"Okay, okay," Evie said, and the sisters stood, watching the silhouette make its way up. As it rounded into form, Kass saw the beam trace clearly into the head.

It really *was* Jakob. Looking haggard and clearly not well, but enough like himself that Kass fought the urge to instinctively walk up and yell at her twin brother. "What the hell, guys?" he said with a laugh, and something about the tone of his voice seemed different from before. Different, as in much more like the old Jakob from high school and college, and Kass could practically see his smirk. "I'm the injured one, and you're making me walk uphill to you?"

CHAPTER THIRTY-SEVEN

EVIE

If only Dad could see them now. If only he could understand how *right* he had been. Knowing that almost patched over Evie's lingering bitterness at Kassie's blatant lie to her about throwing the Key out—not just lying to her, but putting the blame on Mom. But if that had never happened, if Kassie had sent it and Evie had inspected the heck out of the device only to conclude it benign, then it would have likely been sitting in her Buffalo bedroom. And they would have never used the Key to locate Jakob.

So things had worked out. "This," Jakob said, holding the Key, "is how you found me? Where did you get this?"

"Dad brought it back." Evie knelt to get on Jakob's level. They'd walked back to the top of the hill but, for no reason in particular, had stopped there. The whole time, the thin beam of yellow light continued pointing at the back of Jakob's head. No matter the angle, no matter the height, it concentrated on that single spot. "They found him at Lake Kinbote with it."

"Is it like a space phone? And yes, that means I believe you. Both of you," Kassie said, her arm propped under Jakob's shoulder. "Maybe not that part about Jakob being an engineer. You were terrible at math."

"Turns out," Jakob said, "I'm actually pretty good at it. Once I applied myself. I know, I know." Evie offered the Key, and Jakob held it up close. "I know how Dad got this. He didn't want to leave. He was struggling. Grabbing things. Throwing things. They were trying to get him into the transporter," he nodded at Evie. "He must have taken this right before the system activated." Jakob grunted with a wince, buckling to his knees for a moment before straightening up. "I'm okay. It just comes and goes. I figured the headaches out on the X-ray table. Have to keep my head upright and fairly stable, then it doesn't slow me down. That's how I was able to get onto the roof to hide until I headed this way. Police haven't realized to look above them, huh?" He gestured to the space around them. "Or around here."

"Is that why you dragged us out here to the hills?" Kassie asked. "You're hiding?"

"In a developed surrounding, the best place to avoid detection is in an undeveloped region."

Kassie scoffed at Jakob's very soldieresque statement, though he either didn't notice or didn't care.

"This device is just a tool," he went on. "Like a wrench. It's like a really fancy voltmeter. It's a diagnostic tool. The beam is just locking onto the strongest detected material. Helps us scavenge spare parts in space."

"Will it help?"

"No," Jakob said. "At least not like this. But..." He held it up, rotating it around, and his fingers moved over the device, silhouettes slipping over shadows. A trilling noise came from it, and the yellow beam disappeared. "It's got a power source. *That* I could use. In the base piece. Do you have that?"

"It's at the house. Wait a minute, is that why you were buying bomb materials?"

"Bomb?" Jakob stood, and Kass noticed the strange way Jakob held his posture. The wincing and headache attacks from earlier didn't seem as debilitating as before, and if everyone's deductions were correct and Jakob *did* have a micro device plugged into his brain, at least he'd seemed to figure out how to mitigate it.

How about that? Kass thought. Jakob the problem-solver. She would have never imagined her brother being so insightful.

"I wasn't shopping for bomb stuff," he said. "It was to build and amplify an explosive power source."

"Key word is *explosive*, Jakob. The FBI doesn't like that. But let's skip that and get what you need at the house," Kass said.

"Wait, before we go any further," Evie said. Their immediate space lit up as her phone activated, the bright screen nearly overpowering her eyes in the pitch-blackness of the night. "Look at these X-rays."

The three siblings huddled over the tiny display beneath a cloudy autumn night in the middle of nowhere, somehow banded together for the first time in decades, perhaps ever. Evie zoomed in on the images. "There's this," she said, pointing to the *M*-shaped item.

"That's a transponder. It signals the Seven Bells fleet. They're constantly moving. So it's the only way to communicate with them. No base. No central resource. It keeps them safe."

"What about that thing?" Evie asked.

Jakob zoomed in even closer, and rather than watch the screen, Evie observed her brother. Beyond his posture and his expression, the way his eyes tracked the details as he moved around the image, he *was* the Jakob she knew, but so different. Part of his happy-go-lucky charm came from an innocence that drove his life, a quest for sensory experience above knowledge or status.

But now, he looked tired.

"That," he said, "is not good." He handed the phone back over to Evie, then looked skyward. "We'll need to move quick."

"Is that what's causing your headaches?" Evie asked.

"Yeah." Jakob turned to face the twinkling lights of the city below. "But that's not the worst part."

CHAPTER THIRTY-EIGHT

JAKOB

Two different devices. Two separate issues.

The first device, he'd expected. A transponder in his head. With Evie's X-rays, he knew exactly where it was. And now it was a question of getting power to it, which would have been difficult with mere animal-hospital equipment, but easier once he isolated the power source of the diagnostic profiler—the technical term for Dad's device. The process would still be painful but had a much higher chance of success than hacking together Earth medical equipment.

The second device, though… He'd seen that before, a few times, always from the corpses of fallen comrades who'd died the plain old violent way rather than crystallization. Pilots and soldiers were scanned upon return for any foreign objects, but this was always on the list: a different kind of transponder, a Trojan horse of sorts, planted by the Awakened to track an individual's movement. The burst from the decryptor must have triggered it, causing it to drill in a little more. The result was a different pain from the decryptor syncing to his brain as they got close at Half Moon Bay, more of a sharp and direct stab based on the orientation of his head, Earth's gravity, and the environment's air pressure.

Suddenly, everything made sense. Jakob's recovery, the abandoned ship he awoke in, the loss of functional power, all of it must have been intentional. Perhaps even Henry's final moments, a strategic move to give Jakob a personal vendetta, making sure they could rely on him to act as an unintentional spy leading to the mobile Seven Bells command fleet.

But Henry's intel, that was authentic. The mental transference was proof, a process so personal that it couldn't be simulated or faked. And with it, Jakob still had the power to win the war.

Except first things first. Before he could even attempt to remove such a tracking device—or at least safely disable it—he needed to contact the fleet. And that required powering up the transponder.

That meant every second counted. Which didn't allow room for pleasantries as they walked into the Shao home with Kassie's assistant sitting on the couch and Mom upstairs in bed.

"Where is it?" Jakob barked, more an order than a request.

"Easy there, space hero," Kassie said. "Kitchen table."

"Right, sorry. It's just—"

"I know, I know, fate of the galaxy. Evie, didn't I tell you *delusions of grandeur*? Give me a minute." With that, Kassie went up to check on Mom, and Evie nudged him with her elbow.

"I know this is serious," she said, "but, like, lighten up a little. We're here to help." She presented him with a disk-shaped object about the size of her palm.

If the family had never understood the full context of the situation, what might they have seen it as? A paperweight? A vintage video-game cartridge from their childhood? It certainly could have functioned as such. But in this case, Jakob sat with it, holding the warm device in front of him and pondering if his engineer's hunch was correct. "So," he said to his little sister, "do you know if Kassie kept Dad's tools?"

Jakob didn't see his sisters' expressions as he worked, but he could probably guess what they were. Evie paid close attention to what he was doing, the way the mechanics of taking the device apart were similar to Earth logic but in a whole different context. Kassie kept her distance, probably more amused at Jakob's engineering competence than anything else.

They'd settled on the garage given the noise of the tools, and Jakob reminded himself to take a moment and appreciate the irony of trying to save the galaxy in the same garage where he'd hidden his high-school drugs.

Their voices brought Mom out too, and rather than fight it, Kassie let her stay, something about the activity naturally drawing her curiosity. He did feel for Lucy, though, who wasn't getting paid nearly enough to deal with all of this, though at least Kassie acknowledged her with constant apologies for their family's situation.

"Just a few more things," he said. Several more clicks in place, and then he stood up. "Anyone want to do the honors?"

Kassie nodded to Evie. "You're the expert."

Jakob handed the device to Evie, who gingerly took it in her hands. The small circular piece was now dismantled, the smooth exterior shell removed to a core board that worked like circuitry but looked more like a movie prop with its small carvings and glowing lights. On one side, a purple beam tracked to the back of his skull. "Pretty simple. There's a rectangular glyph at the base. Hold it for four seconds to initiate the power transfer."

"That's it?" Evie asked, audible nerves packed into two words.

"That's it. If all goes well, it should power up and open a channel to the Seven Bells fleet."

"What happens if it doesn't go well?" Kassie asked.

Jakob considered telling the truth. He did seem to owe that to them. But at this stage, them picturing the rare-but-worst-case scenario of his skull exploding all over the garage wasn't going to help. "Just stand back."

"That doesn't sound good," Kassie said, sipping a coffee despite the late hour. "Come on, Mom."

"Kassie, I'm helping Jakob right now." Mom grabbed his arm with surprising strength.

"We don't have much time." Jakob pried her fingers loose, then looked Mom in the eye. "Mom, I need to do something. Can you stand with Kassie?"

"I thought you needed my help."

"I did, but you already helped me, remember?" An inherent guilt stung at the way he manipulated the truth to get her to move. On the other hand, his gentle tone and soft words were taken straight from Kassie's playbook. And they seemed to work.

"Oh, right, right," Mom said, laughing to herself.

Kassie tried again to pull her away, this time hooking her by the elbow. "Lucy," she said, "maybe we try to get her inside for this?"

"Okay, should I do a countdown or something?" Evie asked.

"Nah, just do it." From the shoulders down, every muscle tensed in Jakob's body as he knelt.

"Right. Here we go." Though Jakob couldn't see it, he knew Evie activated the power transfer simply from the heat radiating from the top of his head.

"Jakob, what are you doing?" Mom yelled. Despite that, he

remained steady, a pressure building up—not quite painful, but intense, like if a vise grip and heat could combine into a single feeling. He steadied himself with breaths, reminding himself that it'd be over soon one way or the other. Behind him, the sounds of her slippers beat against the concrete floor, and as the pressure ratcheted, he felt thin fingers grab his shoulder.

But it was too late. A pulse of white light came and went, filling the space. An audible "Ow" came from Evie, along with the sound of the device hitting the floor. Jakob stood as the pressure began to release from his head, though a low-level heat remained. His vision blurred, and his equilibrium tilted, and he threw a hand out to steady himself but missed. The movement caused the secondary pain in his skull to jostle, though he fought through all of it to keep his head steady and upright.

"These lights, what do they all mean?" he said, and within seconds, the activation phrase finally worked, internal heat dissipating and bringing a new focus to his vision.

He turned to see his family: Evie, kneeling by the dropped device that gave off steam; Kassie, who tentatively stepped forward; and Mom, who lingered by Jakob but kept looking around, eyes blinking.

In his inner ear, a tiny voice spoke, words translated by the Seven Bells operational AI into communication more suitable for human minds to comprehend.

That part Dad's science fiction had got correct.

"Shao Jakob Human, we have detected your signal."

Jakob closed his eyes, and his shoulders dropped. Though the Seven Bells technology interacted with his physiology, the sudden sway he felt had nothing to do with communications channels or embedded devices. His whole time on Earth had been a clenched fist, a protective stance while he focused on the mission. Every step had involved a goal, a constant churn of strategy to lead to this moment. He held those layers around him tight, always considering the next steps, the best path. But while Jakob's eyes remained closed, the images he saw were vivid: Henry's final moment, the chase through traffic in Reno, escaping the veterinary hospital.

Getting his family to believe him.

Of all the things he'd done in his life, that, more than anything else, may have been the most difficult to achieve. That fact burrowed through, a burst of emotion getting past all the defenses despite his best efforts to maintain an internal neutrality through everything.

Strangely, though, when he recognized that, everything finally lined up.

Jakob exhaled and nodded at the family members staring at him.

"Well," Kassie said, "that's something you don't see every day."

"Are you all right?" Evie asked, still hovering over the dropped device.

"Because your goddamn eyes are glowing," Kassie added.

"Shao Jakob Human, what is your condition?" the internal monitor said.

"This is Shao Jakob Human. I've escaped capture from the Awakened. I have information vital to the effort passed through a mental transference from" and Jakob uttered a series of grunt and breath sounds to pronounce Henry's native name as accurately as possible. "I believe this may be the advantage we need. This is critical, timely information. I need a pickup at my location as soon as possible."

"Acknowledged. We will send a rescue craft within range of compressed-matter transportation. Your signal is weak and requires boosting. We will attempt to calibrate it further. Remain in contact. We will be monitoring."

"Wait. I have a live tracker implanted in my body that I believe is transmitting to the Awakened fleet with the goal of revealing our location. Please advise on disabling it."

The line went silent, and though fifteen years of combat and field ops had hardened him, the lack of response triggered panic until the voice returned. "Can you confirm the existence of the Awakened tracker?"

"I have X-ray imaging that shows it."

"It is a live device?"

"Pretty sure," he said, a casual tone sneaking into the formal give-and-take with command.

"Find a way to boost your pickup signal. Command will decide how to handle the tracker."

"But..." Jakob examined his family's curious looks as they listened to his half of the conversation: this required some delicate phrasing "...does that put this location at risk?"

Evie's posture tightened. With all her years of being inquisitive, she must have understood coded discussion. He met her eyes and shot a quick smile, hopefully to put her at ease.

"Likely. You must leave quickly. Command will update you. Work on boosting your signal for a lock."

Likely. One word put the weight of his entire home world on his shoulders. Jakob sucked in a breath and decided to *not* reveal that the Awakened were on their way unless he could get off Earth as soon as possible. "Understood." That knowledge wouldn't help anyone right now, and he still needed some way to boost the device in his head among the concrete and electronics of suburbia. Across the garage, his sisters showed a mix of awe and curiosity.

"Let me guess," Kassie said. "Aliens?"

"Yeah," Jakob said with a short laugh. "Aliens."

"Fucking aliens." Kassie shot over a knowing smirk. "Seriously, can you—"

"Language, Kassie."

One by one, the Shao children turned to see Mom standing there, her eyes showing a marked difference. They carried a sharpness in their movement as she looked at each of her adult children. "And Evie," she said as she pointed at her, "what have you done with your hair?"

CHAPTER THIRTY-NINE

EVIE

It was a simple question. Taken out of context, it could have been any parent talking to any child at any stage of their relationship.

This, however, was different.

"My…hair?" Evie asked.

"Your hair. You had such pretty long hair. Now it's all shaved on one side. I…" Mom stopped, then looked around her, turning to Kassie, then to Lucy, then back to Evie. "I can't remember the last time I saw you. And you," she said and stepped forward, "your name is Lucy. How do I know you?"

"Mom?" Kassie said, her eyes wide and locked with Lucy rather than focusing on their mother. "Mom, what's—I mean, I can't…"

Jakob rose from his knees, then rested his hand on her shoulder, only for Mom to sharply inhale. She turned, taking in the complete view of her son, then with a purpose of action that seemed impossible for the fragile woman that needed help with stairs, Mom did the unthinkable.

She hugged Jakob.

Which prompted the impossible: Jakob didn't shrug it off.

He didn't return the hug, though. But on the curve of Jakob Shao responses, a lack of resistance meant something. "This is just…" Mom started before her knees buckled. They stayed in place, though their positions tilted, Jakob clearly supporting both of them.

"Mom!" Kassie yelled, dashing in to grab her other side.

"I'm fine, Kassie," Mom said. "Just a little dizzy. Why is everyone in the garage?"

"I think you should lie down." Kassie waved Lucy over with her free hand. Together, they shifted Mom from Jakob to them and headed to the door. "Let's get you inside." Lucy nudged the door open with her hip, and Evie watched as the three shuffled farther until the door shut behind them, leaving her alone with her brother.

Who was now talking with aliens.

The device was still warm when she picked it up off the floor. She offered it to Jakob, but he was too busy discussing something about *keeping it active* to whoever listened on the other side of the conversation. She set it on the floor, unsure of whether to check in with Kassie, who had gone her whole life without ever asking for support, or to offer help to Jakob, who seemed to be in the middle of a conversation about calibrations. Instead, she chose an alternative and pulled out her phone.

As if on cue, a text icon appeared at the top of the screen. She tapped the message, and the name *Layla* appeared in large characters.

We've been monitoring the FBI activity since you

left the vet hospital. They appear to be circling your neighborhood.

Frye said they'd call if they needed anything. But perhaps she'd given them too much credit to just assume they'd back off and leave them alone, especially if they were still looking for Jakob.

"Evie?" Jakob asked, bringing her back to the moment.

"Huh?"

"Hey. Everything okay?"

Evie glanced back at her screen, then at Jakob, who'd apparently started rummaging through the garage cabinets, the dissected power base of his alien device now in his hand. "Are *you* okay? I know we're all on speaking terms again, but I'm pretty sure Kassie doesn't want you going through her stuff."

"Oh, look," Jakob said, kneeling down at a bottom cabinet. "Kassie's got more tools down here." He held up the device in his hand, squinting at it. "I need to boost my transponder's signal. All the cars and electronics around here don't play nice with long-distance transport."

"Well..." Evie said, reading Layla's message again. *Circling the neighborhood* could mean anything, but the fact that Layla hadn't included any puns left her on edge. "I think," she said slowly, "we need a plan B." Jakob paused while sliding out a box of car stuff and finally turned her way. "The Reds say that the FBI are around. I think if we do anything to draw attention to ourselves, it could be bad."

"We can't give them any reasons to knock on the door. That'll slow us down." Lines formed on Jakob's face, a seriousness so unlike his old self. "Options. We need options. Is it too late for one of you to go to the hardware store? I think a car battery and—"

"Slow down," Evie said, palms out. She glanced at the door

to the house. No sounds came through, which could have been good or bad. "Let's back up. What happens if they can't get a lock on you for transport?"

"Either I don't leave, or they try and it compresses my body to implosion."

The word *implosion* produced a mental image that Evie didn't need and certainly Kassie wouldn't appreciate given the relative cleanliness of the garage. "Okay, so that's bad. What's blocking the accuracy?"

"Atmosphere. Any surrounding electrical activity. A high amount of moving vehicles. Radio signals. Phone signals. High-density materials like concrete. Any combination of those. That's why they recruit from remote spots. Each location requires calibration for pickup. It's not something you usually want to rush if you don't have to." Still squatting in his ridiculous flip-flops and *Reno Is for Winners* T-shirt, Jakob held up the base piece again. "But if I could get some more power out of this, it might do the trick. That can connect to the transponder and—"

"Wait, wait, wait," Evie said, a new idea sparking in her mind. Her voice dropped, the rolling whisper to herself that instinctively broke loose when her train of thought started to connect pieces. "They calibrate for a location's specifics. But if there's interference, they have far more parameters to deal with. They need something faster, something with standardized parameters, something they can do quickly as if they..." She jolted up, enough for Jakob to wince at the movement. "Does your fleet keep historical data for locations and their calibrations?"

"Usually. Yeah." His head tilted, and his lip curled, the inquisitive look that Evie usually associated with one of Jakob's terrible and indulgent ideas, not curiosity about saving the galaxy. "What do you got?"

"Listen. We don't need to boost you here. We need to get you to a place Seven Bells knows they can pick you up." It was just an idea. A place. A geographic location, one that saw countless visitors every year. That was, for everyone except the Shaos. For them, it was the epicenter of the end, the point at which everything fractured and drifted apart.

But for now, it was their last, best hope. Evie walked over to Jakob and knelt down. She took her brother's hand and looked at his still-glowing eyes. "We need to get you to Lake Kinbote."

CHAPTER FORTY

KASS

Lucy presented herself so calmly that it disturbed Kass. Because between the light moans and claims of nausea, Mom asked questions.

Real questions. Like "What is Evie doing here?" and "When did Jakob come home?" Which Lucy responded to with complete chill, as though she handled unexpected fallout from alien technology all the time.

And "Why do you look so worried?" That one was specifically directed at Kass. The tone, the timing, the sheer *directness* of it was unnerving. Because before Mom had devolved into a helpless shell of her former self, she'd always known the right questions to ask.

Even when it stung.

They weren't mean or cruel questions. But they were tough. And necessary. The kind of questions to scribble down on a notepad and ask yourself.

Several years ago, a bright, sunny Saturday afternoon had

seen Mom asking Kass a similar question about another life-shifting change. Kass had pulled into the driveway with birds and lawnmowers as the typical suburban-weekend soundtrack. The kind of snapshot for people going about their day as if nothing might ever collapse.

She had made the walk from the driveway to the front door of the Shao family home countless times. Middle school, high school, college summers, staying after Dad died—and visiting after she'd moved out on her own once Mom felt ready to stand on her own.

How many times? Thousands? Whatever the final total, this time felt longer, more impossible than ever before, like she'd scaled up a never-ending cliff to a point in *The Ancient Runes Online* inaccessible to the player. During that moment, the weight of everything bore down on Kass, leading her to consider never logging into the game again. That was their thing, and *their* didn't exist anymore.

Not after what had happened that morning.

Kass put her key in the door, a key that she'd carried with her since she was twelve years old. The metal no longer held any sheen, edges dulled off the various grooves, but it still worked. No new copy had been necessary despite the years and years of use. The door swung open and Kass stepped in, half anticipating the annoyed pitter-patter of Tiger to come charging forward before recognizing her. But that was a long time ago, and though the mini-schnauzer lived to the remarkable age of eighteen, he'd still been gone by then for several years.

Instead, the house had been empty. Kass dropped her purse to the floor and found her way to the kitchen table, the spring afternoon already starting to dim the room. She sat for an hour, only getting up to brew herself a cup of coffee, resisting the urge to smoke out of respect for Mom's disdain for that habit.

At some point, the familiar sound of the garage door started rumbling, soon followed by the slow entry of a car. Kass checked the expected noises off one by one: first the engine stopping, then the slam of the car door, then the rumble again as the large metal door slid shut.

"Kassie?" Mom called out as soon as she came inside. Mom stopped midstep upon seeing her, still holding the door to the garage open. "Kassie, what's wrong?"

That table had seen so many breakdowns in its lifetime, all of the family arguments before and since Jakob had disappeared. About whether or not he was alive. About Evie's choices. About Dad's death. About something as ridiculous as aliens.

And all the while, Kass had never, ever let herself be shaken by it. She couldn't. She needed to be the foundation while everyone and everything else slid into the sea.

Kass's elbows knocked on the table, propping up her head over the lukewarm cup of coffee. "I fucked up," she finally said, head in her hands.

Breaths passed by, and while in most cases the silence might have felt like scrutiny, here it simply marked the passing of time as Mom gave her enough space to move forward. "We all mess up," Mom finally said, coming over to sit by her. "How bad?"

"I cheated on Desmond."

Cheated made it sound small, insignificant. After all, he'd been in Paris for a year with his residency. Drunk, lonely, stupid, that would have made a little more sense. One night of impulsivity, he might even understand and forgive, given enough time and empathy. But Kass had indulged for several weeks. It wasn't a mistake. It was a conscious betrayal born from discomfort.

Mom stood still, the intensity of her stare bearing down

on Kass while she explained. That look had petrified her as a child, and as a teen it irritated her. In both cases, it was because she knew Mom was right. That applied here too. And the thing was, she had two years of being a licensed professional counselor under her belt. She should know the hows and whys of giving in to impulses. Though, she was also the same person who understood exactly why she smoked cigarettes, from the chemical hit to the physical fixations to the subconscious anticipation, and she still couldn't stop.

The quiet finally broke as Mom walked over to a drawer in the kitchen island. She opened it and grabbed a pad of paper, soon followed by the sound of a scribbling pen. Then a sheet tore off.

And then the paper slid in front of Kass. Two questions, written by hand:

How did you cause this?

How will you fix it?

"We'll get through this. You don't have to answer these now. But soon," she said, tapping the sheet, "you will."

The right questions. Always, the questions to push forward—when Jakob went missing, when Dad returned, when Dad died.

When she personally hit rock bottom.

And now as they tried to help their non-deadbeat brother return to an alien war. Kass responded only with blinking and a forced smile. Mom stared at her, her eyes drilling in with a pressure that threw her off. It took several seconds until it hit her: the reason why the whole thing felt like it came from another lifetime was simply because it *did.* "Hey," Lucy said from several feet behind. She waved Kass over, then spoke with a low voice. "Why don't you go check on your brother and sister?"

"Something's weird," she whispered.

"Yeah," Lucy replied at a similar volume. "I'm not sure what's going on, but I'll keep an eye on your mom. Take a minute to regroup."

Kass told herself to take deep, even breaths as she entered the garage, only to find Jakob and Evie talking about…

Lake Kinbote?

"If we leave now," Evie said as she tapped away on her phone, "we can get to Lake Kinbote in just about three hours. Maybe a little less if we speed—"

"Whoa, whoa, whoa," Kass said, a sudden jump in her step. "No one's going anywhere. Something's weird with Mom."

"I need to get there as soon as possible. The FBI is nearby." Jakob didn't even look at Kass when he spoke, his expression seemingly molded in a serious, unmoving frown. "There's no time—"

"Did you two hear me? Something's weird with Mom. She's like…" The right description eluded her. How could she sum up this strange mix of fear, curiosity, and wonder? "It's almost like she's…present." Evie's gasp didn't stop Jakob, who took her phone and tapped at a map. "Damn it, Jakob, are you even listening?"

"We have to go now. I need you to drive me. Or I need your car."

"Hey," Evie said, hands up in full peacemaker mode. "What if we just wait a little bit until the FBI go away? Layla can keep me updated—"

"We can't do that," Jakob said.

"Goddamn it, Jakob, listen to me. Something is very weird with Mom. I know you're this space-hero guy, but this is what's important to me." She paused, something about Jakob's even demeanor causing a spike of uncontrollable venom. "And *none* of you have cared about her since Dad died."

The last accusation flew out, bursting beyond Kass's normal boundaries. It punched hard enough to stop her siblings cold, and while she knew on a practical level that such a generalization wasn't necessarily true, it was still an honest statement. Because Kass had *felt* that way for years, and that singular emotion was authentic.

"Kassie," Jakob said, calm returning to his voice. "Evie. I need you to understand something. And I didn't want to scare you, but this tracker in my head—the Awakened sense it. Their closest ship is on its way. They *shouldn't* have arrived here for decades, maybe centuries, enough time for the Seven Bells to stop them. But unless I leave as soon as possible, that might change. The Earth is in danger. We have to go now. Which means we have to get past the FBI."

"Crystallization," Evie whispered.

"Yeah. And the Awakened are merciless. Relentless. This is life-and-death. If you care about Mom, if you care about anyone, you'll help me find a way there. Look, Command has just given me orders. Keep the tracker active, use it to lure the Awakened into range—but away from Earth. *Then* use the intel I got from Henry. Everything depends on getting to Lake Kinbote."

This was the most serious Kass had ever seen her brother, and it unnerved her just as much as Mom's situation, but in a completely different way. "Okay," she finally said. "You two go. Take my car. But if you cause the FBI to—"

"We won't alert the FBI. Come on, Kassie, I've evaded Awakened strike teams. You think I don't know how to be stealthy?"

Given the stakes here, both personally and galactically, she knew she *shouldn't* argue, but at the same time, butting heads with him came more naturally than working with him.

He probably felt the same way.

"Are you going to end everything with 'me big soldier

man' now?" Kass said with more irritation than necessary. Evie opened her mouth to say something, but Kass jumped in further before that could happen. "Because that is really fucking annoying."

"Hey, you two—" Evie started.

"All I'm saying is that I can figure out a way past the FBI."

"You've been waiting to be the smart one, huh? Dude, you are gloating."

"Hey," Evie tried again. "Listen—"

"No, Kassie, I don't need you—"

"Will you two *shut up*?" Evie yelled, so loud that even Jakob looked startled. "I swear, my entire life, no one in this family has ever let me get a word in. Just be quiet for a second." Silence finally filled the room. "The Reds are able to ping Frye's location and intercept the police band. If we work together, we can get out of here. And get to Lake Kinbote. But you'll need to, you know, actually freaking listen to me."

"What's all this yelling in here?" Kass turned to find Mom standing in the doorway, arms crossed in full-authority mode before stepping forward to confront her gaping children. "I feel like I'm waking up from some fever dream, and all this noise isn't helping."

"Kass." Lucy barged in as well, holding a glass of water that probably was meant for Mom. "Sofia is…lucid."

"Of course I am," Mom said before anyone could retort. "I'm just nauseous. Now, will someone explain why in the world you're talking about Lake Kinbote? It's a terrible place."

Kass remembered a study on electrical activity in the brain, something about how electrical stimulation via a TENS unit or a similar medical device was theorized to help temporarily restore neural pathways associated with dementia. The study proved inconclusive, but the general idea seemed to support Evie's hypothesis that the blast radius of Jakob's power restoration had also boosted Mom's brain. Kass didn't bother to question it: if she could believe her idiot brother was now going to save the galaxy—in addition to being some sort of engineer—well, she might as well just accept everything else too.

Over the course of ten minutes, while Evie jotted down notes from her UFO buddies, Kass and Jakob filled Mom in on as many of the impossibilities as time allowed: Jakob wasn't just back, he had been abducted like Dad had suspected; Jakob wasn't just fighting in a war, he fixed stuff too; Jakob wasn't just trying to get back, he might win the war.

Somehow Mom took it all in stride, her only question being "Will my brain stay this way?" Which they didn't know. And because of that, Mom suggested that they *all* go to Lake Kinbote. As a family.

More like insisted, really.

Kass watched as Mom walked Lucy to the door, an inverse of how Lucy usually guided her. "I don't know how long this will last," she said, her voice carrying so much strength, "so I want to be with my family for as long as possible."

And even from the dining room, Kass could tell that Lucy responded with a hug. "Take care of yourself, Sofia."

"Look at Evie," Jakob said, nudging his twin. Kass turned to see Evie with laptop and tablet up while holding her phone on a video call with several people.

"She's in her element," Kass said. Evie's laptop flashed, half the screen showing a live-video feed of a local street and the other a constant flow of text. "Who knew she could be like this?"

"I did," Jakob said, his response reflexively quick.

Always the contrarian. "Shut up."

"I'm serious," he said, with his usual defiance, but a soft tone woven in. "She's always been capable. And strong. How else could she defy you and Mom like she did? You just never listened to her, so you missed it all."

Her brother's words sank in, and two truths surfaced. First, Jakob was right. Evie had always been her annoying little sister slotting into evolving roles relative to her own life: the one who couldn't keep up, the one who just made things more difficult, the Goody Two-shoes, and the one who ran away.

Second, a very small, very microscopic part of herself was jealous of how this dynamic didn't exist between Jakob and Evie. Their own identities may have evolved, but their relationship didn't fluctuate.

She opened her mouth to respond, but then Evie stood up and approached. "Okay. We're all coordinated. It's gonna be, like, super exact. So I need everyone to follow my instructions. Where's Mom?"

"She's saying bye to Lucy," Jakob said.

"Let's get her ready."

"On it." Jakob turned and disappeared down the hallway.

She offered Kass her tablet. "Team effort. You should leave your phone here too, in case Frye is tracking it. Mine is running through a VPN, but they can still ping the GPS. I need it, though, so we'll deal."

Kass looked at her sister and the unusual way she suddenly took charge.

She hated when Jakob was right. "Okay," Kass said, taking the tablet. "Lead the way."

CHAPTER FORTY-ONE

JAKOB

One in eight hundred and seventy-four.

Those were the odds of victory. If the Seven Bells got to him in time.

The Awakened used eight hundred and seventy-four possible frequencies of sixteen digits each for their specialized fleetwide communications, rotated through an entire cycle at random every forty-two minutes and thirteen seconds. Every single vessel and terminal across their armada used this to stay completely in sync. *How* they managed to handle that sort of real-time synchronization was something that mystified even the brainiest of Seven Bells engineers. Eight hundred and seventy-four frequencies seemed low given the scope of the Awakened's technological capabilities, but perhaps that was the reason in itself—feasibly reaching that many ships may have limited the transmission size of the frequency, and random variability in addition to the number of digits made it impossible to crack. Jakob didn't consider himself among their elite engineers—he wouldn't have been in the field if he were that valuable, but there were many restless hours when sleep refused to come because his mind tried to solve that mystery.

Turned out, it didn't matter. Of all of the things Jakob had gleaned from his experience, *this* was the most vital. Eight hundred and seventy-four possible frequencies, and Jakob knew one of them—a sixteen-number sequence that Henry had seared into his mind.

One big number was the back door to saving the galaxy.

And thanks to his family, they had a chance.

Evie's plan worked, executed with a precision that mirrored some of his best operations with the Seven Bells. She stayed on the phone coordinating in real time with Layla—including stifling her laughs when Layla inserted the occasional pun. In the back seat, Jakob sat with Mom, monitoring an incoming feed of local movement sent by another one of the Reds. Kassie drove, Evie's tablet on her lap showing very specific directions updated in real time to get them onto the highway in relative safety.

And Mom, she didn't say a word. Changed from her slippers and robe to a jeans-and-sweater set she hadn't worn in several years, she simply watched her children collaborate in a way that probably felt stranger than waking from dementia, at least until they'd gone about thirty minutes on the highway.

"Okay," Evie said. "Layla will keep me updated by text. We should shut down the other devices to save battery." Jakob closed the computer on his lap, and Kassie handed the tablet over her shoulder to him.

The clock was ticking. Everything he'd fought for, bled for, suffered for since joining the Seven Bells was within reach. Two hours to go until a rescue ship would be in orbit and capable of transporting him up. And about three hours to get to Lake Kinbote by his estimate. "Can you go any faster?"

"Not unless you wanna alert highway patrol," Kassie said. "Funny how I still remember the exact way there."

"The hardest thing to believe of all of this is how responsible you are, Jakob." Mom reached over and patted the top of his hand, but the sharpness of her tone brought an instinctive cringe, triggering a chain reaction in the car.

Kassie laughed. Of course she would laugh at that. Evie laughed too, a little softer. He even laughed as well: his checkered past of poor attendance and failed promises hadn't exactly made him the model of punctuality or reliability.

It still stung. He'd faced down an armada of Awakened drone ships and rescued half-dead alien brethren from the surface of large asteroids in near-zero-G circumstances, and none of that hit the same way as his mother's comments.

He'd never admit it, though. Every instinct in his core tightened, covered up, deflected, the way they had every day growing up.

Or did they? Jakob looked around, a sudden awareness that the most unlikely of scenarios unfolded before him. Was it the fact that they were in a car together?

No, it was the fact that they were all on speaking terms. And being honest.

"I'm a little better at things now," he said. From the back seat, he looked ahead, catching the rearview mirror where he met his own eyes.

A faint light glowed from them. In sci-fi movies, they would have been a bright green, glowing the way cat eyes did, reflecting a flashlight at night. But here, it was more subtle, a pinch of color showing just enough luminescence to be picked out from a crowd. Compared to fiction, his life was a little less glamorous, a little less flashy, yet much more violent and filled with far more wonder. The things he'd seen and experienced, they'd delivered so far beyond what he could explain or imagine that those events just kind of *existed* in his mind. Even now, reconciling his old mundane life and his current adventures seemed impossible.

Kassie would probably recommend talking to a therapist. "I'm not that person anymore. I've chosen to do better," Jakob said.

"I can see that." Mom turned to him, and despite her gentle tone, Jakob instinctively looked away. "I'm proud of you." He *still* looked away, the uncertainty of how to react to praise catching him in a lurch. His commanders praised him, which was all part of daily life on the battlefield of space. This, though, was different. "I probably didn't say that enough when you were growing up, did I?"

The old Jakob Shao facade refused to appear, despite his best attempts to force it into existence. No charm. No smirk. He remained still, unable to respond to such a personal question.

And it wasn't just him. Evie looked down, the wind seemingly taken out of her sails. And Kassie watched the road a little too closely, fingers tightly gripped on the wheel as the car pushed forward.

They felt this too.

"I could have listened more too," he finally pushed out.

"There's something that I still don't understand," Mom said. Jakob prepared himself for the same deep dive he'd given Evie about the Seven Bells, their technology, the war, all of that. He owed her that too, despite having already explained it to his sisters. He should have made a list for the family when he'd had access to Kassie's computer; it'd be faster that way.

"What's that, Mom?" His reply came in a soft voice, different from his disciplined-soldier demeanor.

"This has been really lovely. It feels like a dream, but not." Any other person would have said such a thing with whimsy. But Mom presented the thought with self-aware bite, and it finally dawned on Jakob after all these years: he understood where Kassie got her attitude from. "Part of me still wonders if it is."

How had he never seen that before?

"I am definitely here driving," Kassie said.

Mom adjusted in her seat as passing lights flashed across her. "Everything makes sense, as much as it can. But no one has told me yet: Why are my children running from the FBI?"

"There was a video," Evie said, her tone suddenly more pointed, as if she'd finally been granted permission to speak.

"Yeah, Jakob," Kassie said, hitting the blinker to change lanes around an RV. "You were here before. You wanna tell us about that?" A thick tension assumed the space between family members, and though she continued to watch the road, Kassie's eyes in the rearview continuously checked on him. "Look, Evie and I are being chased by the FBI too. It'd be nice to know why. So what's up with the domestic terrorism, Jakob?"

"It wasn't terrorism," he said quietly. "It was a supply run."

"Frye showed us the video from Upstate New York. Why'd you blow up the lab? There were weird symbols there."

Jakob launched into a very detailed, very mechanical, very *soldier* explanation about certain materials and chemicals that were needed, scans identifying a location as they flew by Earth, and a plan to get in and out of a research facility in New York specializing in fuel-cell technology. He'd done the same type of transport to get to the surface, waited in a stakeout for half a day, then broken into the facility to tag the necessary materials for ship-out. To eliminate any trace transport signatures, they blew up a section of the facility. He'd burned the symbols in concrete simply as an indicator that the materials had gotten out safely, in case something happened to him before getting back to the fleet.

"It was communication. Not a terrorist threat," Jakob finished matter-of-factly, as if he were giving a debriefing.

"So wait," Kassie said. "You were here for a few hours before you did anything. And you didn't think to call us? Like a public phone or a desk at the facility or *something* to tell us you were still alive?"

"I was on a mission."

"Five minutes." Evie's voice rose to a level that she'd normally save just for Kassie. She'd probably used that tone for Jakob at one point or another, but he couldn't recall ever hearing it. "Five minutes," Evie continued. "You're just sitting there waiting, and during that time you couldn't have left a voice mail? I live like an hour from there. Did you even know that?"

"I needed to focus. I was on a mission. I had to stay stealthy."

"And you never thought of saying something? Calling?" Evie asked. "I mean, if you're just swinging by Earth every few months, you wanna say hello?"

"It's not that simple. Don't you see? If we stay anywhere too long, the Awakened will pursue. Every hour counts," Jakob said, abruptly stopping before his tone became quiet. "We don't have a choice. No government or resources, just a chain of command and hope. We're trying to survive. You need to focus. No outside distractions and no—"

"So you're saying you just forgot?" Kass said, in a tone probably never used with one of her patients. "Like, 'No big deal, I totally have the chance to put a big Band-Aid over the wound I inflicted, but it's cool.'"

"You don't get it." An exasperated sigh escaped Jakob. How could he explain, truly convey, what life was like out there? If only he had Henry's mental-transference abilities. "Everything here is so small, you don't understand what's at stake."
Evie didn't ask any further questions.

He glanced at Mom, who had a scowl taking over her face, one that probably meant she wondered what the hell she'd gotten herself into.

CHAPTER FORTY-TWO

EVIE

A good thirty minutes had passed, and though Evie wanted to ask more—Jakob could transport across light-years and yet he couldn't send some sort of intergalactic email?—she, like the rest of her family, stayed quiet.

"Okay, this is getting ridiculous," Kassie said. "We're all together and not saying anything. There's a notepad in the glove box. Grab it and pens. Three pens."

Evie didn't always appreciate her sister's blunt demeanor, but she'd use it to her advantage this time. Though she wasn't sure where this was heading. Were they going to duel it out with pens? "Okay…"

"Right, so let's just cut the bullshit. This is something I do with families when they're at a stalemate." She glanced over her shoulder and shot a look at Mom, though Evie wasn't sure why. "Doesn't it seem like this family needs therapy? Everyone take one sheet and one pen and write one question down. It can be to one of us or everyone in general."

"I think we've got bigger things to worry about," Jakob said.

"No excuses, Jakob," Kassie said. "We're helping you right now, so you owe us. And Mom is..." She stopped, and though she probably didn't want any of them to see it, Evie caught her expression breaking. Kassie closed her eyes, a quick move that seemed to recenter herself while maintaining driver safety, then she started again. "Mom is here. We don't know for how long. Something is going to happen when we get to Lake Kinbote. I mean, maybe Frye is waiting and takes us all to jail. So yeah, there's some galaxy war happening way far away, but you know what? We are stuck together. And this may never happen again. So screw the Awoken."

"Awakened," Jakob and Evie said at the same time.

"Whatever. They're not in this car right now, so we're sorting this out."

Another motion came from the back, this time the silhouette of Mom nodding in reply. She reached an outstretched hand, waiting until Evie put the pen and paper into her grasp. Jakob sighed, then did the same. A blank, torn sheet stared back at Evie, and she removed the pen cap.

"Where's your sheet, Kassie?" Jakob asked.

"I'm driving. Seems to be a higher priority. So write down any question you have for someone in here. Even if it's, like, *Why did you lie about sneaking into my room when we were kids?* One minute, don't overthink it."

"You give this bedside manner to your patients?" Evie asked.

"Pretty sure none of you are paying me."

"I still have those debit cards." Quiet laughs and snickers filled the car, and though Kassie may have thought it—Evie certainly did—no one mentioned that that money was stolen from Mom.

No need to pile things on right now.

"Okay, pass your sheet to the person on your right. Jakob, you read it out loud first."

The paper crinkled as he adjusted, and Evie looked straight ahead, a flush coming to her cheeks, the nakedness of the moment suddenly overwhelming her. She pulled on her seat-belt strap and awaited the inevitable.

"Jakob: Why did you stay away?" he read aloud. He sighed, and while Evie tried to avoid applying too much meaning to that single gesture, it still infuriated her. "I explained this. I am fighting a war."

"I have a retort to that," Kassie said. "But I'm trying to stay objective here."

"Are you saying…" Mom said. The mere start of her words ratcheted the friction in the air. "You never wondered what your leaving did to us?"

"I mean, of course I did."

"You couldn't have." Evie didn't mean to spit out her reply, but there it was. And in her head, it came with images of Dad—freezing at Lake Kinbote, tinkering in the garage, staring at his computer screen. "You tell us you have this technology to transport down. The thing in your head that lets you talk to your fleet. You could have let us know somehow. A phone call, an email, a letter. Not, like, a Thanksgiving visit. But something. A note. A voice mail. All this time." Thoughts started to undam, all this time, all those hours and days and years while Evie carried Dad's promise forward. "So we can be whole again," she had told Kassie at the airport, but it was clear that hadn't been possible. Jakob's return was a single piece of the puzzle—the corner piece that everything else built from. But their family needed so much more. "You were on Earth for an entire day, and you had time to blow something up but not make a phone call?"

Jakob looked out the window, leaving the car in another silence. For the first time since he'd come back, Evie really, really, really wanted to punch him, and not just playfully on the shoulder.

"Keep going," Kassie said. "Mom, what does Jakob's paper say?"

"It's blank."

"Damn it, Jakob," Kassie said with a groan. "This only works if everyone's on board."

"I'm on board. I just don't have anything to say."

"Okay, look. This whole stoic-soldier thing is really irritating. Is this really what we're doing?" Evie was *so* glad that her big sister felt the same level of irritation as she did. Or maybe it was the other way around: maybe Evie finally matched Kassie's lifetime of irritation at Jakob. Some of that was unfounded or petty sibling stuff, yeah. But a lot of it wasn't. "Okay, fine. Evie, what does your paper say?"

Evie opened the folded sheet from Mom, a single crease across the center. What she saw sparked a grin that refused to be contained.

"What did I miss?" Evie asked, her cheeks bright. But the question itself didn't prompt her smile, it was the quick sketch next to it: floppy ears, sharp eyes, and the scruffy beard of a mini-schnauzer.

Had Mom missed anything? World events happened, things that had dominated the news for days, weeks, sometimes months on end, sometimes changing the way the world turned. Those shifts had happened while Mom's mind lived in a different time and space. But for the state of their family, the needle had barely moved.

Kassie stayed on one side of the country. Evie stayed on the other.

The only difference now was that they knew about Jakob. And Mom was around for that.

"A lot has happened in the last few years. But really, not too much. Not for us, at least."

The weight of Kassie's look pulled Evie into her sister's gravity. Though it was just a flash—eyes on the road, after all—Kassie offered more connection, more approval, more *sisterhood* than perhaps she ever had.

"I was going to say 'You missed a bunch of fucked-up stuff,'" Kassie said with a laugh. "But Evie was a little more thoughtful."

"Thanks," Evie said, unsure of how to take it.

"I mean it. This is the time in a session where I tell a patient 'That was very insightful.'" The car veered as they navigated a turn, then a wide interchange ramp that rose high before returning to ground level. "You're right. We're like the eye of a hurricane. Everything whirled around us, but we stayed the same." Kassie's lips twisted in a way that she probably didn't do with patients. "Every time Evie reached out, I just rolled my eyes and ignored it."

"To be fair," Evie said with a weary smile, "I was usually asking for money."

"See? Nothing changed. But that was kind of our own fault."

Evie chose to stay silent. Not out of awkwardness, not out of frustration, not out of petty spite. But a conscious decision to let that simple truth settle in. Kassie was right. They took their own paths outward since Jakob disappeared and just stayed on that course regardless of the festering wound between them, between *all* of them.

"I own part of that too," Mom said. "I'm sorry."

Evie sat up. Had she ever heard Mom apologize for anything before? It must have happened at some point in her life—if not her life, then Kassie's. But for all the practical advice Mom gave whenever she actually decided to chime in, it always seemed to come with a caveat of moving forward as fast as possible. Even if that meant leaving the rubble still smoking.

"This is good," Kassie said, her voice just above a whisper before returning to its normal strength. "Anything to add, Jakob?"

"No. Not really."

"It fig—" Kassie started, but Jakob cut her off.

"I'm just impressed with you two. That's all. You were both always smarter than me."

Evie shot a look at Kassie, who took her eyes off the road just long enough to meet them. *There* it was. Finally, Jakob's shell broke. He'd probably never give in to a full-hearted apology, opening up and baring his soul in a teary monologue. But he didn't need to. Evie saw it clearly now, and maybe Kassie already had, given her professional training and everything.

They didn't want any of that from Jakob. They just wanted a moment of honesty from him.

"Evie?" Kassie asked after several seconds, her grinning cheeks visible from her side profile. "Did we just get complimented by a *space hero*?"

"He's more than that," Evie said, choosing her words carefully. "He's an engineer too."

The Shaos had never excelled at emotions. No professing of family love, bright smiles, weepy eyes. There were grins at Evie's punch line, a change in the air from each of them. But things fell back to silence quickly. The difference, it seemed, was that *this* silence had finally become comfortable.

That was how their family worked.

"You three are agreeing on something. I see I woke up at just the right time," Mom said after a few minutes. Evie glanced back to see Mom looking like *Mom*, the way she was and always should be. "So now can someone tell me if the world really was that bad while I was out?"

The mood in the car wasn't exactly cheery over the next twenty or thirty minutes—it was hard to be chipper when discussing the strange way the world had devolved before, during, and after 2020—but it provided a conduit for conversation between the Shao family. Even Jakob asked questions, and no matter how much he'd seen in space-fighting aliens, he kept repeating, "I can't believe that."

But the real world had found a way to course-correct, to heal, scars and all, to return patchworked and duct-taped back together. And weirdly enough, simply explaining what had happened to two people who hadn't experienced it somehow brought the Shaos together. Not perfectly, not necessarily at peace, and far from roses and rainbows, but somehow better than when they'd got in the car.

For one second, Evie heard it: the sound of all four of them laughing at the same time. Kassie's exercise didn't really bring about many answers, but it brought them this. And that was good enough for now.

Things settled down in the car, and Evie pulled out her phone to check the time. The screen came to life, first her background screen of a time-lapsed arc of stars in the sky, then a series of icons across the top.

One—no, *four* texts. Three from Layla, all without puns, and one from Edward. Evie's eyes widened as she read the messages, all warnings. Including the latest message that Layla had just sent: Seriously, they're closing in on you. Why aren't you answering?

The whole being-a-family thing had distracted her from the whole chased-by-the-FBI thing.

"I hate to break the mood," Evie said, "but the FBI is back on our tail."

CHAPTER FORTY-THREE

KASS

Jakob was the space hero who boarded ships and fought aliens and stuff. And Evie was someone who talked with enough paranoid people that she probably had an escape plan for every situation.

Kass, however, was just a therapist. So she'd accomplished the hardest task of Jakob's quest. She'd got everyone to talk to each other.

Which was good because, on the other hand, Jakob and Evie were pretty sure that their car was being tailed, and they needed a solution. "Are you sure?" Kass asked.

"That's gotta be them," Evie said, looking at her phone's call log. Apparently Frye had also tried calling several times while they lost signal in the hills. "It's five cars back. Every time we've changed lanes or taken an interchange, they've followed."

"Why don't they just turn the lights on and arrest us?"

"Maybe they think I'm a danger," Jakob said.

"That's true." Evie nodded in the dark. "Like, they might think Jakob took us hostage, and they're worried about aggravating him. So we should go but build some distance. Lake Kinbote is only a few miles away. Wait," Evie said, looking at her map. "This upcoming exit has three off-ramps. North interchange, south interchange, local highway. Maybe we take a roundabout way?"

A roundabout way. Kass had discovered a few of those for Lake Kinbote years ago. But something better sprang to mind.

Even in *The Ancient Runes Online*, Kass wasn't particularly heroic. Aveline was a rogue, mostly stealthing undercover and pickpocketing from unsuspecting characters. Which meant she *did* know how to escape from a tight situation, like when lava beasts chased her as a cave collapsed. Except here, Desmond wouldn't be around to cast a healing spell or give a pep talk afterward.

Maybe someday he would. At least the pep-talk part. That would just involve a little more honesty, a little less sarcasm on her part. If she could get her family to talk, anything was possible.

But first things first: she had to lose the FBI.

"Everyone?" she yelled, the whole being-chased-on-a-highway thing ratcheting up her nerves more than expected.

"Yeah?" Evie asked, answering for the family.

Kass's eyes scanned ahead, then at the bright lights in the rearview that Evie tagged to be Frye or highway patrol or *someone*. She knew this exit, knew the area around it, knew that Lake Kinbote lay about five miles away. Because she had something better than a GPS.

She had the experience of a rebellious teen.

The first exit was the north interchange. The second was the south. The third went to a two-lane rural road that disappeared into the woods and veered around various acres of farmland.

That was the goal. Kass just had to make sure they weren't followed.

"I'm gonna do something stupid," Kass said, eyeing the eighteen-wheeler in front of them. From above, the sign showed a half mile to the junction. She moved casually into the center lane. "Keep an eye out."

"That car moved too."

Did experience with a keyboard and mouse apply to this situation? Probably not, but oh well.

The car gained on the big rig, first pulling alongside, then getting just ahead of it. Kass waited until the junction was in sight, then jolted forward, Evie grunting audibly as her head smacked into the headrest. One sharp swerve moved them in front of the massive truck, then she shut off the headlights and went over the sleeper lines into the junction.

"Kassie!" Evie yelled.

At the first exit, she started to pull into the off-ramp before veering back at the last second. The accelerator on her mid-priced, gas-efficient car roared with what strength it had, then they jolted forward to the final exit. The car descended the ramp, then Kass hit her right-turn signal before turning left. Lines of crops passed by on either side as they hurtled past farmlands in near dark, then she took another turn at the first intersection to go deeper into rural territory.

"Are they still tailing us? Anyone?" Kassie asked, her heart rate much faster than she'd prefer.

"I don't see any lights," Jakob said. "But I wouldn't slow down."

"Shut off your phone, Evie. Just in case. Tell the Reds we're going off-line."

"What about the map? It's pitch-black. Don't you need to

know where to go?" Panic tinted Evie's voice in a way that she'd never heard before—not in the melancholy fear the last time they were here years ago but with a legit *Oh shit, we're dodging the cops* urgency.

"Nah," she said, going far faster than she should have down the thin road. At the next intersection, she turned left, circling around a large mill standing on the corner of the property. "This is the long way to Lake Kinbote. Mom, you know when you'd send me out to get groceries for camping?"

"I remember," Mom said, her voice emerging from the back seat.

"See, it all paid off. This is the way I'd go so I could stop and smoke without anyone knowing. Everyone just keep an eye out for signs of Frye. I know how to get there." They moved through unlit paths, shadows whipping by them under a thin moonbeam and twinkling lights from sleepy houses set back on farmland. "Come on," she said, reaching over to the passenger seat to nudge Evie, "those were some pretty cool moves back there, right?"

Most of the next ten minutes unrolled in silence, though Jakob broke it by mumbling to himself before speaking up. "They're ready," Jakob said. "I just checked. They're in orbit. We just need to get to the lake. They're adjusting the calibrations for tonight's weather."

"Great. No pressure, am I right?" Kass said, barreling through a rare red light.

"Kassie, be careful," Mom said. "They probably have cameras on those."

"I mean, we're harboring a domestic terrorist. Running a red is probably okay."

"She's got a point, Mom," Evie said.

Besides, Kass knew exactly where to go, the turns coming like muscle memory. The hills, the farmland, the long stretches of nothing—they'd been a quiet respite amid the chaos of those trips. Back then, three teens got locked together in a small space while Mom and Dad tried to get the portable grill working. Evie usually went off with headphones and a book, Kass looked for hiking trails, and Jakob, he probably had been sneaking pills on those trips since they were sixteen or seventeen.

But their choice of activity didn't matter. Just being in proximity meant bumping into each other at every turn, until Kass had a reason to head out. Pretending to get lost only gave extra time to sit and smoke in peace before taking the exact route back.

Just like then, Kass sped down the flat straight two-way road, knowing exactly how to get to the entrance to Lake Kinbote camping ground because she'd memorized the route when driving from there. They hit a peak, pausing at the top of a hill, and Kass turned the headlights on low for the final stretch. "We're almost there. So everyone else figure out a plan for what happens next."

CHAPTER FORTY-FOUR

EVIE

They parked about fifty feet from the hiking path that led to Lake Kinbote, getting out at nearly the same spot where Evie and Kassie had sat when Jakob and Dad decided to go on their walk fifteen years ago. "My phone's on and connected," Evie said. "Now what?"

They did all that work—and Kassie's ridiculous stunt driving—just to wind up calling Frye directly. But that extra time proved to be enough to put together a plan. Granted, it wasn't much of one outside of *Everyone pretend Jakob kidnapped us*, but still, that required a bit of a setup.

"Text her," Kassie said. "Tell her the alibi. That'll bring her to you."

Evie pulled out her phone and started the text when she realized something quite strange.

She did it without arguing with Kassie. And it wasn't begrudging submission to her older sister, not the stifled urge to retort, not even a second glance. Here they were, working together to avoid the FBI and go to an alien pickup location. Not exactly family barbecues and trips to wine country, and they were several levels below being a well-oiled machine, but this was good enough.

And good enough may have been the greatest miracle of the past few days.

"There," she said after finishing the text, flashing the message she just wrote.

Jakob is dangerous. He ran off with my family. I got away. Meet me at Lake Kinbote entrance. Please come alone. He can't notice any big groups or noise.

She held the phone out and took a photo of the sign overhead before sending that to Frye as well. "Is that it?"

"We'll do this carefully," Jakob said. "This FBI agent needs to see enough to believe you two. I don't want you getting arrested on my behalf. We should go."

We should go. Just like that, something dawned on her when she looked at Jakob. His eyes still had the faint glow in them, and his demeanor had a certain grace.

Dad should have been there to see it.

"Okay, then. Go save the galaxy. But when you get back, maybe we can eat at Kosmos *without* arguing with each other the whole time." The image of the terrified waiter trying to navigate that morning's awkwardness flashed in Evie's mind, causing her to laugh and shake her head. Several seconds passed before she realized that the rest of her family didn't laugh. And it wasn't like she'd told one of Layla's groan-inducing puns. She'd offered a legit bit of levity for whenever they saw each other again—

Unless…

"You *are* coming back, right?"

In the dim light, Jakob only mustered a shrug. "Evie," he said after a pause.

"I mean, like, maybe in a while. And hey, I don't want to jinx your plan. So, you know, *assuming* things go well and you get everything to shut down and bring peace to the galaxy and all that stuff, then we'll see you."

Jakob looked down, the angle of his gaze hiding the glow in his eyes.

"We shouldn't hold him up," Mom said quietly. "Frye might be here soon."

"Frye can wait," Evie spit out. Her whole life she'd been deliberate and understanding, but of all the opportunities to fight back, melt down, be irrational, this seemed like the right one. "You're coming back. Why wouldn't you come back? We're right here."

"Even if this works exactly as planned, there's a lot to do afterward. This only disables their command. At best we can send a self-destruct to their fleet, but they're *everywhere.* We have to eliminate the threat before the Awakened can regroup. We have to rebuild so many civilizations. We need to—" Jakob stopped, and it was his turn to laugh to himself, shooting a glance at Mom. But his tone was much quieter, much more self-aware. "Fix it," he said, returning to Evie.

"But, I mean…" Excuses of all kinds flooded Evie's mind, each one coming with greater desperation than the last. "Don't you think you've earned a break? You don't have to do everything yourself. Like, you've done your part. Aren't there teams to do the rest? I'd imagine that every system you liberate would all be up and ready to go take care of what—"

"Fallout of this magnitude requires hard work. There's no time for vacations. Not for a long time. And…" Jakob's voice faded, his hands planting a gentle weight on her shoulders "…I belong there. It's who I am. But at least I *am* something now."

"Yeah, I mean—" Kassie's sharp words came in a gentle tone "—we've waited forever for him to get his shit together."

"That's gotta count for something." Jakob looked behind him toward Lake Kinbote. "I need to go." He locked eyes with Evie, the otherworldly glow behind them conveying much more than the simple things he said. "The ship will be ready for me any minute now."

It sank in: Jakob's devotion to a just cause and how fulfilling that must be. The most carefree, flaky person in the world was now the most dedicated, diligent person in the galaxy. And that was a little bigger than a family meal, no matter how much she wanted it.

She chose *not* to hug him—she'd already overplayed that hand when he'd arrived at the Shao house. But something had to happen, something to endcap the surreal nature of the last few days. Yet every second that ticked by meant one less for Jakob to get away, and deep down, Evie knew *that* should be the priority. It felt somewhat appropriate: nothing about their family fell into the category of easy, so their farewell shouldn't either. Evie smiled as a better idea came to mind, quick and simple.

A moment captured in time.

"Wait. Everyone scrunch together." Evie held her phone up once again, this time in Selfie mode. "We need at least one, right?"

"What if Frye searches your phone?" Kassie asked.

Always *so* difficult. Right, but still difficult.

"I'll upload it to my secure storage and then delete it from my phone. Please," she said, her voice cracking in a way that jammed together equal parts begging and anxiety. "We don't have much time."

They huddled, Mom in the front, Jakob and Kassie behind,

and Evie bunched up in the middle with arms extended. "Everyone say *Fucking aliens*," Kassie said.

Which they did. Despite the swearing. Even Mom.

Even Evie.

"Evie, I—" Jakob started.

"Just go. You have to hurry. I have this," she said, tapping away at her phone. Even on a slightly off-center selfie, Jakob's eyes glowed.

Proof.

"Look, it's saving." A bright green checkmark appeared on her phone, indicating the upload completed. "That's all I need. Get going," she said, punching her brother in the shoulder, "space hero."

Evie watched her family start up the path to the lake, though a few steps in, Jakob leaned over and said something to Mom. Even from where Evie stood, she could see Kassie's smirk and nod at whatever Jakob had suggested. Jakob reached over and picked up Mom, her feet dangling as her son carried her like a bride across the threshold.

Small clouds of dust kicked up as Jakob trotted forward. Kassie turned and locked eyes with Evie, giving a thumbs-up and a shrug before following suit.

Somewhere, Frye was inching closer, step-by-step.

A breeze rushed through the surrounding trees, tickling Evie's cheeks. She wanted to look at her phone, at the photo they'd just captured—the sliver in time and space when their family came together in the most impossible way. That could wait. For now, she had a part to play.

Instead, she scrolled through various messages from the Reds, though she paused at the one from Layla.

This is all some wild shit. Please tell me you're doing okay.

Evie *almost* sent the family selfie in response. Almost. The discipline she used in school, in crunching data, in her whole *life* really, took over at this most critical time.

Things are under control. Catch up later.

The Sent icon appeared and vanished just as quickly, and as a gust of wind kicked up, an impulse told Evie to add one more thing.

I'm surprised you didn't make a science pun, but I guess you only do that periodically.

It could've used some work, but it was her first try at a Layla-style pun. Evie gave herself a pass on that.

Sorry, Layla replied almost instantly.

I would have included a good chemistry joke, but all the best ones Argon.

Evie pictured Layla's smirk as she wrote that really terrible joke, and she wondered if they should try talking about something *other* than aliens sometime. The thought lingered as clouds rolled in front of the moon, only bursts of wind and the rustling of leaves to keep her company.

Several minutes later, a car rolled up, its bright headlights blinding Evie. Should she put her hands up? She wasn't a criminal, was she? Not, like, a fugitive, not an ex-con on the loose, but someone who got the FBI and local police out here in the middle of the night.

"Hey!" she yelled to Frye. "We need help! Follow me."

Frye trotted over, the headlights replaced by her single flashlight beam. "Are you all right?" she asked, and Evie got the slightest twinge of guilt for the deception. Acting or any form of lying was never Evie's strong suit; instead she forced out words that counted as truths.

Somehow, that made them easier to say.

"Jakob went to the lake. Where our dad died. He took Mom and Kassie. Kassie called it *delusions of grandeur.*" She turned her face, looking up the path—more importantly, away from Frye as she said the next fib. "I got away and ran until I got phone reception."

"We weren't far behind," Frye said. "Your phone kept pinging in and out, so we had to guess where you were going. We almost lost you on the highway." Evie made a mental note to compliment Kassie on her roundabout navigation getting the job done, though that got jarred from her mind when Frye withdrew her gun. She *did* look badass and everything with her gun and flashlight held in a crossed fashion, a yellow *FBI* emblazoned on her jacket. But still, proximity to live firearms wasn't in Evie's preferred plan. "Let's go. We'll get your sister and your mom home safe. Tell me everything that went down."

Evie's teeth dug into her bottom lip as she reminded herself to stay as even-keeled as possible. Loose dirt and dry leaves ground under her feet as she took first steps and scanned the path ahead. Several minutes had passed, which hopefully had been enough to get Jakob into place—and, if they were lucky, a proper family goodbye between the twins.

Probably not necessarily heartfelt, though. This was Kassie, after all.

CHAPTER FORTY-FIVE

KASS

A lifetime of smoking clearly hadn't been good for Kass's lungs. Despite her efforts to limit herself and do good things for her respiratory system, she knew better. At some point, she'd have to stop and limit any sort of burning to casting fire spells in *The Ancient Runes Online*.

But for now, smoking was the best decision she'd ever made. Because of her sneaking cigarettes during family trips to the lake, she knew a shortcut. "Here," she said, pointing at a sign jammed between a fork in the path. To the left, boating access. To the right, Lake Kinbote campgrounds.

In the middle, a bunch of trees and a hill. "We go straight," Kass said. She turned to the ridiculous sight of Jakob carrying Mom in his arms. It certainly helped in terms of speed—fighting fucking aliens must have kept him in better shape than varsity swimming, because he jogged like he carried a bag of oranges rather than another human being. A senior citizen who only stood a little over five feet tall, sure, but still.

"Up over the hill. The path winds around, but you can get there in half the time if you just go through all the trees and brush. Just, you know, check for ticks when you get back on your spaceship."

"Okay," Jakob said with a huff of exertion. He pumped his legs, and the thin flip-flops he'd never changed out of didn't seem to bother him. "How much time do you think we have?"

"I don't see any flashlights, so that's a good sign."

They started at a light trot, the sound of crunching leaves the only noise the whole time. Jakob said some bizarre code to check in with his fleet, but other than that, they stayed quiet and moved swiftly. Kass gave herself a mental compliment for being able to keep pace, given that her runs around the neighborhood didn't involve lasers or bombs.

Jakob paused for a breather after several looks behind them. "One second," he said, setting Mom down on an empty patch.

"Use the Force, Jakob," Kass said.

"Heh," he said, hands on his knees. "It's not like that. I've seen strange things, but no magic powers."

"Arnold would want to know all about those strange things," Mom said. "You know he came up here looking for you?"

"Yeah," Jakob said, picking Mom back up. "I heard."

Mentions of Dad still seemed to crack his demeanor, and Kass decided to do her brother a favor. Just this once. "Do you know exactly where we need to go? Like do you need to be in the same exact spot?"

"Not necessarily. Only roughly." They resumed as abruptly as they'd paused, Jakob grunting with his first few steps. "I remember, though. I know exactly where we were." Their silent trek proved to be a model of efficient movement, and it only took several more minutes to get to the edge of the lake. Above them, clouds cleared up enough to leave a thumbnail of a new moon shining down, reflecting a beam of white onto the water. They walked to the shore, a mix of dirt and pebbles underneath their feet.

"I can't remember the last time I was here," Mom said as Jakob put her down. "That's not a dementia joke." Despite her wit, her words were framed with anything but humor: fatigue, longing, even a bit of anger. Kass told herself to shut off her therapist brain for a minute, despite this whole situation being an essay straight out of grad school.

Just with aliens.

"Did you come here…" Jakob hesitated, his face dropping "…after?"

"No," Mom said.

"What about you, Kassie? How many times did we come here growing up? Every summer, sometimes Christmas too? Did you come back?"

"I did not. Not after Dad." Kass watched Jakob, the way all of his mannerisms still reflected the person she'd grown up with, and though she understood that he had become someone different, it still didn't matter. Lake Kinbote still stung her with every thought. "I had no reason to."

"What about Dad?" A dry gravel took over Jakob's voice now, a rare seriousness weighed down by what Kass took as regret. "Before he died. Did he come back?"

"Several times," Mom said. "I asked him not to. But he did."

"He came to look for you. For clues." Despite her best efforts, everything she said came out with some additional blame stitched onto it. *Fuck it*, she told herself, *stop fighting it, he's finally listening.* "He was desperate. Just as desperate as he was to get you to finish school. To get your shit together. Look, I know you're about to go back into sci-fi world, but your space adventure had consequences. I mean, look at us. We are fucked-up."

"I understand." Frosty breath rolled out with Jakob's whisper. "Does knowing the truth make it any better?"

"A little? Yes. And no. You still chose to stay while sending Dad back. You still chose not to get in touch when you were in New York." She'd imagined this moment for so many years. In a different setting. And with a different Jakob—the drugged-up loafer who tried to talk his way out of everything rather than the hardened man she saw before her. But it didn't matter. The loser she knew still existed somewhere within Jakob, and that fact eliminated any ability to quell her emotions. "You still made those choices. You chose to steal from Mom. You chose to use us. So even if you have a noble quest, we're still the collateral damage. And you know what? That sucks. There's no better way to put it. It sucks." Kass spoke so fast, so purposefully that it exhausted all the air in her lungs. She took in a deep breath. "So look, you're here. Mom's here. We have, like, minutes left in your second chance. It's great that you said you're sorry, but now what? Is this where we leave it? I mean, it's better than before, and I'll take that, but still. If you have something to say, now's the time."

"I… Hold on," Jakob started before tapping the side of his ear and looking up. He turned to Mom, then Kass, the glow behind his eyes still present. "They're close."

"Jakob, you're different now," Mom said. "We can all see that."

"I couldn't have carried you that far before," he said, his old smirk coming out.

"That part *was* pretty impressive." Kass shot a nod. Truth was truth, after all.

"You know what I'm going to say, don't you?" Mom asked.

"How will you fix it?" Jakob and Kass said at the same time.

How many times had they heard that growing up? Every situation, from fighting over Legos to the times each of them veered dangerously close to failing out of college, that look appeared in Mom's eye, soon followed by that question, the one question she lived her life by. Kass wasn't sure about Jakob, but she knew that part of her loathed that question because it was always, always right.

"See, you did listen," Mom said, and Kass detected a little bit of smugness in her tone, that parental *I told you so* that came up very rarely—Sofia Aguilar-Shao was *not* a gloater, at least until she was. And now, Kass treasured that moment. "Well?"

CHAPTER FORTY-SIX

JAKOB

Mom's favorite question. Jakob had heard that so much growing up that he hated it. He understood, on a core level, why she used that as a response, as a practical way of finding a solution. It was how Mom's mind worked, always searching for a way forward out of the most labyrinthine of problems.

But what Mom didn't know—what Evie and Kassie didn't know—was that he'd started to incorporate that into his own thinking. In fact, the first time he made that conscious choice was immediately following Lake Kinbote, during those first few days aboard a Seven Bells craft.

Arguing went nowhere. Begging went nowhere. All of Jakob's words bounced off Dad, but Jakob knew that this war, the things he'd seen, none of it was meant for Arnold Shao. It was Jakob's purpose, and Dad's presence was a mistake, even though he refused to leave.

Which was why he had made the decision for his new crewmates to apply the decryptor to Dad.

"Let's do it," he had said to the open channel once the bird-like alien working on transporter calibrations and the lanky coral-skinned one with long appendages held Dad. A third alien stepped over too, a female with an orange face, cone-like horns on the top of her head and short white tails draping over her shoulders. She grasped the basketball-sized device and lined it up to Dad as he struggled. "Jakob!" he yelled. "Jakob, what are they doing to me? Jakob, you're not safe here! Jakob, help me—"

His voice faded, and his body slumped, the rapid processing of the decryptor doing its thing. His limp body dragged on the floor, but as they prepped him for compressed-matter transport, Dad's eyes flew open. He struggled to his feet, balance tilting from the effects of the decryptor, and two of the aliens moved in to steady him. Dad swung his arms, all elbows and pushes, totally unsure of who or what he was fighting against. "It's okay to let him go. Just let him go," Jakob called out. "He'll stand on his own." They backed out, and from behind, the compressed-matter transporter initiated its start-up sequence.

Dad looked up, his eyes glazed over and posture swaying. "These lights," he said, "what do they all mean?"

Right before the transporter activated, Jakob saw him reach for something on a nearby stand.

All these years later, Jakob finally knew he'd managed to grab something right before he'd left. Evie and Dad would call it *the Key*. Kassie would call the device *It*. And Jakob knew it as a standard repair tool called a *diagnostic profiler*.

A harsh breeze nipped at Jakob's nose, the smell of Lake Kinbote so familiar, woven into the tapestry of his life. He stood under the empty, dark sky, looking at Mom, then Kassie. How could he fix this? It was more than a rhetorical question.

This was impossible to fix. Some things were. And he'd

known that since the moment he'd chosen to stay with the Seven Bells.

"Dad died because of me," Jakob said quietly. "He died because he was standing close enough to me when they took me. He died because he didn't want to let me go. He died because I told them to use the decryptor on him. Mom, I don't have an answer for you. I don't know how to fix this. Up there," he pointed to the stars, "it's simple. I fight. I fix machines. I pilot. I take orders. I save comrades. There's a start and a finish. Here? It's like my choice created these fault lines between everyone." He turned to Kassie. His twin. They shared so much on the surface—the same eyes, the same bone structure, the same nose. But underneath, he saw someone who'd risen to moments in ways he never could. "Getting everyone back in the same space doesn't fix that."

"That's good," Kassie said after several seconds. "Usually I'm the one who has to lead patients there."

"What do you tell them?" Jakob asked.

"Something like 'If you can't fix things, what would you like people to know?'"

"See," Jakob said, "this is why you stayed in school. And I fought aliens."

"Fucking aliens," Kassie said.

"Language, Kassie," Mom said, but this time with a smile.

Seconds continued to burn away, the finality of it all approaching in the form of a Seven Bells ship above and the FBI somewhere beyond the lake's clearing. There wasn't time for any grand speeches or eloquent proclamations, and even if there were, Jakob would fail at them. After all, he'd only passed his Rhetoric and Communications course because he'd cheated off Kassie's notes. Instead, he blurted out whatever made sense first. "I just want you to know that you're both with me. And Dad. And Evie. All of you. I try to avoid it.

Guilt, you know? But I know you're always there. You pop up when there's nothing else without even trying. I know this isn't a second chance at anything. It's just this slice of time, but enough to show you what I've become. And I hope that's enough." Jakob squeezed his eyes, coming back to the moment Dad transported. Had he known what he grabbed? No, there couldn't have been any way. He probably would have taken anything at that time, whether he intended it for attack or protest or theft; no one would ever know. "Evie said Dad was convinced that that device was the key to finding me. But it was just a tool. I used it almost every day to repair our mechs after combat. In a way, though, it *was* the key. Without its power base, I couldn't contact the fleet or bring this frequency back. All thanks to Dad."

Mom stepped forward and reached over, her hands taking his. "I don't know if I will remember this tomorrow. But I am present now. And I want you to know that, despite everything, I can see something different in you. I'm proud of you." Her frail arms wrapped around his body, a surprising strength. "You've finally become selfless."

He sank into his mother's hug.

In fact, he even returned it.

"Took long enough." Kassie paused, a gesture which was really unlike his twin. "And Dad would be proud too," she finally said.

If only Dad had had the strength to let go back then. To trust him. Jakob wasn't sure if Kassie was right, but he let himself believe it in the moment.

Because it felt right. It felt like what family would do.

No, not family. *Their* family, in all of its messy fractured ways.

"Hey, I gotta know really quick," Kassie said quietly. "While we wait."

"What's that?"

"Are these aliens *really* called Seven Bells? Cause there's that band you'd liked."

"Oh," Jakob said, still holding onto Mom. "Well, technically it's *S'uh-p-ten Be-hellis.* It means *Protectors of the Usurped.* But Seven Bells is easier because they were a really good band."

From a distance, a voice called out.

Evie.

CHAPTER FORTY-SEVEN

KASS

Kass was witnessing the impossible.

A mere week ago, Mom had needed help nearly every waking minute. Jakob was a memory, a dream. In good and bad ways.

But now they stood five feet in front of her, both of them of sound mind and body.

And Jakob—Jakob was goddamn *hugging.*

This really was impossible.

Behind her, a voice rang out. The pitch and tone matched Evie's, and the cadence lined up to the words "Kassie" and "Mom," though echoes and distance made it hard to distinguish. That broke character a little: if they were really in danger, it'd probably be better if Evie stayed quiet and Frye took charge. But her younger sister was probably doing it to give them a hint that they were close, so Kass gave her points for semismooth improvising.

Jakob muttered something indecipherable, probably to his

space crew. "Wait," he said, before doing something that the old Jakob would have done at a frat party while Kass did Jell-O shots.

He took off his *Reno Is for Winners* shirt and held it out.

"This isn't college, Jakob. You can't con me into doing your laundry."

Several seconds later a single light appeared in the sky—not a beam casting down but a dot significantly bigger than the stars above. It moved quickly before hovering above them. In front of Lake Kinbote, Kass could see the changes in Jakob's body: slim, ripped, and covered in jagged scars this way and that. If he wasn't really in an intergalactic war, then he definitely hung out with the wrong crowd.

"No, it's not that. You need to throw this in the lake. Tell them I freaked out and jumped in the water. Say I was talking nonsense about Dad and dove in. They'll find it. That should put everything to rest." The shirt flew across and Kass snatched it out of the air. Jakob's eyes intensified, the glow that backlit his pupils now glowing green dots.

"Hey," Kass said, "I know you told Evie that you've got hero stuff to do up there. But if you ever finish that, you still owe me for that pizza you stole. Got it?"

Mom's head tilted at that, then she shot Jakob a grimace of disapproval. Even now, she wouldn't stand for Jakob's irresponsible shenanigans. He replied the way he always had when their parents had caught him: a shoulder shrug and half smile.

Jakob walked to the shore. Farther away, the faint voices gradually grew louder, a clear sign that Frye and Evie were on their way. She tried to listen, tried to gauge their distance when suddenly everything went quiet.

Everything, as in the air, the crickets, the rustling of leaves quieted as the wind touched them. All of it dropped out into a completely and perfectly silent space.

Then a blast of warmth hit.

Then cold, a chill that tingled at Kass's face enough that she wanted to shut her eyes. Yet she forced them open—if Jakob was going to disappear, she needed to see it for herself.

She stood in the vacuum of sound, surrounded by a battle of extreme temperatures, the whole thing playing out just like Evie had claimed all those years ago. So many times Kass had told her it had been a figment of her imagination, a combination of altitude, adrenaline, panic, and weird atmospheric conditions. But no, this was how fucking aliens transported people.

She looked over her shoulder to the main clearing that led to Lake Kinbote's shore. A thin beam of light came through, and at first Kass thought it might have been related to the ship overhead, but the erratic movements made it clear that it was a flashlight. Probably Frye's, with Evie just behind, and she wondered if they were experiencing the same strange atmospherics.

A glow surrounded Jakob, forming an outline of shimmering color. He turned to face the lake, arms crossed in an *X* over his chest. Something flashed from above, like a strobe shining up across the tree line.

T-shirt still in hand, Kass took her phone out and hit Record. Evie wasn't here to do one of her ridiculous selfies, but this would be the next best thing.

The bubble around Jakob intensified, closing in around him to tightly cover his body. The light continued to shimmer, a web of electricity dancing and cutting rapidly across him, around him. The beam started stretching upward, a trail disappearing some thirty feet into the night sky, and then everything flashed again. A pulse of blinding white. Sound gradually returned, then a pop burst through the area, something deeper but shorter than thunder.

Jakob was gone.

Kass shut off her phone and looked at Mom, then realized that Evie and Frye were now on the other side of the shore. "Mom, we have to act like Jakob jumped. You need to act like you're still unaware. Just stand here, okay?"

"Okay, Kassie," she said. Her face glowed with a warm smile, and she reached over to squeeze Kass's hand. Kass wanted to say something important and monumental about this moment, but nothing could top the light show that had just played out.

Or Mom's simple gesture.

As Kass stared at the now-vacant space in front of them, her eyes adjusted to the rapid changes in light, all leading back to near-zero visibility of a late night by a lake.

She squeezed her mother's hand back.

Evie's voice came through again, this time stronger and mixed with Frye's. They were getting closer, and that meant that Kass needed to play up their end of the alibi. She dashed forward, breaking free of Mom and hands waving. "Jakob, don't!" she yelled in her most convincing voice. She looked behind her and tracked Frye's flashlight to the path at their feet, not anywhere toward where they were. "Jakob, don't jump!" she yelled before balling the shirt as tightly as she could and launching it into the lake. It soared into the dark at an unknown distance—probably not as far as Kass used to throw a softball, but still pretty damn good.

Smoking didn't affect her arm strength, after all.

It was *somewhere* in the lake, and that was all that mattered. She returned, her body language a forced slump, then she turned around and took Mom by the shoulders before whispering into her ear. "I love you, Mom."

Mom's breath warmed against Kass's cold ear as she replied. "I know, Kassie."

"This is some weird shit, huh?"

"Language, Kassie."

Kass nodded, fighting the urge to smile as the sounds of footsteps against a trail echoed through the air. "Frye!" she yelled after stepping back. "Evie! Help! Jakob jumped in the lake!"

In the following hour, Frye was shockingly sympathetic to their alibi. Kass supposed it was because the whole thing made too much sense, much more than the idea that Jakob had beamed back to fight an intergalactic war.

The local police sent out a notice to look for Jakob, and Kass acted unsure as to whether Jakob could have survived the jump and swum all the way across the lake in his current physical and mental condition and emphasized the relevant personal history that Jakob, in addition to being a mediocre student, was a high-school varsity swimmer.

In fact, the most worrying part during the entire time was the way Mom acted—completely silent wrapped in a police blanket, looking off with an unfocused stare. Police brought out a wheelchair to bring her all the way down the opening trail down to the car, Kass and Evie walking behind. "What are you going to tell your friends?" Kass asked low enough to avoid suspicion from the nearby law enforcement.

Several steps passed before Evie looked at her and shook her head. "I don't know."

"I'm fine if you tell them. As long as you swear that they won't pass anything further to the FBI. I know they want to know. And they helped us."

"It's not that," she said. "I just don't know if I need all that anymore."

With that, Evie sprinted ahead and helped Mom out of the wheelchair as Kass gripped the key fob and hit the button several times more than necessary, beeps shooting off into the empty night. She took the first step forward to join them when something tugged at her to wait and turn around.

Across the way, Frye waited, bathed in flashing red and blue lights. "Hey," Kass said, flagging her down, "thanks for helping us out there."

"It's what we do. Still no sign of Jakob," Frye said. Kass reminded herself to look distressed over her brother. A frown, crossed arms, that sort of thing. "Your mom's okay?"

"I think the good thing about her condition is that she won't remember this. It's a long drive home." A heavy exhale let loose, something that was half-real, half an act. "We'll probably stop at a motel."

"I'll stay in touch, let you know what we find. Drive safe. Try to get some rest." Someone yelled Frye's name from afar, and she looked up to acknowledge before taking a step forward. "Oh, I did want to ask you," she said, turning back to Kass, "did you experience anything..." Frye's mouth turned crooked "...strange? Right before Jakob jumped into the lake? Like an intense heat? And, any sound issues?"

Kass looked Frye straight in the eye and offered her surest shrug. "Sorry, no. Probably just weird weather..." The FBI agent matched her gesture, then Kass turned to walk across the street. Right before she opened the driver's door, her hand balled up, and she gave herself a little fist pump.

It started about twenty minutes out, during a quiet moment when Evie was looking up nearby motels on her phone.

"Oh," Mom said, "I can feel it."

"Feel it?" Kass asked. That statement might have meant anything, but any sort of sudden shift in Mom's demeanor or situation raised her inner alarm. "Feel what?"

"I just realized that I can't remember the name of Evie's friend who's been helping us. The one who makes bad jokes."

"Layla?" In the passenger seat, Evie's phone screen went dark, and she straightened at attention. "Well, it's been a really long, weird day."

"I should know this. She's been texting you. I can feel—"

"Don't say it, Mom," Evie said. "Let's not worry about it."

"No, girls, listen. I don't know what's going to happen. I don't know if this was a permanent fix. I doubt it. Something about Jakob's device might have done something to me. But maybe only for a short time. Maybe only while I was around him."

"Mom, we're all tired," Kass said. Which was true, but also any acknowledgment that something might be awry felt like it would give it power.

"No, listen. I can feel it starting to turn. And there's something I need to know. That woman from earlier. Who is she?" Mom's question came out with the authority of a judge demanding compliance.

"Frye?" Kass asked while still watching the road. "She's FBI."

"No, not her. The woman who stayed back home. Who is she? Her name is..." In the rearview, Kass could see Mom's face scrunch up in thought. "Her name is..."

"Lucy," she said at the same time as Kass.

"Who is she? Is she a neighbor? I can't place her. But I feel like I trust her."

With each question, Kass's heart rate quickened, an intensity pounding harder than when she pulled evasive maneuvers on the highway. They'd talked about this already, this very specific thing. Should she bring that up? Perhaps it was all fatigue or the same type of slip that everyone felt from time to time. Her jaw locked up, and she tried to focus on the dashed lines whirling by on the highway pavement. "She's your caretaker," Kass finally said.

"Am I..." Her voice, which still carried the night's strength, trailed off with a new tint. Kass recognized the shift. She saw it in clients all the time: the moment someone realized a question might lead to an answer they didn't want to hear.

"Am I that bad?"

Kass felt the pressure of Evie's eyes on her. "It's fine," she said. "This is what we do."

"No, Kassie. Am I that bad?" Her silhouette straightened in the rearview mirror. "Does Lucy live with us?"

"No, she goes home at four."

"And then what?"

"Then I handle things."

Mom held up her bandaged hand. "This?"

"It was," Kass pictured the dropped mug and its shattered pieces, "just a scratch. It happens."

"What else?" Mom spoke with a sharpness straight out of the times she'd argue with her mortgage broker on the phone about contingency options. Though pieces of her seemed to fade, Kass knew that this was authentic right now. "Have I fallen, got lost?"

"Not lost."

"Kassie, if I'm a danger to myself or you, then I need to know. Before I lose you again."

All of this had to be new to Evie. And given the scope of who was around, where this was heading, that was relevant. "There've been some close calls."

"I know you, Kassie. You think you have these walls built protecting you, but you're easy to read."

Next to her, Evie laughed. Not the kind of laugh filled with spite or schadenfreude, but the understanding that only a childhood together provided. Such a raw moment stole any response from Kass, and though she didn't purposefully try to avoid anything, no words felt right for the moment. No words even came to mind.

Mom finally broke the silence. "I remember that afternoon when I came home to find you so upset about Desmond. And I asked you how you could fix it. But you never figured it out, did you?"

"I'm, um, not sure what Desmond has to do with this."

In the rearview, Mom smiled—and Kass recognized it right away. She'd always parented one step ahead, which created all sorts of infuriating moments. Here, Kass had probably walked right into Mom's trap. "You're always holding everything together for everyone. Not just since Jakob. Even before that." Mom's voice was so even, so measured that Kass wondered how long she'd been waiting to say this. "I worried about you when Desmond was gone. Because he was *gone*—it didn't matter if you two talked every day. He was over there. You needed someone to take care of. Without him, you'd be lost." Kass told herself to stay focused on the road. They'd gone through so much in such a short time that crashing right now because of unleashed emotions would be really, really dumb. But she knew—she *knew*—exactly what Mom meant. "You got lost."

Gears cranked in her head, twisting interlocking pieces in such obvious alignment that Kass felt embarrassed to call herself a professional. "Oh, shit," Kass said. "I'm textbook codependent. How did I miss that until now?"

"Kassie, it's okay to ask for help," Mom said. "Especially now."

"Listen to Mom," Evie said, her voice tiny. "While she can remember me."

"I promised to take care of you," Kass managed to push out with all her strength. *The road*, she told herself. *Don't crash, focus on the road*.

"You're not taking care of me if you're not able to take care of yourself. I am here right now. I am talking to you in this moment. And I am making a choice. I am saying I want you to take care of yourself too. You seem to trust Lucy. I do too. I feel it. That's a first step. So what's next?" Mom sighed, a release tinted with just a hint of exasperation. "If you need permission, then I give you permission. You don't have to save the world anymore, Kassie."

"Yeah. Jakob handles the world-saving in this family," Evie said.

Was she saving the world? Kass always thought she was more in the keeping-things-together business. Except now, she could see how easy it was to mistake one for the other. "If I'm not taking care of you, I don't know what I'll do."

No one knew about Golden Apple yet outside of herself and Lucy. But they were stuck in this car together, and time ebbed away, one grain at a time. Kass took a deep breath and considered all of the options that had suddenly opened up with Mom's permission.

"That's the best part," Mom said. "Let yourself daydream for once."

CHAPTER FORTY-EIGHT

EVIE

Evie had stayed mostly silent during Kassie and Mom's conversation. Part of it was in deference to the topic at hand but also to the personal revelations. Of course she knew that Kassie and Desmond had split, but the reason? Not the usual drifting apart, not distance, not trouble playing nice during *The Ancient Runes Online*, but the loneliness at Kassie's core.

She never would have suspected.

But, she supposed, there was a lot she didn't know about her sister.

During a moment of quiet, Evie opened her mouth, so many questions about Kassie and her life bubbling to the surface in a way that had never seemed possible before. No, not impossible: they hadn't existed before. So many layers of separation seemed to prevent her from seeing Kassie as anything *but* her big sister; it was so strange to think of her as a person.

Instead, she let them come to their own resolution, Evie only offering an opinion here or there. She supposed she technically did have a say in it as part of the family. But this was *their* situation. She'd purposely pushed herself apart from them, forcing their hand by being on the other side of the country.

They pulled into a gas station in the middle of nowhere, long stretches of dirt and nature around them, a clear beam of moon still above. Evie looked through the windshield to the stars, wondering what had become of Jakob and his master plan. Or Kassie, who at the far end of the parking lot with a cigarette butt glowing between her fingers. What was she thinking as she took her final puff before grinding it into the ground?

Her sister gave no clear indication as she walked past the car and disappeared into the service station.

But a more immediate concern came to mind. Something just as important, at least in the small cluster of her immediate family. "Mom?" she asked quietly.

"Yes, Evie?"

"I know why you couldn't remember me."

"Dementia does that."

"No, it's more than that." Nerves tingled Evie's gut, an uncertainty of emotion that acted opposite to the science and numbers she usually immersed in. "Kassie was right. I barely called. I never visited. Other than asking Kassie for money, I just stayed in my little bubble. I thought I was helping us. But I wasn't. I was just trying to tell myself how to feel better." There was more to say, these things surfacing in the hours since Jakob had vanished in a flash. So much more, and she'd wasted so much time, waited so long, only to have a window of a few measly hours. And in that window, hardly anything had felt right. "About Jakob. About Dad."

"I'm here now. Though, honestly, I don't know for how long."

Evie had a hunch this was coming. Mom hadn't acted much

differently since they'd left Lake Kinbote, but the logic of what triggered the memory recall made sense on a night when not a lot did. "You feel it? It's getting worse?"

"Yes. It's like pockets of thoughts and memories disappearing. There's the outlines, but what's inside is gone."

"Shouldn't we tell Kassie? Why didn't you say anything?"

Mom responded with a quick laugh. "I did."

"I mean, you said you felt it. You didn't say it was getting worse this fast."

"I thought about saying more. But I noticed something." Evie turned to face her, despite the awkward twist in the front passenger seat to do so. She wanted to see Mom, not just hear her. "We were quiet. And it was nice. It was… Oh, what's it called? See, it's slipping."

Evie considered the last thirty minutes or so, the way they'd sat together. Mom was right—it was quiet, and there *was* something strange about that. It wasn't exhausted or tense or awkward. It was the opposite, like slipping under a warm blanket on a cold night.

That sort of thing had never happened with the Shaos in a car before.

"A comfortable silence," she said.

"That's it. And I thought, we don't have time to fix everything that's ever happened. I don't even know if we need to. So if comfortable silence is the last thing I experience, that you girls experience with me, is there anything better?"

Kassie emerged from the service station with a cup of coffee and several bags of snacks. "In case you're hungry," she said after popping open the door. "Chips and stuff." She leaned in to put her coffee in the drink holder. "It'll just be a minute while I fill up. You two need anything?"

"No. We're fine," Mom said.

The door closed, followed by the clunking noise of the gas pump.

"I feel like I should apologize for so many things," Evie said.

"Don't. There are many things that I should say sorry about too. I just can't remember them right now." Mom laughed to herself, a quiet laugh that still somehow caught Kassie's eye from the outside. "That's a joke."

Evie closed her eyes, trying to figure out what exactly the soup of feelings inside her meant. Or maybe the exact breakdown didn't matter. She was here, reacting to Mom, and that might have been enough. "Yeah. I got that."

"Here," she said, taking the notebook and pen from earlier. "This is for you. When I can't remember things anymore, you hold onto this." She wrote quickly, the sound of scribbling soon followed by a quick tear of a sheet. "This will outlast me."

Evie took the folded paper, then settled back, the seat belt pulling up click by click with her gradual recline. She opened the sheet, angling it so that the harsh fluorescent light of the gas station caught the handwriting.

I remember you. And I like your hair.

Evie told herself that she would not cry. Not in front of Kassie, not in front of Mom. Instead, she pulled out her phone and set the camera to Selfie mode. She held up the open sheet, the words visible on the reflected screen, and stared straight into the device. It clicked to confirm when Mom spoke up. "What are you doing?"

"This is how I remember things," Evie said. "I capture the moment."

"Oh, yes," Mom said. "I remember that now."

Several more thunks and clicks rattled the car, then Kassie hung up the nozzle. The driver's door swung open, the rattle of keys coming with a burst of fresh air. "Last chance before we go. Anyone need anything?"

"No," Evie said, looking back at Mom. "We're good."

CHAPTER FORTY-NINE

EVIE

Evie's back pocket buzzed, and though she chose to let it go, it buzzed three more times in quick succession. Rapid-fire phone buzzing, but not an actual call.

So it wasn't *that* important. But important enough to ping several times.

The old seat squeaked as she adjusted, the noise loud enough to catch her quantum-physics professor's attention. Evie angled herself to grab her phone and check the notifications. Perhaps it was the maturity of age, but she tried to stay focused the whole time during class. She wasn't the oldest student in the program, but most people still mistook her for a grad student or a TA rather than someone trying to finish the last year of her undergrad degree.

We're scheduling a special to go over the video. Can you join us? We'd like some Ions you.

The pun gave away the sender; Evie didn't need to check. *We* meant the Reds. Who she was still friends with, but no longer professionally associated with, and hadn't even really said much to lately. And *the video* being the video Kassie had taken of Jakob's final disappearance, something that she'd probably seen so many times by now that every frame, every blip of audio seared into her memory—the last true and tangible piece of Jakob for her to cling to. Shot from behind to hide his face, and the specifics of Lake Kinbote eliminated by the dim lighting, but Kassie had agreed to let the Reds have it five months after that night. It came with the agreement that nothing could link it to Jakob or Frye.

So joining them. That might create a bit of a problem. The Reds had gone public with the video last week after spending about a month scrutinizing it, splicing things down frame by frame to isolate all of the details about what had happened to this mystery person—things that the Shaos themselves had witnessed but still totally didn't understand.

Evie probably couldn't add anything helpful to the conversation even if she wanted to, having spent most of that time getting ready for her reentry into lectures, labs, and homework. And really, all of the stuff with the Reds felt like a lifetime ago. She had different types of charts and data now, and besides, the answer she'd sought for years had come and gone.

At this point, she just hoped that someday her brother finished doing whatever he needed to do light-years from home so they might have a nice dinner sometime in the future.

I can't, she typed quickly, I have to study for a midterm. Sorry.

Though she did miss talking with Layla. She missed the puns.

Maybe a little more than just puns.

That was an unexpected thought, and it sparked further

unexpected thoughts. Instead of listening to a lesson on wave mechanics, Evie thought about Layla.

She added several alien emojis to the message, closing it with a big grinning face, then hit Send.

The green check icon appeared, and Evie turned back to her lecture, scanning the professor's notes ahead of her to see where he'd left off. The phone buzzed again, a reply that seemed quicker than usual. She unlocked her phone to see Layla's name again, a new message below.

Too bad. But hey, after your test, maybe you could explain compressed-matter transport again to me. So I can sound smart like you.

Shortly after, a second message appeared.

Or, you know, we could just catch up. The text was followed by an emoji of a red bottle.

So many possibilities had seemed shut off and deactivated during her time with the Reds, during her search for Jakob, when only a singular focus drove her. How it pulled her away from everything, anything else. Discovering each of these possibilities was like lights turning on in hallways she never knew existed—or maybe they were always there and she'd just never bothered to look.

Because, as Kassie would say, *Fucking aliens.*

Evie considered something witty to say, something brilliant to spark a laugh and sigh. Rather than that, she decided to go with something much more benign but also much more honest.

A pun.

I'd like that. It's experi-meant to be.

CHAPTER FIFTY

KASS

She's doing fine.

Kass read the words on her phone screen but they refused to sink in. It'd taken her months to get used to the idea that Lucy and other staff cared for Mom, and despite several visits a week and regular text updates, the whole thing still felt out of step. Not just Mom living in an assisted-living facility, but Kass being without commitment or responsibility outside of the standard bills-and-job thing for the first time since…

For the first time ever? Impulse took over, and Kass typed a quick response.

Are you sure? I can cancel?

Lucy replied immediately, as if she knew that was going to happen and was ready to call Kass on her bullshit.

Yes, I'm sure. It is okay for you to travel. I give you permission.

The message finished with a smiley face, and Kass settled back into the stiff chair in the international terminal of SFO when another text came through. This one from Evie.

Lucy says you're being difficult. Seriously, Mom will be okay with her. Go already.

Figures Evie would still be up. Kass shook her head, marveling at the way that her sister still managed to be a thorn in her side. Though, at least now they agreed. Most of the time.

Some of the time. Which was an improvement on none of the time.

Okay, okay. I get it. Will check in on Mom when I land.

Kass hit Send, the message going to both Lucy and Evie. She looked at the screen at the check-in counter, a clock telling her that she still had an hour before boarding her late-evening flight.

Kass pulled her laptop out of her bag, then fired it up and jumped through the hoops to access the airport's Wi-Fi. More screens flashed until the start-up screen of *The Ancient Runes Online* appeared. Soon the fantasy world of Mystheos appeared in front of her, trees and rocks and buildings digitally terraforming. An envelope icon appeared in the status box above Aveline, and a few clicks later brought up a message from Desmond.

I'm logging out for now to get some sleep, but don't worry, I'll pick you up on time. Breakfast should be just opening up when you get here.

Here. As in Paris, after a fourteen-hour flight with one stop-over in Chicago. Kass gave herself a discreet fist pump, then reached into her purse and pulled out a small notepad and a smaller plastic case. The lid flipped open, and she grabbed two pieces of nicotine gum, then told herself to breathe. She opened the notepad but left the pen clipped to it. Instead, she stared at the message she'd written for herself about a month ago, the thing that she returned to whenever the world needed to return to its axis.

How will you fix it?

Kass turned to the gate's floor-to-ceiling windows. The view of the night sky ignited all sorts of possibilities in her, ideas that formed halfway between dreams and plans. She gazed past patchwork clouds to the light of a single star poking through, bright enough that it might have reached Evie across the country, maybe even Jakob somewhere farther away.

★★★★★

Keep reading for a sneak peek at Mike Chen's next novel.

ACKNOWLEDGMENTS

Stories can spark from unlikely sources, and *Light Years from Home* came from a very unexpected place: a song. This book started in 2017 as a short story inspired by the song "Red" by Belly (off the excellent album King). Tanya Donelly's lyrics spun a tale of someone who wishes to fly away, then actually does, courtesy of aliens. That short story got shelved until I watched Netflix's *The Haunting of Hill House*, which presented a deep character examination of family trauma due to a supernatural incident. Suddenly, the story idea had legs, and a rewatch of *The X-Files* locked everything in place.

That all became an outline entitled "Second Contact" with Jakob abducted at Lake Kinbote (named after *The X-Files* episode "Jose Chung's from Outer Space") while Evie and Kass dealt with the real-world fallout. Fellow gamers might catch that this book's characters are named from the *Assassin's Creed* franchise.

I took this rough idea to my agent Eric Smith and my editor Margot Mallinson, who both deserve a huge thanks for being extremely supportive while I jump around with tone and subgenre. Honestly, I'm surprised they let me get away with what I do.

Of course, a story idea needs a lot of help along the way. Kat Howard read an early draft and rightly suggested starting over (Kat is always right). Wendy Heard and Diana Urban were my writing-sprint buddies as we drafted during COVID-19 lockdowns. Sierra Godfrey and Meghan Scott Molin were there for "I don't know if I can do this" meltdowns about balancing parenting and writing. And there were many, many sessions of complaining and/or brainstorming (world-building, title, or otherwise) with Peng Shepherd, Annalee Newitz, KB Wagers, Natania Baron, Fran Wilde, Jo Ladzinski, Joseph Brassey, Rowenna Miller, Marty Cahill, and Sean Grigsby.

Brea Grant, Lesli Schauf, and Jenny Rae Rapaport helped with the dementia details, with extra thanks to Brea for doing a sensitivity read of the almost-done manuscript. And Jen Silver, who is the best geek/veterinary-tech crossover ever, gave details about X-ray training and certification.

The fact that this book exists is a little miraculous, given that it was written and revised during various stages of COVID-19 lockdowns—including summer 2020, when wildfires obliterated California. It's all a bit of a blur, especially considering that we did virtual kindergarten on top of it *and* managed to keep it together despite every waking moment with each other. So, to my wife, Mandy, and my daughter, Amelia, this book is the culmination of that marathon. We made it—older, wiser, and way more tired.

Finally, the one autobiographical bit of this story is a love for School of Seven Bells. Seriously, Jakob is totally right when he says they're a really good band.

VAMPIRE WEEKEND

Being a vampire is far from glamorous...but it can be pretty punk rock.

Everything you've heard about vampires is a lie. In fact, vampire life is really just a lot of blood bags and night jobs. For Louise Chao, it's also lonely, since she swore off family ages ago—until a long-lost teenage relative shows up at her door. Whether it's Ian's love of music or his bad attitude, for the first time in ages, Louise feels a connection. But as Ian uncovers Louise's true identity, things get dangerous...especially when he asks her for the ultimate favor.

CHAPTER 1

There's one rule we vampires live by: Never reveal your true nature to a human.

Which made sneezing blood during band practice kind of a problem.

Nose tickles are rare for vampires, but something triggered it here, at a *really* inopportune moment. My face squinched, a full-body tension to successfully hold it in, and I continued without missing a beat. My left hand pressed guitar strings taut against frets, my right hand strummed at a steady rhythm, switching to single plucks as notes rang out until going back to chords for the song's outro.

For the moment, I abided by the cardinal rule for vampires. Because as scattered as we were, exposure was *really* frowned upon, enough that rumors of so-called "fixers" swirled—vampires that put others back in line if they got a little too flippant with community secrets. So it probably wasn't great that I'd revealed the truth twice already, first to my late aunt Laura, and second by being honest with my best friend/bandmate Marshall.

And though that last time ended in all sorts of heartache and misery, I vowed *this* time would be different. I'd get close enough to humans to play in a band while being a good vampire citizen.

Because for a vampire like me, music was nearly as important as blood. And I'd starved myself of it for too long. That's why I was here, trying out for Copper Beach—the third band I'd auditioned for in two months.

We sped through the audition set, every beat and note building dreams of jam sessions, set lists, earsplitting drums, and crashing guitars in a shitty empty bar. With each passing second, my whole body felt more in sync, the vitality of band life becoming part of me once again. In movies, vampires were desiccated husks until they drank gallons of blood; I'd starved myself of other musicians for so long that I felt that way, and every chord strummed restored me to full strength.

A cymbal crashed to end the set's final song and our collective noise faded, leaving only the muffled rumbles from adjacent rooms. The run-down Oakland warehouse was filled with bands stuffed into similarly tiny practice rooms, sound-insulated spaces where magic happened despite bad ventilation and faulty electrical outlets. Glances exchanged, an unspoken vibe that seemed to acknowledge that my guitar work fit them well.

The drummer, a scientist-looking guy named Josh, nodded at me while adjusting a snare bolt, and I offered a smile so pleasant my fangs likely showed.

"I think that sounded pretty—" I started before the worst possible thing happened:

Another sneeze came. A full explosion, a clear allergic reaction to something in the air too powerful to stifle.

Suddenly, blood sprayed all over David—David, as in my white Epiphone guitar. I named all my guitars, and in this case, the Epiphone's bright crunchy tone matched the glam sound of David Bowie's Ziggy Stardust/Aladdin Sane period to earn the name. And, in that moment, covered in blood: a light splatter over David's smooth body and the black pickguard.

But what triggered it? Not many odors affected me these days, at least not in the allergic way that plagued my human youth. Vampire life meant that our bodies traded things like functioning digestive and sex organs for a diet of blood, which then increased our immune responses and metabolism to the level of "fairly freaking awesome." *Immortal* wasn't *indestructible*, though; crossing the street or swimming still required precautions. Perhaps more so—at least humans in car wrecks could go to any old hospital rather than a community's secret vampire doctors.

I turned my back to the band, and as I pulled David's cord from the extra amp they let me use for the audition, I caught a distinct smell.

Garlic. One of the few things that triggered a universal allergic response in our bodies.

Goddamn it.

Behind me, lead singer Aidan and bassist Sally talked about how to minimize microphone feedback while Josh carefully tore down each piece of his kit. "Bless you," Josh said without a glance. I looked up to find a vent in the corner of the small practice space, the clear origin of the smell. Though soundproof insulation lined the walls, I heard the distinctive *thunk-thunk* of a microwave, and I remembered that when I loaded in, Copper Beach's practice space sat right next to the break room.

Someone microwaved garlic fries or something similar, a dish so strong it would make humans sweat out the odor.

Another nose tickle arrived, causing my eyes to twitch. My hands clenched as I forced it away, a burst going mute before it could escape. I squeezed my eyes tight, and after several moments, everything relaxed. No one even noticed me wiping the front of David with the bottom of my black shirt, a quick, awkward tug-and-scrub—it didn't restore my gear's usual pristine condition, but that could wait until after work tonight. Some of the blood-snot absorbed into my T-shirt, enough to hide what happened and focus on the much bigger deal:

This audition went really, really well. It might actually work, as long as I left without anyone noticing the blood smears on my guitar.

David's strings pressed against my body as I carried him over to the case in the corner. A few clicks later and he sat nestled in its fuzzy lining.

Audition done. Mission accomplished. I took a breath and hoisted my backpack of pedals and cables. Though an hour remained before my work shift started, it seemed best to escape any lingering smell.

Except a pocket of garlic hit me again after two steps, the ventilation clearly not upgraded to post-COVID standards. That devastating pandemic didn't affect vampires; our immune response proved to be too strong. Garlic, on the other hand, would easily give me fits of bloody sneezes for hours with one good inhale. I fought the oncoming nose tickles before picking up David's case. "Well, I thought that we sounded good together—"

"What the fuck?" Sally asked. Then Aidan glanced over his keyboard rig. Then Josh looked.

"Oh," I said, mind seeking excuses. I'd wiped up David with my shirt, maybe the bloodstains were more obvious than I thought. "You know what? I'd spilled some cranberry sauce on this shirt earlier today, I think—"

"Louise, your eyes are *bleeding.*"

My eyes. I'd been so concerned with David I'd totally forgotten my eyes.

"Shit, shit, shit," Sally said. She walked with purpose, keeping a wide perimeter before throwing the door open.

"Oh, you know what, it's, um, allergies. I have a garlic allergy." Which was technically true. The garlic attack must have produced some tears during my sneezing fit; like snot and saliva, tears mixed with blood for us, and against my paler-than-usual skin, the contrast certainly stood out. "You smell that? I must have, um, burst a blood vessel when I sneezed. It happens," I said, riffing on the fly. "I've got very sensitive blood vessels—"

"I don't care what it is. I'm not dealing with any weird health stuff again." She reached down and put on a mask, then pointed at me. "I'm not taking any risks—get the fuck out. I can't believe you didn't tell us about this."

I blinked, and as I did, I felt the slightest of tears trickle from my left eye, no doubt streaking blood down the side of my face. My knuckles rubbed against it, a poor stab at appearing casual, though the repeated swipes probably didn't help. "I'm serious, it's allergies—"

Not only was I blowing my shot with Copper Beach, if this got out to the vampire community, I could be in serious trouble. I might even find out if the whole fixer thing was real. I turned to hide my blood tears, just in case anyone got the urge to snap a photo of it.

"Get your shit and go," Sally said.

"Wait, I think we sounded great and—"

"Go. Leave now."

Given the state of blood on my face, I tried *not* to face the band, and instead walked in a slow, awkward gait, holding my guitar case. "Hey, um, look, I understand where you're coming from, but can you do me a favor and *not* say anything about my allergy...like, anywhere?"

"*Get out.*"

And just like that, I was forced out, blood smeared across my face. From behind, an argument between Copper Beach broke out, Sally yelling about how she refused to take any health chances while Aidan lobbied that they should give it a try and Josh read off things he'd googled about bloody tears and whether they were contagious or a sign of any infection.

Vampirism wasn't infectious, of course. I couldn't even turn people if I wanted to.

In the end, though, it didn't matter. Yet another chance with human musicians failed, a pattern that was becoming so consistent that I wondered if the universe was telling me something, like I was destined to record at home, the only other living creature in the studio with me being my dog. But, as adorable as Lola the corgi was, she didn't exactly excel at drums.

I blew out a sigh and headed through a thankfully empty hallway out to my car, the hatchback of my white Prius popping open with a beep. The case slid in the back, then I tossed a blanket and several empty reusable bags on top of it. I wouldn't normally leave my gear hidden in my car, but the audition and my work schedule didn't provide a lot of breathing room.

Especially on the second Friday of the month. Also known as blood bag day. I couldn't miss one of those.

As I settled into the driver's seat, I pulled a metal thermos from a small ice-filled cooler on the passenger seat and unscrewed the top, picking off the loose corgi fur that wrapped around the lid. Those stumpy legs were adorable, and the unwavering loyalty was nice, but no one warned me about how much fur corgis shed.

That was the life of Louise Chao, Very Ordinary Vampire: blood and dog hair. In some parallel universe, vampires actually existed like those in movies or Anne Rice's books: cool powers and ornate living while prancing around with luscious hair and Victorian clothes. Here, I dressed like Joan Jett circa the late 1970s, except with Lola's fur clinging to my pants. The closest thing about me to Louis from *Interview with the Vampire* was my name and maybe that one time I traveled in search of kindred spirits. Except, unlike Louis's global search for vampires, I'd followed the Ramones on a few dates of their 1996 farewell tour—until I ran out of money and had to drive for two days to get back to San Francisco.

Not quite as glamorous. But way more punk rock.

The viscous flow hit my lips, a blend of nutrition and hydration that would get me through most of the night. I drank a little slower than normal—blood wasn't particularly tasty, so savoring it mostly wasted time. Here, the mere act of drinking gave space to ruminate, along with the simple rhythm of inhale/exhale to calm my nerves. I watched the building's entrance, hoping a member of Copper Beach would sprint out and breathlessly say it was all a misunderstanding.

I took another sip, watching the small circle of people smoking outside of the building's entrance. Seconds counted by, eventually leading to me finding *anything* on my phone as a distraction. Except the first news headline caused me to pause in a completely different way.

12 Vampire Powers We Wish We Had

Did my phone know I was a vampire? Why else would it pop up? Another semiofficial vampire rule forbade any online mentions of what we were, not even dumb blood puns. I nearly went scorched earth with a factory reset to protect my privacy when the truth hit me.

Of course tech companies didn't know about vampires. Because vampires were superboring. Most of us worried about balancing night jobs (they're not that easy to find) and getting weekly blood needs met without biting people (really not as common as pop culture would have you believe) rather than wielding uncanny powers.

I clicked the link, and it became clear that this had nothing to do with real vampires. Everything people assumed about vampires was wrong.

Case in point, the first vampire power myth from this article: superspeed.

Which I obviously didn't have, otherwise I might have been able to wipe the blood tears so fast they would have appeared a trick of the light.

I skimmed the list, then purged it from my thoughts once I confirmed an algorithm hadn't identified my biology, though it did pull up the related headline of Victim Hospitalized in Bay Area's Third "Vampire" Attack.

I pondered the headline when my phone interrupted with a buzz, a notification appearing on the screen. But instead of Copper Beach inviting back via text, the name Eric appeared. Eric, as in San Francisco's vampire community leader; if there was a fixer, it would have been him. I gave the message a frantic skim, but thankfully he hadn't found out about my bloody tears already. Instead, he wrote about an upcoming meeting, something that I never bothered with.

I ignored the text, then resumed watching the practice space's front door. Another ten minutes passed before my phone flashed a reminder that my 9:00 p.m. shift started soon.

Time was up. And this band wasn't happening.

But it was more than that. I'd auditioned for three straight bands, three really good bands that offered the exact blend of melody and rage that I wanted. And each time, something caused it to fall apart. One band wanted to shoot for opening daytime slots at upcoming local festivals. Another was even worse—needing to meet for weekend daytime practices. And now, an accidental encounter with garlic.

Every time I found a good fit, being a vampire got in the way.

And with my last true band? Being a vampire didn't just get in the way, it destroyed everything.

Marshall didn't deserve what happened to him *or* what I said to him. Perhaps this was my karmic kickback, a purgatory where I never found another band again, let alone another best friend.

I shook off the thought, a conscious pushback at the guilt that had burned for three years. Right now, none of that mattered because I had to get to work. It was a blood day.

My car's battery-powered engine awoke with the lightest of hums while I thumbed through my saved library of music, a snapshot of all of the important stages of my life: Bowie, punk, postpunk, new wave, Madchester, lo-fi and so on. All pieces of my identity; but for now, I needed a warm hug in the form of dance beats contradicting dark emotions. The bouncy synths and thumping bass of New Order's seven-minute classic, "Temptation" began blasting, a wall of melancholy lyrics disguised as pop music, enveloping me as I rolled away, still bandless, in my very practical hybrid car.

CHAPTER 2

Vampire power myth #2: We can bite into anything.

In movies, veins pop like a balloon hitting a nail. But in reality? Kids constantly bonk into sharp objects and get light scrapes. Construction workers work around nails and metal, but somehow buildings go up without anyone bleeding out. I worked in a hospital, so I saw this firsthand.

In practical terms, biting someone for blood was not easy. Newly turned vampires don't exactly have functional teeth. A gradual sharpening takes place over the course of a week, but we're not the instant kill machine from movies.

The so-called "vampire attacks" in the news? Sounded like algorithm-driven clickbait to me. And that was exactly how I thought about it—or *didn't* think about it—when I got to work.

Because today was a blood day. And blood days were literally life and death for me.

Not that I gave off that vibe. Instead, I went about my business, pushing my janitorial cart into the blood bank of San Francisco General Hospital. The automatic door shut behind me, my cart's squeaking wheels announcing my arrival to Sam, the department's night manager, and some staffer who looked more on break than actually working. They leaned over a monitor, attention pulled away by whatever was on the screen. Which worked to my benefit.

Some vampires worked with blood volunteers—usually fetishists who gladly let someone feed off them, likely thinking it was a kink or a new obscure fad diet rather than real vampire sustenance. That still involved the wholly unhygienic and socially awkward process of drinking from a live human. Underground dealers also existed, pumping blood from their arms into a bottle for an in-person transaction.

Me? I went with blood bag theft.

Which, to be fair, I held zero guilt over. Did you know that hospitals waste about 25 percent of blood bags every year? Thus, my weekly pickup during my janitorial rounds hardly made a dent. It all fell within the normal range of lost, misplaced, or expired. In fact, the managers viewed me as helpful for bringing the soon-to-expire bags to disposal. If some happened to make it into my backpack along the way, no one was the wiser.

This, of course, assumed that there were actually blood bags to take.

Today, the usual inventory of expiring blood bags was empty.

As in, nothing on the shelves. Nothing to deliver. Nothing to steal.

Nothing to feed from.

In fact, even the main storage units for in-date blood bags appeared low.

Any stress from the Copper Beach audition evaporated, as things do when food sources suddenly disappear.

I paused the music on my phone and pulled the earbuds out. Some things required a little more professional behavior. I began scouring the other storage possibilities when I overheard the words the vampire community feared the most.

"I swear, it's a vampire."

Eric constantly preached that if humans *did* discover us, racists would find new reasons to fearmonger, while scientists would capture us for all sorts of poking and prodding. Given that we'd all managed to abide by this for centuries, it seemed like a pretty good suggestion to follow.

My hands squeezed the cart's handle tighter as I listened.

"That's ridiculous," Sam said, shaking his head.

"No, think about it." The man turned, the tag on his scrubs revealing the name Turner. "After everything we know about viruses these days, who would actually drink blood? Only vampires."

"Okay, look," Sam said, rubbing his cleft chin. "You're assuming someone drank this guy's blood—"

"Police said he's missing about ten ounces of blood. Same as the other two attacks."

"Alright. Let's assume someone—or some*thing*—drank ten ounces from that poor guy. They said his neck looked chewed, dozens of stitches needed. If you're gonna believe something ridiculous, go with a werewolf."

Suddenly, that headline didn't seem like simple clickbait. Ten ounces. Roughly the same amount my body needed daily, though half that offered cranky survival. So that *was* the typical amount a vampire needed to sustain until the next feeding. And the chewed neck like a werewolf bite? That was a real concern, not because werewolves were real (they're not), but because biting into a human was not easy.

In theory, you first had to properly locate the carotid artery, then make sure it was easily accessible by positioning the head and neck the right way. Then you needed a well-placed bite—millimeters of accuracy here, from an angle where things are hard to see. I challenge any human to try and bite precisely into a piece of Red Vines stuck on a loaf of sourdough to gauge its difficulty. This was in addition to the fangs' fairly mediocre ability to puncture.

Biting humans was messy. Factor in an especially scared nondonor human and tools to make the process smoother and, well, the result could easily be mistaken for werewolves.

With the hospital's blood shortage, their conversation ratcheted my anxiety enough for me to mutter, "oh shit."

That little phrase pulled Sam and Turner away from the screen. Their desk chairs creaked as they turned my way, the headline—San Francisco's Latest "Vampire Attack" Victim Stable In Hospital—now clearly visible on their monitor.

If there was a fixer working in the community, they weren't doing a great job.

"Oh, hi, Louise," Sam said. "Need anything?"

Blood bags. A safe community, one without rogue vampires possibly revealing ourselves to humans. While I was at it, someone to play in a band with—human or vampire—though right now neither seemed to be working out.

"No pickups today," I managed as I pushed the cart through.

"What pickups?" Sam asked, his thick eyebrows furrowing.

"Expiring blood to pick up on second Fridays. You know," I said, switching to a very bad generic European accent, "because I'm a vampire and I need to drink it instead of biting people on the neck."

That joke always worked, but doubly so today.

Both men laughed, and I almost held up claw hands for emphasis. But no, that joke belonged only to me and Marshall.

"I knew it," Sam said, "you're the vampire attacker."

"I thought you suspected a werewolf," Turner said, an Irish lilt to his gravelly voice.

"Sorry, boys. It's a little more boring than that. Management tallies these and I don't want to piss them off." That was a lie; I knew they didn't because otherwise I'd never get away with my theft.

"Right, right. Let me go check in on that." Sam stood and went to the computer on the far desk, his leg catching his chair enough to kick it over a foot. "You're right, our last delivery was low. Must not be as many donors. There's a note saying this might be a thing for a few weeks but it doesn't say why."

Just like that, my food supply went from "comfortably fed" to "empty."

"Cool, cool, no worries," I said despite the onslaught of emerging worries. I built my whole life around a job that provided blood—and that dried up? Maybe in a parallel universe, I might have my own recording studio with session time paid in blood bags. But here?

I loaded my email as soon as I stepped into the hallway. My fingers mashed over the virtual keys, autocorrect pulling all the wrong words and constantly changing *blood* to *brood*, which I supposed was fitting for a vampire. The message went to the local Red Cross chapter's volunteer manager, a request for shifts as a Volunteer Transportation Specialist.

Basically, someone who drove donated blood around.

I'd actually trained for the role when I was in between hospital gigs, but never took any actual shifts since most of them were during the day—which wasn't impossible with proper precautions, but still uncomfortable, and required a lot of extra effort, in addition to messing up my sleep cycle. Circadian rhythm still applied to vampire life.

But this was different. If the supply saw shortages, I'd need alternatives just like the early days when I first started and had no clue what I was doing.

Which really wasn't my fault. Because no guidebook existed for this life, and the woman who made me only came around a few times to check on me before disappearing forever. Despite the physical transformation to vampiredom creating several months of fuzzy memories, I still clearly pictured her during that last visit: a tall, pale woman with long brown hair in peak late-70s punk styling

She'd brought weekly bottles, introduced me to a few Southern California sources for no-questions-asked back-alley blood, gave a very uncomfortable primer on feeding off farm animals in emergencies and offered a very dramatic lecture on the importance of not revealing ourselves to humans in any way. Yet, all of those came during surprise drop-ins and sudden departures, and even her final visit was nothing more than a quick hello before "You'll figure the rest out. You'll be fine."

In fact, she never bothered to tell me her name. Or maybe she did and I just forgot it in my fugue state. Whatever the case, I'd have to rely on those lessons now, to ride out any shortages. I spent the rest of my shift trying to recall how many bags remained in my fridge, and how best to ration them. Hours came and went, a low-level panic setting my night to fast-forward all the way until I stepped into an empty parking garage.

Then my phone buzzed. Multiple buzzes, actually. Though I hoped it was something about the Red Cross volunteer gig, that seemed impossible, given the late hour. No, a quick look showed another text from Eric. And this time, I bothered to read it.

> I've received a few notes tonight about tomorrow evening's agenda. I share your concerns, but there is a plan to address this. Nothing is more important than the health and safety of our community.

Something was definitely up. A blood shortage, someone attacking humans in the wild, texts about "health and safety." A second message loaded up, words pushing the first message off the screen.

If you want to learn more, please come to the event. In the meantime, I encourage you all to download our new community app to stream the discussion. Do NOT discuss the media's 'vampire attack' headlines with anyone, not even jokingly. Blood will be served. Reply to RSVP for in-person attendance.

Did I want to learn more? Of course. Did I want an app that both invaded my privacy *and* knew I was a vampire? No. Did I want to get involved with the vampire community?

Not really. Especially given my history with Eric. But I needed blood, and this was a source, however fleeting.

Besides, maybe Eric forgot about our last encounter.

Still, I refused to download his stupid app. On principle.

Count me in, I typed in a reply text, complete with a little white lie. By the way, I had trouble downloading the app. Maybe later.

On most work nights, I came home just before dawn, changed from scrubs to sweats, let my dog out, and drank blood. Today, that last part remained a sticking point. Lola greeted me as usual, a pitter-patter that told me she needed a potty break. I left the back door ajar for her to go into the small backyard, then checked my blood bag supply in the fridge.

If I'd been more responsible, thorough, careful, and whatever other descriptions my parents threw at me decades ago, I'd have a managed stockpile. Instead, three bags remained, a supply for about four or five days. I *could* stretch it to a week, though I'd be a grouchy, tired mess. After that? Movie vampires went on killing rampages when they needed blood, but in reality, it meant fatigue and delirium.

And if that went on long enough? Death by starvation.

No wonder someone got desperate enough to bite humans.

I grabbed a mug from the cabinet, white ceramic with a

faded photo of a white schnauzer printed on it, Aunt Laura's old teacup, now used for blood. Mostly empty shelves stared back at me from the fridge, daring me to make a choice.

Did I take one now? Did I *really* need to drink or could I wait?

Lola returned from the backyard, hopping over the threshold with her short corgi legs, and her nails clacked on the floor as she ignored my mood and waddled past. The jingling of her collar faded as she went down the hall, and I told myself to do the smart thing. I shut the fridge door and left Aunt Laura's mug on the counter, then followed my dog.

Light flooded the space in my music room as I flipped the wall switch, illuminating everything from the guitars hanging on the walls to the drum kit and keyboard rig sitting in opposite corners. But no dog waited for me. Instead, her collar jingled from across the hall.

The bedroom.

The hour or so before bed normally saw me noodling on a guitar, playing with different pedal effects combinations or trying to work out a lingering melody while Lola stayed at my feet. But as I stood between the two rooms, a crushing fatigue washed over me, something that I knew had nothing to do with appetite.

I peeked in on Lola, the hallway light showing enough that I could see she'd skipped the circular dog bed on the floor to leap straight onto my spot. Usually she'd wait till I fell asleep to pull that off, and perhaps she took advantage of my vulnerable state today. She stretched her little legs into the air, then craned her neck to look at me with ears up, yawning before settling back down.

Maybe she just knew what I needed today.

Instead of going back into my music room, I stepped inside and shut the door, leaving the bedroom in a complete UV-protected blackout state as I crawled under soft sheets. I stayed still, the quiet silence of a moment without vampires, without humans, without blood shortages, just a happy corgi resting against my stomach and worries in my head.

Vampire Weekend
by
Mike Chen

Available January 2023 from MIRA.